LOLA UNMASKED
PART 2
S.K. PRESLEY

Cover Design: RJ Creatives

Edited: Traci Bullman

CONTENTS

Trigger Warning

If you suspect that someone you know, or a child is being abused or is a victim of domestic violence, please reach out to your country and or States' child abuse and DV hotline.

Description of child abuse

Rape fantasy by FMC/MCM hinging on non-consent

Allusion to child starvation

FMC Inner dialogue of feeling "dead"

Consensual non-consent

Forced pregnancy

MCM consensually degrading MFC

Torture

Murder

DEDICATION

This one's for all the girls who don't mind going to hell and back a time or two. Hudson trusts us enough to show us his crazy, so let's go before he changes his mind.

And for the love of God... Don't. Stare. At. The. Man. Too. Long. You'll be in trouble.

I

GETTING TO KNOW YOU

HUDSON

STANDING AT THE STOVE, I stir a reduction sauce absentmindedly as I glance out the big window pane to the right of my stove in the kitchen. It grants the perfect scenic view of the eastern side of my property. The night breeze flowing through the crack in the window cools down my body; a welcome relief as I've been aroused most of the night thanks to Lola.

I narrow my eyes, thinking that just less than a handful of weeks ago, I was staring through another window watching her putting a book up in her shop.

Turning the heat down a bit, I continue stirring slowly, lost in my thoughts.

I smile, thanking God for windows, and that one hopefully gave me a glimpse into my future. As thoughts of proposing to Lola swiftly take over, the woman in question's voice interrupts my musing, drawing me back to her.

"Tell me a time you cried."

I look up sharply at Lola from my spot at the stove, giving her a little smile and an eyebrow raise. "Are you trying to emasculate me, ma'am?" I tease with a laugh.

Her mouth drops open, causing my gaze to drop down as she puts her fingers to her lips. Putting the card down slowly, she meets my eyes rather timidly. Pleasure fills my being. Tightening my chest at the way she sometimes can't meet my eyes, and when she does, she's always flushed. Flustered.

Left floundering and off-center just a little.

I love that I intimidate her, and cause her to feel off balance. It really does so much for my ego. And Lola has no problem stroking my ego either, something else I love about her. However, I love it even more when we're in bed and I lay my body on top of hers and pound into her willing, helpless body.

Lola clears her throat, pulling me from my musing.

Uncaring of her vulnerability, I stare a few seconds too long as I relax against the countertop, watching her fidget with this card game she insisted on us playing.

It's late, the sun's setting, and I'm making us a surf and turf dinner. I splurged on lobster tails and scallops, wanting to spoil her, and right now I'm making the red wine reduction sauce for the steak.

Lola shared with me she listens to mostly clean, older music, so there's a classic r&b soul playing over the speakers. Which in itself is quite amusing because I fuck her so dirty.

Needless to say, the sexual tension between us is thick enough to cut with a knife.

Though we really just met, things have been moving fast between us, and we've been talking daily. Multiple times a day, in fact. I refuse to go too long without hearing from her, whether it's her voice, or a sweet text.

Though she can't always be here with me because of the boys, I've come to enjoy and appreciate the nights where I see her laying in bed with her facemask on as she types on her computer. Backlit by the comforting glow of her bedside lamp in the background. I always wait for her nightgown to slip over her shoulder, gracing me with a peek at her generous curves I love so much.

But I love the evenings where I have her in my home more.

"No!" Lola scoffs, waving her hand dismissively. "Not at all, it's just a question. I can pick another card."

My eyes skim her greedily.

Her hair is loose, hanging in waves down her face. She's in the same blue dress she was wearing when I found her at the grocery story a couple weeks ago, even down to the same tights with the hearts that all I can think about is ripping off her. Her shoes are off, placed neatly in the mudroom, and her purse sits in a stool next to her where she's seated at the island.

Reading me *get to know you* questions off a card game.

"That's not necessary, I was just kidding," I say, putting the spatula to the side and reaching for a knife to begin chopping the mushrooms for the steak. The sound of the knife hitting the board relaxes me, takes some of the pain of this sexual tension off my shoulders. "The last time I cried was when one of my favorite workers died in a work place accident."

"Oh," Lola says quietly, her eyes meeting mine. "I'm so sorry to hear that. I know your work's dangerous. Have *you* ever had a workplace accident?"

I put the knife down and lean forward with my hands flat on the marble top, flicking my gaze across her face.

"I've had *many* near misses, baby. Starting from the time I was a teenager. But thankfully, I escaped every one of them by the skin of my teeth." I quip, tilting my head at her and giving her a smile. "But, that's just the name of the job. As the boss, I don't get up and personal with the builds like I used to. I do a lot of overseeing. You won't catch me on a scaffolding anymore. My mother's *so* happy about it, let me tell you."

Lola gives me a husky laugh. Needing to feel her, I advance closer, rounding the corner to stand in front of her, leaning my hip against the island.

She's nervously biting her lip, and her eyes dart around as if she's looking for something else to say. "It was really nice of you to invite me for dinner," she says breathlessly, tucking a strand of hair behind her ear.

Lola wraps her stocking covered toes around the little foot rest of her stool and her fingers jerk, making the cards slip from her hands and scatter across the counter in front of her. Her little jerk, slapping her hand over the cards to keep them from flying everywhere is adorable, and makes me fill with so much pleasure that it's slightly discombobulating.

I'll never share this with her, but her clumsiness is so endearing.

She glances back up at me with a little apologetic smile and shoulder shrug. "Oops."

I chuckle, thinking she's just perfect.

"You're *so beautiful.*" I say, leaning in, I bring a hand up to caress her cheek. Her skin is so fucking soft, so warm.

I make a little humming noise, tightening my fingers around her jaw, stilling her movements when she goes to turn away from me, blushing. I love making her cheeks tinge pink. Forcing her to hold still, I catch her eye.

"Thank you." I tilt my head at her, knowing I'm making her even more nervous. Good, I want her wrecked just like I am. "So..." Lola gasps, swallowing hard. *"So,* wh-who's this?" Her eyes darts around nervously, referencing the music playing.

I'm not letting her off the hook that easily. "The song I'm going to fuck you to later." I know she can tell in the grittiness of my voice I'm exercising a good deal of restraint.

Her eyes flit back to mine, widening.

"Who says I'm going to let you fuck me?" She arches a defiant brow. Just like she asked the third time I was in her shop.

Chuckling, I grasp her inner thighs and pull her legs apart, working my way in between. "I say." I lean forward, taking her lips in a long, deep kiss. "I *always* say." I curl my hand around the back of her neck, holding her still and enjoy kissing her until the roaster goes off, informing me the lobster tails are done.

Reluctantly I pull away with a little groan, caressing her lips with my thumb before walking away to remove the lobster and flip her steak. I take mine about rare, so it's out resting on the cutting board.

"Everything smells so good, Hudson." Lola calls out, looking over at the spread. "I hate you didn't let me help you make us dinner."

"Ah sweetie, it's not necessary. Let me spoil you." I take two plates out and give her an apologetic look. "I did forget stuff for a salad though."

She laughs again, shrugging her shoulder. "Broccoli and cauliflower is perfect, honey. I'm not picky."

I glance up at her sharply at her term of endearment. She tears her eyes away and shuffles the cards nervously before picking one out and reading it silently. Her face turns so red I smile. She let's out a little squeal, putting her face in her hands and shaking her head.

Laughing, I reach into the broiler getting out her medium rare steak, setting it next to mine on the cutting board. "Give it to me straight, Lo'," I say, beginning to plate our food.

Pulling her hands away from her face, she peeks at me from over her balled up fists, getting a little goofy look on her face that makes my smile broaden even more. I take a drink of my whiskey, then pick up the knife, not wanting to call attention to it, and begin slicing the steak.

"Come on," I encourage her. "Don't be shy with me baby. There's no need." I honestly don't understand how she's so nervous after how thoroughly I've fucked her the way I've been, but I bask in it. Eat it up.

Lola blows out a breath that ruffles her bangs, picking up the card again. "Okay, lets see. *What is your favorite movie sex scene.*" She drops the card to the table and takes a sip of her wine.

This is the most I've seen her drink since I've met her and I am really enjoying it. Her face is slightly flushed and damp, her wispy bangs are sticking in places at her temple, and it reminds me of the first time I fucked her mouth.

"Hmm." I think for a second as the knife cuts through the meat. "I can't remember the name of the movie, but it was this husband and wife scene." I clear my throat, getting a half chubby at the memory of it. "The husband was leading some sort of double life, or used to be some kind of killer. He got out of that lifestyle and married, had kids. She *somehow* finds out about his past, I think some people came looking for him where they lived. Anyways, she was so hurt, betrayed."

I begin plating our food and then start working on her steak. I give her a little amused look seeing her hands keep twitching, like she wants to reach forward and help me.

"She went to go upstairs, and he caught her about halfway up. Grabbed her ankle, pulled her down, yanked her panties off and proceeded to fuck her right there, ignoring her fighting against him. It was passionate, the scene really encapsulated the heightened feelings that one can experience being with another person." I pause, grabbing a piece of steak and holding it to her mouth. I wet my lips as she takes it from me, chewing slowly.

"Yum," she praises me.

I smile, turning my attention back to the cutting board, seriously suffering.

"Anyways, there's this shot where they showed you just her legs and his hips from the entrance of the kitchen, I think it was. And all you can see was him pounding into her, making her take it. It was incredibly, raw. There wasn't any music to break it up, just the sound of them together. It was the sexiest thing I think I've ever seen in a movie."

I finish cutting her steak and then look up at her, reaching over for my scotch. She's got her fingers pressed to her lips, her eyes are wide and she looks quite speechless. I take a deep drink and sigh appreciatively.

"What's yours?" I counter.

Lola blinks, like she's jerked out of a daze. *"Oh."* She sits back and takes a deep breath looking into the counter top. "Uhm, when Beth and Rip get it on in Yellowstone." She bites her lip, averting her gaze shyly.

My cock swells uncomfortably, because I know the exact scene she's talking about.

"That's my favorite TV show." I throw her a wicked smile, licking carefully alongside the blade of the knife as I keep her eye contact. I groan appreciatively at the flavor and give her a wink. "See that? We can skip a card now."

Walking around the island, I turn her on her stool to face me, putting my thumb to her lips. *"Suck."* My voice is hoarse and gritty with desire.

I'm not sure how on earth I'm going to get through dinner, but I'm going to have to, because once I get her back in my bed I'm not letting her out.

Her eyes are big in her face as she looks up at me. Obediently, she parts her lips, allowing me to place the tip of my thumb between them. I grunt in pleasure as her tongue strokes my flesh, licking off the remnants of the steak drippings, causing me to throb uncomfortably in my pants.

I pull my thumb out, and then slide my palms up her thighs until I get into the waistband of her tights where I grip them.

"Lift up." I instruct her, my eyes fall to her mouth which is tilted up in an adoring grin.

She firms her hands on the seat, lifting a couple inches on a breathless giggle, allowing me to pull them down her legs slowly. Lola begins breathing deeper, her breasts rising and falling steadily as I roll her stockings off her. When I get them free, I hold the crotch of them to my nose and then snap my eyes back to her when she grabs my wrists, shooting her eyes to me.

Her playful mood suddenly transforms to one of embarrassment.

"No s-stop , Hudson, *I'm on my period,"* she says in a strained voice, squeezing my wrists tightly.

There's no way in hell I'm telling her I stole her period undies from her house our first time having sex. She has to know though, because I never gave them back. There still tucked away safe in my nightstand. My eyes narrow at her before sliding over to my rare steak on the cutting board a few feet away.

The blood of the steak pools there, keeping the meat moist until I'm ready for it.

Her head turns as her eyes follows my gaze and then she blushes even more somehow. I look back at her, ignoring her grip on me and hold the silky fabric to my nose anyway, inhaling deeply. Treating her to a deep, sexual groan because she loves to hear me enjoying myself, I've found.

She won't be getting these back either.

"Fuck you smell amazing," I say quietly.

Pulling open a drawer in the island, I pull out a long thin box. I put her stockings to the side and then close my hand over hers when she goes to reach for them, trapping her wrist against the marble counter top. Giving her a warning squeeze, I step into her further. "Take your dress off."

"Hudson I-"

"Take it off." My eyes meet hers. "I have a present for you."

She pulls against my hold and then reaches for the side of of her dress, pulling the zipper down. It sounds out loudly between us, forcing her to keep her eyes averted. Normally I'd be irritated that a woman wouldn't hold my eye contact, and be so timid... but with her I enjoy it.

It makes me want to chase her, dominate her.

Her eyes leave mine to follow my motions. I open the box and then hear her suck in a sharp breath. "Wow. What's that?" she asks.

Her hands leave her dress to caress the chain delicately.

"They're diamonds. I had this made for you," I say quietly. Putting the box down I pull out the jewelry, showing her a diamond body chain, and right in the center is a eight inch snake made of diamonds. "I noticed early on that you liked wearing jewelry, and I wanted you to have something that represented me. So, I'd love if you would wear this. Daily."

Lola's eyes go wide as they flick from the body chain to mine then back again. "Hudson is that *real* diamonds?" Her voice is shaky and breathless with nerves. "Those look like real diamonds."

"It is."

Her eyes fly back to mine. "The entire thing?"

I nod my head, placing it back in the box gently. "The entire thing. Well, the *chain* is silver. It'd be too heavy if the chain was diamonds too, and I didn't want you to be uncomfortable wearing it."

Her fingers go to her lips. *"Hudson,* this must have cost you a fortune..."

I smile, because it did. "Don't worry about that." My eyes narrow at her. "I want you to wear it every day, starting tonight."

Lola nods, filling me with a sense of relief because I need her wearing my brand. But right now, this should be enough to scratch the itch that's tormenting me. The urge to continue marking her, however, doesn't abate as much as I though it would.

This body chain is but a drop in the bucket of shit I want to do to her. But I know she's think's I'm doing it *for* her, and in a way, I am.

But make no mistake, this shit is all for *me.* And so is everything else I've got planned to do to her. When I'm done with her she's going to be absolutely dripping in my mark, and in my name. The necklace is easy.

The rest won't be.

Pulling her dress off I toss it over the spare stool and then unsnap her bra, pulling that down her arms as well. I patiently clasp the chain around her neck, showing her how it connects on the sides, fitting the snake snuggly in between her breasts. Stepping back, I eye her with pleasure.

Fuck she's sexy in nothing but her panties, and the diamond snake chain. Representing me.

I bend to her, giving her a brief smacking kiss, and then finish plating our food. We eat, and when we're done, I take her to my bed, lay her down on a bath towel and crawl in between her legs with nothing but sensual music echoing throughout the room, and her snake chain between us.

I lick the skin around it and all the way up her breastbone and up to her throat, pressing a kiss there.

Hitching her leg high up on my hip, I place a hand flat on the bed next to her head, holding myself above her as I smooth my free hand across the fleshy curve of her ass.

"Fuck baby, I'm so swollen it hurts," I say to her, meeting her gaze.

Lola blinks before reaching down between us and wrapping her hand around me, causing me to tense up and buck into her hand. Being she's so petite, her hand doesn't encompass me completely, so she surprises me by gripping extra hard, causing a breath to escape my lungs on a tortured drawn out groan.

"You like that?" she whispers, her eyes flick back and forth between mine.

"Hmm-hmm." I hum, placing my lips on hers. "You've got the best touch."

She spends a minute pumping me from root to tip, squeezing me hard just like I like it. While she's working me, her eyes go hooded and her breathing becomes shallow, letting me know how much she enjoys touching me. I massage her hip while she swirls her thumb against my tip, making me flinch.

Her eyelashes flutter as I narrow my eyes at her. She sucks her bottom lip into her mouth, hiding the grin that tipped her lip up on the right side. But I saw it. Even timid regarding intimacy and sex, she's still a feisty little thing deep down inside. Though she's never outwardly said it, I know at some level she enjoys having this power over me.

I'll let her have it, too. As long as she knows at the end of the day *I'm* the one who's in charge.

Precum is leaking steadily out of the tip of my cock. Needing to sink inside of her I move her hand away, wincing as I notch it into her opening. I pause at how hot she is, damn near scorching me. I suck in a quick breath before going stone still as my nostrils flare at her scent.

She smells like heat, iron, and a deep earthy, musky smell that's so inviting that I'd love to have my mouth down there.

But I don't want to freak her out too bad.

"Goddamn you feel amazing." I take a deep breath, then another, until I'm sure I have a solid grip on my lust. "You *smell* amazing. Have you ever had period sex before?" I ask quietly, my gaze roaming her face.

She shakes her head no, biting her lip.

"Me neither. We'll take this nice and slow, then." I tilt my head, giving her a little wink. "I won't grab the headboard tonight."

Lola nods slowly, running her fingertips across my chest. "Thank you mi-" She cuts off her words suddenly.

Blinking slowly, she averts her eyes again, darting her tongue out to wet her bottom lip.

"Thank you *what?*" I press gently. My heart races, wanting to hear something sweet from her. Putting a finger under her chin, I turn her back to face me.

"Thank you, mi querido."

"What does that mean, beautiful?" My eyes flicker between hers.

She's called me this once before, but I was so angry with her ex that I didn't ask at the time.

"It means, my darling."

My heart skips a beat as I lower my mouth to hers at the same time I lower my hips in a firm, slow movement, swallowing the whimpering gasp she emits. It feels like it takes forever to reach the back of her pussy, but once I'm there, I give her a minute to acclimate.

"I like that very much. Say it again." I whisper hoarsely against her mouth. "Say it again, baby."

"Mi querido," she says breathlessly. *"Me estas amando tan bien."*

"And what's that?"

She takes a deep breath. *"You're loving me so good."*

I treat her with a slow grind.

"Talk to me in Spanish some more," I ask, "don't translate it, just tell me what you feel. I want to hear it from you baby."

Lola does just that, and it flows so beautifully from her tongue that it makes my heart swell. I can only imagine what she's saying, but my heart knows it.

"God you're so sexy." I give her another slow, circle of my hips.

"Hudson," she whines, arching her neck.

I keep our faces close, our lips touching as she pants and digs her nails into my arms. I smile and chuckle against her mouth, giving her a soft kiss. "You're *much* more sensitive this way. Shall I show you how much?"

When Lola relaxes out of her arch, I pull stroke her bangs out of her face as I pull my hips back and give her a slightly firmer thrust, making her lids lower slightly. I dip down to her breasts and nibble at her nipple, grunting at us jerking hard when she suddenly yanks her knees back on a shocked gasp.

I'm finding she this is something she does right before she orgasms, or when I do something that feels unbearably good.

I keep on, giving her soft sucks, lapping my tongue against her nipple in rough stokes.

Once her squirming abates, I let go of her nipple and lower to my forearms, licking deep into her mouth as I rock us until she's delirious. The sound she made when I thrust inside her overstimulated, swollen pussy was enough to make me burst inside her, but no, I need this slow just as much as she does.

I crave this stark, unbidden intimacy that only she can give me.

I'm beginning to think this woman's the only one who can give me anything. But what I want from her is her *life*. The highest form of payment she can give me.

Her.

Through and through.

2

A Woman's Secret

Lola

A couple days later it's a drizzly, calm Wednesday evening. I'm off my period, walking into my house with a couple shopping bags of new clothes, heading upstairs to put them away in my closet. I broke, buying some clothes for my house because Hudson keeps cutting them up. Though he got clothes for me, I don't feel right bringing them here.

Thank God he's a generous tipper.

Hudson is working late on a project and I haven't heard from him for a few hours. Though I'm used to him messaging me frequently, the slight absence doesn't bother me so much. He explained there are construction sites he goes to where his cell phone reception is spotty and he'll be by later to have dinner with me.

As I'm hanging up a pair of pants I hear my phone ring from my purse that's securely in it's spot on my bedside chair.

Walking over, I curse as I stumble over a random shirt that's fallen into the floor and pitch headfirst towards the bed barely catching myself before standing back up. Flopping on the edge of the bed, I dig it out my cell and see it's a facetime from Haley, and I answer it with a bright smile.

She's excited, showing me this coverlet she brought for Nay Nay. I prop her up against my nightstand while I go back to putting away clothes, having a rare relaxing time talking about her day. We've become close. She's a sweet girl, and she just seems to want a big sister and I'm happy to fill that role having never had one myself. We're laughing and talking about her boyfriend when I hear my doorbell ring.

Thinking it's Hudson, I hurry.

"Hold up, Haley, Hudson's here. Can we pick this up next time? I'll call you tomorrow and we can finish talking about Nathaniel." I assure her.

I hang up, place my phone on my bedroom dresser, and race down the stairs to open the door with a big smile that falls as soon as I see *Dominic*. Not Hudson.

I'm so shocked at the sight of him that he's able to push his way in before I even have a chance to say anything. I stand in the doorway, looking outside thinking he's dropping the boys back off, but I don't see any sign of Tucker or Tatum.

"Where are the boys?" I ask hesitantly, feeling a sick, nervous feeling start down in my gut.

Walking back in the house I look down at my foyer table and re-member I left my phone and my purse upstairs where I usually stash it.

Oh no.

I try to tamp the nerves down and swallow hard, wiping my sweaty hands on my thighs. I feel stuck, not knowing what to say.

"We need to talk." Dominic pushes pass me and I wet my lips nervously, stepping back so he can't brush his body against mine.

I close the door with a frown. *"Dominic, where are Tuck and Tate?"*

Dominic barely spares me a backwards glance, already making his way to the back of the house without permission. "They're at my grandma's."

I frown, not liking that he dropped them off with her during a school night and then left them. What's the point of getting them for a night in the middle of the week if you're just going to foist them off on family?

"Okayyyy..." I say, making a mental note to verify this as soon as he leaves. I walk into the kitchen cautiously, seeing he's leaning against the counter opposite the kitchen window. I inch around the table, putting my back to the opposite counter, right in front of the window. "So, why are you here? What do we need to talk about that you couldn't have just called me?"

Like I don't already know. *Money.*

I pause for a second, trying to remember how much I have upstairs because my stash has gotten a bit low. I think I only have about three hundred dollars left in cash. I wonder how I can keep him downstairs so I can go up there alone and grab it, and my phone.

Fuck, I should have listened to Frank when he told me I needed a house phone. It's just so old fashioned it didn't make sense. But *surprise,* Frank was right as usual and now I need one.

"I can't get through to your phone. I'm blocked." His eyes are hard on mine as they flick up from my breasts to bore into my eyes. My spine stiffens as my hackles go up. "And we need to discuss that piece of shit you're fucking."

My heart stops, and I feel my face turn bright red. "That's none of your busi-"

"Does he know you like it to the left?" Dominic tilts his head and as he shifts his stance, I see the bulge between his thighs get bigger.

I swallow hard, feeling my skin break out in goosebumps. Not only does my heart freefall into my stomach, tears spring to my eyes. "Dominic that's *incredibly* disrespectful. You know I obviously am not going to talk to you about him. Why would I?"

He tilts his head and a sneer graces his lips. "Not as disrespectful as the shit you asked me to do to you. Remember that?"

Oh my god. My lips tighten as I begin to tremble. I dig my fingers into my arms, trying to squeeze a semblance of courage into me that'll be bigger than the fear I feel with him.

"That's in the *past,* Dominic. Me and you aren't together anymore, that shit doesn't matter."

Dominic takes a step forward, lowering his brow in a hard set and frowning. "It matters to *me.* I'm sorry I didn't give you what you wanted when you asked me. Lolita, I want you back, those boys need us together."

"Ohh no." Anger colors my tone. "No you don't, *Dominic!* You want a fucking doormat, not a *wife.* Because if you wanted a wife, you would have treated me right when you had me. *When I begged you to love me.*" I feel my face tighten in a hateful expression as rage fills me. "And if you wanted me so bad, if you are *so changed,* you wouldn't be treating our sons like second class citizens!"

"I treat them that way because you coddle them, Lolita!" He snaps at me. "They're boys, they need to be *tough.*"

His eyes widen, and his face morphs into an familiar expression that had become one of the dominate features of our marriage; hate and malice. Within the first year of our marriage, it quickly replaced the fascination he'd once had with me.

"Don't fucking try to cover up what you're doing, *you hate them and you know it!*" I scream at him. "And I swear to God I'm going to fucking take you to court for full custody! *I am done with you abusing us!*"

I can't help it, the spicy bitch in me comes out. If he hits me, he hits me. What's the worst that can happen? I have a hospital bill?

With no kids in the house to overhear I let him have it. My eyes narrow, despite being filled with tears. The hate I have for this man runs so deep that I fear no amount of hail Mary's will be able to cleanse me from this mental torture. The inner anguish I feel.

Dominic's eyes flash as he takes a step forward.

"You will not! You will not take those boys from me. I want you and them back, Lolita." He yells back at me. "*What aren't you understanding you stupid-*"

I take a step forward myself, slapping the side of my palm into my hand. "If you wanted me then you would have done what the fuck it took to keep me. You would have kept it in your pants instead of trying to fuck every *fucking slut* who looked at you sideways. It's not my fault we aren't together. And now that you see I'm with someone who's treating me better, *now* you come to your senses?"

Dominic narrows his eyes at me and a muscle ticks in his jaw. "Well I had to fuck *something* to remind me that I still knew what I was doing. Your bitch ass had me thinking there was something wrong with me." He shouts.

My head recoils. "Get the fuck out of my house Dominic. Don't ever come here, or speak to me again unless the kids are with you." Not able to help myself, I throw him a nasty look. "And I have no problem in the bedroom, by the way. So maybe it was *your* 'bitch ass' that had the problem after all, not me."

My words have the opposite affect as his eyes flash with excitement. "Oh yeah? Then show me."

I scrunch my nose, curling my lip. "You've lost your mind. I said *get out.*"

He gets a grin on his face as his eyes roam my body, lingering on my breasts and in between my legs. The look in his eyes is evil. Sick. I break out into a fresh coat of sweat, shifting on my feet.

"Come on, I know what you want. I see you now... you're red... turned on."

"No I'm not." I press into the sink behind me, fight like hell to keep my hands at my side instead of folded around my torso. I can't let him know that I'm scared.

"Yeah, this is exactly what you asked me for. Slut."

Feeling truly sick, I debate lunging for the trashcan to vomit, but he suddenly moves, walking around the table towards me. True fear enters me, making my knees buckle under a fresh wave of terror. I grapple for a second before gripping the counter top behind me to help hold myself up as I shuffle to the side.

"D-Dominic, this isn't funny." I stammer. "This isn't what I meant at all when I told you about that years ago, *and you know it*. Things are not the same between us at all. Please get out of my house. I don't want you here."

His head tilts, and his brown eyes roam down my body. "Come on babe, this is *exactly* what you meant."

I hold my hand palm up. "No, *no!* I don't trust you. I trusted you when I asked you and that was over *f-five years* ago, Dominic." I'm still inching to the side, desperately trying to keep the table between us.

In my reluctance to take my eyes off him I bounce off the refrigerator, halting my retreat. Holding my hand up to my stinging arm I keep shuffling over, trying to get closer to the entrance of the kitchen, but he's too close.

So close I can smell his aftershave.

"Sweetheart rape is rape." Dominic tilts his head on an evil chuckle that sends chills down my spine. "You can't want it both ways, *chica desagradable.*"

Terrified, I decide to run for it but he's too close.

His fingers brush my my shoulder as I launch myself across the table to get away from him, hearing the vase of flowers that Hudson brought me hit the floor in a splattering of broken glass and splashing water.

"Noooo!" I scream at the top of my lungs as he grabs me by my elbow, yanking me back before I can fully cross the table. Desperate, I struggling against him, feeling tears fall out of my eyes. *"No, Dominic no!"*

I gasp as he works my pants down my hips.

Fresh fear swamps me, and I yank against him again in a futile attempt to get free. He fists his hand into my hair, pulls my head back, and slams my head on the table, momentarily stunning me.

"Ow!" I yell.

"Shut up you fucking slut," he snarls, ripping my underwear down.

Squirming against him, I swallow bile and drag air into my heaving lungs. "Dominic, please don't do this." I sob, feeling tears roll down my face as I dry heave, utterly terrified.

The sound of his buckle clanging as he works to get his pants off bounces around my head in a torturous echo.

Ohhh my God. God please no, don't let this happen to me. I can take a lot of things but please don't let this man hurt me anymore, I pray.

"He knows what you smell like, huh?" Dominic mutters under his breath. "Well, lets see how he likes it when he's sucking my cum out of your pussy later."

I feel vomit come up into my mouth at his words because they terrify me so badly. The blood drains out of my head so fast my kitchen spins in front of me.

I'm going to pass out.

I suck in a deep breath, still jerking against him. "Hudssooonnn!" I scream. *"Hudson!"* I gasp his name over and over, feeling Dominic's erection brush my backside. "H-Help meee! Somebody please heeellllppp!" I sob, pressing my forehead to the table, straining away from him.

His fingers dig into my arms so hard I know I'm going to bruise.

"Quiet!" Dominic snarls. "Matter of fact, scream his name. I don't care, he's not coming for you so scream as loud as you want."

The tip of his erection brushes my center and I brace myself, not believing this is how my fantasy gets played out. I'm never going to be the same.

I feel my heart break in half, right down the middle.

Just then my kitchen door bust open and I hear a blast that has my ears ringing.

A gun shot goes off in my kitchen, causing me to scream once more. I topple to the side, being released from Dominic, crashing to the floor hard with my pants and underwear around my thighs. Shaking, I look up, seeing Frank in the doorway with a riffle to his eye pointing it at Dominic who's standing there with his jaw clenched and his palms up.

"Hey man, we were just talking-" He starts, but Frank narrows his eyes, not having it.

"You want me to kill him Lola?" Frank asks.

My eyes go wide. "*What?* NO! Don't kill him in my kitchen!"

Frank nods. "You heard the woman. Now go on. *Get.*"

Dominic scrambles, running from the kitchen.

"And if you hurt either of those boys tonight I will *shoot you down in the yard the next time I see you!* No questions asked." Frank roars after him.

Rolling from side to side I whimper as I pull at my clothes, struggling to pull them up over my hips in my awkward position on the floor. I gasp, crying big heaving breaths. "Oh my God, Frank. *Oh my God.*"

He come to his knees before me and pulls me into his arms, letting me cry all over him.

"Lola are you okay? Are you okay child?" I nod, the tears and snot making me unable to say anything intelligible. His hand lands softly on my cheek, and his almost silver eyes show nothing but concern as he looks at me. "Did he..."

"No." I shake my head on a sob, trying to fix my top and sort myself out.

Frank narrows his eyes, frowning. "That fucking bastard." Standing up, he reaches into his back pocket for his phone. "I'm going to call Hudson."

I heave myself off the ground so fast that I trip, being snatched up by Frank, who's strong grip keeps me from toppling over into the floor again. "NO!" I yell. Desperate, I clutch at both of his shoulders, digging my nails in, begging him to listen to me. "You don't *understand* Frank, Hudson will kill him! He'll go to prison! *No!* Promise me you won't tell him! *Promise me!*"

"That man deserves it, Lola!" His eyes flash at me, and I can tell he is fuming mad.

Madder than I've ever seen him.

I shake my head. "No! Frank please, please don't make me. *Promise me Frank! I just found him, I don't want to lose him."*

Frank deflates. "You stubborn girl. I don't agree with this, Lolita." He stares at me for a few more seconds, and when he sees I'm not backing down, he relents with a sigh. "Let's get you cleaned up." He turns me towards the hallway, walking me with a gentle hand on my elbow. "Lola we need to do something about him. This isn't good. Dominic's going to retaliate, try to hurt you again.

"I know but, I'm going to take him to court for full custody," I say shakily. "I might lose my house in the process, but at least we'll have each other."

Frank pins me with a warm stare. "No, I won't let you lose your house Lola, you have support. We'll help you through this. But I don't agree with you not telling Hudson."

Shaking my head I stop him just in the doorway of my powder room. "Frank, you didn't see what Hudson did to him in that storage room. There's a side to Hudson that's....different. And I don't want to agitate it."

Franks lips thin into a disapproving line, but he nods his head once, thankfully letting it go.

In the bathroom he wrings out a warm rag and gently washes my face, making me back to being presentable. The adrenaline from the night fades, leaving me crashing. Emotional, I begin to cry once more at how tender he's treating me.

I've missed having a family so much, and his grandfatherly presence does much to soothe me.

Patiently, he holds me to his chest, giving me comfort until my hands stop trembling. The sound of the front door closing causes me to tense back up, and I peer around Frank's arm timidly, scared Dominic's come back to retaliate.

Frank catches my nervous action and sticks his head out the powder room, keeping me behind him with a firm hand on my arm.

"Hello? Lola?" I hear Hudson voice and sag with relief, sinking to the toilet with a hand to my quivering tummy. I hold my other hand to my mouth and focus on breathing deeply. Frank gives me a quick look but I wave him away, shaking my head.

"Hey Hudson. How're you?" Frank calls out, walking out of the bathroom and closing the door quietly behind him, shutting me inside the small room.

Rising quickly to my feet, I turn the tap on and splash more water on my face, straining hard to hear them talk. Their voices get louder as they pass the bathroom.

"Where's Lola?" Hudson asks as they walk pass the closed door.

"She's in the bathroom. She had a little accident in the kitchen so she's just washing her face, trying to calm down-"

"An accident? Is she okay? Nevermind, let me go see her." His footsteps get louder as he doubles back to the bathroom.

I tense, placing a shaky smile on my face, trying to prepare myself for him to knock on the door, but it never comes. Frank intervenes again.

"*No* Hudson, leave her be. We should probably go into the kitchen and clean up the glass vase that broke. She's a bit upset because that vase was a family heirloom. Give her a moment, she'll be out in a few minutes. That girl really likes to be left alone when she's upset doesn't she? Let me tell you what happened."

As their voices fade down the hallway, my shoulders relax and I let out a deep breath.

I give myself another couple of minutes to breathe, willing my color to go down. I fix my bangs, wishing they were a bit longer to cover my red rimmed eyes and swallow hard, feeling my throat burn from the intensity of my screaming. When I think I'm ready I exit the bathroom and walk into the kitchen, seeing the men at the little table and no sign of glass or water on the floor.

Hudson's got his back to me, facing the wall where the backdoor is, and Frank's sitting across from him. Frank gives me a little assessment that I attempt to ignore as I get closer.

"Hi," I say softly.

I come up from behind where Hudson's sitting in a chair at the table, careful to keep my hands to my side so he doesn't try to snatch me to him. I give him a kiss on his cheek before quickly turning and walking to the cabinet to grab a water glass, purposefully keeping my back to him.

"You two want some water?" I wince at how breathless my voice is. Not even waiting for a reply, I grab two more to buy myself a few more seconds of privacy.

"Hey baby, are you okay? I heard you had a accident." Hudson's deep voice penetrates my mind, and as I work to pour water into our glasses, I also use that time to beat back the tears that are threatening to spill over.

"Yep," I say simply, sipping my water slow as I can.

Thankfully Frank sticks around for a while. Tells Hudson a bullshit story about him showing me a gun, and because I still don't know what I'm doing with weapons, I accidently had it going off in the kitchen. Though it's actually a good story, and not in the realm of things that wouldn't really happen due to my clumsiness, I know he's smarter than that.

"Loli," Hudson says in a stern but soothing voice that brings tears to my eyes again. "You can't be setting off guns in the kitchen, honey. *Frank, I don't know if this is such a good idea-*"

"We gotta keep trying, Hud. She needs to be able to protect herself," Frank says gruffly, tapping his hand on his arm in a soothing motion that's really unlike Frank.

Hudson catches it, however, and the movement makes Hudson's eyebrows raise.

His eyes slide over to here I am to look at me through my reflection in the window above the sink. I pray the story is convincing enough to explain away the bullet hole in the wall, and why I'm so shaken up.

"I'm just stupid," I say quietly, turning around to face them both. "I don't think I want to have weapons in the house right now."

Hudson sucks in a quick breath, and his entire body visibly tightens at his first real look at me since coming into the house. His eyes pierce me, makes me tremble so hard the water sloshes in the cup. I bring my other hand up to grasp it and Hudson's eyes dilate as he just stares at me, flickering his gaze down my entire body slowly.

I stand as still as I can as his eyes roam across my face, down my neck, my arms, breasts, seeing my abdomen trembling. When he gets to the center of my legs he stops before his nostrils flare with irritation. I can see the wheels of his mind turning.

I almost piss myself I'm so scared that somehow he knows.

Hudson's eyes flick back up to mine and gives me a frown, before giving Frank a look and they stare off for a minute. For the first time ever I am thankful for Frank's assholery.

After a few seconds where the silence gets almost unbearable to tolerate, his eyes slide to the backdoor. I try to be inconspicuous as I look over as well.

Fuck.

I close my eyes and take a deep breath because we're caught.

The trim is a bit busted, the wood is slightly splintered from where Frank kicked it in and I inwardly groan seeing Hudson's eyes narrow. His fingers begin to rap a steady beat against the table but he stays silent, and it's *quite* uncomfortable.

I clutch the glass harder in my grasp. When you tell a lie, you have to tell like a hundred more to cover up the first. But Hudson can't know about this, especially after the texts he read that Dominic sent me. It's too fresh. Thankfully he doesn't mention the door.

After a few minutes of talking, Frank eventually leaves, and I'm left working hard the rest of the night to placate Hudson.

Hudson knows something's wrong, however, he doesn't push. But he spends the night staring at me a lot harder than usual. His eyes follow me everywhere, and from the look in them I just know. *I know* he knows.

Not the details, of course, but he's paid enough attention to me to know when something is going on.

And I want to tell him, I wish I could.

"Let me," I whisper.

I get down on my knees in the shower and fuck him with my mouth for all I'm worth, but I notice he's taking a long time tonight to orgasm. I'm sucking, tugging, licking; doing all the things I know he likes, but it's still not working.

Hurt, I look up at him. "What's wrong? Am I not doing it...right?"

He looks down at me with a slightly put out expression, and places his hand softly to my cheek. "Yes, I'm sorry but I can't get into it tonight. There's something wrong with you, and I know you're hiding something from me."

I blink, yet again astounded by his bluntness. I lower my eyes in shame, feeling my face turn red. But I can't get up off the shower floor, I'm too weighed down by shame and fear. "I'm sorry." I whisper. "I just don't want to talk about it."

At my weak explanation Hudson grunts, turns the shower off, and clears his throat. Snagging a towel he turns to me, wrapping it around my body before hauling me off the floor.

"You go on ahead and get in bed, okay? I'm going to head out to my truck for a minute."

I nod, feeling a chasm between us I can't seem to make disappear. I can tell he does not like when I'm off kilter, it makes him off kilter too in a major way, it seems like.

Part of me wonders if this should be a red flag.

But I get into bed and roll over with my headphones, putting on a smutty book and will myself to relax.

3

I'm Ready Now

Hudson

I BYPASS MY TRUCK and head straight to Frank's house, because I'm getting some answers. Do they think I'm an idiot? I'm not, and I will not be ganged up on either. I get to his door in about two seconds flat, and before I can even bang on it, it's flying open.

"It's ten forty," Frank says in his stern voice. He's still up and dressed in his clothes from earlier, letting me know he was waiting for me.

He steps aside and I walk in confidently. *"What happened?"* I ask sternly. I'm not fucking around.

His eyes flash at me. "I can't tell you that."

Cocking my head I eye him, not expecting him to have been that honest. "Why not?"

Frank's chin raises as he looks down his nose at me. But it's not a look of disrespect, it's one of resolve. "Because Lolita trusts me. She made me promise, and I am a man of my word." He frowns before raising a finger, pointing at me. "But I will tell you, son, that man needs *taken care of.* I've been patient, even stepping aside and not handling him myself because she's asked me not to get involved."

I bristle at the hint that Dominic is involved somehow. "It's his day with the boys the boys. *Give me something here Frank."* Shoving my hand through my hair I wait patiently, though honestly, I'd love to choke the information out of him.

But I can't -*wont*- allow myself to do that to Frank.

Frank clears his throat, tilts his head and remains silent, pinning me with his cold, gray eyes. His stare is rather eerie, he looks like he's seen some things.

"That man does not play by the same rules that everyone else does." He pauses. "How serious are you about Lolita, Hudson?"

I hold his stare. "I plan on making her my wife." Frank's lips tighten into a straight line, making a shiver of unease crawl down my spine. "Do I have your blessing?" I ask respectfully, seeing he's the closest she has to a father. "I'm ready, Frank. She's the only one for me and I *won't* take no for an answer."

Frank frowns and looks to the side. I know he doesn't like it. I haven't been around that long so I can't blame his hesitancy.

"You know, my Gloria and I only knew each other for a year before we had our first child. We were married fifty years before she passed." I nod, understanding him. His next words take me back a bit. "I gleam that *you* do not play by the rules either."

I stare at him, wondering what he's alluding to as it could be a couple things. I stay silent, letting him give me the answer rather than asking for it.

"Like your late night strolls in the woods out back," Frank emphases.

I fight back a grin. I knew he knew, I was just wondering when he was going to say something. "So you knew about that, huh?"

"Hudson," Frank gives me a weary look. "I knew about you before even that *girl* knew about you."

Well okay then. "So, are you going to tell her?"

"No. I think we can keep that between us, don't you?" It wasn't a question.

I give it to him straight. "Frank, was Dominic over her house tonight?"

Frank gives me a little sniff and then turns, placing his hand on my shoulder in a surprisingly firm grip and begins to walk. I'm beside him step by step. "Let's have a talk son, because I can tell you're incredibly smart and instinctual yeah?"

Instinctual. Sure.

"I guess so, Frank."

He leads me into this room filled with gun lockers and a metal box in the corner of the room. My eyebrows raise at the contents of the small space. Frank closes the door, shutting us inside.

"Son, I was married for fifty years. Sometimes women need their things they keep to themselves, and though you don't like it, you have to respect that they have their reasons for it." He folds his arms, giving me a contemplative look. "Now, I may be overstepping here, but if you want to keep your relationship with Lolita, I'm going to suggest you not try and get her to talk to you about what happened tonight. That woman is as stubborn and as feisty as they come, and she needs a firm hand and a man who knows how to lead her the right way. It's the only way someone with her spirit will submit to you. And Hudson, if you're going to be a man, you need to learn how to straddle the line between what you *want,* and what is going to keep the peace. And right now, you need to be that woman's peace."

I frown. "Hmm-hmm."

"Okay." He points a finger at me. "Don't listen to me if you don't want to, but don't you fucking come running to me when you push her so hard she breaks. Learn to carefully pick your battles. Why get hung up on one battle, when we have a fucking war to see to? So, I'm going to ask you to read between the lines with my next question. *Do you hunt?"*

I look at him and raise an eyebrow. "I've not...not before. Do you?"

Frank nods. "Fourteen bucks in seventy two, eight in seventy-four, twenty eight in seventy-five, thirty-three in seventy-six, and ten in seventy-seven. A slew of bucks in the nineties in South America. Some of my best work."

I grunt impressed, I find myself really praying we're talking about hits in his time in the marines, and not rogue hits, which is what I'm planning.

"You sleep good at night?"

He steps to me, clasping me on my shoulder. "Like a fucking *baby*, Hudson. And so will you."

We lock eyes and everything in me respects this man, because he sees what I believe is the sickness in me, and rather than fear and shame it, he understands and encourages it.

"You let me know when you're ready, Hudson. I'll be here."

"Yes sir."

He leads me out into the main part of the house and I head back to my truck, pulling out my phone as I climb in the drivers seat.

Clayton answers on the first ring. Good man. "Hey Hud."

"Clay," I say, speaking rapidly. "I need you to send me all the security feed from the back of Lolita's house tonight."

Yes, I know what Frank said, but what Lola doesn't know, wont hurt her. He sends it to me and I spend a few minutes fast forwarding through the evening when I see it. Dominic and her in the kitchen.

My blood pressure spikes at the sight of them so close, and alone.

He's got an evil look on his face, no boys.

I can't see her face, her back is to me, and she's got the table between them. She begins to shuffle to the left because of how he's coming at her, and the look on his face is *sick*. He fakes her out and then she lunges across the table to get to the door way.

He grabs her, snatching her up hard and knocking the flowers I got her to the floor.

I'm calm. Way too calm watching this. Because it's decided. His fate is sealed. I just need the boys gone. As I sit there, watching her cry and scream as he pulls her pants down, I let the sickness in me take over and began to concoct a plan. Something to figure out for them to do for fall break to get them out of the way long enough for me to do what I need to do.

Because the man *was* just going to get knocked off and buried. But now?

Oh Dominic, you best believe you are getting absolutely tortured for what you did to my baby girl tonight.

My lips curl with displeasure. I sit here stoically, letting hate fill my being as I see her mouthing my name over and over again. Calling for me, but I wasn't there.

He's getting *truly* fucked up for that.

I'm so angry that I can't even feel relief when I see Frank break her door down and shoot into the kitchen, scaring him.

Making up my mind, I start my truck and make the ten minute drive to his house and park across the street. Sitting there for a second, I contemplate my surroundings, seeing the house is dead quiet with no signs of life. Jumping out, I head to the back of the home and with the simple pick of a lock I'm in, walking into Dominic's house that smells like old food and stale cigarettes.

I quietly go down the hallway and pass a cracked door, seeing the twins in there sleeping on a mattress on the floor. Tucker's lunch box is open next to him, half eaten.

I make my way deeper into the hallway until I get to the master bedroom and walk in. Having pretty good vision, I take in the space before I settle myself in the corner of the room on a wooden chair where I cross an ankle over my knee and breathe deeply.

I can't kill him tonight.

I care about those boys too much to subject them to waking up to their father murdered. Or waking up alone because I took him out of there to kill him. But the fact that we're almost there-so close, gives me comfort.

I watch him sleep for a while. Curious as to how dormant his instinct for danger is, currently asleep right along with his subconscious. He's just *oblivious,* knocked out probably in a drunken haze. I pull out my knife, busying myself releasing and retracting the blade over and over again. Imagining sinking it into his flesh.

The tiny whistle of air of the blade slicing through gives me joy. After a bit, I make up my mind.

"Wake. Up." My voice comes out rough, stern, but quiet.

Dominic's head turns before his eyes snap open and find mine. He sits up with a shout, scrambling up the bed, knocking over the bedside lamp in his desperation to turn it on. The room lights up in a flash before plunging back into darkness as the bulb shatters.

"You don't have to be afraid," I say quietly.

The scent of his fear is thick as he freezes with his back against the headboard. The fear and sleep fades from his eyes, being replaced by pure evil as he sees who's sitting in the corner of his room.

"What the fuck are you doing in my house?" His voice is heavy with thinly veiled terror within his deep timber that soothes my soul just right.

I stay silent for a minute, letting him taste my displeasure.

"I am quite unhappy, and couldn't begin to see how to settle myself after what I came home to. *So,* I decided to pay you a visit," I answer simply.

The silence stretches between us as I let him be aware I know.

"Man, I didn't fucking rape her. She's lying to you." Dominic pulls the covers back, moving as if he's about to swing his legs out of bed.

Tilting my head, I pin him with a stare, seeing his eyes go slightly wide. "Oh no. I'd stay right there if I were you. This will go so much easier on you if you just listen to me."

Dominic pauses, settling his leg back on the bed. He bunches the blanket at his crotch and gives me a slow once over. "So, what... you're here to kill me?"

I shake my head. "No. I'm here to talk to you, Dominic."

He laughs a rough, scoffing sound that scratches that part of my psyche that can't stand to be annoyed. "You want to talk to me, huh? You couldn't pick up the phone like a *normal person?*" Dominic growls.

"I'm not normal. Don't even delude yourself into thinking I am." He blinks as I lean forward. "Now the *last* time you put your hands on my woman," I lean my elbows onto my knees and then point a finger at his face. "I marked you behind your ear. This time, I can't trust myself to put my hands on you, because those boys are here. But I just want to let you know, respectfully, from man to man, that you're going to pay for that."

"Oh please. You're not going to do anything to me." Dominic scoffs with a laugh. "Lolita wouldn't let you. Did you know she told that idiot neighbor of hers not to shoot me? You think she's going to stay with you after you show her how psycho you are by hurting me? How do you think she's going to feel when I tell her you broke into my house in the middle of the night-"

I cock my head, inspecting the features in his face thoroughly. "You think I give two shits about what she would think regarding this?" I gesture between me and him, shaking my head. "No, Dominic. Because she's firmly in her place where she *should* be. Being a woman. Letting her man handle shit. But, I can see where you'd *think* she would have that kind of power over me." The air goes thick with tension between us. "Hmm, maybe so. Because *you* let her have that power over you, huh? That's why you can't let her go."

Dominic's brow lowers even more, letting me know I've hit a nerve.

I sit back in the chair, spreading my legs and folding my arms. "Option A Dominic, I kill you now, right here, and walk out with these boys. Or option B, we shelve this."

"Shelve it?"

"Hmm-hmm. You leave those kids alone, *especially* Tucker. You don't retaliate against him because you're mad at the fact you couldn't have your way with Lolita. We all act like this never happened. Simple."

I need those boys to stay safe until fall break.

"And if I don't?"

"If you don't, *then,* I take the video footage of you assaulting Lolita to the police, and have you arrested."

A spark of something that isn't stupid flashes in his eyes. "Why don't you do that now?"

"Because those boys don't need a prison daddy."

No, they need a dead one.

I can't have him going to prison where I can't reach him. But I don't say that out loud. He'll find out soon enough. As I play my hand, I let him think my love for them is my weakness, and it is, to a certain extent.

"Fine," he snarls. "I won't say anything to her, and I won't fuck up the boys. Happy? *Now get out of my house."*

"Gladly. You're an awful homemaker." I grit as I stand up and pass by his bed. His eyes follow me closely, and I keep my ears tuned for any movement in case the fucker tries to reach for a gun and shoot me in my back.

Making my way out the front door, I leave the house and head back to Lola's.

In no time at all I'm back in her room, seeing her fast asleep. She looks so peaceful, with no hint of the stress in her face from earlier. I take my clothes off and slide into bed silently next to her, contemplating for the next hour, wide awake.

Making my mind up, I turn the bedside lamp on and shift the covers.

Carefully, as to not disturb her, I move between her legs and spread them looking down at the flesh between her thighs. I breathe a sigh of relief seeing no signs of trauma. It appeases me slightly.

And I mean only *slightly*.

Moving lower my nostrils flare as I smell her. I know it's fucked up, but I need to know without a shadow of a doubt. I breath deeply, not smelling anything other than her scent. Pushing my tongue to her opening I taste her unique flavor, groaning with relief as she tastes normal.

The thought of that man's hands on her has got every blood cell in my body on fire.

I began to look her over, looking for bruising that would maybe pop up after the fact. Seeing slight shadows in the shape of fingerprints on her arms, my face tightens so hard I feel like I'm going to have a stroke with how murderous I feel. But soon after, my thoughts turn to something else.

The texts he's sent. How he knows she takes a long time to orgasm.

Should I tell him how hard I had to fuck you to make you cum? He'd said.

No. But I should probably tell you how slowly I'm going to pull your jugular from your neck when your time is up. And I know it's fucked up, but my jealousness takes over. His texts, what he did tonight, he's been inside her... she's had that monsters babies.

My boys.

I'm dying on the inside fighting every instinct I have to erase his very existence from the earth, but what I can do right at this moment is replace his touch.

Lola begins to stir, realizing I'm just hanging out, laying in between her thighs.

"Hudson?" she whispers.

Her voice is raspy with sleep. I answer her by taking her clit into my mouth. She tastes so delicious. I might have actually left again and killed him tonight if I smelled his scent on her.

"I'm ready now baby, I'm sorry I wasn't earlier," I say quietly, murmuring into her flesh.

"It's okay, I want you however I can have you." She moans, moving her thighs restlessly against my shoulders.

Me too baby. And you're about to get it alright.

Right now.

4
EARN IT!
HUDSON

I GROWL, FEELING A hot bead of sweat run down my temple. My pulse is pounding, and I see the veins standing out in sharp relief against my arms as I grip her hips tight.

"Uh-huh, baby. Yeah. You fucking know what you're doing, *huh*, bouncing on top of me like that?" I growl at her. "I feel thicker this way don't I? I know you love this pussy being stretched out. *Harder*, you got some more left to go."

I keep my eyes tight on hers as she works frantically on top of me, screwing our flesh together. Her eyes go hooded and her lips part, responding to my tone. She loves when I talk dirty.

But let me tell you what I love; her complete and utter *earth-shattering abandon* when we're fucking.

"Hudson," she gasps, *"you're h-hitting the back of my-"*

Fisting my hands in her hips, I yank her down harder, making her scream. "We'll make it fit." I growl hoarsely.

I move one hand to her clit and strum it fast, mercilessly. Pinching and rolling it between my fingers, causing her to let out a high pitched moan.

Her headboard bangs hard against the wall as I jack my hips up, making sure she gets all of me in her. The sheets tore off the bed long ago, and we're just fucking on the bare mattress without a care in the world right now except each other. Her breasts slap loudly against her ribcage and I reach up, pulling her down to my mouth so I can take a nipple between my teeth and nip at it.

Lola whimpers and falters in her movements, but I keep making her ride me, getting her back in rhythm while she acclimates to my mouth on her sensitive flesh.

She lets out a tortured cry and it makes my heart skip a beat, so, I suck harder. *Really* making her feel it. And when she squirts all over my pelvic, I help her pound even harder. I want us both wet with her cum, and I want us both sore at the end of this session.

It's loud. Rough. We're being messy, and God, sometimes I honestly think sex is the best thing ever invented.

The smell of it, the sounds, the feel. It's *otherworldly*. For a moment, two souls touch in a beautiful matrimony of physical expression unlike anything else. It's you, the other person, and you're literally inside of each other. It's the physical manifestation of the invisible bond that you know is already there.

But when you are in love with that person?

Well, I stop thinking and start knowing. Because there's nothing better than being inside of Lola.

Nothing.

Lola's whimpering, gasping, clawing her nails into my chest and I couldn't be happier. I'm letting her take the lead with this session of ours.

I think she deserves it.

She deserves to fight, struggle and *strain* for her orgasm. Because when you work for something as hard as what she's currently working for, it's just not right to step in and help them across the finish line and take that little bit of glory away.

"Hudssooonnn!" Lola let's out a cry that I swear almost stops my heart.

"Uh-uh," I chastise. "You don't want to tell me what the fuck really happened? You want to keep stuff from me, then you're going to suffer the consequences."

I jam all the way inside her and roll my hips, keeping her fully pressed against me, ignoring her sharp scream that tappers off into a whimper. My body jerks up and down hard with her movements.

"I don't give a shit about your whimpering. Keep slapping that pussy on me." I throw my head back with a rough growl of my own. "Oh my God, Lo'! *Fuck me!* Jesus *Christ,* baby. You're doing so well. *So wellll."*

Trust me, when you struggle for something the way my baby is right now, she deserves *all* the credit, and I'm going to let her have it. Every beautiful, delectable, painful, pleasurable bit of it. And if I have to cheer her on as she limps across the finish line, well, then dammit call me her biggest cheerleader because let me tell you...

The woman can *fuck.*

And because I'm a jealous motherfucker, it's irritating my soul.

She's fucking me like her *life* depends on it.

I let out a deep groan, my head tilts back once more as my body mists with sweat again and I am straight *suffering* as I concentrate on pushing back my orgasm. My dick twitches inside her hard, once, twice, three times as a hard shiver races up my spine and down the length of my cock, tingling at the very tip. Which she's currently focused on.

She's so hot and velvety.

My ears pick up on the little suctioning sounds of her pussy as she fucks herself on the broad first couple inches of my sensitive cock, stimulating her g-spot. Being fucking selfish at the moment.

The air freezes in my lungs, making me gasp to fight to breathe.

"Oooohhhhhh" I toss my head back on a growl, before cutting it off, feeling strong because I'm successfully beating my orgasm back despite her attempts to throw me off.

I'm not ready yet, but it's beginning to hit me it don't matter what I want right now. Because she just got up on her feet and she's slapping her pussy hard on and off my fat dick. Hitting my pelvic with a little sharp smacking sound, accompanied by a breathy moan like she thinks the answers to all her problems might be found if she can get me just a little deeper.

A little harder.

And honestly baby, the answers just might be there for the both of us if you have the strength to keep looking.

My attention is drawn back to her face as she flinches hard on a particularly rough downswing that I met with a little lift of my hips, surprising her.

"Oww!" she whimpers, biting her lip.

"Does it hurt baby?" I grit up at her, seeing her hair bouncing with her movements. Excitement flashes through my entire being at the thought.

"God Hudson- "

"I asked you a fucking question!" I snarl up at her.

"Yes!" Lola screams, but she doesn't stop slapping her hips down on me.

"Good. I want it to."

Her eyes are wide as she looks down at me.

"Do you like it?" I say, clenching my jaw.

"Y-Yes!"

I feel a bead of sweat drip down my face and my neck as her words unknowingly strike a chord, and I make a pleased sound, feeling her cunt sucking along my length. Her pussy gets super hot around my dick, and my lip twitches because I know she's about to orgasm. And it irritates the fuck out of me, because her orgasms have been starting to come a little faster.

It's not taking her as long as it normally does.

And I don't like that.

She tries to slow down, but I lean forward and pull her nipple into my mouth in a hard suck, making her flinch as she tries to lean away. I jerk her back, tightening my hands on her hips even more, quickening the pace. Her walls flutter around me, throbbing.

I pull away from her nipple to talk to her.

"Lola don't fucking come yet." I grit at her, glancing down, feeling a stream of her juices slicking its way up the v of my pelvic. *"Stop it!"*

I take her nipple back into my mouth and tighten my teeth, making her yelp. Making her just as crazy, feral, and fucked as she makes me. The banging of her headboard is driving me insane.

"No-No Hudson, please." She begs, but I wont relent.

"No."

I want my baby to take her time like she does with everything else. So, she needs to fucking take her time with me like I'm just as important, if not *more* important, dare I suggest. Lola slams herself down even harder onto my dick, making her nipple jerk in my mouth.

Seeing she's disobeying me, I snatch her hips and lift mine slightly off the bed, making her lose her footing. She looks down in shock to catch my eye.

I'm breathing hard, every muscle in my body is locked tight. Those jealous thoughts come back, uninvited. I release her nipple with a rough tug, letting it scrape through my teeth in a slight punishment, making her cry out and dig all ten of her nails into my chest. She lets out a little growl and it thrills me. Been wanting to hear that since the first time I fucked her.

I roll her clit slowly, seeing sweat drip down her chest and in between her heaving breasts.

"Who the fuck taught you how to fuck like this? *Huh?*" It comes out angry, harsh, hoarse, my eyes narrow at her because goddamn she's almost *too* perfect at this and I really want to know why. *"I know that fucker didn't teach you. He better not have."*

Lola lets out a little whimper, suddenly unsure.

Her fingers tighten against me and I give her a little grind, lowering our hips to the bed. As soon as her knees hit the mattress she's trying to scramble back to her feet. There's desperation in her voice that feeds the beast inside of me, and fuck everything I just said about letting someone have the victory all to her own, I'm about to make her suffer for her prize.

"N-no Hudson, I want to come, *I want to come!*" Her eyes are wide, and the whines escaping her lips are panicked sounding.

But just not desperate enough for me.

Victory is always sweeter when a curveball is thrown in and you have to conquer your adversary right when you think your fingers are almost on the trophy.

I pick her up by her hips and make her bounce up and down on me hard.

Too hard.

Hard enough to beat back her orgasm a little bit. She lets out a screech that I know is going to make her throat sore later, but I don't care. I give her a few more of these hard thrusts, and when she tries to lift her knees to get her feet back under her, I elbow her legs back down how I want them and slap her thigh.

Because my baby is going to fight me to the death for this orgasm.

She's not going to limp across the finish line, I'm going to make her *drag* her way across by her finger nails. The ones currently embedded in my flesh.

"I *said* who the fuck taught you to fuck like that?" I shout at her, snatching her by her hair to jerk her to my face. *"Was it him?"* My eyes narrow.

Unwanted visions of them fucking fill my head and it sends my hatred and lust through the roof. How dare he touch her. Ever.

How dare *she* not feel like she could trust *me* enough to tell me?

I grunt, pumping her up and down in my arms, working us together hard in a harsh rhythm. This bed's going to break. I tilt my head, seeing her hair beginning to mat to her skin and tangle. Her fingers slip along my wet skin, and she falls forward crashing into me hard on a cry. I push her back, getting us back in rhythm.

She doesn't get a get-out-of-jail-free card because she's clumsy.

"Lola, stay right there." I chastise her.

But I want to ask her. *Did he try to hurt you tonight, baby?* God, I wish she would just tell me what happened. But we can't even get past the first question I asked her because she's biting her lip to keep herself quiet.

My anger and desire swirl in a fucked up tornado of lust. I'm so upset that it makes me fuck into her even harder, hearing a rather concerning crack indicating a piece of her headboard might of just split. *Cheap piece of shit.*

Lola shakes her head, her eyes going even wider.

My eyes narrow at her. *"You better fucking answer me Goddamnit it.* I said was-" thrust, *"it,"* thrust, *"him?!"*

She's strains against my hold, and it's beautiful sight. "No! It wasn't him, Hudson. *God!"*

We're staring at each other, only a foot away, but she's just not close enough for me.

"Are you sure? You're too good at this baby, *I don't like it.*" I raise a hand to fist in her hair and yank her to where she's just a couple inches away from my face. Her belly rubs intimately against mine as she undulates on top of me. "I know that fucker didn't teach you how to suck dick the way you do, or how to fuck the way you are, *so, answer my question.*"

"No!" she yells.

Her hips jerk, straining into mine.

I let her have the control back, just for a second, and right when I feel the right hot clasp of her pussy, I take her and drag her off of me backwards from the finish line again. I know her hips are going to be bruised tomorrow.

"You don't tell me no! Who the fuck do you think you are defying me?! Huh? I ought to rip out your fucking tongue for ever having had it on his dick!"

Mentally I feel like a fucking animal. All instinct, as I work to fuck this woman so good that she ever forgets she ever had anyone inside her before I got to her.

I'm back to making her bounce on me. I'm completely aware we're struggling against each other with everything we've got. But even if Frank *himself* came in here with a gun to my head to tell me to stop, he'd just have to shoot me at this point.

I'm too far gone.

"What?" she gasps, furrowing her brows.

I shake my head at her one time. "You heard what the fuck I said," I say roughly.

I spend a couple minutes thrusting, the squeaking of her bed sounds loudly in the room driving my insanity to greater heights.

"Ohmigodohmigod," Lola shudders as tears fall down her face, splashing against her breasts.

"Your bed's a piece of shit. I'm replacing it this week," I say to her, curling my lip as I watch her breasts bouncing. "I can't hear your breasts slapping the way I want to because *the shit's so fucking loud!"* I shout, gripping her hips even tighter.

Lola throws me a dirty look, but I meet her with one of my own. "Say something," I taunt her. *"Give me one good reason to fuck you up, girl."*

"Goddamn it l-let me! Hudson let me cooommeee!" she screams, thrashing on top of me.

Her fingers claw at my hands to try and force me to break my grip, but I'm too strong. I tighten even more in warning.

"I'm not just letting you have nothing," I snarl at her. "You'll have what the fuck I *tell* you you can have. And right now I am pissed, baby girl. There's *no way* I'm going to let you fuck me the way you fuck anyone else. *No way, Lola.* Straighten your ass up and fight for it! *You want me?* You want what this dick can do to you, then you better fucking *earn it!"* I shout this last bit at her, and I swear I'm at my breaking point.

But so is she.

Magically, suddenly, she's slapping at me. Her palm connects with my face so hard I see swear I see stars. I suck in a sharp breath, turning my face back to her and bracing myself for another slap. This next one really hurts as she doesn't hold back.

Fuuuck.

I love being hit, and she is delivering it just how I need it.

She's slapping my face, the side of my head, my neck, my shoulders, and as an added bonus she's scratching at me. Rough, sex-crazed sounds mix with Spanish and I have never, and I mean *never*, heard another person lose her mind sexually the way she just did.

I think I actually broke her.

She bends forward and latches onto my neck with a low grunt, right over my vein. My body breaks out into another mist of sweat, and shuddering, I snatch her to me by one arm around her ass with another arm around her shoulder, just grinding into her.

I let out a rough sound. "That's right baby, bite *harder. Harder!*" I shout as she whimpers and tightens her teeth so hard I feel her break my skin causing my entire body to tighten viscously. I growl, pressing her mouth even harder against me. "Suck like you mean it, Lolita."

With every hot pull of her mouth, my dick jerks hard inside her. We struggle for a second; her tearing into me, and me tearing into her pussy.

I love it.

She yanks on my hair as I move under her, relentlessly treating her to those thrusts I know she loves. And she isn't even aware, because she's so lost in attacking me and it's amazing. I let out a growl, reach between us, grab her throat and pull her off my neck, seeing her eyes roll to the back of her head.

"This how you like it, huh? Like me fucking you this rough? Want me to make you bleed?" I lick across the seam of her mouth as I tighten my hand around her throat, cutting off her breathing so she has to strain to answer me.

She makes a strangled sound and I let up, hearing her suck in a ragged inhale.

It hits me then that we've never established a safe word, and God-damn it the thought alone makes me swell even more inside her sweet cunt. Making me wince at how sensitive my shaft is. Because I don't want a fucking safe word with her.

I want this dynamic between us just the way it is.

"Uhhnnn, I like it, I like it Hudson!" She sounds feral, crazed.

We're almost there.

I tighten my hand again, cutting off her words. "Beg me for your next breath," I grit out. She scratches at my forearms, the color slowly draining from her face. *"I said beg me."*

Lola makes a sound that almost stops my heart just as a slow stream of her juices slicks over my abdomen, and keeps going and going. Her eyes meet mine and widen as she jerks hard before her hands fall away. Her body heaves as she strains to take a breath through the grip around her throat.

Her thighs grip me tightly as she wiggles. *"P-Please,"* she whimpers. Her throat convulses under my hand.

"No!" I say, tightening minutely more and watching her eyes slam shut as more wetness travels between us. I let go as she begins to go limp.

She tosses her head back and weakly wails something in Spanish that sounds like *help me,* and I know that I wont have long before I need to have my release. Because we're fucking so good she's screaming for help? Yeah, baby's lost her mind. *For me.*

It's a bout damn time, because *my* mind was gone a long time ago concerning her.

I hear her desperate, guttural sounds as she drags in precious air into her lungs, and I make it worse. *"Help?"* I mock her, teasing her through the blood roaring through my head.

Lola's wiggling on top of me with everything she's got. I chuckle at her as I relent, letting her have the control back for a second. She makes a happy, desperate sound as she slaps her hands against my chests and finally gets her feet under her. And as she's lifting up, I'm yanking her back down by her *throat.*

The fact this woman gets turned on by me doing the same thing that fucking piece of shit did do her has got me ready to take this up a notch for both of us.

I pull her head back by her hair and meet her shocked eyes.

"You don't need help. Help yourself, Lolita. *Take it,*" I grit out, yanking her harder and *harder* as I begin to swivel and circle my hips with every smack into her body. I know this shit has to hurt on some level, but she's not complaining. Her small hands wrap around my wrist and forearm and just hang on.

This is the roughest sex I've ever had. The type of sex I only ever dreamed of a woman letting me have with her, and I hope to God she can meet my eyes later.

"Shit, baby, are you okay love?" I groan, feeling my ears start to ring and my head goes almost stuffy as all the blood decides to flow south, and I become somehow even thicker inside her. My hips churn relentlessly, my cock burns, aching for release.

My heart bangs so hard against my chest that I think I'm going to have a heart attack.

"Yeessssssss," she lets out a tortured sound and I know she can feel me preparing to come.

It's pure fucking bliss, what's happening between us.

I let myself feel it; stop pushing my orgasm back and let my body have what it needs so she can take it from me. I feel my skin sizzle, my chest tightens as my heart goes from being where it's supposed to be, and being lodged in my throat then back again.

I treat her to a whimper and gasp of my own because she deserves to know what she does to me.

What she's working so hard for.

"Yeah baby, yeah! You're fucking my cock so well. Look at you. *Fuuuuck.* Goddamn it, you drive me wild. Pound yourself on me, Lolita. Goddamn."

I tighten up. My breaths saw in and out through my nose hotly, making me feel even more lightheaded. My dick swells even more inside of her, and she whimpers right along with me. Her eyes widen, and I just know she's feeling a burning sensation as I stretch her out even more.

My baby gets even hotter around me and I growl, feeling her freeze up, and then she lets out a shocked, crying noise that strikes that chord inside me, making me feral.

"Ugh!" I grunt, yanking her down to me with a resounding slap, and see two tears fall down her face.

Suddenly everything stops.

She stops breathing, I stop moving, and we're just jammed tight against each other silently when it happens. She flinches on a weak, shuddering moan. My jaw clenches on a growl, and we come together, looking into each other's eyes.

My fingers flex against her hip and throat, keeping her right where I need her.

Keeping her eyes on mine.

It's painful, what's just happened. What we're currently sharing...because we've somehow went a level above pleasure that I didn't even know was there. And I can tell you that this level is nothing but pain, desperation, and fear.

The throbbing of my release counteracts her clasps and sucks around my dick, and I settle us back into the mattress, keeping my hand around her throat. Not letting her up.

Because we're going to explore this level for a little while longer. Together.

And she's going to let me.

That's the least she can do since I've decided to murder her ex-husband. Because fuck if that man will ever take this away from me. That's why pain is a level above pleasure. Because when you finally find your happiness, all you can think about afterwards is how to keep it, the fear of losing it, and what are you going to do if you can never have it again.

I've spent my entire adult life wanting this, and I won't just kill Dominic if he tries, I will absolutely burn this *world* to the ground if it's taken from me now that I've finally got it.

When I release her a few moments later we're *both* trembling.

I pull my cock from her slowly, seeing a small smear of blood on my dick.

Laying back on the bed for a minute with my chest heaving, I secretly eat up that little bit of blood on my skin. Happy that the beast within me is finally having some meat to chew on instead of a bone, and he likes it rare.

Getting up, I grab a couple of hand towels and wet them, coming back to join her on the bed. I take the time to clean her pussy, being careful because I know she's sore as hell based on her sharp hiss of air and the way she closes her legs against my hand.

Cleaning my dick off, I pad back into the bathroom to throw the towels into the hamper before crawling back into bed with Lola who is almost completely limp, relaxed into the bed.

I roll to my side and pull her to me, rubbing her hair, her hips. Soothing her with long strokes before I smooth her bangs back and put my lips to hers.

"You are the best thing that's ever happened to me." I admit to her, not afraid to be vulnerable with her like this. Her eyes are hooded as she stares back at my quietly, made heavy with her satiated desire.

"You're just saying that because you just got some good sex," she breathes, sounding weak and tired.

It makes me unbearably happy because I like her worn out after sex.

"Hmm...it was some *really* good sex. The best I've had so far," I chuckle, brushing my knuckles down her cheek and pushing her hair off her sweat dampened face. Both our breathing is still slightly labored, and I feel like the luckiest man alive.

"Yeah," she chuckles, blowing out a slow breath that washes over my face.

I smile slowly. "It doesn't scare you, fucking this hard?" I ask, genuinely curious.

I don't want her to feel like she has to, and in a quiet moment of self reflection, I realize I'll bend for this woman. She's the only one I've ever felt like I'd change for, if I had to. I guess it's true what they say about love. It makes you consider things you didn't use to, throw away your selfish desires.

"Oh, no. Not at all, Amor. Not with you. Never with you," she whispers, closing her eyes and snuggling deeper into my arm.

Hooking her leg over my hip, we work to sink deeper into one another, arranging our limbs to accommodate our size difference. She's warm and soft, and smells just like how I like. Hard sex that mixes both of our scents together, seeped deep into her flesh.

I take her fleshy ass cheek in my hand and grip, massaging her firmly. We're both still slick with sweat, and my fingers glide over her skin easily. Pressing myself into her body harder, the feel of her nipples against my chest makes me wish I could go again, but baby girl has thoroughly drained me.

Lola moans as my mouth closes over hers, and I nibble, tugging her bottom lip in between my teeth. "You didn't get enough?" she murmurs into my mouth, letting me explore her slowly with my tongue.

"It's never enough where you're concerned baby. I won't be satisfied for a long time I don't think." Keeping my voice low, I relish the intimacy of our moment. Here in our dark bedroom the world and it's burdens feel so far away. Right now it's just me and her, and I take full advantage of it, treating her to slow kisses and little nibbles to her lips. "I want us to sink so deep into each other till there's nothing but you and I left."

I want to tell her I love her so badly, but she's guarded.

Hitching her leg even higher up my body, I press a palm into her ass and pull her even further into me. "Are you sore, beautiful? Does your pussy hurt?"

Lola blushes. "A bit."

A pleased rumble escapes my chest because fucking hell, that makes me feel so good. My response makes her blush harder, and she sinks her fingers into my hair and hides her face into my shoulder. I brush my hand down her hair and pull her back gently to look into her eyes, letting myself be even more vulnerable with her.

"I like that it hurts." My eyes flicker between hers. "It might not hurt well enough for me... does that scare you?" Sleepily, we stare at each other in the darkness, and I hear her breath hitch right as her nails sink into my scalp, and just like that, I feel my dick stirring again. Responding to her. "I love when you touch me like this," I say.

I have to let her know. because it's important for me for her to know that she affects me.

"It excites me." Lola admits, but her speech is slurred as she fights sleep hard. "So much about you excites me."

Leaning forward I press my lips to her forehead and keep them there, feeling her body completely relax into sleep.

It excites me. Her words echo in my brain, lulling me into the abyss of nothingness right after her.

So much about you excites me.

5

LOVE IS A CHEMICAL

LOLA

THE NEXT DAY I'M cleaning aimlessly at the shop, taking it slow as I'm in pain from how roughly Hudson fucked me last night. And all I can think about is what us women have to sacrifice and put up with in relationships.

Because try as I might to keep things casual and easy between us, Hudson proves time and time again that he's not having it. Demanding something deeper than surface level; knocking down wall after wall. Barreling his way into the very core of me, as if he has the right to be there. As if he's earned it.

Like he told me to earn it last night, and it's got me really, *really* thinking.

Women go through so much in the name of love. We raise babies by men who couldn't give a shit less about us and our children. We put on a brave face, and damn near staple a smile on our lips so our loved ones can't see we're absolutely buckling under the mental strain, mom guilt, and invisible burden that society likes to act like doesn't exist.

And as I do my best to keep a smile on my face for my patrons, I can't help but wonder about the shit we have to endure all for the sake of saying we have a man who loves us.

All day my mind has been whirling. Sobered by the fact that I was actually almost assaulted by the person I have children with. The same person who stood in front of that priest eight years ago, and promised to love and cherish me to death do us part.

I pause in putting a new liner in the coffee machine, shaking my head against the memory. Fucking shoot me in the head if I ever decided to get married again.

Love. I let out a scoff at the thought, slamming the lid to the machine closed and starting a fresh brew. *Love is a chemical.*

A bit later, not able to help it, I'm still obsessively thinking about it as I tinker around the shop, absentmindedly walking through the isles and straightening a book here, watering a plant there. Still busy thinking about the absolute raw intimacy that Hudson and I shared last night.

What we indulged in was borderline inappropriate. Something that him and I probably should have had an *extensive* conversation about beforehand.

What's confounding, however, is my reaction to it. Seeing as it basically paralleled what almost happened with Dominic, and I loved it. Ate it up. Wish it could happen again. And again. And again. I also replay everything he said to me last night, how manic he acted with me, what he forced me to endure. And I wasn't scared.

On the contrary, I was so turned on there was a moment that I came so hard on him I wet us both up so bad I was forced to scrub my mattress the next morning seeing we were so rough we tore the bedding off.

The trust I have in this man must qualify me as insane. So, I hesitate to call what we have love.

Because to me, love just *isn't* the word for this thing between us.

No. This is some sort of chemical imbalance that scientists have yet to offer us an explanation for. And I didn't use to believe in aliens, but now I do. Because just as I'm sure as shit that there's a cure for breast cancer, polio, and sclerosis, I know there's a extra chemical composition greater than love that whoever runs this fucking world won't let be known.

Because it's dangerous. This thing between Hudson and I.

"Love is a chemical."

I remember one time when Dominic's aunt Barbara told me that. We were hanging out by the kid splash pad at the public pool in the middle of the hottest day of the year when she said it out of the blue. I'll never forget it because I was sweltering, absolutely suffering. But the kids were loving it.

They were four years old, and I remember not wanting to be outside. I wanted to wait until that Sunday when it was supposed to be about ten degrees cooler, before we went to the pool. So, you know, *I* could actually enjoy the day with them all, too. But Dominic spent all night the night before wearing me down, promising me he would help pack up. He'd take a twin, I'd take a twin. Claiming that if we tag teamed them it'd be a fun day for us all.

I reluctantly agreed, seeing how excited he was.

I spent that morning packing up everyone's lunches and filling the cooler by myself. Making sure we had extra clothes, towels, our first aid kit, plenty of sunscreen and hats for all of us. I made an extra ham and cheese sandwich for Dominic. Peanut butter and jelly sandwiches on white toast with the crusts cut off for the boys.

I brought the entire twelve count box of capri sun because I just knew they were going to suck it down, and I wanted to be prepared. Then on the way to the pool, I'd stopped by the corner store to buy a gallon of water and some ice because I was terrified someone was going to get dehydrated.

And don't you know I was so busy putting the boys in the vehicle by myself to notice that Satan's brother didn't load the fucking cooler in the back of the SUV? He had one job and couldn't do it.

I was angry, but I slapped a smile on my determined, sweaty face anyways. Because love makes you overlook a multitude of faults, and we were married, and exchanged wedding vows that was supposed to *mean* something.

"We can buy some food at the concession stand!" Dominic said, giving me an eye roll.

As if money is just supposed to solve everything.

As if it doesn't eventually run out if you aren't careful. Like it just willy nilly falls off trees or some shit. And I guess for Dominic, he thought it did.

When he got with me I had money. *Lots of it.* More than what most people see in a lifetime. But I was young, and five million dollars stretched across what would hopefully be a long life, give or take six decades, doesn't amount to a lot. Not when you have two kids that will want to be in sports, hopefully college, be able to take a trip or two.

Let's not forget the fact insurance is high, and boys always hurt themselves, and before you know it that money is gone.

Then, he started realizing just how prolific my brother was. That's really when the problems started. Because Dominic didn't meet my brother until the twins turned three years old. Right around the time the abuse really started to become unbearable. I took him and the twins to California to meet him.

Dominic seeing Alejandro's California mansion for the first time was the craziest experience I think I'd ever had with him up until that point.

The man had literal stars in his eyes. But he quickly realized my brother was an asshole. He really is.

As much as I love him, Skee's a *fucking asshole.*

But he loves my boys, and he loves me. Enough to give Dominic probably what would have amounted to the total cost of my inheritance and insurance money that should have lasted me at least three decades had I been able to invest it right, save it, put some in CDs, etc.

We had more than enough to be comfortable, but Dominic was greedy.

And once he realized Alejandro was an asshole, he decided to be a *bigger* asshole. He began to make my life a living hell. Spending, spending, spending. And when I tried to move the money to another bank without his name on it, the fucker found out a way around that because we were married. Literally got a *lawyer* involved.

To spend my money.

The money began to dwindle and then suddenly the boys couldn't see my brother unless 'he paid for the privilege.' But it didn't quite start off that threatening. It began gradually, then escalated to the shit it is today.

Dominic is a monster. Plain through and through.

So love is a chemical, because chemical compositions change, and love can turn to hate real quick under the correct duress.

I believe that day at the pool was the real beginning of mine and the boy's duress. I was sitting next to Barbara, only in the half shade of the umbrella because I didn't want her to burn and she was twenty five years older than me, and kind enough to sit by me while I watched the twins *alone.*

Because Dominic abandoned me and the boys to play water sports with a group of people who were our age but didn't have kids.

I remember the pain I felt seeing him that day. He had a perky, twenty something year-old with big tits in a bikini sitting on his shoulders in the adult pool, hitting a volleyball over the net. While his wife sat in half shade, the other half of me getting sunburnt, trying to watch over two rambunctious twin toddlers while his *aunt* gave me company.

Feeling sorry for me.

Explaining to me why love is a chemical.

And she told me that while I was checking out Tucker's back, because despite the massive amounts of sunblock I put on him, he got a huge blister. I was trying to take care of it with my first aid kit, carefully reading the chemical ingredients on the tubes to make sure I wouldn't fuck up and make the burn worse.

I was smearing the stuff on, half listening to Barbara ramble on, when Dominic appeared out of nowhere, snatched Tucker out of my arms, and threw him in the adult pool. When Tucker couldn't swim.

"They're boys! He needs to toughen up!" he'd snapped.

Barbara was so horrified she stopped talking to Dominic afterwards. Said there was something wrong with him. Warned me to get out of the marriage. His own *aunt* said that.

I'm fortunate that it actually didn't take as many years as it does some other women for the concept to hit them, that sometimes you can do better by yourself. Because I got the fuck up out of that relationship about two years later. So what the hell do I look like getting into another one?

An idiot. That's what I look like.

6

I Can Make You Like Anything

Lola

"Hudson!" I squeal and put my clenched hands to my face, taking a step away from Champ.

This weekend we're solo. Hudson brought me out to the stables, wanting to take me for a late evening ride on Champ. He reaches for me, and tries to bring me closer to the huge beast. Though he's magnificent, all I can envision is him running me over and trampling my five foot one frame to death.

"No, no no no, Hudson! *Oh my Goddd..."* I pull against him, scared to get any closer to the tall steed.

Though I've come in here and talked to them, I've never been in the stall with them. Never directly stood next to one of them. Have you ever stood next to a huge animal with no protection between you? It's terrifying, and I think I might cry.

Hudson gives me a slow once over before tightening his fingers on me. "Come on, baby, I've got you."

I eye him warily. He's got one hand on the saddle horn, and the other stretched out holding my hand where I'm leaning back as far as our arms allow.

"Hudson I'm s-scared!" I whine.

"Hey, *look at me,*" he says softly, walking up to me now and putting his hand on the side of my face. I tremble as my eyes flicker back and forth between his. "There's nothing to be scared of. I promise you'll like it."

I shake my head rapidly. "No, *no I wont.*"

Dipping his head down at me he raises his eyebrows. *"Yes.* I'll make you like it."

"You can't make me like something, *Hudson!* That's now how things work-"

His eyes harden as he wets his lips "Oh I can make you like it alright. I can make you like whatever I do to you."

The low growl in his voice is my undoing and just like that, I'm wet. I lick my lips and I shift my feet, feeling my heart begin to pound. "Well..." I gesture a hand down my body, his eyes follow my agitated movements tightly. *"I-I'm too little to get on-"*

His eyes snap to mine, making me flush. "Size has got nothing to do with it. You spread your legs just fine when I fuck you."

My heart skips a beat as it's made very clear I've lost this round.

He drops my hand to turn and grab a folded blanket that's hanging on a nearby ladder, before walking back over to where Champ and I stand. I wring my hands, already knowing this is one fight I won't be winning based off the tone of his voice.

"B-But-" I stammer, biting my lip as he glances over at me with a hard set to his lips. His Stetson hat covers his brow, putting half his face in shadow, giving him a mysterious, sexy look.

"No. I want to go for a ride with my girl." His tone leaves no argument. "So, you're going to oblige your man and get on the horse so we can enjoy a nice evening ride and watch the fireflies." That sells it for me, and I say quiet, watching as he hoists the folded fleece blanket over the front saddle.

Flicking my eyes to the tall beast next to me, I let Hudson pull me around to the stool that Champ is standing next to and help me mount the double saddle. He mounts behind me before I even have a chance to react, sliding an arm around my waist and pressing me into him as we take off at a slow gait.

My eyes widen at the feel of the Champ under me as Hudson efficiently steers us to the right of the barn and to a path within the tree line of his property.

"Are you okay?" he asks, pressing his hand tighter into my stomach.

I nod and look around, noticing that I *do* feel safe.

It helps there's a million lightning bugs out here helping me to relax and feel content. We ride in silence for a few minutes, and I see why he wanted to do this. His property is so beautifully backlit with lavender, pinks and dark blues with the stars just popping out, twinkling so prettily. It's such a treat.

I wish my boys were here to see this. They deserve this view, and it makes me feel sad that they aren't hear to see it.

As always, when I start feeling down, I work to distract myself from my musings.

Throwing a look over my shoulder, I catch Hudson's gaze. He gives me a sly look along with a rather wicked crooked grin that causes butterflies to erupt in my stomach.

"Hudson, what's your favorite food?" I ask hesitantly.

Just because we're seemingly in a whirlwind romance doesn't mean we shouldn't know these things about each other.

Hudson gives me a laugh before tearing his eyes away to look ahead. He steers us between two oak trees, and we dip slightly as the trail inclines downward. His hand slips under my shirt, and his calloused thumb brushes over my belly button in slow strokes, making me tremble.

"Meatloaf, potatoes, a side of buttered peas with corn, and a good old fashioned *roll,*" he says in an amused voice. I can hear the smile in his words.

Placing my fingers to my lips I snicker, and can't seem to stop.

"You laughing at me ma'am?" He digs his fingers into my stomach making me yelp and grab onto his forearm.

We turn into a clearing making our way through two feet tall grass, hearing crickets as we journey along. I wonder if he knows how incredibly blessed he is to call this home.

"Yes." I titter. "I sure am."

"What's so funny?"

"Because I just *knew* you were going to say something that had no *spice* in it. And I was right."

He bends down into my ear and it makes me suck in a breath. "I have something spicy enough in my bed, beautiful. You don't need to worry about that in any way at all."

"Oohh," I say quietly, "I'll take that as a compliment."

"As you should."

I feel him swiftly harden against me, and his hand slides high up my torso to cup my right breast over my bra, tugging the cup down and freeing me. The bouncing causes me to become even more sensitive, and he begins to rub the pad of his thumb against my nipple.

I let out a soft sound of pleasure, closing my eyes and resting my head back against his shoulder.

"Like this." He rolls my nipple between his fingers, causing white hot pleasure to shoot down to my clit, making it throb. "You didn't think you'd like me doing this and now *look at you*. I can make you come just from playing with your nipples alone."

He's so right, and I'm on fire for him. I open my eyes to ask him to take me to bed, but I already see he's heading back to the stables.

"Well that was a short ride." I toss back over my shoulder, flinching as his hands become more demanding. I moan, feeling my center ache. The wind whips around us, making my flesh even more sensitive and attuned to him.

"I've got a long appetite I need satisfied. Time to go inside." His hand lowers to grab my hip where he gives me a lewd squeeze, rubbing firmly across my thigh and to the center of my legs where he cups me firmly.

I turn and look at him sharply. "I want a shower first, I smell like Champ now, and don't want to get in bed like that."

He gives me a dark chuckle, nipping my earlobe. "That's fine beautiful. Whatever you want."

"Whatever I want?" I grin.

"Whatever you want."

We enter the stables and he jumps off first, reaching up to grab me. But as I lean forward to slide off the horse into his arms, my right foot slips through the stirrups. Of course.

Offf course it does.

"Oh my godddd!" I yelp, throwing my arms out to Hudson in a panic.

He catches me, but my leg is aloof as I work to kick my foot free.

"Shit. " I curse. "Hudson, what if he starts walking?" I begin to panic, clutching onto Hudson's jacket and kicking harder.

"Damn girl," Hudson huffs. "How'd the fuck did you manage to do that?"

"I'm sorry!" I yelp, trying to use my other foot to help move the stirrup over my heel. We spend a second struggling before he grunts, trying to maneuver me so he can grab the reins and then get to my foot. He tsks his tongue and hauls me completely to his left arm while he reaches forward fast and wiggles my foot free.

He's breathing hard by the time he gets me free and it just adds to my embarrassment.

I keep my eyes averted as he places me on the ground and then shakes his head with a chuckle. I wait patiently, my face on fire with shame as he gets Champ back into his stable and locks it.

I point at him as he makes his way back to me. "See! *I told you.*"

"I made you like it though," he says, grabbing my hand and tucking me under him.

"Up until my foot almost got ripped off," I scoff, rolling my eyes and ignoring the look he gives me as we walk over the grass to the main house. We bicker all the way until we step in the shower where he shuts me up shoving my mouth over his cock.

He's offended, because we're still talking about it in bed an hour later after he indulged me in a seriously long shower. He's swiveling his hips nice and slow, and I can feel his heart beating hard against my breast. I feel so close to him in a way I've never felt with anyone else.

I'm laid so bare and raw for him, it's discombobulating.

"Challenge me again," he says roughly in my ear. "Come on sassy girl."

"I don't think you can make me like just *any old thing,*" I giggle against his neck.

My brows furrow as I work to beat back my orgasm, trying to extend it out a little. Can you believe that? Couldn't orgasm to save my life, and now I'm trying to hold myself off from orgasming.

The man is a God.

But I think I've hurt his feelings, because he's not laughing back. He gets eerily serious instead of humorous. "I *can* make you like anything I do to you."

I grin against his neck again and nip at his skin in just the way he likes. "Aww, did I hurt your ego? Ayyy, papi. You might *think* you can make me." I unashamedly goad him.

"Oh baby." Hudson's dark chuckle is enough to catch my skin on fire if we weren't already burning up between the sheets. "I *know* I can make you, and there's not a thing in the world you can do about it either."

My heart skips a beat at the carefully veiled roughness blanketing his words. However, something changes in his voice that catches me off guard, and my eyes meet his warily as he pulls back to look at me.

My pussy contracts on him as he pushes himself a tiny bit deeper inside me, making me arch my neck on a gasp. He grinds a bit deeper despite my whimpering. It's a clear warning, however, my body recognizes it as a threat. My lips pout, and a shuddering breath escapes me because the look in his eye is wicked.

It's something *different*.

And to be honest it scares me a little.

However, my fear feeds my excitement and I make the decision to continue to tease him, because I just can't help myself. All I can think about is how he attacked me in my shop, throwing me to my knees and dragging me into my storage area to ravage my mouth.

It was the hottest, most sexiest night of my entire life. Aside from the other night, when he made me bleed he fucked me so hard. That's going into the *Hudson Hall of Fucks* as number one for us as far as I'm concerned.

"Oh you really think so, *do you?*"

He smiles at me and begins to rock our hips side to side in a slow, lewd motion that has my face turning red because it's vulnerable and intimate.

I mean the man is acting like his dick isn't touching every single inch of me. He's moving. Stirring it inside of me before suddenly pressing against that spot he found the other week in my storage area that I didn't even know I had. I tense, slapping an arm around my breasts and a hand around my mouth as the feeling reverberates through my body.

"Hmmm," Hudson growls, his eyes flashes at me in a warning.

My eyes widen in shock and my nipples pull unbearably tight at the sound.

Hudson grunts, tugging my hand and arm away to pin my arms flat on the bed. His broad hands wrap around my forearms, not my wrists, somehow making me feel even more captured. It's almost *just enough* to appease that part of me that wants something nasty and forbidden, but it's not.

I want more. So much more.

He watches my breasts bounce for a minute, the suspense killing me, because I know he wants to suck them. He's just making me wait for him to decide when.

As if he read my mind, his eyes leave my nipples and meet mine as he sinks his cock deep and holds himself tight against me. I let out a pained whimper, because he normally doesn't do this as he knows he fills me too full. Something about that extra inch of him all the way at the back of me is just too much for me to bear.

I need to come so bad I can taste it. However, that look in his eyes, that something *different* I can't explain, captures my attention and holds me back. And fuck it all to hell if I don't want it to come out full force and make me be a good girl. So, I let the feisty part of me come out to play.

"You can't make me because I'm a bad girl," I whisper up at him.

Hudson bends down to my ear and gives me a chuckle that has me grasping at his cock. "A bad girl, huh?" He grunts before yanking himself out right before I'm about to cum and tears fill my eyes.

My lips quiver because oh my god, *I'm right there*, and this man likes to deny me every time. *Every fucking time.*

Doesn't he know I'm hot? Needy?

My vagina is almost in pain with the feeling of his thick dick inside me stretching me out, making my skin too tight for my body. Goosebumps are all over me. I'm suffering. I let out a whine.

"*Bad girls get punished,*" he says.

I shudder, knowing this man can feel my heart beating out of my chest. The look on his face as he gazes down at me has it racing even faster.

"Let go of my arms. Let me touch you," I gasp, jerking my arms against his hold.

He releases me, and I loop my arms around his broad shoulders and revel for a second at the feel of his hard muscles bunching and flexing under my touch.

"You want to be my bad girl, Lolita?" Hudson's lips graze the side of my jaw. The use of my full name causes me to flush even hotter.

"Yes," I say quietly, meeting his eyes. "Oh Hudson you feel so good inside of me. You're so s-strong," a whimper cuts off my words at the next expert circle of his hips against me.

I yank my knees up and back at the feeling, sending him even deeper inside me. Making *him* groan into my neck.

For a long, drawn out second, all we can hear are the sharp slaps of our bodies meeting. Overcome, I clutch desperately at the back of his hair, prompting him to whimper again. I flex my fingernails into his scalp, feeling his hips falter in their movement before he picks up the pace, slapping even more heavily against me.

Jesus he's pounding my pussy so good.

I dig them in even harder, feeling him shudder.

Hudson doesn't mind, he never does. He always shows me he's as wild for me as I am for him, and I love that about him. He doesn't hold back like some men do in the bedroom, he's right there with me just as vulnerable, but in his own way.

I tremble, about to give Hudson a piece of me I promised I'd never give away again. I need him to prove to me that I can push him to the limit, and he can attack me but he won't break me like Dominic tries to.

"I want you to... I want you to...*to...*" Oh god, I can't say it. *Can I?* I look away shyly, but he turns me back to face him. A silent understanding passes between us.

"You want me to *what,* Lolita? I need to hear you say it." His drops his lips against my ear and his face turns slightly, letting me know he's waiting.

But I can't say it. I can't say it exactly the way I know I should, for clarity's sake. No, I have to trust that he understands me.

"I want you to...to *force* me...to be a good girl."

Something changes within him, his body tightens, his fingers flex against me, his movements become slightly predatorial...

"Force you, huh. Against your will?"

My pulse pounds hard in my ears, stealing my breath.

I nod.

"Then say the actual word." His voice comes out rough, gravely, and makes my heart skip a beat. Making my throat tight.

"Uh-uh." I shake my head, nervous.

"Say it." Hudson teeth are sharp as he nips my ear. His breath tickles me, giving my already sensitive skin goosebumps.

I take a deep breath, but it doesn't help. "I c-can't. Hudson I *can't.*"

"Ask me-"

"No, Hudson, *no.*" At my interruption, I stiffen as his hand wraps around my throat in a warning. *"Oh God."* My eyes widen as his narrows at me. "Please," I beg.

His brows lower, pinning me with a hard stare. *"The more you resist me, the harder I'm going choke you."*

My breasts slap loudly against my ribcage as he begins to fuck me harder now. At my silence his fingers tighten, harder than what I expected, and I let out a surprised moan at his viciousness.

"It's such a simple sentence baby girl. All you have to say is 'Hudson, I want you to rape me'." His voice is gritty with lust, and looking into his eyes I see he's a breath away from losing control.

Fucking God, I can't believe he's making me do this.

A shiver races down my spine and I hear our sex sounds become sharper, louder with how wet I'm getting at his rough actions. "Hudson, please!" I plead. "Please, baby please, *I can't.* I don't think I c-c-can," I stutter.

Hudson tightens his hand even harder and he leans down, sealing his lips to mine in a possessive kiss. It's so hot, sensual. Making me so turned on that for a second I don't think I'm going to survive this.

"Fucking hell, you're throbbing so hard around me, sucking me in. I told you this cunt was greedy. *Didn't I?*" His voice is stern making my pleasure soar to greater heights. He smacks his hips forward on a thrust so hard I squeal, tossing my head back. He yanks my head back to face him. "Didn't I? *Answer me, woman!*

"Y-yes." I sob.

"Fucking damn right I did. You just want to be hardheaded sometimes, don't you?"

I shudder, clenching down on him. "Yes," I breathe.

He lowers his hand, smacking me hard on my ass cheek. The sound cracks out loudly in the air. My face pinches with pleasure, and I moan as he alternates crack after crack against my ass with a hard thrust. The pain spreads through my body like wildfire, boosting my pleasure almost unbearably.

"Fuck Hudson that feels amazing," I cry out.

"Imagine how happy you're going to be once I give you what you crave sweetie. But you gotta say it first. 'Hudson I want you to rape me.' "

He pulls back and then catches my eye, and something I see make me feel safe, and brave.

I let out a long whimper as I resign myself to trusting him, feeling my eyes well with tears, making his vision blur in front of me. However, he stays silent.

"I want you to r-rape me Hudson." My voice is barely above a whisper but I know he heard me.

Hudson chuckles and places his lips against my ear. "Are you sure about that?" I nod my head, feeling euphoric. "Good fucking girl." He praises me.

The look on Hudson's face softens just a bit, but his fingers don't loosen around my neck, adding to my pleasure.

"I am?" Tears well in my eyes at how badly I want this.

His thrusting stays steady, delivering such insane pleasure throughout my body that I know I'd let this man do whatever he wanted to me.

"Ohhh *honey*. You're the best girl. You know that?" His tone sounds different, more calculated, rough. And it turns me on so much that my pussy flutters around him, giving him my answer without me having to. But I give it to him anyways because he has a thing with hearing me verbalize it. "You want me to fuck this sweet, tight cunt without your consent?

"Yes."

"The way I want?"

"Yes." I squeal, bucking under him. *I want you t-to do it to me the way you want to, Hudson!"*

Oh God, I just know he's going to make it good. Honestly, I don't know how it can get any better than this right now, but my body shivers with anticipation at what he might do to me. Force me to endure.

"Ohhh baby, *gladly.* "He hitches my legs slightly higher and thrusts a tiny bit deeper making a small growl escape my throat.

Then my eyes widen as what just transpired between us processes through the haze of pleasure we're cocooned in, and vulnerability takes me over. One thing I just learned, if the earth opens up and and swallows you, and you have a man inside you when it happens, he comes with you.

There's no escape. I'm actually asking for this man to take me against my will. My deepest darkest fantasy.

Rape.

The one thing a woman is not supposed to want to happen to her. And I've only known him a few weeks. It took me *years* to ask Dominic, and I had babies with him.

Am I crazy?

I should have done this while we were on the phone, so I could have hung up on him afterwards. But no, he just had to say he could 'make me' the way he did, and my dumbass brain decided to snatch the one opportunity she thought she might ever have to get what she really wants.

But wait; did this man just say *gladly?*

He rams back inside me on a low grunt and starts those sharp slapping thrusts that has me tightening in excitement. Bends his head to my nipple with a groan and nibbles. Sucking and tugging at me with no mercy.

"Ohhh," I whine, feeling a tear sleep down my cheek. "You're so big it *h-hurts.*"

I bite my lip and shudder as the hot feeling of my orgasm beginning to rise inside me. I'm close. So close. He looks up, searing me with his eyes.

"I know. You like it too, *don't you?*"

I nod. "Hmm-hmm."

"Filling you too full?" I nod again and he responds by thrusting so hard that my hips roll off the bed as he puts his body weight into his hips, rolling against me heavily.

I pant, my eyes go round as he places a hand at the top of the headboard and uses it to press even harder, making a high pitched gasp leave my lips. My abdomen trembles with nerves.

"You sound so pretty when you're near panicked sweet thing." His head stills, tilting as he assesses me. But he remains unmoving, keeping my orgasm in limbo. "You want me to take this sweet body, baby? Pin you down and make you take it?"

I nod because I do, I really, *really* do.

He lowers our hips and begin to thrust again, pulling out halfway and then back in repeatedly. "Do you want me to make you scream?"

I nod again.

"Do you want me to make it hurt?"

Oh Jesus yeessssss! "*Hmm-hmmm.*"

My eyes narrow when I feel it. It starts in my clit, and works its way to my vaginal muscles. I become almost numb down there before an unbearable, sickly-hot feeling drapes over me. Suddenly he pushes a tiny bit too far and I hear myself make a small sound. My eyes widen as we hold our eye contact.

My muscles lock up under him, and my hearing fades slightly as a ringing begins in my ears. He grabs me under my chin and forces my face up to him, fluttering his thumb across my cheek.

"Do you want to know when it's going to happen or do you just want me to take you?"

"I don't think I wanna know! Oh God, *Hudson! Fuck I need to come!*" I arch with a gasp.

Everything feels so hot. I feel my orgasm looming, about to strike in the dark to tear me apart. Hudson's still talking, so I can't succumb just yet.

"You want me to make you cry when I do it?"

Oh god, oh god, oh god, it's the sexiest thing I've ever heard in my life. "Yes!" I yell.

"Can I ask you something in return?"

"Yes, yes anything!" I sob.

"I don't want you to just let me have it. Make me work for it, *fight me* while I'm possessing you." He licks up the shell of my ear, as if he's sealing the words deep inside my brain.

My heart stops as a ragged moan leaves me.

"You gotta trust me baby." Hudson growls into my ear, and the sound is so sexy I feel my nipples tighten painfully. "Even when I scare you, you have to trust me."

"I *want* to trust you!" I whisper, slapping my hand over my mouth because I can't control myself.

I'm proving it time and time again.

"Oh baby, you can trust that I'm going to give you everything your little heart desires. I promise you. I'm going to give you everything you won't let yourself have. And if it's against your will, *well,* even better."

My hands smooth down the hard planes of his back. "I'll relish the shocked look on your face when you realize you can't run from me while I tear you apart so thoroughly you won't even recognize yourself anymore beautiful. And when I put you back together, you'll be mine. *In every fucking sense of the word.*"

He pulls back to look at me, and I struggle under him. Lost in pleasure so acute I didn't even know it existed. He pins my forearms down to the bed and squeezes tightly, forcing my eyes to open and find his.

"And baby, if you ever dare to give yourself to anyone else after I make you mine, I promise to God I'll make you pay for the rest of your life. Do you understand me? I'll kill Dominic so we wont be having competition over who gets to fuck you up. That privilege will be completely *mine.*"

Whoa.

"F-f-fuuccckkkk....*Hudson!*" I clench down, sucking hungrily along the length of his cock.

I close my eyes against his admission and I jerk in shock, feeling his wet mouth suck at my nipple, rolling it between his teeth.

"I do want to tell you one thing I'm going to do though. Just so you aren't shocked." He buries his head in my neck so he's speaking directly into my ear. "I know you said you aren't sure you want to know. So, when the time comes, I'm going to wipe you down there so you won't be so wet, and that's how you'll know how it's happening and won't be too scared."

As visions of him doing the exact thing he just described fill my head, so does the pleasure I believe I have to look forward to. The fact that he cares enough to let me know something that will put my mind at ease about the whole situation touches me, and I also fill with a different kind of warmth that meets and strokes the flames of my sexual desire.

My orgasm hits me scorching hot and I break. I arch under him and I don't scream, I'm straight *crying* my release out in a desperate wail full of sobs and pleading. Hudson works me through it patiently. It's almost unbearable.

I collapse back down into the bed and I'm shaking.

My legs are shaking, my arms are trembling against the hold he still has on me, and as if to reinforce what he just said, he bends down and takes my nipple back into his mouth just because he can. And fuck if I don't suck a sharp breath in and squirt, because he just gave me another orgasm.

I just had a back to back orgasm. My first ever.

I'm worn out, just the way he likes me.

7

TWO BOUQUETS

HUDSON

IT'S WEDNESDAY AFTERNOON AND Lola's admission rings a torturing echo throughout my head. Somehow I lucked out and got a woman who wants me to take her the way I crave, and if that's not divine intervention then I don't know what is.

However, her vulnerable admission so soon on the heels of what that fucker almost did to her gives me pause. I take a second to turn away from my employees and pull out my phone, wanting to do something that would put a smile on her face.

It bugs me though, that she didn't trust me enough to tell me what Dominic did, but she *did* trust me enough to tell me her fantasy. Which, as fantasy's goes, that's a pretty taboo one and it makes my blood *hot*.

And you know what, Lola's right on both ends.

She was probably right to not tell me about Dominic because I think hearing it from her lips, seeing the fear that would be no doubt in her eyes as she does it would probably be what sets me off and makes me hurt him prematurely. But her telling me she wants me to do to her what she so obviously was in fear of with him, makes me insanely euphoric.

So euphoric, that I know I said some fucked up shit to her in the throes of our passion last night, but I just can't help myself. She does something to me.

I further torture myself with how to implement an amazing session that will leave her stunned, fulfilled, and craving more. The fact that I'm sure I'm going to be fulfilled as well leaves me going throughout my days with a steel rod in my pants it feels like.

This woman is absolutely a breath of fresh air, and I cannot wait to explore our fantasies together. But I want to do it in a way that isn't the status quo. I want to throw her off guard and give us something we *both* need. That's why I worded what I said to her the way I did. Operation Lola takeover is full in effect.

She's not going to know what hit her.

I'm at the job site, standing in an extra sturdy pair of work boots, looking down at my phone and flipping through bouquets of options of a local flower delivery company. I'm contemplating on buying Lola a weekly service where the company automatically picks the bouquet and sends it to her, or picking it myself every week. The automated delivery package is cheaper.

I don't care about the money, but I do care about them sending her a bouquet that I won't think she'll like.

Flipping through the options, I find myself lost thinking about what she's doing at this very moment when I hear work boots crunch their way across the gravel to where I stand. I don't bother looking up, already knowing who it is because I recognize the pattern of his footsteps.

"Well, *well*. Thinking about buying yourself something pretty?"

I grunt looking up at Tyler, my right hand man. "Now why would I do that when I have *your* face to look at most days?" I rib with a wry smile.

The man's been so nosy in my love life the last few years that I've been contemplating playing a prank on him and setting him up on a blind date with Clay. They rival each other in sniffing into my business.

Tyler heaves a laugh and bumps my shoulder good naturedly, making me click on a bouquet and see they have differing size options. I can get Lola bigger bouquets, and the thought makes me smile.

"You got a picture of her?" He actually takes a step back at the look I shoot up at him. "Hey man, it's just friendly curiosity please don't think any different."

I know my look was fucked up, I can tell by how narrow my eyes are but I can't help except to feel protective.

My gaze pings around the job sight, observing dozens of male employees working. I've spent a million hours listening to them dog whistle and wolf-call at women throughout the years. While that just seems to be a construction man's thing, a byproduct of the trade, it won't be a thing for my woman. That's why I haven't brought her around.

Planning to kill a truly fucked up human is one thing, but I can't afford to start knocking off employees over jealousy. That's taking it too far.

Reluctantly, I pull up a picture of Lola and show him.

"Oh man. She's Latina?" Tyler whistles then steps back a few feet quickly at the look I give him. "Okay Hudson, shit *come on* it's a compliment! I mean no disrespect." He saddles back up to me slowly. "All I meant was maybe you should bring her around? She can bring birria tacos for us men, or carne asada tacos...you know how Latina's love to cook." He rolls his eyes at the look I give him.

"Don't be fucking racist." I growl at him, curling my lip. "You think I'm going to have her cooking and shit for y'all just because she's Latina? Isn't that the most stereotypical thing?"

Tyler, who's a Latino man himself, throws me a "you know damn good and well" look. I know I'm being unduly obnoxious, but still. It's the principal of the matter.

"Hermano," Tyler beams a bright toothy smile at me and chuckles, bumping my shoulder with his. "Come on, bring her around, let the guys see you're happy. I'll tell them all to be respectful and if they aren't, I'll fire them. How's that sound?"

"It sound's like I'll *think* about it."

I go back to my phone dismissively and pick a delivery service option, deciding she's going to get the best of both worlds. Two bouquets a week; one for the house, and one for the shop. I'll do delivery for the shop, and I'll pick the flowers weekly for the house. Easy peasy.

I'm busy scrolling looking for something else to buy her, when a text comes through my phone.

> Hey Hudson... Sorry to bother you while you're at work but I'm going home early so I won't be here later. I called Dominic to pick the boys up from school so Frank doesn't bring them to the shop. I know you like coming after work, but I can't do it today. I'm sorry. I really don't feel well. -Lola

Frowning, I click out of the text thread, pulling up her number and calling her. She answers on the first ring.

"Hey..." Lola's voice is low, strained. She sounds tired, and a bit breathless.

My smile dissipates immediately. "Hey sweetheart. Are you okay baby, what's wrong?"

"I don't know..." she sighs, sounding like she's crying, *"I don't feel well."*

I nod at Tyler, turning and making my way off the job site. "Okay. I'm going to come get you and take you home-" My house that I think of as our home.

She sniffles, *"No,* no please. You're still at work. It's okay. I'll pick up some medicine on my way in and go lay down."

"No. I'm coming now. I'll get the medicine on my way. Put your closed sign up and I'll be there in about half an hour."

"Hudson-"

"Don't talk back. Just do what I asked and I'll be there soon okay, baby?"

She heaves a deep sigh. "Okay, Amor."

My eyes widen at the term of endearment.

Hanging up I make my way in record time. Racing to the drugstore, I buy everything my fingers can touch; Gatorade, pain medicine, tums, cough drops, a humidifier, chicken noodle soup, tampons, nose spray, sleep aids, even magazines and chocolates at the register. Like an idiot I also buy her a *'get well soon'* card.

The clerk looks at me like I'm crazy as I keep grabbing shit to put on the counter, not sure what Lola means by "not feeling well," and want to be prepared.

I pull up at the shop behind her white SUV and see her through the window curled up on one of the plush seats under a blanket, She doesn't look good.

I walk in, concerned. "Lolita, baby come here."

I bend down and take her into my arms, blanket and all. Her hair is out of it's usual bun, flowing long and wavy down the sides of her face and over her breasts. As she presses her forehead against my neck, I feel she's slightly hot. I lock up her shop in record time and get her into my truck, putting her seat down into an incline.

"Oh Hudson..." Her voice sounds weak as she tries to talk to me. "You don't have to do this for me. I could have made it home."

Giving her a kiss on her flushed cheek, I ignore her griping and shut her door before clambering in on the drivers side. I hit the highway and settle in, seeing she's already fallen asleep. When I pull onto my property, I carry her straight upstairs and put her into our bed.

I take a second to make sure she's comfortable under the covers and crack the window to give her a nice fall breeze to help refresh her. I bring in all the bags, and then start some soup for her on the stove before carrying up her medicine.

Seeing her laying there with her brow furrowed as she tries to rest bothers me. I don't like the thought of her being in pain.

"What is it sweetie? You on your period, or about to start?" I don't think she's due for another couple weeks, but you never know with women's cycles.

She shakes her head.

"Upset stomach," I press, "you feel feverish?"

"No... I have a bad headache. Bad. My eyes hurt." Lola breathes, rubbing her face into the pillow.

"Hmmm." I reach over and put my hand on her cheek again. "Here take this." I hold the painkillers to her lips along with her water and wait until she drinks them down.

"Thank you," she whispers, and begins wiggling out of her clothes.

I help her, pulling it all off and putting it into a hamper. I run downstairs to grab her soup, bringing it to her on a little lap tray along with some Gatorade, and place the other bags along with her purse on the chair close to the bed. It's only when I start taking off my clothes to crawl in next to her does she speak up.

"Hudson you don't have to. I think I just need to sleep. You don't have to babysit me." She takes a slurp of her soup, and then sighs as I cup the back of her head, kneading into her nape and the muscles of her shoulders.

She lets out a little moan and rolls her head back, heaving out a sigh that I'm surprised her soul didn't come out with. You can't tell me she's not feeling the after affects of the stress of her attack.

"Baby, I'm here for you. Whatever you need Lola." I need her to know that I care about her. I cherish her unlike anything I've ever held close to myself in my life. This woman somewhere along the way has become my heart. "Come here," I murmur, setting her tray aside and then pulling her down to me, cuddling her to my chest.

I press a kiss to her temple and smooth her bangs away. After a second she lets out a sob, and then another. Her poor body is trembling, and I can tell from the tension in her shoulders that she is currently holding on to so much.

"Hudson," she says in a small voice.

I keep my body language calm, however I know she can feel my heart race under her hand. "Yes baby?"

I'm not sure what she's going to say, but if she is about to tell me about what happened when Dominic came over, I need to prepare myself. I only want her to ever see that I can keep it together.

I need to be her strength, because she can't just consider only herself any longer. With two boys to think about, I know she's constantly surveying her surroundings with the 'mom lens' first.

"Please don't treat me like he does..."

That is such a loaded sentence that I don't even know how to respond at first. My hands rub her hair where it's cupped around the back of her head, and the other rubs up and down her forearm, giving her soothing stokes. I grip her chin, tilting her head up to look at me.

"That is something you will *never* have to worry about," I swallow hard as I feel something shift in my chest. I know I have to make this woman mine. I have no clue what that looks like though, because honestly I need more than a wedding ring and a piece of paper. "Just watch my actions sweet girl." I caress her cheek gently with my thumb, holding her stare. "Just keep your eyes on me, and let my actions speak what words can't express."

Lola takes in a shuddering breath, holding my stare.

"That's it baby, keep your eyes on me."

I haul her in between my legs and settle us a little deeper against the king sized pillows propped behind me, stroking her bangs back over and over in that way we both like. Not feeling the need to say anything else, because I know my girl understood me. We just stare quietly at each other, drinking each other in.

Eventually the medicine kicks in and Lola's eyes flutter tiredly. She fights it like she does everything else, but eventually she succumbs to sleep.

I'm thankful. Selfishly wanting to take time to hold her and think while she's in my arms. Because I never want to let this feeling go.

After about two hours I make sure she's sleeping deeply enough, and head outside to check on my horses. I round them up, put them back in the stables and brush them, muck their stalls, and give them food and fresh water. Satisfied they had enough fresh air, I make sure their classical music is on and head back to the house just in time to see the delivery person dropped the food I ordered off onto the porch.

I pick it up and bring it inside, seeing Lola's in the kitchen and looking into the freezer. She grabs a package of chicken out and places it in some water in the sink to defrost.

"Hey baby, feeling better?" I call out, placing the catered bag of spaghetti and garlic toast on the island. I take it out the bag and put it into the warmer before coming up and grabbing the pack of chicken back out the sink and placing it into a drawer in the refrigerator for tomorrow. "I ordered dinner. I don't expect you to ever cook when you don't feel good." I pull her into my arms and rest my hips against the counter behind me.

"Yeah, it's mostly gone. Thank you, I really appreciate it. I forget sometimes what it's like to be able to call and order food just because." She giggles. "I haven't been able to do that in so long, I'm just used to pushing through."

"Well, you don't have to push through anymore. How're you feeling?" I rub my hands down her head gently. "You seem like you suffered a pretty bad headache. Do you normally get those?"

"No," she shakes her head, "every once in a blue moon maybe, but nothing like today."

"Okay, just wanted to know if it's something I need to be on the lookout for." I step away and snag down a cup from the cabinet and fill it with fresh water. "You know I never see you drink a lot of water. Drink this entire glass for me, we need to make sure you stay hydrated."

I turn to her and then hand her the glass, ignoring her sassy eyeroll. But she takes it from me and drinks a few deep gulps, swishing some around her mouth and making me smile at her quirk.

"Would you ever swish my come around like that?" It comes out before I even think to filter it.

"What?" Her mouth drops open, forcing me to chuck her under the chin to close it.

"Sorry, those intrusive thoughts get the best of me sometimes. As I'm sure you've seen." I tease her. She gives me a trembling smile before bringing the cup up to her lips, sipping carefully without swishing which makes me sad. "Hmm. Better?" I tilt my head.

"Well I wouldn't know yet, now would I?" She places the cup down and tries to grab the spaghetti but I pull her back gently, mindful not to jerk her around and exasperate her headache.

"Hey, I need you to drink more water. Ryan is right, you don't take care of yourself enough, *and not just on Wednesdays.*" I cup a handful of her ass and haul her to me, causing her to tilt her head back to look at me. "You need to prioritize yourself more."

"Oh really?" She scrunches her nose and smiles, one corner tilting up more than the other.

"Hm-hm. So what can I do to help you do that?" I arch my eyebrow and lean down, growling as I take a little nip out of her neck making her squeal and try to shrug me away.

"Hudsoonnn!" Lola chastises me, but I don't let her get away, I haul her up my body until we're eye level.

She wraps her legs around my waist, and I hold her there as my thumbs firmly caress her ass cheeks through her leggings.

"No, don't 'Hudson' me. We need to talk about what it's going to take for you to take better care of yourself. If you need me to come sit with the boys a couple nights a week so you can get a massage? Get your hair done, go shopping? What do we need to do?"

No I'm not letting this go, and we're not going to eat until she gives me something to work with.

"Hudson, I can't afford to-"

Shaking my head I tsk at her. "Uh-uh, that's not what I asked. I said *what do we need in order for you to start making yourself a priority.* I gave you a solution, will you take it? You don't need to worry about money."

She gives me a sad smile and a shake of her head. "Hudson, I can't just keep letting you spend your money on us."

I feel my jaw tick and narrow my eyes at her. "I don't need your permission to *let* me do anything for you, or those boys. If it needs to be done then I'm going to handle it. *Understand?*"

Her eyes go wide, and her lips part on a surprised breath at my stern tone. *"Yes, Hudson.* I'm sorry."

"No need to be sorry. I set you up a biweekly massage and facial at a local place up this way. So, I'll just drop you off on Sundays, and that'll give me enough time to tinker around the area until you're done. I'll do grocery shopping for the house or something."

The face Lola gives me can't really be described, but it makes me chuckle.

"What?" I laugh. "What did I say?"

She snickers. "You're going to *tinker around*. Did you turn into Frank while I wasn't looking?"

"That man." I tsk and put her down, turning to grab the food out of the warmer. "I want to do something romantic for you so come on, let's eat in the cellar this time. I haven't showed it to you yet."

I snag the food and a couple plates and utensils and usher her through the door that leads to the cellar in the basement.

8

CELLAR TALKS

HUDSON

"ROMANCE? WHAT'S SO ROMANTIC about a cellar?" Lola teases me.

I smirk at her and turn the corner and lead her through the iron and glass doors leading into the great room downstairs. It's a circular cellar, filled floor to celing wine bottles backlit with soft, glowing light, giving the room a beautiful ambiance.

"Nevermind, forget I said anything," she says in a hushed tone, and I smirk as she looks around the space.

It's an intimate space, made even more so by the circular table in the middle of the room. I place the food and dishes down and hurry to the little bar area, snagging a couple tall candles, a lighter, and two wine glasses.

"Pick one. Any one you want," I say to her, working to light the candles in the middle of the table.

She throws me a teasing look and a smirk. "I dunnooo, I'm not really much of a drinker. What if I pick wrong?"

"There's no way you can pick wrong, this is all good quality wine." Glancing up at her, I see she's leaning forward, craning her neck to see all the ones out of her reach. "A lot of them were gifts. The only wine bottle I'd rather you not pick though, is on the eighteenth row, second bottle from the top. Other than that, knock yourself out baby." I begin to plate our food.

Lola stops her perusal to look over her shoulder at me. "Why? Did some woman give you that?" She lets out a little laugh.

I frown at her, because I don't think it's funny. "No. I bought that *myself* a few years ago for me and my wife to break open on our wedding night." I sneak a look at her as she's still walking slowly along the circular wall, keeping her back to me. She's silent for a second.

"*Hmm*. Lucky woman she will be, to have a man so thoughtful."

I snap my head up to narrow my eyes at her. *Is she fucking serious right now?* "You better be thankful you have a headache." I breathe, covering the spaghetti back up.

"What was that?" she says sharply, turning her face to look at me again with an arched brow.

I give her an arched brow of my own as I place the container at the bar so it won't be between us while we eat. "Nothing important."

She comes back with a decent white wine choice and I take it from her, twisting the wine opener into the cork and tugging it out with a pop, making her squeal.

"So you've never been married before? *Ever?*" Her tone is full of curiosity as she puts an elbow on the table, and props her chin in her hand, raising her eyebrows.

I reach forward and tuck a lock of hair behind her ear, smiling at her blush. I love I can affect her this way, it makes me feel like the luckiest man in the world. "No," I say simply, pouring her a glass first.

"Not too much." She takes a slender finger and tips the bottle up when she thinks I've poured enough. "So, would you mind if I ran a background check on you then?"

The question throws me off guard, but it shouldn't, because I did the same thing to her, she just doesn't know about it. "Absolutely not. I would expect you to, honestly, considering you've got the boys."

She takes a sip and nods, twirling her noodles on her fork. "Wow, that wine's amazing, Hudson. It's so refreshing!"

Fuck, the way she says my name makes me feel like a God, yet another thing I won't allow to be taken away from me. "Thank you, can't go wrong with a good white."

It's a tad too sweet for me but there's no way in hell I would ever not drink or eat anything she ever offered me. I'd rather cut my tongue out first.

"So, when you run it, are you going to tel me all the dirty secrets you've found out?" I chuckle, putting another bite in my mouth.

She grins around chewing her food and swallows quickly. I spend a second praying she doesn't choke as she rushes a little too fast to answer me. "Depends on if I find out if you have a secret family or not."

"*My,* you're curious about this whole me never having had a wife thing aren't you? I promise I'm not lying to you Lolita." I take another small swallow of my drink and just watch her observing me.

Her eyes are tight at the corners, probably because she's been bat-tling a tension headache, but those eyes are bright on me, giving me her undivided attention.

"Well, I'm just wondering what a sexy, well spoken, charismatic, ambitious... *handsome...*" her eyes flick down to my chest before coming back to rest on my eyes, making me feel tight. I beat my erection down with some effort because her tone is *way* too feisty. Her words and more like an accusation, not compliments. I frown, not pleased. "...*obviously* successful man such as yourself is doing still single in his forties-"

"Just turned forty." I correct her. Putting another bite of spaghetti in my mouth, the urge to pull her to me and make her soften her tone is wild, but I beat that back too.

"Sure, same difference." She shrugs a shoulder and gives me an arched, defiant eyebrow to match the feisty tone she's treating me with. "It's just odd is all."

I feel my eyes narrow as I give her a little grin, tapping my finger on the wineglass and turn my gaze to my plate for a moment. "You get off on testing me with your tone." I look back up at her, seeing her head tilt and her eyes fall to my lips, before rising back to mine. "I'm going to ask you one time, *nicely,* to correct yourself when you're speaking around me."

I keep my voice purposely low, only with a tiny hint of threat.

Her lips part on a gasp as she meets my eye for a quiet second. "No I don't-"

"It wasn't a question, love." I interrupt. "Just please be mindful of your tone with me. That's all I ask."

I sit back in my chair and exhale deeply. Placing an ankle over my knee I turn to face Lola head on and rest my elbow on the table. She presses her lips together and her eyes fall slightly. Clearing my throat, I decide to give her a little of my past.

"I was around your age I suppose, when I was with a woman... in a serious relationship. It was right around the time I was becoming successful, something I'd been working so hard for for many years. I had bought my first building, not the one I'm at currently, but it was still nice. Though smaller." I tilt my head at her, seeing her eyes come back to meet me. "I was starting to give my parents more money on a regular basis, and was getting more employees and jobs under me...making a name for myself." I take another swallow and put the glass down, deciding I want whiskey instead.

Standing up, I walk the few feet to my bar and pour myself a couple fingers of whiskey and return back to the chair, getting myself comfortable again. Lola's pushed her plate back, finished for now.

"I spent all my early twenties just immersed in school work. My parents took out a second mortgage on their house to put me through college, so, I had to stay on top of my game. They didn't have much growing up but they made sure we traveled, and that I got to experience some of the world in person and not just see it all in textbooks."

"That room upstairs are tokens from your travels?" she asks quietly, a little too subdued.

Seeing the change in her I reach forward to take her hand.

"Yes." I clear my throat and my eyes shift as I think about my earlier words to her, seeing her demeanors changed a little bit. "Baby, I know I can come across...*intense,* but I don't want you to feel chastised by my asking you to fix your tone." I tilt my head as we regard each other quietly. "I just want you to live in your feminine with me. You don't have to have this tough exterior, not with me. And I'm not *him,*" I say softly, running my thumb across the back of her hand I see her swallow hard before looking away. "You know that right baby? *I won't do you like he does you.*" My eyes flicker between hers. "You can be sweet with me, you can relax and let me take the lead. I have no reason to lie to you, nor do I want to."

"I know," she whispers, twisting her lips as she glances away for a second. I squeeze her fingers harder, bringing her back to me.

I continue. Not wanting us to get too caught up in that. "Amber was her name, we were already having problems in the bedroom-" Seeing her look, I decide to elaborate. "She didn't like what *I* liked in the bedroom. We weren't compatible-"

"Do you think *we're* compatible?" Lola blurts.

She closes her eyes, tilts her head slightly away, and sucks a breath through her teeth as if she's mentally beating herself for speaking up. I tighten my hand on hers hard once more, enough to get her attention back.

"If we were any more compatible I'd think we'd burn this entire place down, don't you?" I chuckle at her, feeling better at her hesitant grin. "Come here," I whisper.

Leaning forward to take her lips I kiss her softly. She whimpers into my mouth and I feel my blood boil at the sound. I pull back, keeping a tight reign on my desire.

"So what happened to her-Amber?"

I exhale and shake my head a little. I don't like thinking about the woman, much less talking about her.

"Well, things weren't going fast enough for her, she wanted to go house hunting, wanted the ring, wanted the lifestyle that my status and money could bring. And she was upset because I put my parents up first, having been content with my condo. I wasn't exactly rushing to be a homeowner when I was busy trying to build this mega construction company and all. It took up a lot of my time, getting started. I actually went and bought an engagement ring thinking to appease her, even visited my parents to tell them I was going to ask Amber to marry me." I look away from her briefly, replaying the last moments with my last serious relationship.

"Something happened didn't it?" Lola whispers, her thumb now moving over my fingers gently. I nod, clearing my throat again.

"I had gotten into a small fight with my mother. She didn't want me with Amber, said she was money hungry, and she was going to ruin my life. Confirming what I already knew, really. I went home to Amber, told her I wasn't ready, and she retaliated by hitting me. First time being hit for me, and I realized I'd liked it-*a lot*. It brought out that sickness inside of me... in our passion we ended up screwing, and I was so mad at the entire fucked up situation that I fucked her rather...*hard*. Rougher than normal for us. Hate sex, you could call it. I guess you could say I had pent up frustration."

"Sickness?" Lola whispers, tilting her head at me.

It's my turn to swallow hard, afraid of how much to tell her.

I pause, thinking about that night and how Amber looked at me when we were done. I had lost myself so deep in my feelings that I couldn't see her anymore, and that's when I decided to start wearing my mask like armor.

"It's okay, Hudson, you can tell me. You can trust me." Lola's soft voice brings me back, and I flit my eyes to hers once again.

That light inside her eyes beckons me closer.

"Yeah...that something inside me that demands satisfaction, no matter the cost. I felt pulled in so many directions that I snapped. Afterwards, she said I was sick, for liking the kind of sex I do. I was caught off guard, blindsided really... then she broke it off. Called me cheap because I wouldn't get the house she wanted in her time frame. I never even had the chance to ask her to marry me, or give her the ring I'd bought. In the end, she ended up marrying a wealthy friend of mine that I'd introduced to her one time at a party. I'd found out a little later that she'd been pregnant with his baby in the last couple months we were together, and was trying to trap me into marrying her because the man was married at the time, and she didn't want his wife to know about the baby. It was a fucked up situation. My mother was right, after all. As moms usually are." I give her a little wink.

Lola's lips part as her brows furrows and she looks away, staying silent for a minute, letting my words process. Our fingers work to thread together and she holds on tightly to me, her thumb fluttering over mine. My mind goes to when Lola tried to break up with me, and how I took her afterwards in a storm of anger and lust.

Is she going to draw a parallel to that? It wasn't the same situation at all.

Anxious, my lips tighten and I take a deep slow breath to steady myself, but before I can say anything Lola beats me to the punch.

"I'm sorry that happened to you. And *for what it's worth,* I don't think you're sick. I love the sex we have," Lola says in a swift voice, and I spend a good second staring into her eyes. "And though it's been intense been us, I believe if I'd told you I had a problem with anything that you do... that you'd respect that."

I tighten my lips, not really sure in her words to be honest.

"Yeah but I've never taken you the way I did her. I'm ashamed to say took her body without a single thought for her feelings. I've never claimed to be perfect, and I'm not, by a long shot. But with you, it's always about you first, sweetheart."

Because love, and maturity, makes you look and act different.

"Hudson I...." Lola stares at me with those light gray eyes and I meet her gaze calmly, giving her the time she needs.

"What is it?" I ask softly.

She flicks her gaze away for a minute and wets her lips. "I don't want you to think that that's something you have to worry about with me. I don't want to get married again." Her eyes land on the wine bottle I told her not to grab, and my fingers tighten on hers ever so slightly as her words process.

My blood suddenly runs cold, and I feel my mask skip momentarily as my face turns to stone. I don't know what I expected her to say, but that wasn't in the realm of possibilities. Somehow she's still talking, making it worse.

"And I already have *two* kids- so I'm done there. You don't have to worry about me trying to trap you with a baby...or trap you for your money. I had money before and it didn't make me *any* more happier."

My eyes narrow, but she doesn't notice.

Oh God. Please stop talking.

Slightly thrown off guard, I feel my breaths beginning to come a little harsher. So, I work frantically to put that mask back into place. Her voice fades in the background of my mind as it takes almost every bit of my concentration to get control over myself.

Because she's saying the exact opposite of what I want.

Her fears are unfounded, but the more she speaks the worst it gets. It wasn't until she told me she was done having kids, and it became a tangible thing that this is something that I could not look forward to with her, that it hits me just how badly I want to see her pregnant with my child.

And as far as her not wanting to get married again- no.

   Just no.

I'm momentarily grateful for her headache because I'm scared of what I would do if she didn't have it. My entire body is locked down when I realize she's not talking anymore, and she's back to sipping her wine. Lola picks up her fork, taking a small bite of her food. So many thoughts race through my head, and it plays as if in fast forward, blurred and unfocused.

"Hudson. *Hudson,* do you hear me?"

I suck in a harsh inhale, hearing her address me, and I'm pulled firmly back to myself with just the sound of my name from her lips. A muscle ticks in my jaw as I feel hot shivers race up my spine. I clear my throat to try and ground myself.

"I'm sorry sweetie, what?"

"I said do you need me to warm up your food for you? You're not eating," she says quietly, putting a hand to her temple and rubbing on a wince.

"No, be right back, I'm going to get your medicine."

   Standing up quickly, I hightail it to the bedroom and snatch up the bottle of pills, using the time to get a grip on my sanity that I'm fighting hard not to lose. Because what the fuck am I going to do if she won't marry me? I return to the cellar, seeing her looking over my stash of hard liquor curiously.

"*Ewww,* you've got the good tequila with the worm?" she says, wrinkling her nose.

"Yeah, but I wouldn't suggest trying it right now when you don't feel good. But we should try it-one day. In the future."

Because you're not going anywhere. *Nowhere,* Lolita.

No fucking where.

Lola scrunches her nose at me as I hand her her medicine and we sit back down. When I feel like I have better control over myself, I begin to eat again, and we're silent for a moment when it hits me.

I'm struggling so hard because I don't *want* to have control over myself with her. I want her to accept me as I am.

If I want to interrupt her meal, throw her to the ground and fuck here on the floor of this cellar, I want her to not only let me, but enjoy it. I think she would, because of our conversation the other night when she revealed her fantasy to me. But, what happens if we go through the motions and she decides she doesn't like it after all?

That we aren't compatible in *that* way?

The thought is *horrifying.*

I want this woman to desire that sick thing inside of me I've been able to control for years until she came along. That's why I'm struggling, not because I can't hide it. Because unbeknownst to her, she's calling me out of my hiding spot.

Oh Jesus. I don't want to lose her. I've waited so long for her. She's perfect for me, and I think I'm perfect for her, too.

As I work to figure out her role in my life, we continue to eat in silence, and this time it's rather comfortable. Except for this feeling of uncertainty, a feeling I'm not used to. She looks over at me and gives me a shy smile that I return with my own.

One thing I've picked up about Lola, she doesn't feel the need to fill up the conversation with random chatter like Clayton does, and I'm oddly appreciative. Our silences are often comfortable, and it gives us time to settle into our nonverbal cues and learn more about each other. After a couple minutes though, I'm ready to break the silence between us.

"How're the boys doing? School treating them okay? Is Tucker's grades still holding strong?"

Her eyes light up at any mention of Tucker or Tatum, and that spark is so bright it's almost enough to cast away the heavy darkness I feel in my soul sometimes.

"They're doing good, they both have straight A's this year. Tucker was doing bad for a bit, but I've really been helping him with his homework. He just needs patience, and someone to really give him time to think things through. He processes a little slower, really soaks it in and thinks about things, you know."

"Hmhm...sounds a lot like someone I know."

She's mid chew when her eyes meet mine. "Oh yeah? Who?"

"You," I say on a dark chuckle. I run my fingers through my hair, trying to rid myself of this sudden disconcerting feeling that Lola might be distancing herself from me. With all this talk of no more marriage and not wanting more babies.

My teasing makes her smile, and it lights up her beautiful face. *"Stop."*

"You do take your time, with *everything.*" I can't help but clench my jaw, thinking about the time she spent forty nine minutes to orgasm. I just know her body was sensitive, and that night continues to torture me to this day.

"I do not!" she gasps, giving my arm a little slap.

I hold my hands up and chuckle. Leaning back I take a swallow of my wine. "There's nothing wrong with taking your time baby, I'd prefer you exercise patience. *Especially* when it comes to sex and the intimacy we share."

Her face goes bright red, and I can't help but give her a devilish wink to make it worse. She takes another small bite, and I quickly get lost watching her lips move as she chews.

"So," she swallows her food. "How long have you lived here? Seeing you ended up buying what I assumed she wanted to end up with."

"Here?" I clear my throat, leaning back and picking up my wine glass. I take a swallow.

"Yeah...*here.*" She meets my gaze and holds it. Good girl.

"I've lived in Bainbridge Island for eighteen years, but I had a condo for while I was getting my business going. I didn't need much, never really did. When I started making my first real money and expanding my business, I invested, saved, and made sure my parents were put up and comfortable first."

That impresses her. I see her eyes light up at the mention of taking care of my parents, and in this moment I remember she hasn't had parents since she was eighteen years old. Has been on her own for eight years.

"That's sweet."

"Thank you." I give her a smile. "Then about ten years ago, I bought this house-"

"Mansion," she interrupts with a little laugh and smile. "Come on, be real. It's a *mansion.*"

"Okay fine, *mansion*." We both laugh and taking a minute to drink in her directness, I cover her hand with mine, squeezing lightly. "How's your headache baby?" My thumb rubs over the delicate bones at the top of her hand.

"It's okay... thank you for asking, mi querido."

Lola's eyes drop down to her plate and I wonder briefly if her keeping things from me of this magnitude is something that is just limited to the shit she goes through with Dominic?

Her life seems very cut and dry, not drama filled. She keeps the same schedule, takes care of the kids and her shop, and doesn't deviate from routine. I plan to change this. I have the means to inject her life with fun and excitement, and I can't want to show her how spontaneous we can be, even *with* the kids.

"And Hudson...thanks for taking care of me today. I really appreciate it."

"Anytime." I lean in and kiss her, taking my time and really extending out. "*Hmmm,* you taste like spaghetti. It's a shame you aren't feeling good, I'd love to take you upstairs and take my sweet time with you tonight."

She let's out a little exhale and treats me to a smile.

We finish our meal in peace, but I can't help but think about the fact that the next day she's going to be with the kids, in her home. When all I want in the world is to have them here with me, in *my* home. So, my thoughts turn to how to make this happen.

But first, I really want to know what my parents think about her.

9

Forging Ahead

Lola

He wants me to meet his parents.

My eyes go wide as I continue to stare straight ahead at the television in front of us on my dresser. We're lounging in bed at my house half naked on a rainy Thursday night. Perfect weather really, for cuddling. Both the windows are up, letting in the cool misty breeze, and we're under the covers soaking in each other's body heat.

Just being together.

My boys are sleeping their last night with me ahead of their weekend with their dad, and we had a good day, followed by a great dinner with lots of conversating and laughs.

For the last few weeks, Hudson seems to have become a permanent fixture in my life. But for some reason, it's just now hitting me how thoroughly he's enmeshed into my-*our*-world.

I'm reclined on him, and he's got both arms wrapped around my torso, holding me so close.

He's busy talking, lulling me into the rhythmic cadence of his deep voice. Hypnotizing me. Telling my about his family and their previous travels, sharing what he's told them about me, and how they're eager to meet me. His mom apparently loves my name, his dad wants to visit my bookstore, his cousin might flirt with me if he comes around.

"My dad's a former principal," Hudson explains.

I nod my head quietly, trailing my nails down his forearms. The crisp hairs tickle my fingertips. He feels so warm against me, but it's not enough to drive the chill away that's settled deep inside, paralyzing me.

Though I'm quite relaxed, I'm freaking terrified.

But like everything else, I try to hide just how scared this all is making me. I don't know how to do this, how to be a normal girlfriend, in what sounds to be a normal family. Dominic's family was dysfunctional, and the ones that *weren't,* didn't stick around with the other members.

I never knew what it was like to have normal in laws, to be able to count on my ex husband's family to help guide us as a young couple. Not having had parents of my own, I was truly floundering as a new mom.

"I think you'll like them, they're nice," Hudson rumbles in his deep voice, tickling my ear. "I already know my mom's going to love you."

"Hmm-hmm," I hum, rolling and biting my lips.

I'm not offering much to the conversation, or asking any open ended questions about his family. I know it's not fair, and maybe even a little rude, possibly even a little hurtful to him, but I'm currently dying on the inside and I'm not sure what to say. Because he's expressed to me a few times already that he's not been happy with how in my head I get. I can't blame him, either.

I can come across really stoic at times, especially when I feel cornered, or when I'm operating from a place of hurt.

And I'm a wealth of hurt, to be perfectly honest.

It's not been easy to catch when I fall back into old patterns. To unlearn the way I've had to toughen myself to survive Dominic. It's not fair to make Hudson suffer for Dominic's sins. But on the other side of the coin, this relationship Hudson and I have made has happened so fast that I haven't had time to truly heal to feel confident enough to be in a healthy relationship.

While Dominic is alive I may not be able to.

"Hey," Hudson says, turning me around so I can face him. He lays me over my lap and pushes my bangs back, making me feel weak. "What is it baby? You're awfully quiet."

I bite my lip, my gaze moving from his eyes to his mouth.

Biting the inside of my cheek I take a deep breath, then another as I attempt to gather my thoughts. But it's not happening, my brain feels scrambled. Yet, Hudson waits me out patiently. His eyes stay warm and green on mine, like a soft, plush meadow.

Seeing I'm struggling, his hand comes up to my face and his thumb strokes my cheek slowly, softly. "Is it another headache?" he asks, his brow furrowing.

I shake my head. "No," I whisper, closing my eyes. When I open them his image is blurry, swimming in my tears. "Hudson I-" My voice catches and I avert my gaze. I can't do this. Can't tell him the depth of my hurt.

"Uh-uh. No," Hudson says sternly. His lips tighten in a straight line and his eyes darken. "You don't need to be scared."

My chin quivers hard, forcing me to bow my head to hide. I curl in on myself but Hudson refuses to let me cut myself off from him. He leans into me, wrapping me in his arms.

"I c-can't."

"That's too bad, because I'm not letting you go," he whispers down at me, pressing his lips to my forehead. "I'm not letting you go sweet thing. Ever."

Why, and how, does he always know what to say to break down my defenses? I'm so scared. I am *terrified* that my drama is going to ruin his life and everything that he's spent two decades building. I don't want that on my conscious.

But... Hudson's not giving me a choice.

I sniff against chest, my fingers are clenched hard in his shirt as I give in. "Okay, I'll go meet them."

His chest shudders against me and I realize just how emotionally strung tight this man is for me. "Thank you," he says, and I just know that even if I wouldn't have said anything, I was still going to be meeting his parents. *"Kiss me, Lola,"* Hudson groans, fisting his hand in my hair he pull me back slightly making me arch my face up to him.

He lowers his head slowly, rubbing his lips against mine, refusing to deepen it just yet.

"Hudson," I whisper. "Are you sure? What are we-*what are we doing...*"

"You're mine. And those boys are mine," Hudson says against my lips, darting his tongue out he licks up my top lip but still refuses to deepen it despite me trying to inch closer.

He keeps my head pinned, and his eyes on me. My brow furrows as I feel a slight tugging on my right shoulder as Hudson fists the material of my nightgown and yanks it down, baring my breasts to his gaze. My nipples harden immediately at the feel of the crisp breeze licking over them.

I flush as a little growl escapes his chest, informing me of how aroused he is. *"Jesus,"* he groans, shuddering slightly against me.

He tilts his head as he just stares at the naked, round globe of my breast.

For a few hot stopping seconds there's nothing but the sound of rain, and our breathing between the two of us as he just stares at me, drinking me in. My nipple is distended, so vulnerable looking between us.

"I love your breasts, woman." His voice is rough, barely restrained. When his eyes flicker to mine, my lips part at the raw, feral need in it's depths. "They're my favorite part of your body. Soft, round, nurturing. *I love them,*" he emphasizes again. "And I think I'm going to spend some time showing you just how much."

I'm so lost in him and the fervor of his words, the heat present in his eyes, and the feel of his thick erection pressed into my hip that I'm not prepared for him to touch me. Inhaling sharply, I jerk against him on a low cry as his fingers enclose and pinch my nipple without warning.

I let out a ragged whimper as he plays with me, treating me to tight rolls of his fingers before he cups my entire breast in his hand and squeezes hard, making my brow furrow.

Hudson's eyes flicker back and forth between mine as a little grin graces his mouth. *"You want me to stop?"* He arches his eyebrow at me as he rubs the calloused pad of his thumb over my nipple repeatedly, causing me to shiver against him.

I shake my head, clenching my jaw at how much stimulation he's giving me. My heart pounds hard in my chest and I squeeze my thighs together tightly, needing relief.

"Good, because even if you would have asked me to stop, I wouldn't have." And with that he dips his head, taking my erect nipple in his hot mouth.

Treating me to little nibbles and soft sucks so pleasurable I throw my head back and moan, feeling a weak orgasm take my by surprise. I can't believe I can come by nipple stimulation.

Overwhelmed, I sag down heavier into his arms, but he just firms his grip, hauling me tighter against him.

"Come here," he mumbles against my flesh, sucking me so good and so long that it hits me that this isn't about me.

It's about *him*, and what he gets from me when he has me like this. My most sensitive part of my body, held up to him in his arms, not able to move, only able to take what he has for me. As he takes what he wants from me.

He doesn't fuck me tonight. Instead, he just feasts himself on my nipples until I'm sore and pulling at his hair, rolling under him in desperation to escape his mouth. Proving to me yet again, that he'll take me where he wants when he's ready, on his terms.

I'm coming whether I like it or not.

Problem is, I like it too much.

I whimper as I place band aids on my nipples the next morning.

They're so tender from Hudson over stimulating them that they won't go down, and I don't want them rubbing my bra making them even more raw than they already are. Not bothering to pull on my bra yet, I take a second to brush my teeth and do a light coat of makeup, keeping it natural today.

It wasn't until I was almost crying with need last night that Hudson told me he'd bought us plane tickets to California that morning, and we'd be taking off shortly after he dropped the boys off at school so I can have a few extra minutes to myself to get packed.

Then, he buried his head between my legs and licked my pussy for so long until I couldn't discern where he began and I ended.

As I'm taking a painkiller, my phone pings from it's spot in the vanity and I look over, seeing Amanda's picture pop up with a facetime call. I answer, picking up a paddle brush and begin to run it through my hair.

"Tell me *WHY, Lola, why!?* Just when you think you're going to get some, he pulls his pants down and has a itty *bitty* wiener!" Amanda bemoans into the camera. She's at her own vanity, doing her eye shadow.

I burst out laughing, because out of all the ways for her to greet me, this wasn't one I'd thought about.

"I'm going to take it that you didn't get laid last night then?" I say sympathetically, wincing as I hit a snag. "Fuck, I've never had as many tangles in my hair as I've had since meeting Hudson!" I huff, running it through again and making sure I got all the knots. "What do you think Amanda, up or down?" I hold the camera up with one hand, and hold one half of my hair up with the other hand.

"Girl why you do you have Band-Aids on your nipples?" Amanda gasps and lunges for the phone. "Bitch, what the hell!? *Hudson's doing you like that?* Ooohhh I'm jealous!" I giggle, pulling the camera up slightly. *"Ugghhhh,* you naughty, *naughty* woman! Send some of that magic my way. I want tangles in *my* hair!" she gasps. "I want *my* pussy to hurt! I want mind numbing orgasms! I don't want to be able to talk the next day because I've been screaming all night the night before-"

Hudson appears in my peripheral making me yelp and almost drop my phone. I slap an arm over my breasts, but not before he sees the band aids.

His face is the epitome of amusement. He leans against the doorframe and arches an eyebrow on a wicked smile. *"What* are you two talking about in here-"

"Get out!" I grit, pushing against his chest and slamming the door on him. My face flushes bright red. "Oh my God," I moan, holding my hand to my mouth as Amanda and I break out in giggles. *"He sawww!"*

I prop the phone up on the vanity and work to pull my bra on, snapping it right when the door opens again.

Hudson walks back in, sparing Amanda a quick glance before stepping into me, pressing me into the wall behind me and tilting my head up with a finger hooked under my chin. He gives me a hot, knowing look before leaning down for a sensual kiss.

"Hudson if you don't leave my friend alone!" Amanda sputters through the phone. "Hudson *move*-I can't see her!" She snaps.

Hudson looks over his shoulder and gives Amanda a grin. "Hang on Amanda, and I'll be out of you girls' hair." He turns back to me then leans forward, rubbing his nose along mine. "Your nipples hurt baby?" he says quietly.

"Uh-huh." I breathe, tilting my head back even more, our lips barely touching.

"A shame. Wonder why?" he chuckles darkly, teasing me. He bends down and seals his lip over mine. "I want them off tonight. You understand?" he says against my mouth. My lips tremble as he releases me. "We gotta be out of here in twenty minutes sweetheart. I've already packed your bag and made you a breakfast wrap."

He backs up, and I can't help but stare as he retreats through the bathroom door.

"Yooo-hoo!" Amanda sings, waving her hand in the camera. *"I'm still here!"*

I smile, picking the camera up and heading into the bedroom to find something to put on, seeing an outfit already laid out courtesy of Hudson. It's a boatneck sweater dress.

"So you didn't sleep with him because he's got a small pee-pee huh?" I tease. "I mean, *good for you,* you have to have standards!"

I giggle, pulling on my dress and adjusting it on my hips slightly before frowning, seeing it's cinched in my waist just a bit, making my boobs look even bigger.

We finish up our conversation, hanging up just as Hudson walks back into the room. I pause at spraying perfume on my wrist and tense, seeing him walk up to me and his gait is so fast it makes me take a step back.

"Baby girl we gotta go or we're going to be late," he says, the rough bite in his voice makes my eyes go round.

He grabs my wrist and pulls me behind him causing me to drop the perfume on the bed.

He looks back at me, and the playful glint in his eyes makes me giggle as I realize that he's excited for me to meet his parents. Seeing his abandon causes a lot of my nerves to fade as I realize this is a big deal for him. I don't want to ruin this for him. I hug myself close to his arm, letting him bundle me into his truck, and we give Frank a wave as we pull out.

Two hours later we're high in the air, set up in first class when he tells me he booked us an air bnb. Not even a hotel room.

"We're not staying the night with your parents?" I ask curiously.

He's looking down with his brow furrowed, and tapping something on his tablet. He's got a very official looking page with bar and pie graphs with dizzying numbers pulled up that make my eyes cross.

"No. Not this time." Hudson taps something else, and the screen fades to show him picture after picture of the development of land that his company has been busy working on. "But if you want a hotel next time, I can book us something five star. But no, we're not staying with my parents."

He stops a picture quickly, blowing it up before staring intently. I watch slightly mesmerized as his eyes flicker over the image. He's very thorough.

"W-Why not?" I whisper quietly, feeling bad for breaking his concentration.

He continues to stare at the tablet before pulling up another screen and beginning to type on it. I give him a second because obviously something's going on that needs attending to. He's been spending so much time with me and at my shop, that I'm sure it's something that could have been avoided had he been more present at work.

"Because, I didn't fuck you last night and I plan to tonight. I don't want my parents hearing, and I don't feel like being quiet, or going easy on you. That's why."

He continues to type, but my face is bright red as I look around at the seats around us. We're in the back row, and from what I can see, no one has heard him.

"Hudson, shhh! Other people might hear you!" I whisper furtively.

He turns his green eyes to me and I see he's deadly serious. I tighten my lips and then turn back to the front, shoving my air pod back into my ear and settling in to hopefully finish my book. I have a new blog due.

We spend the rest of the flight in silence, and it's only when he puts his hand on my inner thigh and squeezes that I see that even though he's immersed in his job at the moment, I'm not far from the vestiges of his mind.

His hand rubs and squeezes rhythmically, making the muscles of his forearm shift and flex seductively.

When the airplane stewardess comes to get our drink order I whisper to her that Hudson would like a whiskey. The entire time he's knee deep in whatever report that he's looking at that I don't think he even hears. When she comes back, I pull down his lap tray and set it down in front of him.

"Thank you, sweetheart," he says.

I smile. So he *has* been paying attention, he just trusted me to get him what he needed so he could take care of business. The thought makes me smile.

We get off the plane and at the car rental place I sit back and watch him do his thing, interacting with the clerk as he picks up the keys to our rental vehicle. He smiles brightly when the clerk tells him that he's able to upgrade him to the truck he wants, and I feel myself getting a little wet at just how he handles himself around others.

He's smooth, in control, suave. Presenting himself with a touch of charisma that a lot of people could only wish to have, and he makes it look effortless.

In the rental truck he makes me sit right in the middle so he can put his hand in between my legs, cupping my thigh as we settle in for the almost hour and a half drive to his parents house.

Ironically, I feel like I'm riding to my doom.

10

WHAT I WANT

LOLA

"OH YOU'RE SO BEAUUUTIFULLL!"

Leaning to look around Hudson who opened my door, I smile, seeing the source of the voice.

Hudson's mother Annabelle, a beautiful, plump older lady in her mid sixties, comes out the front door of a sprawling, ranch-style brick house with an equally impressive sprawling front yard. I smile at her simple green dress with capped sleeves. Her feet are in a pair of slippers and she's got a very loose scarf draped over her arms to combat the chill.

She's followed quickly by a taller, well built man who is obviously Hudson's father. Except he's silver, and has spectacles on his nose. It's dusk, and the lights on the inside of the home glow, giving the property a romantic ambiance.

"Hellooo!" I smile shyly at her, feeling Hudson's hand squeeze my shoulder before letting me go.

I'm not prepared when she walks right into me and hugs me hard, making me gasp and hiss as she inadvertently agitates my sore nipples. She pulls away quickly.

"Oh dear, did I hurt you? *I'm so sorry!*" Annabelle's gray eyes are worried as she looks me over.

"Oh no, no, no, it's *fine!*" I half laugh, "It's so nice to finally meet you. Hudson speaks so highly of you two!"

Annabelle gasps. "Well he'd better have nothing but nice things to say about his momma." She throws Hudson's father a sly look. "Now his *dad* on the other hand, you take what he says with a grain of salt!'

The two of us burst out giggling as his father, Charles, steps around her to give me a rather wicked grin, and I see where Hudson gets his charm.

"Oh Annabelle. Don't scare the poor girl off before she can even get in the house!" Charles chastises. "She looks terrified! Come here kid, I don't bite!"

Rather flustered, I try to keep my smile from wavering as Hudson's father steps into me. He gives me a much gentler hug before stepping over and embracing Hudson. They spend a second patting each others back, and I can hear his father whispering something to him.

I can only make out "son" and "good to see you my boy", however, their embrace is such that I can tell Hudson doesn't come around much.

Though he talks to them at least once a week that I know of anyways.

I bite my lip and put a hand to my chest rubbing, I feel this odd warmth start in my heart and my eyes sting. I miss my own father. My mother. I haven't felt a parental embrace in over six years. I miss it.

Hudson's mother pulls me into the house and pretty soon I'm distracted by my grief as I'm shown all over the house which smells like chicken pot pie, and being shown pictures of them on their travels. Which his mother had meticulously documented. Hudson's old report cards, which his father obsessively kept.

But it's a picture of a teenaged Hudson, bare chested and in a hardhat, holding swinging a hammer as he straddles a beam on a roof that takes me back. The iconic Habitat for Humanity sign is in the background.

"Your love of construction was born from volunteering?" I say quietly, shuffling through all the pictures. "You never said!"

Even as a teenager he was strong. There's picture after picture of him doing stuff I'd never seen another person his age doing.

"Mom kept me grounded," he says, pouring a cup of coffee.

Charles laughs. "You mean she always had her foot on your neck?" The men trade a laugh and then he turns, taking the pot holders from Annabelle who is busy waving the steam out of her face, to bend and grab it out of the oven for her.

"Seriously you two? *I wasn't that bad!*" Annabelle puts her hands on her hips and gives them a glare that makes me smile, because it's how I assume I look at my boys when they're being annoying.

"Mom, go sit down," Hudson says sternly, making her smile.

Anabelle sits in the chair at their oval kitchen table and gives me a bright smile. "So Lolita-"

"Ohhh, call me Lola, *please,*" I say, waving my hand. "I don't usually go by Lolita, unless I'm in trouble." I giggle.

Annabelle leans forward, and pats my hand warmly. "Oh, but you have *such* a gorgeous name! Why don't you want to use it?"

Biting my lip, I shift my eyes away from Hudson who's putting the pot pie on a corkboard in the middle of the table. "Well, my name is just not looked very good upon...in the book world," I say softly, feeling my face warm.

I see Hudson pause and tilt his head at me, furrowing his brow in a 'what the fuck' look.

"Really?" Charles asks. "How so?" He looks over his spectacles at me.

I hurriedly look down at the table in front of me blinking. That hot flush of embarrassment creeps down my chest. "U-Uhm," I whisper. *How do I say it?* I clear my throat, tilting my head. "Well... there was a book written back a few decades ago with my name, and it was sort of about a underaged girl, who was groomed by a much older man...and the book was banned it was so bad."

Hudson's brow raises and his eyes roam my face, no doubt thinking about our age gap. I know I am., maybe his parents are too. Fourteen years is a bit of a stretch to be honest. My heart pounds, wondering if they're going to bring it up.

Annabelle's eyes go wide. "Oh myyy. Sounds like drama!"

Relief fills me, and I fight the instinct to cross myself. Thank God.

I nod, biting my lip. "Yeah...well...I mean *I* haven't read it. I didn't want to," I say rather breathlessly as relief fills me from head to toe.

Hudson catches my eye and gives me a little wink. I'm suddenly hyper fixated on the little wrinkles at the corner of his eyes, the sharp cut of his jaw, how broad and muscular he is. Thoroughly seasoned and hardened by life. He's lived a life before I was even born and had so many adult experiences well before I even dipped a toe into adulthood.

My breath comes faster, as I become turned on. So inappropriately.

"So how is it, owning a bookshop? What's your stance on banned books?" Charles asks, startling me out of my thoughts.

I turn to look at him and smile. "Oh I make sure to follow what books schools are trying to ban, and I make sure I get them for my bookshop. I am not for suppressing education, culture, and knowledge."

Not wanting to be idle, I get up, looking in the cabinets and finding the plates and cups.

They'd been so eager to start showing me the house and the pictures that no one thought to set the table. It's the kind of chaos I like. I don't even ask, I just start setting the table with whatever I can find, and listen to them talk about the time Hudson fell off the roof of a house and had to go to the hospital.

"Thank you dear," Hudson mom says as I begin to start plating everyone's food. I smile and lean further to plate Hudson's dish when her next words make me pause, biting my lip because for just a moment, I forgot I was in the spotlight. *"Oh my,* you have beautiful collarbones my dear. Did you ever model at all?"

"Oh," I half laugh. "No. But I guess I could have been the next Bella Hadid if I'd wanted to. I did have a chance, thanks to my brother. I just didn't want to, it wasn't for me."

Hudson's eyes go straight to my bare shoulders and then lower before he sits back and takes a sip off coffee on a self-satisfied groan. I see a muscle tick in his jaw, that familiar heat enters his gaze that reminds me of his words to me on the plane.

"Oh really? Who's your brother?" Annabelle's eyes sparkle as they meet mine.

I realize they're as eager to learn about me, as they are to share their lives with me. My eyes flicker to Hudson who gives me a little grin and a wink, letting me know that I'm safe with him and his family.

"Alejandro Perez." I say quietly, taking a bite of my pot pie. "He's a director."

Charles frowns. "The director of Sand Time Down?" I nod, and she gets a slow smile. "That was a damn good movie, tell him I said it, too."

"Okay, I will."

"So tell me about the *boys!"* his mother says, leaning forward and patting my hand once more.

I melt, the mere mention of my boys letting me relax, and we spend the rest of the evening chatting. And I feel so at home, more at home than I've ever felt anywhere else.

Though I feel at home, try as I might, I can't feel *calm*. Because every good thing that happens to me, gets taken away.

Seeing how comfortable we all are together births an anxiety inside of me that is much different than what I'm used to. And I spent the rest of the time obsessing over why I had to meet his parents so fast.

Though I don't know what the timeline is on meeting a boyfriend's parents, common sense alerts me that it's too fast. I have never been blessed with this kind of luck. I fear that the more things feel seamless, the more chance everything has to rip apart.

I can't afford that.

A few hours later we're driving to our rental house, and I'm picking at my nail, still dealing with anxiety that won't let up.

"What's wrong?" Hudson asks me.

It's quiet, the radio is on low, and based on how tight his hand is on my leg, I wont be trying to get away with lying.

I peek over at him and see he's studiously staring at the road as we drive. His hand goes just a little higher until he's pressed firmly against my pussy.

"You gunna answer me Lo', or are you going to make me force it out of you tonight?"

Looking over I roam his face, seeing his features are tight. He turns onto a residential street and before I loose my nerve I wet my lips. "Why'd you bring me to meet your parents, Hudson?" I ask quietly.

His thumb strokes me nice and slow, a little hard so it bunches my flesh up and he squeezes with every pass. A minute later he still hasn't answered my question. We pull into the driveway of a very nice house, opening the car door and pulling me out. He keeps a hand on mine as he reaches in the backseat and grabs our duffel bag.

He packed our stuff together since we're only going to be here for two nights. We walk up to the dark walnut wooden door, and I watch silently as Hudson puts the code into the home. My mind is in a whirl. I don't know what to think and I can't stand when I get like this.

It feels like the Tasmanian devil has been let loose in my brain.

Putting a hand on my lower back, he ushers me in first, and right when I'm getting ready to walk through the house to explore I hear the duffle hit the ground and then gasp as he picks me up.

"Legs around me beautiful." Hudson growls, making my pussy twitch which is made even worse by his eyes staring into my soul. This man knows something I don't, I guarantee it. "Get used to them being open tonight, yeah?" He arches an haughty eyebrow at me.

He begins to walk us to the bedroom, keeping his eyes on me. I'm so vulnerable in this moment that I'm trembling, my anxiety forcing me to press my forehead against his shoulder. But all too soon we're entering into a bedroom with a giant four poster bed.

The sight of it makes the blood drain from my face, though I'm not sure why. We've been in bed together almost every night the last few weeks.

He sets me down on my feet and I back up quickly, still cognizant that he didn't answer my question. Or rather, ignores my question. I give him a shaky grin that I honestly don't feel.

What I do feel is trapped.

At the raw, open look on his face, I turn my back to him, clenching my trembling hands together. The sound of his boots hitting the hardwood floor as he advances towards me reverberates through my body. Putting me off kilter. I can't get a grip over myself where he's concerned.

Could I ever with him, though?

"What do you want from me?" I whisper.

Bringing my arms up to wrap around my torso, he steps into my back and and unzips the back of my sweater dress. He doesn't answer me, and all we can hear interrupting the silence between us is the zipper as it hisses as it goes down slowly.

So slow that I know he's admiring my skin being revealed to him.

"I want your body raw from me worshipping you," he says. "That's what I want."

He pulls off my dress, my bra, and turns me to face him, pushing my hair behind my shoulder. I tense as his gaze lowers and he gets his first look at my nipples, swollen and red from his incessant sucking last night. His eyes darken.

"And it looks like we got a good start on that last night." His eyes flicker back up to mine. "Get on your knees and open your mouth. I want you to be a good girl for me tonight. That's your only job. The *only* thing you're allowed to think about right now."

I shudder, inhaling on a ragged breath as I feel a stream of my juices run down my thigh. *"H-Hudson why did you bring me to meet your parents-"*

Goddamn it I just need him to *say something. Anything.* To validate what I'm thinking before I go absolutely crazy.

He bends down, getting inches away from my face. "On your knees, and open your mouth as wide as you can. And I don't really want to hear another word from your lips."

My eyes widen, and my heart pounds. There's something new in the bite of that authoritative tone of his that's got me even more on fire for him. I love when he's like this. Like that elusive thing that flashes in his eyes, I like this part of him.

I like all parts of him. Crave it. So when he tells me to get on my knees, that's what I'll do.

For him though, only for him.

"Yes sir." I whisper, sinking to my knees and unbuckling his pants.

"Hhhmm," he growls. *"I like the sound of that."*

My mouth waters as the smell of him hits me and my sex gets heavy and hot between my legs, the force of my arousal makes me whine around his thickness. His hand comes down to caress my cheek as I swallow the first few inches and a tear falls down my cheek when he reaches lower and rubs his fingers across the tips of my tender nipples.

"Ohhh baby." Hudson chuckles, pinching me so slightly.

The action causes me to jerk, and I hear a muted splash as I squirt on the hardwood, but Hudson wraps his hand around the back of my head and forces himself even deeper.

"You're wetting the floor up sweetness." His voice is raspy with desire.

I look up at him through my bangs, feeling my mouth stretched to the max as he goes a bit deeper. Nervous at this new thing between us, I try to pull back, but his hand tightens on my head, halting my retreat.

"Uh-uh. *No.*" There's a warning in his tone that's new. "You stay right there."

There's a second where I can feel our wills clashing like a tangible thing. Saliva floods my mouth, and I feel my nostrils flare as I attempt to breathe, to suck in enough oxygen to replace what's being forced out of me.

Hudson bends his knees slightly, grips my head, and pulls me deeper on him before he pulls out then begins to fuck my face *hard.* Just like the first time. I moan, this experience clashes with the last and I feel my eyes roll into the back of my head as I dig my nails into the front of his thighs.

"Keep your hands *down.*" He snarls, feeling my fingers curl into his pants.

Obediently I lower my hands palm flat to my thighs, letting him pound my face until I'm gasping on every upswing. He's unrelenting, and my mouth is beginning to go numb. It's going on for so long that I'm unsure what he wants, but I know he wants something. Tears and saliva stream down my face and neck, but still he continues.

Then, without warning, he pushes into my throat and all the way down. Panicking I screech, jerking and flailing against him.

"Are you ready, Lola? Hmm?" Hudson's eyes flash as he looks down at me but I'm struggling, trying to cope. "Why're you fighting me? I whimper weakly around his dick. Hudson tilts his head, refusing to give me mercy. "What's the matter... did you stop preparing for me baby?"

Through my panic his rough, sex-hazed words seep into my consciousness, and I realize he's referencing my blog. My knees are slipping on the hardwood, and the only thing holding me up is his grip around my head. I'm moaning wildly, trying to get a hold of myself but I can't.

His thick length abrades my throat as he pulls me off him and lifts me up. I cough hard, my lungs are heaving and gasping for air as I weakly clutch at him.

"Hudson!" I cough again, trying to get a lungful of air but I *can't.* There's too much that's overwhelming, and he won't stop. He notches the tip of his cock into my opening, bearing me down on it. I let out a ragged shriek that he cuts off by thrusting two fingers into my mouth and my head tilts back as he goes past my throat.

My eyes are wide as I stare at the ceiling, and as he slams into my aching pussy, his fingers go down my throat, until he's finger fucking me while he pounds into me.

It hurts so *good*.

I squeal around his fingers, trying to jerk my head away. My fingers dig into his arms and shoulders, scratching him.

"Gag," he says. "Gag and I'll stop it."

I try to talk around his fingers but it comes out garbled.

Pulling out his fingers, he licks up my chin, then sucks my tongue into his mouth before he pulls back. I shudder weakly. He walks to his duffle bag and zips a side pocket, taking out a small tube of lube. He pulls out of me gently, and my eyes go wide as he reaches between us. Hearing a squirting sound, I lower my head to his shoulder.

"What are you doing to me?" I whisper. "Why?"

"God, there's so many why's tonight, baby," Hudson tsks and shakes his head. I whimper feeling him notch the tip of his dick to my ass. It's slippery and slick with lube. "I thought I told you I didn't want you to think about anything?"

My eyes widen and I wiggle, trying to squirm out of his grasp but he's too strong. "No!" I whimper. "No Hudson, no. *You're too big."* My heart begins to beat out of my chest.

"Bear down," he says, firming his fingers tight on my thighs. "Bear down and breathe for me Lola." He presses harder and I push, feeling my mouth drop open as he spreads me unbearably wide.

My eyes focus on a singular bead of sweat that travels down his temple and slicks past the engorged vein in his neck.

"Now," he says, "Lets try this again." He puts two fingers to my mouth again and presses back in.

Back and forth, in the same rhythm he's fucking into my ass. Inch after inch he saws in, and this time I gag for real. The sheer size of him magnifies his presence in my mouth, and I quickly am swept away. I claw at his arms, feeling hot tears stream down my face. One after the other.

"Yeaaahhhh," he growls, "that's right baby. That's my good girl." He tilts his head. "See, all I wanted was for you to give me something that no one else has gotten from you. That's all baby."

I let out a squeak as his pelvis hits my ass with a little slap and stays there, settling balls deep.

He's just standing there, rocking us side to side while he leisurely pumps his fingers in and out of my throat. My heaving stops, and I calm. The burn lessens, and then turns into a hot, heavy throbbing.

He pulls his fingers out and I loll my head to the side, eyeing him warily.

"I'm not sure you're going to be able to satisfy me," I whisper before common sense hits me.

I slap my hand over my mouth, mortified.

"Oh really?" he says, in a tone so scary that I clench hard trying not to lose control over my bladder.

The action causes a wince to flit across his face.

Oh God. "I didn't mean to say that out loud," I say quietly. "I don't know...I don't know what I was thinking..." I trail off, seeing his features tighten even more.

"I keep telling you *and telling you* to watch your fucking tone with me," Hudson says, his chest is tight against my breasts and I can feel the muscles swell even more against me.

"Well just like you refuse to answer my fucking question, I refuse to fix my tone." I snap.

His eyes narrow at me, and mine widen in response. However, he stays silent, choosing not to acknowledge my outburst. Placing his hand over my mouth. Hudson proceeds to fuck me slowly, leisurely, at his own pace.

And not only am I forced to not speak, I also can't think about anything worth anything. He only fucks my ass for a few minutes, as I've become so limp in his arms I just hang there, taking it. He pulls out, cleans us up and then lays me on the bed and fucks me some more.

A couple hours later, when he's pulling himself out of my aching pussy carefully on a groan, and all I can do is sob I'm so boneless and spent, he rubs my hair tenderly, and asks me if I still feel like he can't take care of me.

And the answer is, of course he can.

Why I every doubted him is beyond me. I snuggle deeper in the covers, relaxed and trying to fall asleep. But Hudson's hand lands on my cheek, caressing me softly, telling me what he's going to sew my mouth shut the next time I back talk him like I did. My eyes snap wide open in shock, and I clutch the covers to my breasts tightly, because I'm pretty sure I read that in a book somewhere, or seen it on a show.

"Uh-huh," I say, blinking sleepily. "Don't you have to know how to sew first?" I tease.

He meets my stare unwavering, staying silent.

It hits me like a ton of bricks that he says some truly fucked up shit when we're in bed together. This wasn't the first occasion that he's said something off the wall, and I don't believe it's all out of lust either. He watches me until I fall asleep, safe in his arms.

Because little bit by little bit he's revealing more of himself to me, and I love it. I love *him*. Making it official that *I'm* the crazy one.

Go figure.

II

No Rest

Hudson

I LAY AWAKE IN the wee hours of the night. I'm relaxed with my back against the pillows, watching Lolita sleep. Her thick black lashes lay peaceful on her cheek, her dark pink lips are just slightly parted, the round swells of her breasts rise and fall gently, rhythmically. Her nipples are soft, their color is starting to go back to normal.

I can't say I like that, but I did my best to leave them alone especially after the way I treated them the night before.

Running my fingers down the ends of her hair I briefly wonder if she's dreaming, and if so, what does she dream about? She looks completely at rest, and I love this for her. But there's no rest to be had for *me.*

I lay here silently, just thinking about how much I love this woman. I love her.

I move closer, caressing her hair back off her face as she sleeps so deeply that I get hard again knowing she's only like this because I fucked her so good that I put her to sleep. However, that's nothing new. She always look so at peace when she's with me. The anxious thoughts are at bay while she sleeps, relaxed in the cocoon of my arms and the heat of my body.

"If you only knew how I see you, my beautiful girl. What a blessing it is to know you." I caress her cheek with my knuckles, careful not to wake her.

I tilt my head, assessing her quietly. What it was about her that drew her to me that night I stopped dead in my tracks in the middle of the street over just a glimpse of her face.

These thoughts plague me endlessly, but tonight the ache in my chest has become almost unbearable, watching her with my parents.

I can't view my life anymore unless it's through her lens.

"There's a hymn to who you are, a softness about you that I think only you let me see." I whisper, feeling my chest tighten. "Am I worthy, Lola? I wish to hold the pieces of you together so that with time you'll come to forget what it feels like to be broken...."

I stoke a hand down her hair, careful not too disturb her too much.

"You have taken over me so thoroughly that I can't sleep, can't relax without wondering what I can do to settle you, to give you what you deserve. I want to give you everything sweetheart...the world, if I could."

My jaw tightens as I think about this thing inside me that drives my desires. Why I've been so successful. What has enabled me to fight for whatever I've ever wanted throughout my life. Feelings of insecurity begin to cloud my sanity, and I clutch her to me just a little harder.

"God," I gasp, putting my lips to her temple I feel myself break. A singular hot tear makes it's way down my cheek. "I want you to love me. Why won't you say it?" I whisper, yet she's there lost in the bliss of unconsciousness. "Please stop being scared." I close my eyes, swallowing hard. "....I want you to choose me. *Will you?* Even though I know sometimes I think things that maybe aren't...right."

"I want you to accept me baby."

"I want you to grow my child inside you."

"I want to wake up to you everyday."

"You're done living life without me, I'm making you my wife, with or without your consent. I hope you can forgive me."

I talk to Lola until I fall asleep with my lips to her temple. The next morning, my mother pulls me aside and demands to know when I plan to ask her to marry me. Heat fills my being at her question, because I'm *not* asking her. My mind flickers to my secret time in bed with Lola just that morning.

"I bought you a ring."

Those were my last words to Lolita before I finally drifted off early this morning in her arms.

I can't do this life without her. I refuse.

12

Confessions

Lola

After what happened between Hudson and I in California, I'm feeling more vulnerable and insecure than ever and I feel like I need space. Dominic is overbearing, constantly asking for money, and I'm too nervous at this point at the vitriol between the two men to confide in Hudson about what's going on.

Not to mention Hudson is almost *always* with me.

The closer we become, the more I feel like something inevitable is about to happen and I don't want him, myself, or the boys to become collateral damage. This thing between Hudson and I is getting too serious too quick, so I pull back.

Scared.

Unsure if this fast paced romance is something I should even be indulging in, considering everything I'm currently going through. As much as I care for him, I don't want to lose myself in the shadow of another person. And Hudson's shadow is fearsome.

That thing inside him is fraught with a wide terrain of of unknown territories dotted with little divots of secrets which in turn shelter hidden pockets that hold caverns of icy cold pools filled with a substance unknown. As I've observed him, I've gleamed that some of those caverns within him are shallower than others, some are deep.

But for some reason he seems to be leading me straight to the deepest, darkest, shimmering one. A chasm so deep I can't see the bottom it's so endless.

One that I just know if I dive in, I won't have any hope of finding my way out. Every passing day he edges me closer and closer, until I balk at what's inside. Could be poison, could be love, could be both.

All I know is that just like he told me before, that a snake's bite strikes fast and deadly, I wonder if *his* particular venom works when you're already assigning yourself to a life of being dead.

Because no matter how much I've fooled myself into thinking I'm alive, my body continues to prove to me that it's very much killing me. From the inside out. Viscous headaches begin to overwhelm me until pretty soon I deal with them almost daily.

I confess that I unfortunately allow my fear to begin to get the best of me, and I do my best to hide it from Hudson.

As he stands there next to me in front of that metaphorical chasm that might as well be an abyss, gesturing for me to see what's inside, I keep my eyes on *him* instead of what he's offering me. Knowing it's only a matter of time before he strikes.

Only a matter of time before his next bite truly takes me out. Have you ever seen a snake attack a dead corpse?

It swallows it whole. No mercy.

Poetic, and ironic.

Lolita/Hudson's Text Thread

Are you busy baby? I haven't heard from you today. -Hudson October 2nd 3:33p

I'm fine, just busy with an order and trying to reorganize books in the bookshop. How're you? -Lola October 2nd 5:20p

Missing my baby. -Hudson October 2nd 5:22p

Look at the building going up, isn't it neat? Hey, are we still on for dinner tonight? Hudson October 5th 2p

Yeah, that's so cool. You've gotten a lot done in such a short amount of time and it's coming along great. And no, I'm going to watch a girlie movie and turn in early tonight. -Lola October 5th 4p

You don't want company?- Hudson October 5th 4:02p

I have a headache and I want to go to sleep. I'm sorry, I won't be good company tonight. I'm closing the store early by the way, so you don't waste a trip coming by. – Lola October 5th 4:57p

Another headache?- Hudson October 5th 4:59p

Yes. I just want to sleep.- Lola October 5th 5:15p

I'm coming over. -Hudson October 5th 5:16p

Hudson, no. Baby it's okay.- Lola October 5th 5:25p

No, it's not okay. I'm not letting you shut me out, Lolita. I'm coming over. -Hudson October 5th 5:26p

Hudson/Clayton's Text Thread

Clay, I need you to hack Lolita's account please. Tell me what her transactions are. You know the one I'm looking for. -Hudson October 5th 5:30p

Sure thing. Hang tight. -Clayton October 5th 5:34p

There was a random four grand withdrawal on October 4th. -Clayton October 5th 5:55p

What's her account down to? -Hudson October 5th 5:57p

Nine thousand today. -Clayton October 5th 6p

Thanks man. Appreciate you. -Hudson October 5th 6:02p

No problem. You okay? -Clayton October 5th 6:02p

Peachy keen, friend. -Hudson October 5th 6:04p

I'm at home on the couch, didn't even have the strength to climb up the stairs because I feel so emotionally drained and so weak, that all I can do is lay here and cry.

It was all I could do to fight with the medicine bottle in order to get it open and take three pain killers. I drug the small trashcan from the corner next to me just in case I'm overcome with nausea. All I can think about was the dollar amount I saw in my bank account.

What's going to happen when the amount gets to zero?

The thought is enough to cause a flash of pain in my skull and I moan miserably. Putting my hand to my temple, I pray that the medicine kicks in fast.

I hear a knock, and it isn't coming from inside my head. But I can't move to answer it. I just lay there, thinking that Frank's just going to have to get a clue today because I can't do it. I don't have it in me to get off this couch.

After a minute I hear a key in my door and I'm so shocked and terrified that I sit straight up, causing my entire head to throb. The feeling takes me over so fast that suddenly I'm on the floor, hunched over the trashcan heaving.

But nothing's coming out because I haven't eaten.

"Oh baby."

I hear Hudson's voice coming closer, concerned. He approaches from behind me, and I feel his strong fingers brush the nape of my neck as he works to gather my hair back.

I'm crying. *Ugly* crying, and heaving and gripping the trashcan like my life depends on it. I'm shaking so bad that I can't do anything but sit there on my knees, whimpering. Hudson thankfully gives me a minute to settle before he bends, lifting me into his arms. The action makes the room spin and I moan.

"Hudson, you shouldn't be here." I hear myself whisper miserably. "I don't want you to see me like this."

Staying quiet, he takes the steps slowly, which I'm grateful for because everything hurts.

"I think I'm coming down with something." Pressing my fingers to my temple again I moan. I've never head headaches like this in my entire life.

My body is betraying me.

"No, Lolita," Hudson presses his lips to the top of my head. "You've been off since the other day."

I know he means the night Dominic attacked me. Though I never did tell him exactly what happened.

I sniff miserably as he walks us into my bathroom, sits me down on the toilet, and turns my shower on. Just the feel of the steam and the humidity alone begins to soothe me. Turning to face me he toes out of his shoes, stripping himself bare before he works to take my clothes off too.

Picking me up gently he steps us under the spray and then sinks to the floor, settling me against him. Hudson's fingers encase my scalp and somehow he expertly hits every pressure point as he tenderly massages me for long minutes.

Between his massage, the medicine, and the shower, my nausea begins to disappear until I am completely relaxed onto him. My nose is buried in his neck when he speaks.

"I'm not going to force the information out of you. I'd much rather you trust me enough to tell me. If you don't want to tell me everything, I'll accept that you have your reasons, but I need you to answer two questions for me. Can you do that?"

He's still kneading my scalp deceptively calm and I nod, hypnotized by him.

"Yes," I whisper.

"Have you given him any more money in the last week? Since the time you gave him the four grand at the shop when he came to pick up the boys?"

My heart begins to race, and I just know that he can feel it.

"Yes."

Hudson is silent, but his pec beneath my cheek is stone hard, betraying his tension. "Thank you for telling me the truth." He pauses, still stroking my hair. "Has Dominic put his hands on you since I came into the store a few weeks ago... when he attacked you in the storage room?"

Hudson goes completely still at how stiff I become at his questions.

I nuzzle deeper into him, ashamed. So incredibly ashamed of myself.

Guilt at keeping this from him fills me from head to toe, and it's so massive that it renders me mute. I don't want to hide things from him, it feels unnatural. But I also feel there's a wealth of unknown when it comes to Hudson, and I don't want to trigger him.

We're quiet for a long time as he exercises an ungodly amount of patience and waits me out.

I can't even say it. I just nod my head, making that suffice as my reply, but he feels it, and the relief that raises off me feels like someone took a concrete block off my chest. With it's removal, all the emotions flood the space it left behind, causing me to break down for the second time with this man.

The faint beat of his heart against my chest breaks me.

"Oh Hudson!" I cry, shuddering despite the heat of the shower. "I don't know what to do. You shouldn't have to deal with this. It's too much to ask of you-" My words are cut off with a choked sob. I'm such an ugly crier, and to my horror, Hudson pulls me gently away from him to make me face him head on and I just know I look awful.

To my horror, I start hiccupping.

"Baby, *I choose you.*" I shake my head but he just continues, ignoring my protests. "I choose you, and I'm not going anywhere. Do you understand me? So stop pushing me away."

I pull away from his arms completely though it kills me to put any space between us, tightening my lips with how upset I am.

"No now...*now* you aren't going anywhere!" I emphasize harshly. I slap the side of my palm with my fist, my eyes flash as I glare at him. "But you're making me feel-" I gasp, cutting my words off. I won't say the words. I won't. "-You're going to make me attached to you, and then you're going to rip what's let of my heart out! And I need it for the boys, *don't you understand?*"

"*I need your heart too, Loli!*" Hudson growls at me as his hands tighten around my head, refusing to let me loose. "*Lola look at me! Don't you dare deny me the ability to look in your eyes.*"

Obediently, my eyes fly open. "I can't give it to you!" I gasp, "I don't have anything left to give anyone! Cant you see that? I'm barely a shell of who I once was." My eyes well up and overflow with tears. "You want an empty, dead girlfriend?"

"Then let me fill you up." Hudson's fingers tighten on me as his eyes crinkle at the corner, and his face flushes, betraying the depth of his emotions. "I will make you whole, just give yourself to me. That's all you have to do baby. That's all I require from you."

"Hudson, I-I," Trembling, I shake my head against his grip, whimpering as he pulls me forward to press our heads together.

"You asked me the other day to fulfill a fantasy of yours and you said you wanted to trust me." He presses his lips to mine, swallowing my sobs, and speaking against my lips. "Well now I am asking you-no-*demanding* that you trust me. Let me give you what you deserve. Baby, I will give you and those boys the world."

My eyes widen, seeing his eyes well with tears and I'm just staring at him, because I don't know what to say. My brain is completely fried. Hudson pulls me deeper into him, and he presses his lips to mine forcing his way into my mouth on a harsh groan. Tilting his head and licking even deeper, causing me to whimper.

"If you don't come to me willingly, then I will take what I want. But I want you to come to me willingly *first.*" Hudson whispers against my lips.

I raise up on my knees, pressing my hips forward to notch the broad head of his erection to the entrance of my pussy.

My movements are hurried, clumsy, and I sway as I attempt to wrap my leg around his hips to make him fit. He surprises me by slamming his hips upwards and sinking himself inside my aching core, making me jerk against his tight hold. My nails sink deep into his shoulders as he splits me apart. His possession feels so rough, heavy.

At my loud cry he fists his hands in my hair and pulls my head back to look down at me.

"Hmhm, I'll fuck you," he says quietly, "but I wont be distracted. You're not going anywhere, and you're going to stop closing yourself off because you're scared. You will not leave me." His thrusts are slow, measured. *"Do you fucking understand me?"*

Hudson rolls us till I'm on my back, entwining the fingers of our hands together intimately. Staring into my soul, he carefully fucks me on the floor of my shower, my safe spot.

For the next hour our battles of wills is viscous as we attempt to prove to each other that I won't let him in, and he refuses to stay shut out.

Neither one of us wins this round, I don't think.

"We're not done with this conversation, not by a long shot," he says in my ear, keeping me still while he empties his cum inside me.

I'm weak, broken down, and I know if I get pushed any harder I'm going to break.

The next day I'm busy checking out my afternoon customers, having had a line for quite a while now due to a special I'm running on half priced books, and sneak out into my storage room as soon as the bell dings as the last customer shuts the door.

Walking into the storage area I blow a breath and haul myself up on the wooden table and lay down on it. Pressing my fingers into my eyes and rubbing, as if by sheer will I can force the pain and mental exhaustion away. I've never in my life have had stress headaches before, but I guess there's a first time for everything.

I sigh, hearing my phone ding. I dig it out of my pocket and see it's Amanda.

> Hey babe! We're still on for dinner at Hudson's tomorrow? Are we making anything sweet for the boys?-Amanda

> I can do a dirt cake, can your boys have chocolate? It's just oreos, and pudding but it's so sinfully good!-Lola

> Sure! Why don't I come over tonight and we can make it together? I'm frying some chicken strips and I can pop some French fries in the oven. We can have a drink maybe and girl talk?-Amanda

My heart pounds, because I can't believe I'm actually texting and making plans with another woman my age. I haven't had a chance to make any close friends, and the fact that she might become one, and have boys just like me, is almost too perfect. I bit my lip as anticipation fills me.

> I'd love that! I don't get home until about seven thirty usually, but tonight I was going to lock up a little early. Can you be at my house by six? Is that too late?-Lola

> Hell no that's not too late! Where do you live?-Amanda

I text her my address, seeing the little bubbles pop up immediately.

You only live twenty minutes away! You're so close! Okay, I'll be there at 6 with a bottle. -Amanda

Nice, let's not tell the boys. Let's surprise them!-Lola

I grin to myself and hop off the table, sauntering back into the shop feeling much better at the prospect of gossip and a glass of wine. I text Hudson to let him know I'm closing down early, and when Frank drops off the boys I tell him my plans so he doesn't have a conniption fit that our schedule is slightly altered today.

"Aw, you having woman time? That's nice Lola, that's nice," he says, patting my shoulder affectionately as he walks me out of the store, waiting patiently as I lock up. He pins me with a stern stare. "Don't let that man crash your party tonight. He doesn't always need to insert himself, Lolita. Keep something to yourself, you hear me?"

That man? I frown, pausing on the sidewalk outside the shop and looking over at him. "You mean *Hudson?*"

"Yeah. Him." Frank clears his throat and then looks rather awkwardly to the side. "Sometimes we men like to encroach, you know. Become a little obsessive. Overstep our bounds. And you definitely have one who likes to take over Lola." He turns his head to gaze at me rather contemplatively. "I know I complain about your feisty spirit but...don't let him kill it completely. Leave him guessing a little."

I fold my arms and look up at him through my bangs, giving him a cheeky smile. "I don't know, Frank. He seems to want quite the *feminine*, soft spoken woman by his side."

Frank chuckles and shakes his head. "Ah, God. Don't you *dare* give that man what he thinks he wants. It's alright to let yourself be a little softer. But stay *you.*" His eyes nail themselves onto mine. "Keep his blood pressure up, lass. Thank me later." Frank hugs me hard, giving the boys hair a ruffle and then turns to his truck.

"Come on little men," I say cheerfully, "we have to stop by the shop."

"For what, Mami?" Tucker looks up at me as we make our way to the car.

When I get in the drivers side, I catch their attention in the rearview mirror. "Because we're going on an adventure!" I say, making them laugh.

We journey to the store where I splurge on all kinds of fun stuff for the boys to get into and the ingredients for the dirt cake, making it home just a mere ten minutes before Amanda pulls in my driveway.

The boys almost bowl me over seeing we have a visitor, and when her sons' amble up behind her they get real excited, trying to beat each other to the back yard to play catch. My face breaks out in a smile seeing how excited she is.

"Hii!" We both sing.

"You're place is adorable!" Amanda sings, leaning forward to wrap me in a hug.

I grin. "You smell like marshmallows." I tease.

"The best scent everrr!' She squeezes my hand before giving my house another curious once over. "It's so...*clean,"* she says in a little awed tone.

"Thanks. I do it myself." I feel my face heat up with the compliment.

My face hurts from smiling so hard, and with my happiness, I feel the remnants of my stress headache melting away. Frank steps out onto his porch to wave hello at Amanda, giving her a quick assessment before he inclines his head in a little nod. Just when we turn to make our way inside, Hudson comes driving down the street.

I snort in amusement, holding my hand to my mouth. *"No,"* I whisper. *This man.*

Does he have separation anxiety or something?

Frank looks over at me and raises an eyebrow. His face twitches as he gives me a little knowing look. Pulling at Amanda's arm I stall her from walking through the door. She turns, sees Hudson parking against the curb, and then furrows her eye brows giving me a confused look.

"Did you invite him?" She leans into me, whispering.

I shake my head, hearing his truck door slam as he exits the vehicle, shoving a hand through his hair before saying hi to Frank. He turns to me, snapping his eyes over at Amanda gets a grin on his face. He's wearing a rather expensive looking light tan cowboy hat.

"Am I interrupting something?" He drawls, walking up to us slowly and then pulls off his sunglasses, towering over us both.

I look over at Frank who has a seriously rare amused grin on his face as he stands there, bracing his hands against the railing of his porch and chuckles.

"No..." I say slowly, meeting his eyes once more. "Not me. *Him.*" I jerk my head over to Frank.

Hudson gets a confused expression on his face before glancing over at Frank who is chuckling so hard his shoulders are shaking. "How am I interrupting Frank?" His eyes snap back at me.

I giggle, step into him and then raise up on my tiptoes, pulling him by the nape of his neck to peck my lips against his. "Because you're *not* crashing our girl party. Vagina's *only.* Go have dinner with Frank," I say, giving him a wink.

His eyes flash at me and he steps down a step, giving me a once over. "Are you serious?" he asks in disbelief.

"Come on Hudson, I could use some company. Leave that girl alone for one night." Frank calls out. "Give her something to miss. *Damn,* you youngin's got a lot to learn." Frank shakes his head and then walks inside his house, leaving the door open.

Hudson gives me another slow look before stepping back up and swooping down for a kiss that burns me from the inside out. "You two have fun. I'll be calling you, and you better answer the first time it rings."

The threat in his voice makes me shiver. "Or what?" I counter, giving him a smile.

He's at the driveway, looking over his shoulder when he calls out, "Oh, you'll see."

He takes Franks steps two at a time before disappearing.

I turn, catching Amanda trying to contain her absolute glee. "Girl, am I supposed to be this turned on?"

Snorting, I push her through the doors. "Stop it. We've got some dirt cake to make."

"And some gossip to talk about. *Girl I read your blog!*" She wags her eye brows at me. "What the hell do you be reading?"

I throw my head back and laugh, walking her into the kitchen. "Well, on a scale of one chili pepper to five chili peppers what do you want to hear about?"

Her mouth drops open into an 'o' and her eyes sparkle. *"Five.* Gotta be five."

"Oh shit, we're going to be here a while!" I laugh.

We spend the rest of the evening laughing, cooking, talking, and getting to know one another. And at the end of it, I'm pleased to see I'm not the only one who's made a new friend. Tatum and Tucker are the most joyful I've seen in a long time. And we part ways with a promise to do it again the next week, this time at her house.

When Hudson calls me that night, I let it ring a bit before I answer. The hunger in his voice makes it worth it.

"You like playing with me, huh Lola?"

I smile into the phone, flinging myself across my bed and giving him a self satisfied sigh. "Yes. *Yes I do.* " I confess.

13

You Don't Get It, Not Yet.

LOLA

A WEEK LATER MY joyful mood has passed and I am once again suffocating under an avalanche of stress. And this time it's not just Dominic and my money troubles. No, it's Hudson's turn to have me feeling like I'm topsy-turvy. Causing me to be all over the place emotionally.

However, I don't like to rain on people's parades, so I keep our dinner date with Clayton and Amanda.

It's my weekend with the boys. We're at Hudson's hosting Clayton and Amada and her three seven, eight, and nine year old boys for dinner. My eyes dart side to side, seeing everyone laughing, drinking, joking around with each other, and for some fucked up reason it causes that black cloud over me to darken.

I'm bothered because it's *too* perfect. I don't trust it.

I'm not sure why, but my feelings of self doubt are hitting extra hard today, and I'm completely off center seeing how well Hudson is doing with the boys. All the kids, really. And how playful he is with Clayton, and his sister. Friendly, outgoing, but not flirting with Amanda.

I keep looking for signs, or a red flag... starting to truly wonder if I'm missing something. I'm beginning to not trust myself.

Our shower conversation has been on a torturous repeat in my mind, making everything worse. Surely Hudson should have shown me something by now that could give me a clue that there *is* a red flag, something wrong with him.

Everyone's got them right? Or, am I just so used to seeing them with Dominic all the time at this point, that I've lost my ability to see them at all?

Off and on I've flirted around with the idea of breaking things off despite Hudson demanding me not to, because again, I have a maniac for an ex. And honestly, if shit feels this good with Hudson, then I know I'm setting myself up for a heart break that I am sure will probably more than likely actually kill me.

I barely survived my divorce with Dominic, and we hated each other at the end. So, what the hell is going to happen to me when Hudson decides to call it quits when the going gets tough and we actually like each other?

I just... I don't know. I don't know if I can subject myself to that.

I hunch my shoulders, feeling off center. Hudson is laughing and joking around with the boys when Clayton mentions something about plans for the wintertime, and they trade each other a knowing, playful look.

Amanda giggles, gives me a nudge with her elbow and whispers, "here we go," to which I frown. Because *what?*

What's she know that I don't?

Then they make the announcement, causing my blood pressure to sky rocket.

"We're all going on a five day skiing trip to Aspen for winter break over Christmas!" Hudson says, smiling widely at the kids excited yelps.

I blanch.

Winter break. *In December.* Two months from now.

My jaw drops. I feel my anger drape over me in waves, and my body temperature heats to near boiling. In the back of my head I can hear the boys yelling, and celebrating they're so excited. But I can't think straight. Everything sensible is pushed to the back of my brain and I'm so angry that I can't help it.

That sassy bitch Frank always bemoans comes out before I can stop her.

"Excuse me?" I say, and it doesn't come out nicely, either.

Hudson turns his head to look at me with an arched eyebrow, and his smile fades seeing my expression. We both ignore Clayton and Amanda's shifty looks.

I narrow my eyes. "Who the hell asked you to do that, Hudson? Oh my fucking *God."* I exclaim. Folding my arms I sit back in my seat, my eyes widening as I regard him from across the table. "You keep bulldozing with your *shit* and we don't know if I'm even going to still *be with you for Christmas!"* I half-yell.

I'm shaking I'm so angry, and frustrated.

Hudson narrows his eyes before placing his knife and fork down on the table. His face twitches slightly and he tilts his head, narrowing his eyes at me. *"What your tone of voice with me."* He says in a *very* clear warning tone. The air shifts around and between us, going from playful and joyful to oppressive and thick in a nanosecond.

I heave out an indignant gasp at how stern he just spoke with me. His words fuel my anger to the point I can't comprehend that his voice softened with his next sentence.

"Lola, I think the boys would like-"

"Shut the fuck *up,"* I hiss. The table goes deathly quiet, and I see a muscle tick in Hudson's jaw as he cocks his head at me. I lean forward, feeling the color coming high into my face. "You don't even *have* kids, how would you know what they like? They'd like to not be jerked around. So, don't promise stuff you don't even know you're going to be able to deliver on."

"Ohhh." Clayton makes a little noise. Like a *'you fucked up'* noise, and it places me firmly back in the present. I'm suddenly reminded of how irritable it makes him when my tone of voice isn't checked. So, to talk to him like this, in front of *everyone,* has probably unlocked a new level of Hudson I haven't found out about yet.

And it sobers me almost instantly.

I blink, feeling the overwhelming wave of anger begin to cool off as the table goes somehow even quieter. Clayton and Amanda trade a look, and Hudson keeps his eyes tight on mine as he takes a slow bite of food. I know without anyone telling me that it was purely to keep himself in check from reacting to me right away.

My gaze lowers slightly, seeing his chest rising and falling slightly more. As my eyes flit back up to meet him, he holds my stare unwaveringly, continuing to just stare me down. Not saying a fucking word. Embarrassed, I turn my head slightly, looking out my peripheral as shame begins to fill me.

Tucker and Tatum's eyes go wide. They haven't seen me lose it like this before. I don't even lose my temper in front of their dad. We always argue after they've left the room, and he's never hit me in front of them. I keep it all away.

So I don't know what exactly came over me just now to lose it like this, especially in front of Amanda who I was hopeful to become friends with. My anger deflates a bit as regret and shame fills me, forcing me to avert my eyes from his smoldering stare.

I go to open my mouth to apologize, but before I can say a word, Hudson beats me to it.

He glances at Clayton and Amanda who are still staring, stunned, waiting on his reply. Which they all are. The five boys are looking over at us, being incredibly nosy. He then flits his eyes at me just long enough to let me know that I'm in some big fucking trouble. It swirls in his irises like a tangible thing.

His pupils are wide, and the only characteristic present is danger.

His eyes turn back to the rest of the table and his face changes slightly, more warm, as if what I said didn't affect him. But that look in his eyes was a promise of things to come.

"You know, Lola is such a good cook." Hudson gives the table the brightest smile I've ever seen another person have. "I mean, she makes the best lasagna in the world. Doesn't she boys?" His eyes now turn to the twins.

Tatum and Tucker smile and explain that yes, yes I do.

I sneak a look out of my peripheral and notice that they don't look nervous at all. Not like me. My stomach is in knots, because it just hit me that I just embarrassed this man in front of company, and why on earth I let my bitchy side out like this at the dinner table is beyond me.

We could have had this conversation in private, but no. My fucking big mouth had other plans.

Because I can't just live in my feminine energy, just like Hudson claimed when we first met.

"Oh really?" Amanda smiles, taking another bite of steak. "I love lasagna! I can never get the layers right for some reason," she says with a giggle, obviously not understanding the seriousness of the situation I have embroiled myself in.

"Yup," Hudson says, "and that is the first meal she's going to make when we're on our trip. In Aspen." He loses his smile and as he turns his eyes to me, there's that something different that flashes in his eyes. But instead of disappearing like it usually does. It stays there. *Oh fuck.* My eyes widen, my heart begins to pound heavily as my head recoils slightly at the intensity of his stare. *"Isn't it?"*

Oh fuck.

I've never heard two words be so emphasized in my life.

"W-Well, u-um," I stammer, "I-I can double the recipe and show you how, Amanda. It's not hard." I somehow manage to speak above a whisper.

The intensity of his stare has got me throbbing between my legs and glancing away from him. My eyes shift everywhere but at him, because *oh my God* I'm going to die.

He's going to *kill me.*

Hudson smiles before getting up to round the table to me. I shiver at his advance, so hard that I wonder if Amanda can see it. His eyes flash in a warning as he leans into me to give me a sweet kiss, really making a meal of it.

As he breaks it off, he rubs his nose along mine, but I'm not fooled. That look hasn't left his eye yet. I never expected it to make an appearance like this at dinner in front of other people so, I'm thrown so far off guard that I don't know what to do *but* just sit here and let him kiss my forehead.

He looks over at Amanda who's still eating nonchalantly. The picture of minding her own business. "She makes the best chocolate chip cookies, too." Hudson finishes with a wicked grin.

Amanda smiles so hard it looks like her face could break in half. *"Does she?"*

Amanda! I try and shout at her telepathically, widening my eyes at her. *Help! This man is psycho, can't you see it?*

Clayton makes a happy noise. "Ohhh! Something else for her to make in Aspen." He interjects.

Hudson turns his fake, phony face back to me and loses his grin once again. I meet his stare more boldly than I feel and narrow my eyes at him.

"Okay Hudson I get it! *God.* "I huff as I side eye him, frowning. *See Hudson, you're not the only one who can empathize words.* I'm tempted to stick my tongue out at him.

His lip twitches, as if he heard my secret thought. "Do you? I don't think you get it. Not yet anyways. But you're about to though. Because that's the last time you're *ever* going to insinuate you're breaking up with me, baby. So, I hope you enjoyed your little temper tantrum. Hope it was worth it."

My stomach finishes freefalling into hell at his words.

Oh. My. *God.*

My eyes widen as I stare down at my plate silently. Hudson stands fluidly off his knee where he was kneeling besides me and smoothly picks my plate up, bringing it back to his side and stacking them.

"Hey Amanda." Hudson calls across the table. She looks over at him from taking another bite.

"Yeah Hud?"

"What's your opinion? Do you think I know anything about kids? What I'm doing, and all that?" His eyes are piercing as he stares at me instead of Amanda. I groan, tilting my head back.

Oh here we fucking *gooo.* Why did I open my damn mouth? I'm mentally slapping myself, because when am I going to learn to get a hold of my attitude?

"Hey kids, go place your plates in the sink please." Hudson address-es all the boys who are buys back to being kids and having fun.

I start to relax a little, probably prematurely, by Amanda's en-couraging look at me that did a lot to make me feel less alone in this moment. Her bright eyes are warm as she regards me fondly before turning to face Hudson.

I mean you do wonderful with my boys!" Amanda gushes. "Always have from the moment they were born." She turns her gaze back to me one more and I try with all my might to give her a sweet smile in return. "Do you know he actually helped me change their pampers a few times? It was *so* hard having three babies under three. Honestly, I didn't know how I was going to make it sometimes." She ends with a little laugh.

Amanda leans over to take another bite, still trying to finish her food. I'm busy thinking about how I love that she eats slower than I do when Hudson's next words make my soul leave my body. "Well thanks for the compliment, Amanda. I'm sure you'll be returning the favor next year for us."

Huh?

My jaw drops. Clayton snaps his head to look at me, Amanda tilts her head to look at Hudson, and I ironically stop seeing anything *because what the fuck did this man just say?* Allude to?

He's off his rockers. There's that red flag I've been looking for, flying nice and high.

I feel my lips pull back as my eyes flash at him in a warning, and my heart starts pounding at the sheer audacity that this man had, announcing to everyone we're going to be expecting a *baby* next year. His green irises meet mine and I can see he means business.

If I haven't learned anything else in the few weeks I've known him, it's that Hudson stands on business.

"You're fucking loco-" I snarl, moving to get up off the chair.

At this point I'm ready to launch myself across the table. I don't care if I physically can't take him, I want to claw his fucking face off trying. But I'm quickly stopped in my tracks by two eight year olds who are barreling towards me.

"Mom, *mom!* Can we go spend the night with them? Please, please, pleassseeee?" I'm quickly interrupted as Tuck and Tate both bowl into the back of my chair and start tugging at me, begging to spend the night at Amanda's house.

The other boys are doing something similar to Amanda and I'm quickly overwhelmed by all the noise. Hudson meets my eyes calmly, not betraying any inner thoughts at the fact that I almost hurled myself across the table at him.

"Boys, lay off your mom a bit. You're being too rough," Hudson says gruffly.

But I clutch them to me desperately. They can't go, I can't be left here alone with him after my outburst. I'm fixing my mouth to say no, but Amanda opens hers first.

"Sure, we'd love to have them over!" she says loudly, laughing as Tuck leans over and smacks a kiss on her cheek.

I shake my head, pure panic is filling me, making my hands start to tremble around my son's arms. I try to speak but it's so low that I can't inject any power into my voice. "I-I don't think that's a-"

Hudson interrupts me. "Sure you two can go. Be on your best behavior, and I'll take you to get ice cream when we pick you up tomorrow. How's two o' clock sound?"

Wait. My lips tremble. *I'm the parent, Me. ME!* I yell in my head, but I can't bring myself to say anything.

Amanda glances up at Hudson. "Can you make it five-thirty? I'm taking them to a movie at three tomorrow. I'm buying Tate and Tuck their tickets now to make sure we can all get seats together." Amanda's on her phone, clicking away.

Am I the only one who can tell I'm in danger?

I look over at Clayton. Nope, *he* can tell. He gives me a little grin followed by a wink, slaps his hands on his thighs and stands up. "Go on boys, grab your pajamas and a change of clothes so we can head out."

"I'm going to go pack a lunchbox for Tucker," Hudson says, turning to walk out of the dining room with our dirty plates.

"Why? I've got plenty of food at my house. You know I won't let them go hungry," Amanda says, getting up to walk to the kitchen with him.

"It's his thing," I hear him say. His voice fades. "He feels better with it. Promise me if he wants it, just let him have it?"

Their conversation fades the further they get down the hallway and then I'm left alone. Reeling. I've made not one single solitary decision tonight and I am floored. But then I realize, I rarely make decisions when it comes to Hudson.

I frown, contemplating this new to me revelation.

The house is bustling. Kids are stomping around upstairs, Clayton is down the hall in the powder room, and Amanda and Hudson are chatting and laughing at something in the kitchen. My eyes shift restlessly.

What the hell do I do?

I'm so discombobulated, running over the last half hour in my head. My blood starts pounding in my veins, and, lifting my arms, I can see I have goosebumps. I rub them briskly, as if that's supposed to help matters.

No. I think I'm officially beyond help.

Thinking about help, I'm suddenly hit what the memory of a couple weeks ago when we were having some really rough sex. Way rougher than I'd ever experienced before, and I'd been so strung tight, so sexually overwhelmed that I screamed for help.

And with that memory, the hair on the back of my neck stands up, knowing that if this man fucks me tonight I'll be way past screaming for help. Another memory hits me of him telling me he was going to fuck me like he hates me.

Oh my God. Can it get rougher between us? Can I really trust this man like I've let myself believe I can?

I decide I can't be here alone with him. Not after what I did, and not after that look that came in his eyes to let me know I'm in trouble. Soon, everyone comes back downstairs, and the boys almost kill me smothering me with kisses.

"Promise me you'll be good?" I say, seeing Hudson hand Tucker and Tatum each a lunchbox and ruffle their hair, making me soften a little with the sweet gesture.

I feel Hudson's hand settle under my hair at my nape, and his warm grip causes me to break out into a sweat.

Without a backwards look they're all out the door headed to their cars, and I feel it.

The air shifts once more, becoming hot, heavy, and sweltering. It crackles between us and strikes through to my bones. I realize the only thing that was a buffer between Hudson and I was their presence. It gave me a false sense of security, and the further they walk away, the more oppressive the space is around us.

I turn to look for my purse, because I obviously need to get the fuck out of here, when I suck in a sharp breath at the feel of his fingers tightening hard on my scalp, holding me fast.

"Hudson!" His name is a guttural protest as it escapes my lips, and my eyes widen as they meet his.

I yelp in shock, putting my hands over his, trying to tug him off. The sound of the door slamming shut is almost enough to throw me into a full blown panic attack.

I don't know what Hudson is like when he's angry, I just realize.

Flicking my eyes, I find him out the side of my peripheral and pale, seeing it's there front and center, the red flag I've been looking for. It's in the hardness of his eyes, the firm set of his jaw, the furrow of his brow, the tightness of his lips.

"Where. Do. You. Think. You're. Going?" Hudson says, sounding like the devil himself.

I whimper, because what else can I do? He turns me to face him, and there's that look in his eyes. Holy Mother of God, I don't think I've ever seen a psychopath before, but I think this is what it looks like.

I lick my lips, feeling them tremble as I'm firmly reacquainted with weak Lolita. Apparently, the only time she comes out is with Hudson.

"Home." I manage to spit out. *"I'm g-going home."*

He tilts his head and I blanch, seeing his eyes harden even further. "This *is* your home," he growls.

What?

Panicked, I tear at his hand around my hair and feel myself pulling out strands. My eyes water in pain, and fear, because let's be honest, I pushed too far.

Maybe you wanted to, you've been wanting this, Lolita. That voice whispers in the back of my head. The one that tells me I want my deepest, darkest fantasy fulfilled with someone I trust and love.

My nipples pull tight, and I let out another pained whimper. His eyes narrow and in an unexpected move he roughly slams my back into the front door on a harsh grunt.

He's staring into my soul as his hand plunges between my legs, snagging down my panties underneath my dress. Refusing to break his hold on my hair, he takes his foot to wedge it over them, then pushes them down until they pool around my ankles.

"Step out," he growls.

"Fuck you!" I his at him, tearing at his hand again.

His free hand wraps around my throat and then lifts me a few inches, amazing me with his strength. My panties are kicked to the side, but before I can slam my legs shut he wedges a boot between them, keeping me slightly spread open.

My eyes widen as I feel all my body weight suspended between his two hands. His green eyes go stormy, and I truly know I'm fucked.

That thing...whatever the hell that's in his eyes is fucking *scary.*

"Y-You better not fucking t-t-touch me!"

I'm dripping down my legs, and the fact that he knows I'm turned on by this also scares me, because how far is he about to take whatever this is between us?

The sound of the metallic clang of his belt as he frees his dick sounds out loudly between us. He steps into me. Pressing every hard ridge and muscle against me, flattening my curves against him. Leaning into my neck he sniffs, inhaling me in.

"You disrespectful *bitch,"* he says, making all the blood drain out of my head. "I already told you that I can do whatever I want to do to you."

My mouth drops open in shock as I die and crawl back inside my grave because I did *not* think that I was into degradation. But, according to how violently my pussy just spasmed, apparently I am.

I lift a knee, wedging it between us and trying to kick at him, but it only makes him haul me up slightly higher, making me gasp and wrap around his wrist to hang on. His eyes narrow as our gazes clash, and I wonder for the first time what the fuck I was thinking asking him for this without really knowing him for real.

And we have no safe word?

I'm crazy. Got to be. That's why I attract crazy.

I shiver. *"H-Huds-"*

He turns and drags me by my throat to the nearby powder room, snagging a hand towel and wetting it in the sink. I continue to squirm against him, my fingers pluck at the grip he has on my hair but he refuses to budge. Reaching out I smack his face, but he ignores me, pushing me up against the corner of the little room and then reaches between my legs with the towel.

"What are you doing?" I whimper.

His brow is furrowed as he concentrates, keeping me pinned with one hand. With the other, he's busy wiping me hard, taking my wetness away. My eyes go round at the realization as to why.

Oh God.

"No!" I let out a small panicked noise as I plunge between my legs, trying to find my clit to play with it, to make myself wet again. But Hudson moves quickly, slapping my hands away and pushing me into the wall hard. I put my hands between my legs and whimper. "No Hudson." My eyes are wide on his as I work to shake my head around the grip on my neck. "You c-cant. *I'm too dry-"*

My words cut off as he leans into my ear.

"Move your fucking hands before I make it worst, Lolita." He bends, hooking my thigh over his arm.

I bite my lip, refusing to relent. If I take my hands away to hit him, he'll have access to my pussy. I'm stuck.

But before I can make my mind up he rears forward, taking my jaw in his teeth biting down hard, making me scream and throw my hands up to his face to try and push him away.

Pain shoots through my face and I panic, feeling his dick probing at my now mostly dry opening.

"Nooo Hudson-" I cry out, but his body tenses as he levels himself up with my vagina and shoves himself in me so hard on a feral grunt, making me slide up the wall on a scream so sharp it cuts off his name.

My leg dangles uselessly. And right there, staring into this man's eyes, I'm thoroughly possessed. I knew he said he would do this to me and that's how I would know...but in the moment it's quite over-whelming. But I like it.

Love it.

"Oh, oh..." I gasp.

Because I'm not slick enough his possession burns. He feels much bigger than normal, thicker. His dick pierces me between my legs like a dull knife, and I can tell he's not all the way in, he's not even *halfway* in.

And it burns so hot, so sweet. My pulse strums, beating heavily in my pussy.

My lips quiver feeling him lower, pulling out of me slightly before thrusting back in harshly on a grunt. His nose twitches, his jaw is tight, and his eyes are hard giving me no mercy. I'm breathing hard, feeling a tear slip out of my eye as he lowers again, pushing himself repeatedly, grunting with each thrust. I match each grunt with a high pitched moan.

But he can't get all the way in.

His lips pull back as he stares at me hard, taking what little breath I had away.

"You sat there at that table-" His chest heaves with how hard he's breathing. "-and spoke to me like I'm no better than your fucking ex in front of those boys. *My* boys."

Uh oh. He is angrier than I thought. I shake my head. "No," I whimper, "No, I didn't mean to baby! I'm sorry-I'm sorry-*I'm sorry-*"

He leans forward, pressing his lips to mine and silencing me. "Uh uh. Be quiet," he says into my mouth. We spend a second breathing into each other and I feel my pussy spasm around him, sucking him in just a little bit more. "You're going to learn to control your fucking bullheaded mouth," he says so quietly, and in a tone so final that it scares me.

My nipples harden painfully, and his forehead rests against mine as he grunts, pressing so hard against me that I cry out seeing he isn't willing to relent the resistance of my flesh.

"Ay!" I yell, but still he persists. I feel him slip harshly a few more inches inside, his dick tugging uncomfortably at my sensitive tissues. "Ohh *Goddddd,"* I yell, feeling my throat burn almost as bad as my pussy.

My body responds to him, and my pussy throbs before slickening, trying to ease the way for him.

His chest is heaving with emotion, and I know instinctively that he's got a point to prove. I've hurt his feelings, and for that, I'm going to pay dearly. God, *I want to.* I want this man to fuck me senseless. Eat me alive.

And while he's doing it, I want him to make me tell him thank you for slicing me open to bleed all over the ground for him.

"I wont...tolerate," his brow furrows as he lowers me a bit down the wall before bending his knees and then snapping his hips forward, *"disrespect."* The word come out strangled as he pushes hard against my unyielding vagina.

My eyes snap past his and see our reflection in the mirror of the vanity, seeing his hips barrel forward several inches as he forcibly sinks the rest of the way inside me, causing me to break out into a full sweat as he grinds his outer sex against mine.

It's somehow incredibly pleasurable and painful at the same time.

Stunned, I whine and whimper through it because I'm so shocked.

He's so big, throbbing hard and heavy inside me. He keeps his eyes on mine, and then pulls out and thrusts back in hard, holding himself there for a few seconds before pulling out and thrusting again, this pause longer than the last one. Letting me know I'm trapped. His to do with what he wants. Another tear falls down my cheek and splashes against his wrist.

"You asked for this," he says simply, and I blink, keeping quiet because he's right.

Staring into my eyes he begins to thrust rhythmically, slowly, silently, making me feel it. Beating my hips against the wall with a sharp thudding sound. My lips quiver and I manage a whine through the grip around my throat. Grateful he's letting me breathe.

I honestly don't know between the eerie quietness of the moment, his obvious possession of my body, and that fucking look in his eyes if I'd be able to tolerate this if he took my breath away too. Knowing that this is probably the reason he's letting me breathe, because on a deep level he really meant what he said about knowing me, makes me trust in him even more.

My body heats up almost unbearably with the knowledge that I trust him to take my will away because he wont in fact hurt me or abuse it, and I moan, feeling myself about to orgasm again.

Leaning into enjoying my fantasy, I work to bend my knees back and open my legs wide, letting him truly hit the back of my pussy and that spot that drives me wild. *"Ah God that feels amazing,"* I whimper, clutching his shoulders hard.

At the first clasp of my pussy he slips out with a bit of effort on a small grunt, surprising me.

Suddenly his hands are gone. He pulls back, standing back a couple feet. Just like that. Making me devoid of his touch and his possession. My mouth drops open as we stare at each other silently. His eyes burn into mine, stripping my common sense and setting me even more on fire for him. But where there was flaming hot desire, is also red-hot attitude.

Fucker is denying me? Denying my fantasy?

I'm going home.

But before I do, I step forward and slap him across his face on a sharp cry. His head barely moves, but I see that vein in his neck stand out, and to be honest I'm ready to tear it out and let him bleed out all over the floor. I feel so fucking betrayed in this moment that I can't think straight.

"Fuck you," I whisper to him, my emotions making my voice thick.

Hudson ignores me. "Your purse is in there." He points to where it's sitting in the living room down the hallway just past the formal dining room.

I stare at him hard, almost biting my tongue off with the effort to not cuss him out. However, I just nod, throwing him a filthy look, turning to head for it. The sexual tension and anger between us is thick, but I have to get the hell out of here.

I can feel I'm wet between my legs, but I'll just take care of it myself when I get home

The thought of my house comforts and makes me sad at the same time, and I hurry down the hallway to collect my things. Nabbing it up, I go inside it to look for my keys when suddenly the lights turn off. I look up, curiously.

"Hudson?"

I hear his footsteps, sounding like they're fading away from me.

Peeking my head out the living room doorway, I see Hudson isn't by the front door anymore. It's eerily quiet, as if he's disappeared. I can hear his footsteps somewhere near the kitchen I think, but he's not saying anything. There's just a shuffling movement.

A tingle makes it's way though my spine at the thought of walking in the dark to the front door, and I swallow hard. My heart is pounding, and that feeling that chases me down in my shop when I run to the front door at night after I close up finds me.

"H-Hudson..." I stammer. "I'm going to go. A-And I'd rather go pick up the boys by myself tomorrow."

After I delete your number.

My eyes flicker around nervously. Oh God, it's so dark...and quiet. I somehow am able to get my voice above a whisper though I don't know how.

"You just can't stop being hardheaded. Can you?" His voice is sarcastic, making me even more upset. I hear him obviously somewhere in the back of the house, moving around doing God knows what. "Grab your purse Lolita, I know you like to have it on you."

I frown. *He does?*

I purse my lip, irritated now because he's going to leave me in the dark, barely saying a word to me, and then just ghost me in the house? Not even walk me to the front door?

Asshole.

"Okay, Hudson. Sure. I'll work on that." I make sure to really insert all the nasty attitude I can into that retort as I walk out into the hallway, trying like hell to not let my feelings of being chased in the dark take over me. I break out into a sweat, reaching for the doorknob, breathing a sigh of relief as I get the door open and take a step outside.

Into freedom.

14

CUTTING TO THE
WHITE MEAT

LOLA

THROWING A LITTLE LOOK over my shoulder I see nothing but darkness behind me. Turning to face the front yard, I breathe out my tension, feeling a small twinge of relief when I feel my feet hit the porch and I hurry as fast as I can down the stairs, stumbling down the last two.

Of course.

"Ow!" I yelp as I roll my ankle, but I keep going, determined to get to my house in one piece. Plunging my hand into my purse, I half limp over the pea gravel of the decorative walkway leading to the drive where my car is parked. The sun's about gone, and I'm fumbling quite blindly, unable to find my keys. My ankle throbbing uncomfortably mixes with the irritation because I keep them in the same spot. So where are they? *"Dammit,"* I mumble.

Lowering my purse to my thigh with a groan I half turn, seeing the barn floodlight come on suddenly in the distance. I squint my eyes, trying to see what's out there that caused the lights to come on, when suddenly I hear movement behind me. I turn quickly, ignoring the twinge in my foot and my eyes widen, seeing Hudson running towards me.

I'm so shocked all I can do is lift my hand up in a weak attempt to stop him. But rather than slow when he gets to me, he slams into my middle, causing me to fly off my feet as he tackles me to the gravel. I screech as we roll a few times, before coming to a banging halt against my vehicle.

"Hudson!" I yell, seeing him bare chested, covered in a sheen of sweat and he looks crazy.

Manic.

"You trying to leave me?" he says back, his tone rough, quiet.

Resigned.

All I can do is stare up at him. I can't even blink my eyes are so greedy staring into his, so I damn sure can't speak to answer him. His green eyes are hard, being swallowed up by his irises and his brow is low, furrowed into a stern expression that takes my breath away. At my continued silence, his arm moves so quickly that it makes me flinch in fear, however his hand lowers to his side, and I see him take a knife from his boot.

His chest his rising and falling rapidly, and keeps my eyes locked with his. I begin to shake my head rapidly as fear makes my throat so tight my vocal chords are literally paralyzed. With a grunt he slams his fist into my tire. Stabbing the knife into it. My jaw drops.

"What are you dooooiinng?" I screech up at him, bucking up into his hips.

It's no matter. He's much heavier than I am, and has what feels to be all his body weight pressing down on me. Hudson ignores me, and that rattlesnake tattoo flexes as he tightens his muscles, ripping the knife through the tire. The air hisses as it deflates.

"You're not fucking leaving me. Ever," he snarls.

He jumps off me, his boots crunch into the gravel and then bends down to grab my non-hurt ankle, pulling me over the gravel to the other tire. Slashing that one. Then pulling me around the back of the car to the other tire. However, when he slashes that one, I kick at him, buckling his knee and then freeing my foot enough to crawl away.

I get exactly two feet, before he grabs my other ankle and flips me.

"Ow!" I yell, raising up and trying to grab my foot. *"Hudson my ankle."*

Hudson's eyes flick to me and then narrows. He lowers back to his knee and then grasps my ankle carefully, pulling it up to his face. "You fucking hurt yourself trying to run away from me?" Hudson says, our eyes meet and I see something in them that's more than whatever this thing he calls his sickness is.

What he's got is more than a sickness, it's a *cancer.*

There's a possessiveness there that's dark, abnormal, and it terrifies me to the point that on a last ditch effort to get away I kick out at him with my other foot, nailing him in the side of the head.

He groans as his head snaps to the side hard, and, ignoring the burn in my foot, I ungracefully claw my way to my feet and take off. I'm panting harsh, desperate breaths as I work to run across the gravel, but Hudson's quicker, snatching me back again by my hair. I turn and lash out, scraping my fingernails across his face, giving him a red slash across his cheek that bubbles up and begins to drip blood.

His fingers tighten on the back on my scalp, instantly making my eyes water. He pulls me to him, yanking my head back as far as it'll go as he lowers his head to me. My eyes widen and I jerk, feeling a sharp, cold blade against my throat.

Oh my *God.*

My knees buckle.

"I'll kill you." He licks his tongue over my bottom lip before pulling away. "I'll slit your fucking throat myself before you even take one step away from me," he whispers down into my face.

My heart draws to a stop as his words sink deep into my psyche.

Terror meets pleasure, mingling with my desire for something taboo and forbidden, curing the blood racing through my veins with something new. Sick, wanton, and devious. With his words he stole my breath, and as *his* breath flushes over my lips, making the wet spot where he licked me tingle, he breathes a little of himself into me.

Bringing me back to life.

"You're fucking crazy." I whisper back up at him.

"I know. I never claimed to be sane, Lola."

The blood races in my body, pure pleasure fills me from head to toe. The realization that I'm probably just as sick as he is is a bit disconcerting. Taking a step back I claim a tiny bit of that power I know I have over him. He meets me step for step and we inch slowly over the gravel.

"It's like that, *huh?"* I whisper, walking back slowly.

"Hmm-hm." Hudson hums. "It's like *that. It's always been like that, baby."*

His grip tightens as he pushes me down to the ground. "Spread your legs."

I spit on his face in reply, scrunching my nose up at him. "I'm not having your baby," I whisper. *"I'm not going to-"*

I cry out as the knife presses harder into my neck, and I lock my neck muscles down to keep from swallowing. Scared the bob of my throat is going to finish me off. The force of me holding myself back causes me to tremble, and my breath shoots out hot and fast through my nose as I try to cope.

He wipes his cheek, narrowing his eyes at me. "See that's your first mistake. Thinking you have a say in anything."

He presses a thick thigh in between my legs and undoes his pants again, pushing them down just enough to get his dick free and then he slams into me silently, grinding my ass into the gravel underneath us.

I scream a tortured, strangled cry as he splits me apart.

Our gazes hold as he enters me, but when he gets to the back of my pussy he grinds roughly against me, grunting in the back of his throat.

A small sound rips from my own throat as tears swim in my eyes, making his face blur.

At the sight of my tears he takes his free hand, turning my head to the side and then presses down hard, grinding my face into the gravel. The little digs of pain cause me to gasp harder, and as he begins slapping his hips against me, making me bob up and down with how hard he's fucking me, the rock scratches into my temple, and my cheek.

Blood runs down my neck as with every thrust, I'm treated to a little slice. The tiny pinpricks of pain send me deeper and deeper into this man's poisonous web.

My body tightens up, and I orgasm fast and hard with a long drawn out cry. But he keeps going. A harsh grunt leaves his lips with every slapping thrust into me, uncaring that I'm obviously overstimulated.

"Pleaseee!" I dare to cry, flinching as I feel another hot rush of blood slick down my neck.

He fucks me harder, his hips meet mine with a dull thudding sound, causing me to moan and ripple around him. On a particularly hard thrust, I scream, feeling the knife slice deeper and suddenly it's gone. And Hudson's hot mouth seals over the cut, sucking, licking the blood away.

"Fuucck, your pussy is somethin' else," he groans, his breath washes over my neck in a warm mist. I tense up and scream, my eyes going wide as he presses the knife to my neck and gives me another shallow slice. The feeling of my skin burning as it opens for him it unreal. Un-

like anything I've ever felt before and I come on him hard, wetting the flesh between us with my excitement. "God girl, your taste is...*fuck!*" he growls. *"How fucking dare you taste this good?"*

His hips pound harder, splitting me apart from the inside out. My pussy contracts around him, trying to suck him deeper with every withdrawal of his hips.

"Hudson you're so deeeeep!" I wail, completely overcome. "Oh *fuck,* you're so deep in my pussy!" I yell, tapering off into a cry as he sucks even harder at my neck.

The desperate moaning sounds as he works to lap and suck my blood off my neck is the hottest thing I've ever heard, but right when I think it's over, I feel a pinprick against my nipple.

"No!" I gasp. "No, not there." I beg.

I breathe out a sigh of relief as the pinprick goes away, only to return at the edge of my acerola where he slices once more. Causing me to arch and scream underneath him, digging my body into the gravel to try and get away. He lowers his head fast and takes my nipple into his mouth, sucking my nipple along with the four little dots of blood pebbled there.

My body tenses and I lock up in shock as I orgasm once more, feeling my vision waiver. "Hudson!" I gasp, digging my nails into his forearm. *"Hudson! Help me!"*

He smacks one more time into my body and then stills on a groan as he comes deep inside me. As he raises his head to look at me, I tremble. My nerves becoming even more frayed at the sight of him. There's blood smeared on his cheek from where I slashed him. Blood on his lip from where he's been licking it off me.

"Get up," he grits, pulling out of me, yanking me up, and proceeds to walk me backwards to the stable.

My legs shake so hard, but I don't dare to ask him to pick me up. He's never had a problem carrying me before, so I assume he isn't wanting to right now for some reason. My knees knock together as he works to open the stables and then resumes walking me backwards through the threshold.

Nay Nay and Champ blow, neighing at our presence but Hudson ignores them, turning me to face the opposite side of the massive room from where he keeps the horses. I dig my feet in and whimper, seeing a new wooden plaque hanging above what I thought was an empty stall.

Burned into the wood is my name. Lola. And next to it, a lollipop.

"Aren't you so lucky?" Hudson breathes into my ear, giving me goosebumps. "You get your *very own stable.*"

The silence grows between us. I blink. Not sure what to say, or what to do. What this means.

But before I can muse on it too long, he marches me inside where I see a small couch, a leather chair, a stainless steel table with various instruments that I can't make out. Tons of whips and riding crops hanging on the wall, and hanging from the celling is what looks to be a meat hook.

The blood leaves my head. The sight of that hook causes me to immediately panic. And I turn, getting reach to plead, to fight against him, but in a surprising turn of events Hudson snaps his hand out and smacks me in the face so hard I go flying to the floor.

As I crash down onto my hands and knees, sinking to the floor onto my side the first thing that hits me is that this doesn't feel anything like the times Dominic hit me. Nothing like it. My body is alive, burning from the inside out. And he's the only one with the power to stem it.

The door slams shut, before he locks it with a key that he pockets in his dark denim jeans. I let out a little moan as he reaches to where I lay, yanking my dress over my head, along with my bra.

"You fucking animal," I breathe, glowering at him.

Before I know what I'm doing I slap his hand, trying to dislodge his grip. He's too strong, so I slap then his face. Twice. The groan that escapes him at the contract of my hand on his cheek sets my blood on fire, and all common sense leaves me as I crowd into his space and press my breasts into his front.

Because I'm not going down without a fucking fight.

"You wanted me to fucking fight?" I hiss at him. "I get you're upset, but I didn't ask you for a fuckin' trip to Aspen. And this is not my house. And I am not having your babyyyyyy!" I yell. "Asking the love of my life to fulfill a rape fantasy is one thing, but just moving me in without talking to me about it? Telling me you're going to get me pregnant without my consent? You've lost your *fucking minnnddd!*" I shout, putting my hands against his chest and push hard with all my might, letting my anger out.

I stand up on my toes and yell in his face, ignoring the deathly still look in his eyes as I blatantly challenge him. Because fuck all the shit he said, I'm not dealing with it. The vein in my temple throbs, and I'm sure I burst a blood vessel at how loud I got, but Hudson took care of that.

His hand flies out to wrap around my neck and cut off my words along with my air supply, pressing me hard into the wall behind me before pressing his chest into mine. He's close enough now that I can see the look in his eyes, and my own widen as I struggle against him.

"No! No, Hudson. *NO!*" I have tears in my eyes.

He can't do this, *he cant!*

My mind races as I realize he's doing it. He's taking my will away.

Quite literally.

"I'm piercing you, fucking you, and when I'm done we're going back to the house, I'm taking you upstairs, and I'm going to *crawl* between your legs. I don't care if it hurts, how loud you scream, or what you fucking say to me. And Loli, I'm not stopping, at all, until I'm done using you."

My jaw drops. "Piercing me? *Where?"* I cry out, feeling faint.

"Your nipples," he growls.

I gasp, almost wetting myself. Because *what?*

I'd rather him slap me into the floor a million times.

Ignoring me gaping at him and staying silent, Hudson pivots on his heel, dragging me to the stainless steel table where there's a small cabinet. He grabs a small bag out of the cabinet and opens it. I see all the condom's that he'd bought and we never used, and before I can open my mouth and rip into him about using one now he pulls out a roll of duct tape.

I recoil, my teeth begin to chatter as I jerk in earnest against his strong hold. Hudson ignores my struggling and gets my wrists bound in front of me.

My eyes are wide as I stare at him, and my throat strains from all the screaming I've been doing.

However through the anger of him asserting his dominance in a...well...pretty unorthodox way, my body responds to his. I feel myself become even wetter, my nipples pull tighter, and I become almost faint with the fierceness of my arousal.

This man can't really force me to move in with him...can he? He can't just pierce my nipples like he owns me... *can he?*

He lets me go and I stumble back a few feet in absolute fear.

Hudson jaw clenches as he stays silent. His muscles are huge as he works to remove his clothes, flexing and contracting. And I just know,

I pushed too hard tonight. So, he's going to push me as well. My eyes flit to the door.

Catching my line of sight he turns head to meet my eyes.

"You won't make it," he says, matter of fact. "And besides, it's *locked.*"

His eyes flash, however, he remains silent as he waits for me.

My entire body breaks out into an embarrassing sweat at the thought of Hudson shoving a needle into my most sensitive area. It dots on my forehead, my upper lip and on my hair and in between my breasts, making the diamond snake rub. Slightly abrading the tender skin there. And the effect is as if he'd reached out and stroked down my breast bone but no, he's still sitting by the inclined leather padded chair waiting.

I wet my lips. "I-I can't do it."

"You mean you *won't* do it." His voice is measured, patient.

But I know better. His patience runs out with me regarding certain things.

I shake my head rapidly, hearing my earrings click almost as if they're taunting me. "No, I mean I can't." My eyes meet his. "Hudson, they're too sensitive for piercings." I cross my arms stubbornly, drawing his gaze down to my cleavage.

I lower my arms but it's too late, the damage has been done, I'd inadvertently made that piece of him that works to get whatever he wants more desperate. Greedy. His eyes raise back to mine, narrowing.

"This is the next step, baby girl. Now sit down."

His patience is waning.

He pushes off his perch, to advance to me. I take a few rapid steps back, begging to tremble as he reaches out lightning fast like a snake striking it's prey and grabs my elbow firmly putting me ahead of him and walking me to the chair. Where he pushes me down and then lifts a thick leg, swinging it over me, straddling me hips, and then settling his body weight on my thighs.

He leans forward, pressing into my chest hard as he works to reach behind the seat. After a second I hear chains rattle and before I even know what's happening, he's looping chains around my neck, tightening my head against the seat

My eyes narrow at him. "Get the fuck off me! You don't have to sit on me like a child, I can be still." I snap.

And just like that, he's got me hook, line, and sinker.

He gives me a smirk. Pleased at my accession to his desire to literally infiltrate my body with him. "Watch that attitude, missy. Or I'll be forced to adjust it."

"You're already adjusting it, asshole."

He bends down into my face. "You're damn right I am." Narrowing my eyes at him, we stare at each other for a few tense seconds where my heart begins to pound against my breast bone in a fierce tattoo. Unconcerned with my irritation, he goes back to his little table of instruments, pouring me a double shot of vodka. "Here," he says, handing it to me. "Shoot this back."

My lips tighten because I'm already envisioning a huge needle going through my nipples, and I doubt a shot of vodka is going to help matters. "No!" I gasp through the tightness around my throat.

He makes a growling noise, reaching forward to dig his fingers into my jaw, forcing my lips apart where he pours the liquor into my mouth.

"Fuck you." I gurgle around the liquid.

"Fuck you too, baby," he says back with a devilish grin.

I throw him a dirty look, taking it from him and tossing the shot back, feeling my eye twitch at the burn. "Blech... gross!" I cough, feeling a tiny trickle of liquid seep down my chin. "What kind of vodka *is* thaaat?"

Hudson gives me a little laugh, staying silent. I swallow hard, clearing my throat as a weird, ice cold trickle of unease crawls it's way down my spine. And then I feel my body flush hotly.

"Oh wow, I don't think I drink enough to be taking a double shot like that." I turn my head to look at him, but my head sort of lolls lazily as I catch Hudson's gaze, blinking slowly. He looks... on *fire* for me. He's got the same kind of look in his face that he gets right before he fucks me.

"You're going to look so beautiful when I'm done with you," Hudson says as his eyes slowly caress down my body.

My brows furrow as I try and pay attention to him, but he suddenly sounds like he's talking through a tunnel. Is that wind in my ears? Where's it coming from? "Uhm, I feel strange Hudson..." I slur, feeling my head tilt further down.

"Good girl, you know I wouldn't put you through this pain if you didn't have to," Hudson says from far away, but I'm slipping slowly away from him.

The fucker drugged me, but only enough to make me loopy.

There's a whirling noise, and I feel my seat lowering to almost parallel position. "Hudson I don't want my nipples pierced. It's going to hurt," I whimper, feeling tears come to my eyes.

I watch warily as he pulls the table closer, and what I couldn't tell before, are trays of piercing instruments. And a clit sucking vibrator.

"This is for you. To help," he says. Picking it up he pulls my legs apart, inserts it into me, and then settles it over my clit. He turns both sections on and I feel a buzz deep inside against my g-spot at the same time my clit gets sucked into an evil suction.

I tilt my head back as far as the chains allow, arching my neck off the headrest and feeling the cold metal pull at my skin. "Uhhhnnn..." I complain.

It's almost too much after the orgasms I'd already had tonight. But, before I can open my mouth to say anything, Hudson swipes what smells to be an alcoholic pad over my distended nipple, and then takes a tool and pinches me tight. He stands there next to me, clamping my nipple with one hand and a needle with the other, waiting.

I gasp. My chest heaves hard as I'm hurdled towards another orgasm.

I feel my thighs are wet with my juices and I moan wildly. My head lolls to the side as the effect of the drug mixes with the fierceness of my orgasm making me feel like I'm having an out of body experience. But my pussy heats up almost unbearably hot with need, bringing me back down to earth, throbbing incessantly.

I feel a string of drool escape my lip, and my eyes become unfocused.

Right when I open my mouth to scream as my pussy clenches hard on the worst orgasm of my life, Hudson moves quickly, piercing my right nipple so fast that the pain is a slight blip.

I moan as the needle shoves through. My eyes raise up to meet him and as I pant, I see him staring at me hard with such a look of lust it actually scares me.

"The toy," I gasp, "I need..." My brows scrunch up as the toy just sucks and sucks, taking my voice away.

I throw my head back and screech, barely discerning that he pierces the other nipple. I'm lost in this insane pleasure, when he tugs the toy out and then lays his body over mine, keeping on leg extended to the floor because he's so big he can't fit on here with me.

I look down, seeing his initials, H and M, swinging from the bar piecing my tender flesh. They throb, in the same beat as the throbbing in my pussy, and my throat.

"We're not done," he says, settling against me. His thighs rub against the inside of my legs, and his hands push my knees up and back for him. *"Ughhh,"* he grunts roughly, snapping his hips forward.

The force of his thrust causes me to slide up the seat about a foot, and I feel my hips shake and my breasts slap against my ribcage before his hands dig into the flesh at my hips and lock down.

"You *territorial* motherfucker," I whisper up at him, feeling my bottom lip quiver.

He answers me by rolling his hips even harder into me, then pulling up on my bound arms, and hooking my arms around the headrest then pulling me down further, trapping my arms, and forcing my newly jeweled breasts higher.

He's breathing hard. The sweat on his chest rolls down into his muscles as he shakes his head at me. "I don't feel like hearing your fucking mouth right now." He makes a sound deep in his chest that causes me to whimper. "You need to fucking shut your mouth some-times."

My eyes widen at his words. "But you like it, right? *Right?*"

He shakes his head but I can tell he's hiding a grin. Reaching over to the table next to us he tears off another piece of tape and then places it over my mouth, shutting me up.

I whimper and moan into the tape around my mouth, feeling my abused tissues stretched almost unbearably. I'm so full there's no room for anything else. I'm suddenly concerned, because he swells a little when he's about to orgasm, and I just know that tonight's going to be rougher than the other night.

By a long shot.

Hudson's lack of noise is eerie. It's as if he's just single mindedly focused as he begins to tear into me.

All I can hear are the slaps of our bodies meeting echoing around the room, the scrapes of the chair legs on the wood floor, and my whimpers and sobs. He raises the seat more into an incline and then flips me so I'm on my knees, staring into a mirror hung on the wall. Entering me again, Hudson just pounds and pounds.

And it hurts so good.

I wait a long time for him to let up, but he doesn't. He keeps his gaze on mine in my reflection in the mirror, watching my breasts sway, his initials tapping my areola with every hard thrusts into my body, and his balls tapping against my pussy. I mean he's straight *pounding*, and the force of it is shocking.

I feel a tear fall down my face. Then two, then three. Until I'm crying nonstop through the insane pleasure pain of him taking me over. He's making me cry just like I asked him to, and it feels so good, so utterly delicious and perfect I can't help but cry.

And he acts just like he doesn't care, ignoring it.

The slabs of muscles in his arms and shoulder look like he's made out of stone as they bunch and contract, slamming my hips into his.

"Lola," he says harshly, looking up from where he was watching him sink his dick into me, he catches my eye and my attention once more in the mirror. "You're going to take my name. None of that Lolita Perez-Montgomery bullshit. You're going to be Lolita Montgomery. *That's it.*"

Everything disappears with his statement. The pleasure, the pain, even the discomfort of my arms straining as I'm tied down.

Completely shocked, I make a surprised noise, and then break out into a nervous sweat that has my skin becoming even more sensitive.

Que?

What the hell's this man talking about?

My heart gallops inside my chest and I freefall straight into hell. My new home. Because I've seemingly been seduced by Satan himself.

"This isn't what I meant when I said I wanted you to take my will away!" I try to tell him, but the tape prevents me. It doesn't matter, he ignores me regardless, still thrusting into me. Finally electing to talk.

"We'll apply for the marriage license on Monday, and have the courts marry us by Friday."

His next thrust is so hard it draws a guttural grunt out of him. "Aw *fuck,* Lola. This pussy is so sweet." The back of my pussy flutters around him and I let out a pained moan, already knowing I'm not going to be able to walk tomorrow. "We can have your dream wedding at a later date, but I'm sick of the shit, Lola. You and the boys are moving in, and we're working on having a baby. Starting tonight."

I jerk against his hold, screaming with everything in me against the tape, but he ignores me. Concentrating on the sight of my ass jiggling as he quickens the pace, proceeding to fuck me the hardest he's done so far.

"God the thought of your belly swelling with our child..." he cuts off with a long groan, and I feel his dick jerk inside me hard before he jams back in then stills, pressed all the way into the back of my sex, causing me to whimper in pleasure pain.

I attempt to shift to the left for relief, but he just follows me, causing me to feel like my body bursts into flame. My screams cut off and I'm left sucking air through my nose, heaving sounds I'm so thankful the tape is muffling.

Hudson lowers his head and I see his features tighten and his chest flexes momentarily as he works to get a grip on himself. We pause like that for a few moments before his fingers tighten on my hips and his gaze lifts to meet mine in the mirror.

"You're so beautiful when you're helpless for me baby." His voice is thick and tight, and for a second I swear he sounds almost like a different person.

My heart begins to beat painfully in my chest as he continues to talk.

"I followed you, almost every night after I met you. I hunted you down because you were mine, from the second I saw you in that window. And the biggest mistake you could have ever told me was that you wanted me to force you because baby, you opened the door wide for me to walk through." His eyes meet mine, still as the night. "And there's no going back, for either of us. Do you understand me? You're not getting out of this." My chest tightens to the point of pain, hearing the rawness of his confession. "I'm sorry that I'm like this but I meant what I said outside. I won't let you. There's no corner of this Earth you will be able to run from me. I have too much money, too many resources. You're mine, and you're not going *anywhere*. And there's nothing you can say or do to change that. So, I need you to start accepting this."

H-He... what?

The information barely has time to sink in because I'm so lost in his eyes I can't hear much. The only physical warning I have before he starts pounding back into me is his lip twitching and the tattoo on his arm flexing, making me feel like it's going to leap out of his skin and sting me.

Well, I guess it already has.

I've been poisoned with something that only Hudson can give me. Injected with a serum that has firmly and decidedly brought me back to life. I'm straight having a heart attack and he's still talking. Something about school districts, pediatricians offices, baseball lessons nearby.

And he's fucking me mercilessly through all of it.

I'm screaming myself raw against the tape and he doesn't care. Sweat dips down Hudson's body, and that bulging vein is prominent in his arm and neck. He's crazy. But I can't do anything but hang on. I'm making a mess on the leather seat beneath us. I'm so wet that it's splashing between us with every smacking thrust inside my body, and I quickly realize I'm in a constant state of orgasm.

After a few minutes I hear the unmistakable sound of his phone ringing. he pauses and reaches into his pocket to pick it up, still hard and heavy inside of me.

Narrowing his eyes he answers, putting it on speakerphone. I'm happy to see that though he hasn't been making any noise in him trying to nail me through the chair, he's breathing hard. I take the second to hang my head, desperately trying to get a handle on myself. My pussy is throbbing, sucking him even deeper into me.

My breath is shooting fast and hot through my nose, and I weakly lift my head up, seeing him smile into the phone. I'm surprised to hear Hudson's voice and not the demon that has surely taken over his body.

"Hello? Is everything okay?" He pauses for a minute and then grins, putting the phone on speakerphone. "Hey Tuck, are you having fun? Oh that's good... sure you can. Here she is, hang on."

My eyes widen and I moan against the tape.

Hudson meets my eyes through the reflection of the bathroom mirror and puts the phone on mute. Reaching over, he peels the tape off my mouth carefully, waiting for me to stop gasping for air. Tangling a hand in my hair, he tips my head back all the way back so I can meet his eyes upside down.

My throat burns with the stretch pulling against the little cuts, but it serves it's purpose as I can feel myself submitting for him before even even says a word to me.

"Are you going to behave? *Put that sassy ass bitch away and act like you've got some sense when you're talking around my boys.* Not like how you were at dinner." Hudson's eyes flash at me in warning, and he's seemingly back to sounding like a psychopath.

I nod frantically. "Y-Yes, yes, Hudson!" I cough weakly. "I'll behave, *I'll behave!*" My voice is hoarse, and thankfully he believes me. I wet my lips before the holds the phone up to my mouth, unmuting it. I clear my throat, trying to talk through the burn. "H-Hi, mi amor! You having so much fun?"

"Yes, mami. I just wanted to say goodnight, and te amo."

"Aw, I love you too baby. Thank you for calling, and tell Tatum I said Iove him too, and goodnight."

You may not have a mom to come home to, by the way, if Hudson succeeds in ripping me apart that is.

"I will." He replies. There's a backdrop of boys talking and laughing behind him. "Can I talk back to Hudson?"

Hudson pulls the phone back and he's so patient it's unnerving. "I'm right here buddy."

"I love you too, Hudson."

My eyes widen as my entire body breaks out with goosebumps as I'm suddenly hit with a wave of deja vu so clear it's like I've heard him say those words a thousand times before. Hudson goes completely still behind me.

It's so quiet you can hear a pin drop. Tears spring to my eyes and Hudson's face flushes as Tucker's words process. "I love you too little guy, we'll see you tomorrow." Hudson sounds choked up.

He puts the phone down and then meets my eyes again. Something passes between us, and I just know he's mine. I gotta have this man. If that makes me just as crazy as he is, then so be it.

"Do it," I whisper.

We continue to stare at each other. I know what I screamed at him just a bit ago, and all the fucked up shit he's said to me tonight, but this man broke through to my *baby,* and now all bets are off.

I flutter around him, feeling my womb trying to welcome him in and pushing back, I wiggle my hips enticingly.

His hands tighten impossibly hard on my hips, and begins those slapping thrusts that have me straining, crying out in pleasure. I feel him reaching forward, grazing his fingers over his initial hanging from my nipple and then I seize up, yelling out my orgasm.

Feeling myself break apart under him.

Sagging into the chair, I'm breathing hard as I attempt to find my sanity but it is firmly nowhere to be found.

Hudson picks me up and carries me back into the house and to the bedroom where he fucks me senseless. Pouring so much cum into me over the next several hours that I know no amount of plan B would help if I wanted to.

Soon it's the early hours of the morning, and he's got me folded half, pinning my knees back to the mattress with his arms. Keeping me spread wide for him.

His arms are wrapped under my shoulders and he clutches my hair hard, making me stare deep into his eyes as as he pulses for the last time inside me before sinking all the way down onto me on a tortured groan. My eyes are wide as I feel the lash of his semen inside me, and I whimper in shock when he grunts and quickly pulls out a couple of inches to make room for his seed to stay deep inside me without it leaking out.

He leans down and gives me a kiss. Several in a row before speaking. "You're so damn perfect, my beautiful girl," Hudson whispers, leaning down to give me another smacking kiss.

He tilts his head and swiping his tongue along mine on a groan that leaves me with no doubt that he desires me, and everything that comes along with me.

Pulling back to meet my eye, he stays close, causing my heart to skip a beat at the intimacy between us.

Though we're only inches apart, Hudson keeps eye contact, and there's so much nonverbal communication between us in this moment that it causes me to well up with tears.

He leans forward and kisses them off my skin softly, soothing and comforting me. As he kisses me, he begins to rub himself gently in and out of me. I realize he's keeping me stimulated down there, coaxing my vagina to open for him and accept his seed.

Knowing it doesn't matter, I don't bother to tell him to stop because I'm one hundred percent sure we've conceived tonight. I just know. Just like I knew with Tatum and Tucker.

I'm pregnant without a shadow of a doubt by Satan himself, because this man is slicker and way more deadlier than his brother.

Appropriate and ironic, as it was a snake who enticed Eve to bite the fruit from the tree of knowledge and baby, I just took my biggest bite yet.

So though I won't tell him, I dub Hudson's alter ego, Lucifer. I also won't tell him that I won't be able to keep the initials in if we're really serious about getting pregnant. I'll save that conversation for another time.

"Baby," I whisper, sinking my fingers in his hair like he likes.

"Yes sweetheart?" He rubs his nose along mine intimately. I swallow hard as a shiver races through my body. My eyes flicker between his, and my heart begins to pound. I'm unable to speak. "It's okay baby. You don't have to say a word, I hear you."

Just like that, I settle, knowing he does. "Fuck me again," I whisper, relaxing my body into the pillows and clenching myself around him.

Hudson arches an eyebrow, giving me a sexy grin. "Oh baby. *Glad-ly*. But I need a second to recover. You really took me for a run tonight. Kiss me for a bit."

"Make me," I mouth, arching my own eyebrow in a challenge.

My face tightens as he suddenly fists my hair hard in his head and pulls me back slightly, making me gasp. He tilts his head slowly to mine. The kiss he forces me to endure is sexy, full of promise.

And the best part?

Hudson makes me beg for my next breath before he lets me up, and by then, he's ready to ravish me all over again.

15

PLANTED SEEDS

HUDSON

"No, keep it in."

She gets a shocked look on her face as I gently push her back into the bed, gather up her legs, wrap my arms around them, pulling her knees to her chest and just cradle her like that. We stare at each other, aware that in our passion we didn't use protection and she's not on birth control yet. I lean forward and run my nose alongside hers. Silently willing her to let me do this, not change her mind now that we're done fucking.

My ass actually might die if I can't plant a baby inside this woman. But I meant every *every* word. She'll be my wife by the end of the week.

We lay here like this and my thumb strokes alongside her outer thigh, I press a kiss to her knee, resisting the urge to push back inside her and force my semen back even further in her vagina. I'm that fucked.

Her eyes ground me though, and I'm so unashamedly possessive that I won't look away. If she wants to address what's happening between us right now I'll respond, but in this moment I need to think about how I feel that my seed could be making its way to do its job in her body, and every male instinct is fighting against fucking her all night. Tying her legs back so she can take all my cum.

I can see the hint of fear in her eyes, and it's not unwarranted fear either, if this woman gets pregnant with my baby it's game over. I won't be nothing like Dominic, but there's a part of her that knows that I'm every bit of domineering, just in a different way.

I place two fingers against her and press, pushing it deeper, finding the spongy spot of her cervix and massaging it. Fuck it.

Her eyes go wide.

"Let me uuppp!" Lola complains, squirming against me. "I need to pee after sex Hudson, and wash up."

I pull my fingers out reluctantly to let her loose, and lounge against the covers with a knee up and an arm tucked behind my head. I grab hard on to the sheet that she's trying to haul off with her and I hold fast, making her pout and crinkle her nose at me.

I suck the two fingers that were just inside her into my mouth and narrow my eyes at her.

"You don't need to cover yourself. Go on. You can go pee, but no shower." I call after her as she pads into the bathroom. Her ass bounces perfectly when she walks.

"Hudson, I'm going to smell!" she yells from the bathroom. I can tell from the vanity mirror that she's closed the toilet closet door completely. I smile and stroke my hand down my beard.

I keep my eyes on her because if she grabs a hand towel I'm going to be upset. Her eyes turn to mine and I give her a little head shake no.

Obey me, I think.

She walks back into the room, and damn if the sight of her walking back with her arm over her breasts, and a hand clamped over her sex doesn't make me hard again. Seeing the object of my desire attempt to cover herself from me even though I know I just had her on her back, with her legs up, forcing her to keep my come inside her just feeds that sickness.

You can't hide Lola, I'm inside you.

She climbs into the bed, I admire her softness as I pull her against me. "Why won't you let me shower?"

"Because I like the smell of sex and I'm not ready to take it off you yet."

She's quiet.

"What do I taste like?" Her voice is soft and hesitant because she's not used to this level of intimacy, but she's trying. I turn my head from its gaze at the fireplace in front of us.

"Your pussy tastes like the earth," I say simply.

"Que?" Lola makes a slightly offended sound, and her eyes narrow as she furrows her brows. I remind myself again to talk to her about never fucking with her eyebrows.

She's wiggling, worried about my answer because she has no experience. And that's my fault, because this whole time we've been together, I haven't had my head near as much as I've wanted between her legs. I take full responsibility for that. I just can't stop thinking about that spot on the inside of her thigh that would be perfect for what I want. I can't look at it too long or it physically hurts.

I chuckle, putting my lips to her ear and nuzzling her.

"You taste like like you've been planted so long that you're extra sweet, and I got to see what true nourishment tastes like. Because the things that have been planted for longer are more luscious, delicious, expensive... rare because they're more difficult to harvest."

You know... like asparagus, truffles, that sort of thing. I want to sink into that dirt she complains she's buried under and let the nutrients take me over.

"Oohhh," she turns bright red.

I smile against her jaw and spread my hands on her rib cage. "What do I taste like?" I'm curious.

She pulls back and licks her lips. "You taste like rain. Life."

I smile, because Lola is good. "And I'm going to give it to you."

Just did as a matter of fact.

I relax into the pillows and pull the covers up on her, seeing her curl her little hands under her chin, and snuggle deeper in my bed. I took her hard tonight, for hours. And though I have this instinctual desire to keep pumping her full of my seed until I'm sure the job is done, she's tired and deserves to rest.

I've never had a woman in my bed, and I think it looks good, refreshing. Lola brings life into this house that has been sorely missing. I busy myself stroking her bangs out of her face, she melts even more and her eyes start to grow heavy and flutter shut.

I quickly gleamed that she liked this earlier on, but didn't realize how relaxing she found it until just now, and I grin. Because this is the kind of intimacy I want. Someone to place into my bed, pull the covers over and know all it takes is tenderly stroking her hair back and then she's asleep in our safe space.

Ours. Because it's ours.

Frank is going to be an asshole about it, I already know. But now that I've gotten a taste of what she's like in my house, in my bed, we've got no choice.

I'm marrying her, and her and those boys are moving in.

And if I have to yank Frank's old ass along with us then that's fine too. We can be one big happy family, so long as she's where she belongs.

Rolling into her, I lower myself down so my face is smushed between her breasts and her leg is draped over my ribs, and tucked under my arm. It's perfect. I curl my arm against her ass and breathe deeply, saturating my lungs with the perfect smell of us she wanted to wash off.

Her heat lulls me in and I am off, following her into sleep.

16

A Turning Point

LOLA

THE NEXT MORNING I wake up to the biggest rock on my ring finger I've ever seen in my life and I'm thrilled, but I'm also terrified. Like utterly *terrified*. You see things different when you're not in entangled the haze of lust. And in the morning light of the sun I cannot believe I let this man come in me the way I did with a plan for no contraceptive measures.

I'm toying around with the idea that I should get a plan B anyways, because surely all the unhinged shit that he said last night was fueled by lust, too, and he didn't mean it.

I mean, we just met. Literally *just met*. What the entire fuck is wrong with me?

He catches me staring at the diamond. "Do you like it?"

I nod my head, eyes wide, still glued to the ring.

"Is it big enough?"

I nod.

"Is it pretty enough for you?"

I nod.

"Is it the correct cut?"

Okay *damn Hudson*. My eyes fly to meet his. "It's gorgeous, thank you." And perfect on my hand. It's a gold band, too. I smile, feeling a nervous shiver race up my spine.

Skee's going to absolutely murder my ass. I don't know how I'm not already dead yet, what with all the testosterone in my life threatening to choke me out.

Hudson won't leave me to my thoughts.

He carries me out to the stables because surprise, *I can't walk*, and places me gently on the table there while he goes about taking care of them. Seeing him talk to Champ, Nay Nay, and Beauty brings a smile to my face and the way he's so insistent on them listening to classical music is a little bizarre and touching.

But he must be doing something right because these are the most calming horses I've ever seen.

He carries me back into the house and makes us breakfast burritos, putting extra picante on mine. As we're sitting there I'm fixing my mouth to talk about last night because we really really need to discuss if he meant any of that shit or not, when he pulls out his phone and makes a phone call to someone named Tyler.

He's leaned back in the chair with his legs spread looking delicious, so, I can wait a little bit because he gives me such yumminess to look at and it makes it bearable.

They're talking about work, he's delegating tasks and checking to make sure everything's running smoothly for the upcoming week. I'm waiting patiently, because I *can* force myself to be patient when it comes to him, when he says it, "Hey I'm going to need you to oversee the job tomorrow morning, I have to take Lola to the courthouse."

My eyes widen and I recoil my head slightly. I wet my lips nervously, flicking my eyes around. Hudson makes a grunting sound and then chuckles into the phone.

"No *you fool*, we're applying for our marriage license. *Uh huh.* Thanks man. Yeah, you too."

Wow. He wasn't kidding.

I'm breathing hard when he finally hangs up the phone and stands up. He picks me back up and takes us straight to the tub where we spend at least an hour in silence. I do not know what to say, and I get the feeling he doesn't want to say anything. He's going to clobber me over the head and drag me to the altar one way or another, and I don't know if I should be worried, or *flattered*.

We eventually get the boys back, and we still haven't said a word about *any* of it. Barely said three words to each other.

I can't drive, so I have to leave my car at his house. Hudson makes plans to stay the night with me and the boys before they go to spend the night with Dominic before fall break starts. He gets the boys for two nights, then they come to me for the rest of the time. I didn't tell him, but I bought them tickets to go see my brother for the other seven days.

I'm tired of this man controlling me and telling me what I can and can't do with my own children. They miss their Uncle.

We have an amazing night together, and I'm pleased to see that Tucker is all over Hudson, and to watch him warm up a little makes my own heart warm. They all play catch in the backyard, and I sit on the patio with a heater going and a small glass of wine, watching them enjoy themselves. I have music playing and it just feels like an amazing evening.

Frank sits in the chair beside me, finishing up another disgusting sandwich and looks over at me with a stern look. "Well I guess congratulations are in order missy."

I look over at him with an arched brow. "What are you talking about Frank?"

"Ain't you two getting married?" He stares pretty blatantly at the ring on my finger.

Oh yeah.

My jaw drops. We literally hadn't even talked about it, and then Frank comes at me. Hudson got to him and told him first. I hunch my shoulders, feeling stuck.

"We talked about it last night." I turn incredulous eyes on the backyard and see the boy's breath slicing in a white fog throughout the air. They're having so much fun so I decided to not blow a gasket for the second night in a row and just let them be. I turn my eyes back to Frank's. "We *talked* about it."

Did a lot more than talking, but that's neither here nor there when Frank is concerned. What am I supposed to say? I let Hudson fill me up with at least a pint of cum and I'm sure I'm pregnant? No. I can definitely not disclose that.

"That rock is a little bit more than talking missy."

"We *talked* about it." I'll repeat it until I'm blue in the face and actually die. Because we did, and they can carve the shit directly on my tombstone as far as I'm concerned.

Frank grunts. "Well that's not what I was told. I was told you're going to be Mrs. Montgomery at the end of the week." His eyes turn back to me and I twist my lips.

"Hmm-hmm." I say, taking a sip of my wine. Watching Hudson laugh as he tosses the ball far for Tucker to catch.

The fact that Frank's got nothing to say, not even a smart ass re-mark, tilts me a little more off kilter and makes me wonder if this really isn't so crazy after all.

The next afternoon I'm contemplating my life, at the shop. Dusting shelves. Thinking about whirlwind romances and men who just take over. Hudson drove us straight to the courthouse after the boys got picked up by their dad this morning. When Dominic got here, Tatum was excited, showing off the new glove and ball that Hudson had bought them, still on a high from last night when they were playing catch in the yard.

Tucker was subdued, hanging back and not saying anything as usual while Tatum was giving Dominic a play by play of their game.

"And dad, Tucker is a really good catch! He caught every ball that Hudson threw him!" Tatum was gushing over his brother.

Tucker furrowed his brow and mumbled. "Tatum, *stop it.*" Throwing him a nasty side eye.

Obviously hurt, Tatum had caught his look then bit his lip, looking rather ashamed and blinked silently as if he didn't know what to do. It was hard seeing my boisterous baby so unsure, his small face flushed with embarrassment making me tilt my head, wondering what's happening there. Because I've also noticed that some things have been off with their bond I can't pinpoint.

They leave, and Dominic thankfully didn't make any nasty comments about Hudson or him playing with the boys. It surprises me, because I would have expected some form of vitriol.

After they leave I'm quickly whisked off to the courthouse where we actually do it. I'm at Hudson's side, in a daze, as we apply for a marriage license and they tell us that it's going to be ready in three days. I breathe a sigh of relief, thinking about once I get off work to have Hudson take me to the drugstore where I'm going to get a plan b pill, and then we're going to go home and talk about this.

About if this is something we will want eventually. And if so, we need to talk about living arrangements, blending our families. He hasn't even met my brother, I haven't been around his parents that long. I haven't even seen his office. There's so much we need to *discuss;* finances, assets, all of it. Hudson said he needed to run to get some feed for the horses and I'm expecting him to come back any minute. Where hopefully we can talk.

I'm busy dusting, staring off into space when my phone rings.

There's a thin line between love and hate. And let me tell you, when I get the phone call from Tatum's watch... three of them in a row, and hear the screams of my baby Tucker in the background. Tatum's desperate, panicked voice trying to be heard, telling me to come quick because Tucker is hurt.

Well, I can tell you there's a point where that line is not even thin, it's *nonexistent.*

I call Hudson on three way, who is thankfully only around the corner from me when he answers. He's confused, because of the utter chaos on the other line that I didn't have time to prepare him for, and I finally am able to tell him I need him. *Tucker and Tate needs me,* when I see him flying around the corner almost taking out a man jay-walking.

I'm locking the office when he flings his truck door open, I climb in and we're off. I'm trying my best to give him directions amidst the terror. My heart pounds uncomfortably in my chest, the blood rushing in my ears makes me feel like I'm talking through cotton.

The next thing I know, Tatum's watch goes dead and it's silent.

"No!" I gasp, trying to call back and get no answer. I pull up Dominic's number and he thankfully answers.

"What?" He snarls into the phone.

"What is Tatum talking about Dominic? What's wrong with Tucker?!"

I can hear him screaming in the background, hoarse cries that I can tell he's trying to bite off, but it's not working. Pain is pain.

"Nothing Lola he's fine. He just fell!"

"He's not *fine* you asshole! Listen to him! What happened?" I yell, completely aware that he hits me when I raise my voice at him but I don't care because I'm getting my baby.

"He fell down the stairs!"

I pause.

"Dominic...you don't *have* any stairs." I said dumbly.

My eyes go to Hudson's. His narrow and I see a muscle tic in his jaw. Then I realize he's been driving for quite a while with no instructions.

"Dominic, he sounds like he needs to go to the hospital." I'm almost whispering because the sickening cold feeling of truth is finally making its way through my body. And because it started at the top of my head and made its way down, my throat currently feels like it's being frozen, and I'm losing my ability to speak.

And I just know, I know whatever happened, Dominic did it to him. He waited until he got my kids alone to retaliate for Hudson playing with Tate. I know it in my soul. Anger unlike any before I've ever felt enters me. I reach down and snatch Hudson's switchblade from his boot.

Hudson shoots me a look and then wisely turns his face back to the front.

"He doesn't need a hospital. He can sleep it off." I hear Dominic turn his head and say, "Grow up!" to Tucker, who's whimpering, and biting back his moans.

"Dominic, I'm on my way."

"It's not your day, Lolita."

"I'm on my way you asshole." I hang up on him and try Tucker's watch, since Dominic has Tatum's.

It's Tatum that answers, and I can hear Tucker saying, "ow," "ow," so close.

"Mami..." he bites out a sob.

"I'm here baby, Mommy is here. *Oh Tucker...*" I put my hand to my mouth, fighting back the feeling of being sick. "Come outside, Mijo. Tate, get your brother outside!" I yell into the phone at Tatum.

I see we're turning onto his street and I don't even ask how Hudson knows which house is Dominic's. I jump out the truck before the vehicle even comes to a complete stop, and I run at a dead sprint to his front door and see Tatum hunched over. He's got Tucker's arm around his shoulders, and he's dragging him for all he's worth through the front door.

"Get your ass back here!" I hear Dominic yell, before he comes around the corner with a beer in his hand. But it's too late, because while he was distracted, my boys got out of the house. I go to grab Tucker but then I stop, drawing up short. All the blood rushes out of my face at the sight of Tucker's left arm.

To say it's bent at an odd angle is putting it mildly.

I look up and meet Dominic's eye and for a heart stopping moment, *every fucking memory* I have with him flashes through my mind. But the one that sticks out the most, is that day at the pool in that hot ass sun, when he didn't give a damn about Tucker's blister that popped open, and he threw him in the pool that had too much cleaning chemicals in it.

I blow out a breath and my eyes go to Tucker. "Baby, I'm here. Mommy's got you."

Dominic comes up behind them and he's sneering. *"Punk ass little bitch.* Can't even fall right without breaking something."

I'm around the boys before I know what happened and in his face. I might be the next one with a broken arm, but I promise you, I'm going to take out a piece with me before I go.

"If you don't let me take my baby out of here I will gut you where you stand," I snarl. I look at him in his eye and they widen as he feels the prick of the knife I've stuck the tip into his side. I grind it in, to let him know I'm serious. His face winces, but he doesn't cry out or even act shocked that I'm holding a knife to him.

He just takes a swig of his beer and steps back. "Fine, but I'm coming to make sure you get your facts straight about what happened, *eh Tuck?*" I turn around and see Hunter looking murderous, pulling Tucker carefully into his arms and jerking his head at me to get back in the truck.

The look that's in his eyes is back. Very *different*. I wouldn't call it evil, but it's seriously something you don't want to memorize because you might see it in your nightmares.

We get in the truck and we race off to the hospital, and Dominic follows closely behind.

"Tuck what happened?" I plead for everything I'm worth.

Hudson's trying. I'm trying. But neither boy is relenting. It's all "I fell down the stairs."

"He fell down the stairs."

"You have no stairs at your dad's house! Please tell me what *happened?*" I twist around in the front seat, facing the back, trying my hardest to get the truth but they just won't do it.

"I fell at Mona's!" Tucker whines.

"Who's Mona?" My eye's fly to Tatum, who widens his own and looks down. His tell tale sign that he's lying.

"One of dad's girlfriends," Tatum whispers.

I look at Hudson, but he's scrubbing his hand over his jaw and looks clearly deep in thought. I say screw it and call the police. I tell them that I suspect that my son's father might have broken his arm, and they agree to meet me at the hospital.

We pull into the emergency room in record time, and thanks to Hudson carrying Tucker, we're in there with no problem. But Dominic is close behind trying to pull back on Tatum's arm. I wrap my fingers tight around my baby, seeing as his dad's trying to get him away to obviously coach him. However, because the nurses are talking, and they manage to get Tucker in right away, the tug of war between the three of us doesn't last long.

Soon the police comes and I'm pulled aside with Tatum. I proceed to tell them what I think happened, and it's utter chaos for what feels like forever.

There's nurses, x-rays, bones being set, hospital staff asking questions, police taking Tatum to the side, wanting to talk to him alone. Then wanting to talk to Tucker alone. And the whole time I'm *terrified*. So terrified that I can't even feel Hudson rubbing my back, because I'm busy staring across the space at Dominic. Staring into his eyes.

And we're promising each other something that is special to only us.

We're telling each other that the way forward isn't going to end pretty.

And because I'm finally alive, I decide to keep it that way.

I don't know how, and I don't know when. But Dominic is going to pay for what he did to my son. Even if I have to take his ass out myself.

17

ACKNOWLEDGING HUDSON

I HUNKER DOWN EYE level with Tate in the corner of the room. My eyes roam over his brown ones, and though he keeps his face in a blank, impassive expression, I see nothing but pain, and fear.

"Did he do it?" I ask softly.

Lola is currently verbally ripping into Dominic. The both of them are busy fighting in Spanish and I can't discern what's being said, so I keep an eye on Lola while I focus on Tatum.

Dominic is unfortunately still here because neither boy will say what really happened. The fact that Tucker has to lay here in this hospital bed, while the man who hurt him is just a few feet away, makes my blood boil in a way I don't even feel when I'm inside my girl.

And that just doesn't sit right in my spirit.

Tatum's chin trembles, and have you ever seen a little boy cry? It's slightly different from girls.

With girls, they cry over everything. *Every little fucking thing.* They're emotional, supposed to be. That's what they're born to be like because they're our nurturers of society, our beautiful, soft understanding persons who we come home to at night and they just make us feel safe, taken care of, loved.

We lay our heads on their breast and let the cares of the world melt away.

But boys? We don't usually cry. And when it happens, it's stoic. The tears might come but you'll get a hard stare to accompany it. We don't want to be looked at while it happens, or seen as weak. We want to be left alone to endure our emotions by ourselves because it's ingrained in our very psyche to be strong.

Tatum's lip quivers and I see his eyes flick quickly to Tuck, then Lola for a long moment, and then finally settle on Dominic.

I watch quietly as the fear in his features morphs into hate. His eyes harden for a moment before Dominic looks at him and the fear is right back. But that's all I needed to see.

Tatum turns his face back to me, and the nod he gives me is so slight I barely, *barely* see it.

I snatch him to me, wrapping my arms around him tightly so some of my strength seeps into him, and I stand straight with him in my arms. Tatum wraps his little arms around my neck and he hangs on for all he's got. He's silent, but I hear him loud and clear.

And I'm not sure about the power this man thinks he has over these kids, but I can *guaranfuckingtee you* it's no match for the sickness that's inside me. In this room, with a piece of my future in my arms, I finally embrace that dark side of me I'd forced myself to ignore and beat back all these years.

The room suddenly goes quiet as both Lola and Dominic whip their heads to stare at me. But I've got my boy in my arms, so I let it roll off for a moment and hold him.

Lola's eyes flick to me and then to Dominic in fear of him, when the man suddenly takes a step towards me. His face is contorted in a nasty expression.

"Get your fucking hands off my son-"

The vicious rumble that leaves me is enough to shock him, and he stops walking immediately. A look of shock crosses his face before his hateful look is back. Lolita's breathing hard, scared of the man who just hurt her baby in an unimaginable way. She turns her face sharply to address him, but I don't give a fuck. This is between me and him right now. This is personal. "Domin-"

I snap my fingers hard to silence her. Dominic recoils his neck with a slightly confused, yet angry expression on his face. Lola gasps, closing her mouth.

I let the mask slip, unconcerned that she can see and I take a step closer to him, grinding my foot into the floor. "There's nothing to say," my voice is clipped, stern as I address this vile fucker. "Because I warned you *already.*"

As much as I want to walk to Tucker in this moment I tighten my arms and hold Tatum tight to my chest, keeping his face turned away from Dominic as we stand down in this little room.

Because let me tell you, through this all, all the concern has been on Tucker.

Tucker the *victim*... the one who's been abused.

But Tucker has had a savior that placed himself in between him and his abuser the best he knew how. No one ever checks to make sure the strong one is okay. And I see clearly, while my mask is *my* sickness, Tatum has a mask of his own, and his mask has been his *strength*. He's used his charm and his favoritism with his dad to keep Tucker safe.

As safe as he could for an eight year old.

But Tatum *is* only eight, and his mask is beginning to slip because he's just a child.

Keeping my eyes on Dominic, I step back out of earshot to put my lips to Tatum's ear and begin to whisper to him. Speak life into him. I tell him how proud I am of him, how brave he is, and how strong his spirit is. I thank him for protecting his brother, even when he thought his brother hated him because was the favorite. I tell him I understand his pain and how it ends tonight.

I tell him to leave his fear with me, and let me take it.

Because I'm never going to let anyone hurt him, his brother, or his mom ever again. I ask him to trust me, and at the end of it all, I tell him I love him. When I'm done, I put him down, look him in the eye, and I give him a gift that I hope I don't regret.

"Go hug your dad and tell him you love him," I say.

His eyes are wide as he regards me, as if he's unsure.

"Trust me," I whisper in his ear.

He gives me a lingering look, but eventually he turns and walks to his dad, gives him a hug, and tells him he loves him just like I ask. Lola looks at me, shell shocked. To be fair, I would be too, if I didn't know the circumstances. Because you see, that was the last hug Tatum will ever give his dad.

Unbeknownst to any one in this room aside from myself, that was their goodbye hug.

Because tomorrow they are going to Skee's for a seven day break, and by the time they get back, their dad will be dead.

That's a promise.

Lolita's angry. "We can talk about it when the boys are away to Skee's for fall break. "

Dominic's lip curls back. "They're not going anywhere."

"Yes they are. I've already bought the tickets. You can't tell them they can't see their uncle!" she whispers furiously, however I remain unconcerned.

In my head, I'm flaying the man's skin from his muscle. Because he broke Tucker's arm. *My* boy. And Tucker has to live with that memory for the rest of his life. So yes, you can bet your bottom dollar Dominic is going to get what he's got coming, and I'm going to try and not cry tears of joy when I finally am able to execute my plan.

"Well, their uncle is in California!" she snaps, her voice raising. "And per our divorce agreement you need my permission for them to go out of the state!"

The nurse comes in to check on Tucker who's knocked out from the pain medicine and tucked in the hospital bed carefully in his cast. I throw her a friendly smile, making it the one all the ladies love to really lay it in thick, because I need her attention.

"Hi ma'am, sorry to keep you here on a Monday evening. What's your name?" I speak lazily, like I'm really concerned.

The nurse throws me a little smile. "It's okay. I'm used to it, been doing it for years now. Name is Jane."

I nod. My distraction makes Dominic feel comfortable to keep talking with Lolita.

"Why won't you let them go? You think my brother Alejandro is going to hurt them or something?"

The nurse is trying, but failing, not to be nosy. Her eyes keep flickering over here.

Dominic leans forward. "You know why, he needs to pay me first, and so far he hasn't paid me shit to see them this time."

Lola lets out a frustrated groan. "So we're still on that, right? Hasn't he already given you almost a hundred thousand dollars this year to see them? It's not enough? How much you want this time?"

The nurse is really taking her time. I'm still asking her a little question every once in a while. Shit that doesn't have anything to do with anything, and to anyone else, it might even seem like I'm flirting with her. But I'm not, and thank God for Dominic's foolishness because any normal person world have waited until the nurse was gone to have this particular conversation.

But Dominic is truly a stupid dumbass if I ever saw one. Thank God for divine intervention, perfect timing, and Dominic's clear lack of boundaries and respect for Lolita. *In this particular incidence anyways.*

"Tell him two hundred thousand dollars, and the boys can go."

The nurse pauses in her task and frowns, casting her eyes over Tatum, who is sleeping peacefully. I let out a displeased, disbelieving noise. Not because I really want to, but just letting them all know I'm listening.

Lola lets out a gasp, leaning forward in her seat with her arms tightly crossed. "The hell I am! I'm putting them on a plane tomorrow night. *Fuck you.*"

She's pissed. My thumb rubs soothing circles on her back and it's everything in me to not to step in. My body burns with the effort of holding bad. My tongue throbs with how hard I'm biting it to stay silent. I tap the toe of my foot against the shiny tile floor to get rid of some sort of energy and ground myself.

Dominic forgets himself in his anger. "The hell you are! *I'll kill you first bitch.*"

Lolita sucks in a shocked breath, the shock plain as day on her face.

My eyes narrow, the tapping stops and my thumb stops moving. I stop breathing. I think even the blood stops flowing in my veins.

The nurse cracks her head to look at him, but Dominic doesn't notice her.

Let's pause.

I can't break his face open because we're in a hospital and they will save him. So, I take comfort in the fact this man won't do anything right this second because we're in public. They're just words. Hudson. Breathe and tamp the beast down. The rage inside me swells to insane heights as I force myself to sit there calmly and let the nurse hear all the bullshit, and while she's taking notes, she also sees I don't retaliate.

Right now I'm the comforting boyfriend. I put my arm tighter around Lolita's shoulder and openly caress her. "Why the hell would you say that *again*, in front of the kids at that, Dominic. Don't you care that they hear you threatening their mother?" I say quietly.

Though it was never verified he's actually threatened to kill their her, instinctively I just know he has, and that's why they haven't said anything. They've both been protecting their mother. But the nurse doesn't know that, and what she doesn't know can't hurt her.

My performance is literally Oscar gold worthy. I'll need to see if Skee will let me hold his gold statue.

The nurse stiffens, and Lola tightens her lips in shock. Perfect. *"I'm sick of you using my kids against me, Dominic!"*

The nurse leaves discreetly. Pleased with how effortlessly everything is falling into place, my thumb flutters over the back of Lola's hands. I couldn't have handled this better myself.

Lola and Dominic keep going back and forth until Lola texts Skee to send the money. Skee sends confirmation of payment and then as if the heavens threw us another miracle, security walks in the room. Dominic stiffens and his eyes fly to mine, as if I did it.

I didn't do it dickface, I *orchestrated* it, and you guys just played right into my trap.

Oddly enough. I shrug my shoulder.

"Sir," the officer says. "We just received a call that you threatened this woman's life."

"What?!" Dominic throws Lola a nasty look and then turns his eyes to the man. "I did not, and *SHE* will tell you I didn't." He's so confident.

The cop turns slightly, motioning to the hospital door. "Sir, the report came from a witness here in the hospital. You'll need to leave."

Another officer comes in and asks Lola to come with him to give a statement.

She throws me a worried look. "I-uhm, *why?* It's okay."

And it's perfect, the officer can see she's scared of Dominic and this is just what we need. She throws me a shocked look. She's shaking, her eyes slide to Dominic's and he throws her a look so promising that I text Clayton and have him install camera inside the house this time.

"Ma'am it's hospital protocol," the officer responds.

Lola throws me another look and then glances at the boys. "Don't worry." I say. "I'll watch them. I'll be right here when you're done."

Lola stands up, bends down and gives Tucker a kiss on his cheek and then pulls the blanket further up on Tatum before following the police officer out.

She's gone for about forty five minutes before coming back. Her face is pale, and she looks distraught, and tired. I hold my arms out and she climbs into my lap, settling against my chest and sniffing. I hold her close, placing a kiss to the top of her head.

"Fuck I'm in trouble, Hudson," she whispers hotly against my neck. "He's going to retaliate, he already hurt the kids I don't know what to do."

I take a second to carefully consider my words. I don't want her to know my plans. "Let him try."

We get the boys home that night around ten, and on the drive there I buy my own plane ticket to help her drop them off in California the next day because fuck if I'm letting her go by herself, especially after all of this She went back and forth on the decision to let them go, especially after what happened to Tucker, but the boys pleaded her down, and Skee promised to take care of them and make them call her several times a day.

We pull into the driveway, and Frank is already there waiting at Lolita's front door.

His arms are folded and the man's stern face looks carved from stone. I pick up Tucker from the back seat. He's limp in my arms, knocked out from the pain killers. Lola grabs Tatum who's also asleep. Careful to not jostle his arm, I manage to get him to the front porch without him waking up and look up just in time to see Frank's eyes soften as he gets a good look for himself the fucked up situation we're in.

I look into his eyes for a minute, just silently communicating with him, and his eyes harden swiftly as he steps aside to let Lola open the door. We all make our way into the home without a word to each other.

I flick on the light in the foyer, and catch Lola's eye. They're red, as she's cried the entire drive home.

"I'll be at the table." Frank says in his stern voice disappearing down the hallway leading to the kitchen in the back of the house while we head up the stairs. After we get the boys situated and their door closed. I pull Lola into a hug outside in the upstairs hallway. Her eyes are welled with tears again. I'm worried about her.

I know how her headaches get when she's stressed.

"If the situation were different, I would have walked behind you and helped you shove that knife into him earlier for doing that to Tucker," I whisper to her.

I need her to understand that I'm holding myself back. I need her to believe I can restrain myself, because I'm still not sure if I'm ready to unveil the true sickness inside of me in all it's entirety. I don't want to traumatize her, she's already been abused enough, her and those two kids. She pulls away and huffs a shaky breath. Her fingers are trembling when she brings them up to wipe under her eyes.

My poor baby.

We hurry downstairs, because anyone with sense knows you don't keep Frank waiting. Rounding the corner we see two bologna sandwiches with lettuce on a paper plate, and a small black case.

"That man in jail?" Frank's eyes are hard on us as we go to join him at the table. Lola whispers a thank you to him and then lifts the bread up, to look inside.

"No, and thank you for the food." My voice is strong and sure as I take a big bite out of my sandwich. Shit, it's good. Fried, too.

Franks eyes widen ever so slightly, and his brow lowers. A ripple of unease crawls down my spine at his expression. I would not have wanted to have this man as my superior if I ever served.

"Why the hell not?" he asks.

"Because they won't talk, Frank." Lola sighs. I place a hand on hers, rubbing.

She looks so tired, mentally exhausted. Strain is all over her face and that worry deepens. I can't have this.

Frank grunts and takes the black case and turns it to him. At the same time he pulls out his phone. We stare at him while he dials a number. "Hello, is this the police?"

Lola's eyes widen.

"Yes. Well I don't know if it's an emergency, but I just saw this gray vehicle drive past real slow on the cul-de-sac and he stopped and is just staring at my neighbor's house. She's a young woman, lives by herself with two boys in that house."

I'm nodding, impressed as Frank pulls out a shiny pistol, and motions for Lola to lean forward.

"I get that but the issue is this is the twelfth time in about two months this same person has done this, and I don't ever see him get out and actually go up to the door. Windows are tinted. Yeah...yeah I got the license plate number, let me know when you're ready."

I'm even more impressed when Frank rattles off Dominic's plate number by heart. Lola and I chew silently, patiently. I keep my hand on her knee, needing to feel connected with her.

"Yeah..." Frank is silent for a minute as he puts the gun back in it's spot in the case and then snaps it closed, sliding it closer to Lola. She takes it hesitantly, but I reach over and slides it out from her hands and closer to me.

"Dominic Patrick? Yeah that's her ex-husband's name. *Hm.* I wonder why he's been stalking her." And just like that Frank planted another seed with the right people.

Frank finishes up the phone conversation, giving his report, and then he hangs up and looks dead at Lola. "I'm giving this gun to you for your protection. You aim the fucking barrel right between his eyes and you do not hesitate. Pull the damn trigger, you hear me?"

Lolita rolls her lips and nods her ascent. But I'm not letting my baby have to shoot anyone.

"And for the love of God, please don't shoot yourself. That's the last fucking thing we need to deal with next," he says. His voice comes out sarcastic as he looks away for a minute out the backdoor window, but I know better.

Frank hasn't been happy with the fact Lola hasn't allowed him to take care of Dominic.

And this has gone on far too long. He's got a major soft spot for Lola, and sometimes I wonder why. Why his loyalty to her runs so deep. What's the history here that I'm missing. Because according to Lola, he's been her neighbor since they moved here eighteen years ago. She's known Frank since she was the twins age. But the way he acts, there's something more personal here I can't place.

"Frank, I'm going to need my curfew to...not be a thing. I mean, we are getting married in a few days." I state. Folding my arms, I spread my legs and pin him with a stare, ignoring Lola stiffening.

His head turns to look at me. "Hudson, your curfew hasn't been in effect for about a week now."

My eyebrows raise. *Well okay then.*

"Are we still up for skinning that deer this weekend?" Franks says, eyeing me, not blinking.

My head tilts, because we never made plans to go deer hunting. Lola frowns and then throws me a look.

"Yeah. Bright and early Sunday morning," I say slowly. "We're going to be headed out at four am, right?"

Lolita's eyebrows furrow and she throws Frank a inquisitive look. *"You guys are deer hunting?"*

Frank gives her a grin. "You betcha, bright and early." He turns his gaze to me. "Stop by and see me in a couple days, Hudson. We need to make sure we got the right equipment so we aren't wasting our time. You know I don't like that."

And just like that, Frank, my newest ally, has joined my ranks and we are preparing to take Dominic down. He gets up and makes his way out the house, without a goodbye as usual. As he stands, I see the butt of his gun in the back of his pants. Smart man.

Lola looks at me. "I didn't know you hunt."

"*Ohhh,* I love to hunt baby girl." I get up from the table and grab our trash, tossing it into the bin and then grabbing her hand, helping her stand up. We set the alarm via the keypad, and I make sure all the windows and doors are secure before I follow her upstairs, seeing her getting ready for a shower.

It's been a long day and I roll my shoulders, trying to release some tension.

I check in with Haley on my phone, double checking that got the horses taken care of. Walking into the bathroom, I watch as Lola takes off her clothes and then works to pin her hair up in a sloppy bun on top of her head. She keeps her eyes averted, obviously deep in thought.

"Hey, I need you to pack a bag for the week," I say. "We'll go to my house after we drop the boys off at the airport. You're going to stay with me until the weekend." I start stripping my own clothes, tossing them into the bin with her dirty laundry.

She gives me a humorless laugh. "Hudson, come on. I can't not come home for a week. Frank will freak."

"*No,* Frank will the thankful you're not home alone by yourself, and a target for your piece of shit ex. And you heard him, he said curfew's over." I pull out my phone again, checking the feed from the cameras around the house, and double checking the alarm is on. Because I don't trust that fucker, period.

Lola gives me a little look over her shoulder as she reaches in to start the shower, and the look has got my blood boiling because my girl wants to defy me. I know it. Any other day I'd answer that call but the boys are near, and there's been way too much tension during the day that's concerning.

"I'll kidnap you."

She lets out a giggle that turns into full on laughter.

It goes on and on.

And on.

I frown, not seeing anything funny, honestly.

She's snickering because she just doesn't understand that sickness inside of me is real. Not only will I kidnap her, I will actually lock her ass up to make sure she's safe if I have to.

"You don't believe me huh?" This really has her laughing.

"No! But you're hilarious Hudson, thanks for the laugh I really needed that." She steps into the steamy shower and adjusts the spray a bit.

I see the water hit her hair and begin to weigh it down. Rivulets of water cascade down her body, and I hop in with her, wanting to make sure I don't miss a bit of this. Shower time with Lola is my weakness.

"Think about it, I can fuck you every night after we get home from the shop." I place my lips against her neck, letting my hands encase her ribcage right under her breasts.

By the way, the shop is about to go away for a bit, but she doesn't need to know that.

She squeals and tries to shrug her shoulder up to dislodge my latch onto her ticklish spot but I growl, persisting. Nipping at her, I'm encouraging her to give me my way.

"Think about it, beautiful." I breathe in her ear. "We can come straight home and you can lay down, spread these legs, and let me bury my face into your pussy for hours. Let me lick and suck at you for as long as you want. As long as you can stand it."

My erections so swollen it hurts I'm so turned on by just the smell of her. The feel of her soft, wet naked skin against mine. My dick feels like its own alive creature that's attached itself to every nerve in my body and is making me suffer.

At the thought of my mouth between her legs, I sink to my knees and hook her leg over my shoulder and go on ahead and bury my face down there like I want to. I don't care I'm about to drown.

Wait. I need to care about stuff like that for at least another week until I get the job done.

Frustrated, I groan and I maneuver us so the spray isn't going to drown me after all. I appease myself by fantasizing about her sitting on my face so hard I can't breathe. I have other fantasies I want to explore with her, yes, but God damn... I want this woman to fuck my face, take her pleasure from me. Grind her juices and her smell into me.

Mark me so that she has no doubt that I'm hers.

The hairs on the back of my neck stand up as other more forbidden, sick thoughts come back. I shudder, getting even more aroused at the thought of branding me, branding her, so we know we belong to each other.

Because I need her to know I belong to her, without a shadow of a doubt.

I slip my tongue into the apex of her thighs and it's so warm, so fragrantly her that all I can think about is getting deeper. So, I take a hand and spread her plump flesh wider for me, making her whimper and attempt to recoil in shock because my beautiful thing has very sensitive bits that overwhelm her for me to suck and bite at.

That's something you're going to have to learn to get over pretty thing. I lift her slightly, put her other leg over my shoulder, and bear her body weight completely. I love it.

I pull away from her enough to talk, still treating her to slow licks. "Do you know how much I love you, baby?"

Lola stiffens, because I got her stuck, and she can't run. Just like how I like her. Her legs began trembling and I smile against her flesh.

I spread her apart gently and I tease her, flicking the tip of my tongue against the hard tip of her clit and I stroke it just long enough so that with every flick I hear a whimper, I feel it swell just a bit bigger against my tongue and that's my cue. I seal my mouth around her and suck.

Because I have the world's greatest wiggler on my hands, it forces me to tighten both my lips and teeth in warning.

I nip her, letting her know to be still. The action causes her to seize up and I hear a strained sound leave her throat. She's biting her lip to keep from being loud so the kids don't hear. But I don't let up. I have to do this, because the shit she just went through today, as a mother, seeing her kid hurt the way he was, she deserves reverence.

To be worshiped.

There's no reason why a woman should have to be subjected to having to press a knife into their abuser's body in order to ensure they get their babies, but my love did. So brave.

I would have killed him with my bare hands in his front yard had he retaliated, but I let her have her moment. Because being able to know that you can be brave is such an important part of life. It's crucial, I would argue, to know that if you absolutely had to, you can stand up for yourself.

And I gave her that gift, because for the rest of my life she'll never have to stand up for herself ever again, because I'll be doing that for her.

But I wanted her to have that knowledge for herself.

And though I'm more of a man of actions than words, I give her what I should have done when I was busy fucking her late into the night intent on imparting a piece of myself into her body.

"I love you," I mumble against her flesh. Because she deserves to hear it, even if she doesn't believe in it. "Hmm baby? You know that?" I burrow deeper and just suck and suck. She sags against me, flowing down my throat.

Her fingernails bite into my scalp, making me growl because it's so fucking *good*.

I wait until her orgasm wanes and then I slowly kiss my way up her body. Keeping her legs in the crook of my elbow, I line her up to my aching cock and I give her a whimper as her heat envelops me. I lower her down onto me, slowly, taking my stretching her out. I love how much she enjoys hearing how much I enjoy her, so I give it to her any chance I get.

I let out another groan, and my eyes flick over her face watching her bite her lip. "And I love those boys, too."

Lola sucks in a ragged breath as her face breaks with her emotions. She turns away so she can hide from me, but I pull her back to face me.

"I love you." I'm not even moving. We're staring at each other, pulsing around each other. Deeply entrenched in one another. "I love you, and I've got you *and* them. Do you understand me, baby?"

She's still staring, sadness burned deep into her eyes, and it tugs at my heart that this man broke her so badly that she won't let herself acknowledge this thing between us. But it's too late. It *is* here, and we're going to acknowledge it.

"We can stand here all night, pretty thing, if that's what it takes," I say.

I bottom out inside of her, and her lashes flutter as she clearly struggles emotionally. I rock her side to side, and much like the time we were in her foyer and our battle of wills were put to the test, I hold her through this in the safety cocoon of our shower.

It's just me, her, and this thing we have to prioritize.

She lets out a small, hurt sound and I lean forward to press my forehead into hers. There's tears running down her face and I swear, I've never felt so much for anyone before, ever. And just like I let her hear what she does to me in bed, I let her see how much she affects me in this regard, too.

I let my own tears run free, because fuck it, she has my heart in the palm of her hand. She's watering me with her tears, and I feel so fucking nurtured that I can't do anything right now but cry. Show her that she does this to me.

This thing that men just aren't supposed to openly do.

But if I can't tell this woman I love her, if I can't show her my tears, then what really is this?

It's so quiet, and it's in Spanish, but it happens.

"Te amo, mi amor," she says, sniffing.

I feel it with my heart, more so than understand it with my ears. I swell everywhere in response. My chest puffs out, my heart itself swells, my dick swells, my tongue wells too, because suddenly I'm choked up. No one's ever told me they've loved me before.

I mean, not a woman, anyways.

I believe her. I just know she loves me for *me*. Because she saw my mask slip and she's still here, still letting me touch her, be around the boys, love her, be inside of her. She trusts me.

"Thank you," I bite out, somehow.

I want to say that feeling loved is like floating on a cloud. But no...this isn't like that, not for me.

It's swelled inside me, every Goddamn, spare inch of me is full to capacity with Lolita. It's not a floating feeling, this is a *grounding* feeling. Almost like all the dirt she claims she was buried under got poured into my body and now I'm forever cursed to carry its weight around.

I grind my foot into the tile of her shower and let it overtake me, fill me up, make me heavy with need, want, desire, desperation.

Determination.

They are my family, and there's nothing that anyone could say to change it. I may not have given her the seed for her to make those kids, but you'll be damned sure I'm going to be the one to ensure their growth and pluck them up out of the ground when they're ready.

But there's something that needs culling first, I acknowledge.

A weed that's poisonous, winding through the three of them and trying to choke them out. Trying to make them rot from the inside out. And before I can enjoy the fruits of my harvest, I need to eradicate the infestation first.

Lola's brother and I assess each other in the space of the private airport terminal. Meant for fancy celebrities and people who have more money than God. I eye his security team seeing he's got four people with him, and behind him, there's a limo in the background through the glass doors.

I smirk. "What, no red carpet? How so *first class* of you."

Skee laughs and then tension is broken. I like him. Don't like how him and Lola cuss at each other and call each other names, but I see it really is all in love.

Skee and I trade a look and a brotherly hug.

"We good on the plan?" he whispers in my ear.

"I'll let you know if we're not, okay?" I handed him a thick envelope with the documents, every piece of it, every coordinate, burner phone, all of it.

"It won't, but just in case things go wrong," I whisper in his ear.

He nods, casting the boys a glance and then leaning forward to hug Lolita. "You take care of yourself, mami." He pins me with a look. *"You take care of my sister."*

I nod, a hard look passes between us and I turn my attention to the twins, feeling my heart tug. I already love them so much.

"You be good for your uncle, you hear? I'll have a huge surprise for you when you get back!" The boys smile and give me a big hug with excited grins. They love my surprises.

I step back with Lola and we watch Skee make his way through the glass doors with the boys.

I smile as they're already laughing and playing around. Lola pulled out the little piece of paper with the itinerary Skee gave her off their activities for the next seven days as we walk to our gate. We touch down back in Washington and as soon as she turns her phone on, we see it.

"Oh my God!" Her hand covers her mouth.

"What is it?"

"I just got alerted the bookshop is on fire!"

I give her a concerned glance but honestly, I've went through every possible retaliation Dominic could attempt and the bookshop, her, and the house, were all up for grabs. I just knew as long as she was with me, it wouldn't be *her*. So the bookshop had to go.

"I'm sorry Lolita," I say, giving her hand a squeeze and pulling her head to my shoulder.

If only you knew the bookshop you're going to have in the future.

I'm pained at taking this from her because the look on her face is devastated.

"That asshole!" she cries.

I wince. It breaks my heart to see these kinds of tears in her face.

"I'm sorry baby," I whisper. Pulling her deeper into my chest, I kiss the top of her head. But that feeling enters me, the one that lets me know we're close and every little detail needs to be paid attention to.

"Come on, I'll call Frank and let him know." I pull out my phone and begin to tell Frank everything from beginning to end I make the call last a good hour. While we hang up I text Clayton.

> Hey what's for dinner? Our usual?-Hudson

> I'm getting burnt out on deer burgers-Clay

I smile, because what perfect wording.

> I'll order in then.-Hudson

Back in town, we stop by the bookshop, survey the damage, and give a report to the officer. Since we were both in California at the time, we couldn't give much information other than we were out of town and the shop was closed down.

"*Officers, was it a piece of equipment?*" Lolita's tearful, clinging on to me. *Hold on tight to me baby.*

The office looks, at her and his face softens. "No Ma'am. I'm sorry to say this was arson."

Lola throws me a look and it breaks my heart. "No! No Dominic can't do this! He can't do this to me!" She collapses, sinking to her knees with her head in her hands.

I look at the officer and hold out a hand to stop him when he bends down to grab her elbow. I try to keep my face neutral as I pick her off of the ground and cradle her, sobbing, in my arms. "It's okay, we just had to file a report with the hospital yesterday because her ex-husband threatened her life while we were there with her son," I say softly. "We think he broke the boy's arm, but they aren't talking so we can't know for sure. I walked in on him grabbing her by the throat a few weeks ago, and he's just getting more and more violent I think."

The officer gives me a pitying look. I fix my face into a sad expression, keeping up the façade that I'm ever the innocent boyfriend.

I'm letting every fucking department that's involved in this mess know what the other department knows and is doing, and I'm about to build us a case so big the shits going to go nation wide.

He nods. "Ex-husband got a last name?"

"Patrick."

"Thank you." The officer nods and speaks into the walkie talkie at his shoulder before holding his hand out to us. "Thank you again. We'll be in touch should anything arise. In the meantime, you'll need to get ahold of insurance."

Because Lola is so distraught, I shake hands with the officer and pour her into the truck.

"What the hell am I going to do?! I have no business? What am I going to do?" she whispers, more to herself than anything.

You don't even need to worry about that Lola, because I know what *I'm* going to do. And that's all that matters right now.

18

PLANS TO HUNT

LOLA

TO SAY I'M MENTALLY fucked up is an understatement.

I look over at Hudson, who looks cool, calm, and collected as per usual. Though I've seen him in some truly passionate scenarios, the man is like a beacon of strength. It's like he's got it all worked out in his head, and if we just lean in hard enough, we'll emerge out the other side perfect.

I wish I had his bravery, his confidence that everything is going to be okay. Because I am not calm at all. That fucker hurt my baby, and now he's taking my livelihood away from me. What else is he going to attempt to try and take? My cheeks flood and I think about my house, then ironically about Frank.

I pull out my cell, needing to speak to him.

"Yello'," he answers right away.

"Frank." I put my hand to my chest and breathe. I'm so fucking worried about the man but honestly, he's got enough guns and ammo, and I think that big box in the back of that one room might have been a bomb or something. I'm sure he's probably the safest one on the block.

"Lolita, are you okay, lass?"

I frown, lass?

"Uh...yeah Frank I...I just called to let you know what the officer said about the bookstore. Half of it's burnt down. The police say it's *arson.*"

"Put him on speakerphone," Hudson says, and I do him one better and connect my bluetooth to his truck.

"Frank, it's Hudson."

"No shit Sherlock."

There's an awkward pause because Goddamn, why can't Frank just be nice throughout *one* entire interaction?

"I'm bringing Lola to my house for the week. She'll be back on Friday night, and then me and you will head out to go hunting Saturday morning."

"What I don't understand is," I say. "Is why the hell am I going to your house for the week, and then you take me home Friday night to go hunting Saturday morning. You don't think anything's going to happen to me *Saturday?*"

Make it make sense! I screech in my head. But Hudson just places his hand on mine and squeezes.

"Now Lola... Hudson's been doing so much to take care of you," Frank says in a kind, grandfatherly voice. "We've got your house secure, you've got protection. We can be boys for a few hours I think. Besides, do you really think that dumbass is going to be up at your house at four in the morning? No! He's going to be hung over from drink and screwing into some rank pussy till probably three in the morning."

I recoil my head and wince. Jesus. *Rank pussy, Frank?*

Hudson's sly grin is enough to make me roll my eyes. "God, is that how you men talk to each other? Ew." I'm totally judging, but I don't care.

Frank clears his throat, sounding slightly ashamed of himself. "I'm sorry about the bookshop, Lolita. Did you have insurance on it? I hope you did."

"Yes, but it wasn't much, honestly."

"Enough to rebuild?"

"Sure, but not enough to rebuild and then sustain myself through the time for the claim to go through and the time to rebuild and all of that."

"No one's going to let you starve, Lolita. I've got plenty of hog head cheese here. Don't worry about it."

"Bye Frank." I'm disgusted, and Hudson is laughing.

I'm glad one of us can laugh.

"I don't even know why I worry about him." I shake my head, seeing Hudson's property come into view. It hits me then that I don't have any clothes. And then it also hits me, amongst all the chaos, I've missed my threshold for getting my contraceptive. I look back over to Hudson.

Fuck.

Does he actually want this?

19

I NEED SOMETHING

HUDSON

I TAKE LOLA'S HAND and lead her out of the construction zone. I bop her on her hard hat that I had to manhandle on her, and I take her safety glasses off when we get into the safety zone, making our way to the truck. I heave our duffle bag and our lunch cooler into the bag of my truck. I'd made her hang out with me all day at the construction zone after we spent a couple hours at the office.

Her face when she saw the building I work out of was priceless.

"Stop it," she teases, slapping my hand away.

Her phone beeps and she takes it from her back pocket seeing it's Skee, facetiming her.

"Hey bro!" She smiles big into the camera, tilting it so I can see him as well. They're lounging in the backyard of his mansion, and I see a huge pool, and lots of water spitting everywhere in cool designs.

"What are you two wearing?" Skee slips his sunglasses down and takes a better look into the camera. She laughs as I pull the hard hat off her and ruffle her hair, putting her bangs back into place.

"Don't be fucking rude, Skee. We can't all be in Oscar de la Renta and walk the red carpet fifteen times a year."

"Well you *could have* been. Did you tell Hudson that when you came to Hollywood years ago, you were offered the lead role in Binding Desires?"

I throw Lola a sharp look and she blushes and rolls her lips. "No, can't say I did."

"No she did not." I interjects. "And I'm glad she didn't because she wouldn't have given me the time of day." Lola turns and delivers a playful smack to my arm. I smack her ass so hard she stumbles forward a few steps and throws me a horrified look.

Thank God for her playfulness, she cried for a day straight about her shop.

I pull her back, giving her a kiss to her temple. "Let me see my boys Skee. I know you don't have Tucker in that pool getting his cast wet."

I see Lola sneak a look at me and I nuzzle her with my nose. Those boys are mine, and as soon as I can, we're filing adoption papers and I'm giving them the Montgomery surname.

"Hudson you motherfucker do you think I don't know better than to put a kid in a cast in a pool? *Look at him!*" Skee turns the camera, and in the background we see an insanely famous wife and husband duo with their kids in the pool with Tucker, who's in the shallow end pulling a toddler in a floatation device.

He's got plastic taped around his arm protecting him from getting wet, and a smile from ear to ear as he plays with the little child.

Lola's eyes widen at the sight of the famous couple. *"Hey is that-"* Lola starts, but Skee turns the camera around fast.

"If you don't shut your bitch mouth-"

"Hey!" I admonish in a hard tone, grabbing the phone and cutting him off now. "No one's allowed to call her that but me."

Skee gives me a rather hard look, and his mouth thins into a straight line. "I know you don't call my sister a *bitch,* motherfucker-"

"Not like that..." I rush. *"Not* in the context your referring to. Only in the bedroom."

I wince as Lola heaves an outraged gasp and pushes my chest, her eyes furious. Oops.

"I'm sorry," I whisper to her.

"Ohhh." Skee slides his sunglasses back up, clears his throat and then lays comfortably against his lounger. "Wellll, good for you guys. Lola *never* fucked her ex. I'm honestly surprised she got pregnant with twins."

Lola's mouth drops open and then she turns, climbing silently in the truck and slamming the door and staring straight ahead out the window with her arms folded. Goddamn it.

I heave a deep, long suffering sigh and put my hand to my nape, squeezing hard. "Thank you. Thank you so much for that, Skee. It's going to make tonight sooo wonderful."

Skee gives me a shit eating grin and puts his arm behind his head. "Boys, come here and say hi to your stepdaddy."

The acknowledgment warms me enough I might not punch the man in his face the next time I see him. The boys climb out the pool and run up to the phone. I knock on the window so Lola can roll it down, heaving myself up so I can show her the screen.

"Hi babies!" She's all teeth, it's wonderful.

"Mami! The weather is so nice here, you have to come down next time!" Tatum is trying to hog the phone, but I see Skee pull it away and let Tucker have some screen time too. "Sharing is caring." I hear him say to Tatum.

Tucker gets into the phone. "Mami, Hudson, *hi! I miss you two, I have a question!"*

"Sure thing bud, what's that?" I grin at him, I feel myself settle at seeing him so carefree right now.

He squints into the phone. "Can I have a little sister?"

Skee suddenly turns the phone and gives us a 'what the hell' look, before turning the phone back to the boys. I look over at Lola and see she's bright red, and she's stuttering, trying to figure out what to say.

"Sure bud," I smile brighter at him. "We don't have control over if it's a boy or a girl, but we're trying okay?"

Looking back over at Lola I give her a wink, seeing the color high in her face. I've never seen a woman blush so hard in my life, and for a moment, I'm actually concerned she's going to pass out. Hearing some ruckus in the distance, I turn my head, hearing my employees start to yell their goodbyes as they all head to their own trucks.

"Yay! Did you hear that Tatum?" Tucker yells towards his brother excitedly. He turns back to his phone, smiling the biggest I think I've ever seen. "Bye Mami, bye Hudson!"

"Bye mijo! Love you," she chokes out.

Skee puts his face in the phone again. "Whew boy. Well, you see they're taken care of, so, good luck yall. Have fun baby making." And with that he hangs up in more of a dramatic exit than Frank, ironically.

I turn my face back to her and then peruse her face slowly, she's studiously not looking at me. I let my eyes travel down her body slowly to linger on her tummy, and just to reinforce my point I place my hand over it.

Hard to believe we met just two months ago, and now, she's the center of my entire world.

I give her tummy a little rub, then place my hand on her ring finger and straighten her engagement ring. She throws me a shy look, and her face is just so adorable I can't help but reach up and caress her cheek.

The sun is pounding down on me, but I can stand here fussing over her all day. My phone rings next and I answer it, no nonsense. "Hey Clay, I got word that Dominic is out of town until tomorrow. Perfect time to ransack his house tonight."

I grunt, stepping off back into the dirt rounding the front of my truck. "Okay, let's get to getting. Meet me there at seven?"

"Sure thing, Hud."

Hanging up, I climb into the drivers seat and turn to Lola. "Hey, do you think you could have dinner with Frank tonight and I can pick you up at about eight or so?"

Lola wets her lips and gives me a rather relieved look.

I'm sure she was expecting me to bring up the fact she might be pregnant, or even the fact that we're going to be married the day after tomorrow. I smile at her, because we don't need to talk about stuff that's inevitable.

We just don't.

But to make her feel better, I'll bring it up when I'm inside her later.

"Yeah, let me call him real quick." She pulls up Franks number. "What are you doing?"

"Hm?" I let out a little grunt as I start my truck and pull off.

"I said what are you doing?"

"I'm running an errand with Clayton."

"Oh. Doing what?" Her tone is light, but I know better.

"Digging information on your ex that we need."

As I said before, all she's gotta do is ask. Her silence is the loudest I've heard yet. She pulls her leg into the seat, turning to face me, her eyes flash with a mixture of determination, and anger.

"I want to go with you."

"Absolutely not." I interrupt her. Has she lost her mind? "You'll have dinner with Frank."

Her eyes narrow at me. "Fuck that! That man hurt my child, and I want to be apart of whatever you got going on!"

She's adorable.

"So here's the thing." I throw her a look as I maneuver us down the highway. "I know that you're feisty, you want what you want. And rightfully so sweetie." Turning back to the front, I move my hand to her leg, curling around her inner thigh and squeezing. "I'm not ever going to deny you your comeuppance, okay? But I need you to trust me to bring you what you need."

Lola is silent.

"You need to trust me on this," I say to her quietly, throwing her another look to implore her.

"Fine. But I *am* trusting you, Hudson." She huffs in the seat, crossing her arms and stares out the window pensively, her brows furrowed together. I tug at her arm and thread my fingers through hers. I don't want her closing herself off from me.

"Good girl. That's my baby."

I drop her off at Frank's, and make sure she's in the house before I take off to Dominic's.

"This fucker is *gross*," Clayton says.

I've never seen Clayton's face so scrunched up before, but my face feels just as balled up, honestly. My skin is crawling, and I feel like I'm going to be scrubbing extra long in the shower later.

If the situation weren't so serious, it'd be funny.

I grunt in reply. We're in the middle of ransacking Dominic's place, seeing he's taken off to Florida for two days. One thing I do know for sure, I'll never tell Lola the state of this man's house. I just can't do it. Nothing in me wants to subject her to the truth to how this sorry excuse for a man makes her sons live while they're here.

I make my way out of the kitchen and head to the boy's bedroom. I know what it looks like from when I was here last time, but honestly, I just want another look so I can see how it is without anyone in the house.

As I walk into the threshold I pause for a second, looking around.

Their mattress sits on the floor with one fitted sheet that doesn't look like it's been washed in months. The dirty stained carpet is more black than grey, and there's only one, three-tiered plastic bin with all the boys clothes shoved in haphazardly.

The walls are dirty and peeling paint. The closet door is missing, and chock full of cardboard boxes. There's no life in this room. No happiness. No baseball glove hanging up on the wall. No fun curtains on the window with their favorite cartoon character.

Nothing that'll make a boy smile when they get ready to snuggle in bed after dinner.

That fucker needs a bullet in his brain.

I leave, because there's nothing else to look at in the boy's bedroom, sadly. I slowly make my way to Dominic's bedroom, seeing a trashcan a third of the way full of used condoms and tissues, with no liner. I look in his drawers and see half folded shoved in clothes, clothes all over the room on every spare surface, random bits of squares of toilet paper strewn on the floor.

But what throws me off is the picture against the far wall. It's the only one.

It's of him and Lola, and they look young. Eighteen, maybe nineteen. She smiling, has a adoring look in her eye. I pick it off the wall and shove it under my arm. I'm going to hold this in front of his face while he dies.

"Hey Hud, you need to come look at this."

I inwardly groan because I know that tone.

It's not good, whatever it is.

I walk to where he's standing in Dominic's closet and see he's broke open a box and has manila holders and papers everywhere. He's clutching a folder in his hands, holding it out to me. However, he holds it fast when I go to take it. Making me meet his eye.

"Hud, I'm going to need you to not lose it. Promise me."

I raise an eyebrow at him. "Since when have I been in the habit of losing my temper, Clay?"

Clayton gives me a look, and I know it's not good. His eyes turn wary as tries to pull the manila folder back, forcing me to tug it from him.

"Give it to me, Goddamn it." I say in a hard voice. "Fucking shithead." I throw him a dirty look.

I turn to walk back out into the bedroom, not liking being in the small space with him. I stand there, fighting rising irritation and open the folder scanning the contents inside. My eyes narrow in concentration before my blood freezes in my veins, causing me to feel nauseated.

No this motherfucker didn't.

Inside the folder are documents of Lola, and the boys. Multiple monetary figures litter the paper. As I look closer I see their demographics, and then there it is; the life insurance amount on each of them. The boys have a ten million life insurance police on them each, and Lola has a thirty million dollar life insurance policy.

But that's not what's made my blood run cold.

The man recently put a hit on them.

All *three* of them, even though he's not even a beneficiary on Lola's. But he is on the boys. I grit my teeth so hard I feel pain erupt in my skull. I turn and look at Clay, who's leaning his shoulder against the closet door, giving me a look of concern. I feel my face twitch and I clear my throat.

"Let's get the fuck out of here." I see Clay go to bend down to put the papers back in the box but I stop him. "Leave it," I bark at him. "I want him to know I know."

Clay tosses the papers into the floor, scattering them everywhere. With that, we head out the house, and I leave the door wide open.

Letting him also know we're open for business.

Bang. Bang. Bang. Bang. Bang. Bang.

"Open your legs wider," I growl.

"Hudson *I can't-*"

"Wider, I said." I rub my lips and tongue along her jaw, drinking in her taste, her scent. Memorizing her. "Obey me, Lolita. *Now.*"

I'm fucking her too hard, and I didn't tie her up because I knew I might. I'm breathing hard, my heart is pounding, and I can't stop.

I won't stop.

I fit my elbows into the crook of her legs and double her over my damn self when I see she's truly struggling. I sink all the way into her on a smacking thrust, holding myself there. I grunt, growl into her ear, and for good measure I bite her and tug her earlobe.

I move my gaze to her naked pussy where that bare strip of skin has been the bane of my fucking existence since I saw her.

My hips sink even more heavily into her, and I keep my eyes on that tan strip of skin just teasing me, making me suffer. Small rumbles escape my chest as I fight with everything in me to get control over myself.

Lola shudders on a high pitched whine, digging her nails into my back, and I snap out of it, pulling out a fraction, having observed that she can't handle me pressing into the back of her the way I am for longer than a few seconds at a time.

I spend a second breathing hard, placing my lips to hers.

As much as I love the rough sex we engage in, I don't want to purposefully bruise her unless we're having one of those nights where it's an understanding between the two of us.

Her eyes flicker between mine, going wide at whatever she see's in there. In me.

"Hudson, what's bothering you, amor?" Her voice is small, hesitant.

The fact that she can read me so well let's me know that she's the one. Lola's the only one that's been able to see through my mask.

I keep still, making sure that I don't hurt this woman.

Do I tell her?

Tortured, I lower my head to her neck and struggle desperately to get a handle on my emotions. I tighten up when I feel tears prick in the back of my eyes, and I work to get my arm under her to press her to me, my other hand going to the side of her head and stroking her gently.

I got my breathing under control, but my heart rate wont slow down. I press my body harder into her, needing her softness.

Her love.

"Please tell me you love me," I say. My voice sounds tortured and I hate it. I never want to appear weak in front of her.

I only ever want her to feel like I can protect her.

"I love you, Hudson." She puts her hand to my cheek, caressing me. "You know I love you."

The tears come easily, and now I'm the one shuddering against her as I fist my fingers into her hair and hang on as tight as I can.

"Hudson? Oh baby what's wrong?" Her voice is unsure, and her fingers go into my hair. She strokes me, giving me comfort.

I pull away from her neck to look down at her. My heart swells too big for my chest as I regard her, and another tear slips out, thinking of a future with her. Her hands immediately go to my face, her thumbs wipe my tears away almost reverently.

She's so beautiful it hurts.

My heart pounds at the knowledge that this woman holds the power to give me everything I've ever wanted.

"Lolita," I hold her eyes, aware I'm still intimately inside of her, however I keep my thrusts slow and unhurried. "Baby, do you think you're pregnant?"

Lolita's eyes widen and then she bites her lip. I'm sure if she wasn't already flushed from how hard I was taking her, she'd be blushing from my question. Her eyes drift down my face, and she takes her time processing my question before giving me a reply.

It doesn't bother me at all.

My baby can take as much time as she needs as long as she tells me the truth.

"Yes," she whispers. "I think I might be." Her own breaths become labored between us as we're finally speaking about this unspoken possibility between us.

"Do you...do you want me to be the father of your children? Not just the one we're going to have, *but all of them.*"

My firmly believe that my heart would bang out of my chest if it weren't caged in.

Lola stares at me for a long minute before nodding. I feel my heart soar. Put my hand to her head, and then push back her bangs in that way we both love. Leaning down I press my lips to her forehead.

"It'll be my absolute honor and privilege, my love. My baby." I begin moving faster, keeping her eyes. "I need something from you. Just one thing."

Her eyes go wide. "What is it, Hudson?"

"I need you to let me brand you."

She stills and it makes me still too, sensing her seriousness. "W-WH-*WHAT?*" Her mouth gapes open. "What do you mean brand me, like I'm a fucking cow?"

I give her my most serious stare. "I want my initial's on the upper crease of your thigh, right next to your pussy."

Her brows furrow next. *"Hudson!"*

"Lolita."

"You already pierced my n-nipples!"

"I don't care." That awful desperation fills me, making me even weaker. *"I don't care, I need this."*

"Dios mío, lo dices en serio, ¿no?" Her words come out too fast for me to understand much. "¿Qué diablos quieres decir con que quieres tus íntimas junto a mi coño? ¿Cómo? ¿Como un tatuaje?"

I shake my head. "Slow down, sweetie, I can't understand."

Lola takes a deep shuddering breath, pinning me with her gray eyes. *"I said,* what the hell do you mean you want your initials next to my pussy? *How?* Like a tattoo?"

My jaw clenches. "No, I'm going to burn it into your flesh."

She gasps hard, blinking up at me. The air shoots through her throat and her eyes get wide as she just stares at me silently.

"I *need* this Lolita." I emphasis. "Just two initials, it won't be that bad." I rub my lips along her jaw, trying to coax her. Seduce her. I can feel her indignation from the inside out, I press my lips to her ear lovingly, trying to convince her. "Please baby, I just need this one thing." I beg.

'It won't be that bad? Hudson-" She gaps up at me.

"I'm getting your name as well. Directly on my chest."

This takes her by surprise and I bite back a grin, feeling her throb around me. Her wetness gushes between us, and I begin to move with renewed purpose. Building her pleasure back up. Leaning down to place my lips against hers, I talk to her in between lush, wet kisses.

"Come on baby girl, I'll make it sexy. One mind blowing orgasm in between each letter."

"Who...." Her voice cracks. "Who's going to do it?"

I pull back. "I am." I rake my gaze down her face and back to her eyes. "You think I'm going to let someone else down there seeing what's mine? *No.* I'll do it here."

Her eye brow raises, and something flashes in her eyes that I've grown to know is that thing inside of *her* that demands it's own satisfaction.

"Oh." She wiggles under me, prompting me to lower my head and take her nipple in a hot suck. Piercing and all. I tug on it with my teeth, hearing my teeth clang against the silver.

I give her a dark chuckle. "I bet *that's* not in that fucking book. *Is it?"*

Lola gives a little squeal and then smacks my shoulder. *"No it is not!"*

I take her wrists and pin her arms to the mattress. "I warned you, from the very beginning. Didn't I?" Sensing how excited she is, I begin to thrust harder, working us up to what we were at in the beginning before our talk.

"Okay, baby. Fine, since it means so much to you, I'll do it," she whispers in my ear, making my dick jerk inside of her.

"Yeah?" Oh God. Pure unadulterated joy fills my soul.

"Yes."

"You've made me one very very happy man, woman," I say into her ear, pulling away to kiss her lips where I spend time just worshipping her, letting her know she's adored.

"Hudson?" Her eyes flicker between mine as I pull away.

"Yes love, what is it?" I caress her cheek, seeing her eyes fill up anxiously. My chest tightens, I don't like it when she's like this.

"My bookshop..." she gasps as a tear falls over her cheek. "I don't want to give it up."

I pause, stilling my movements so I can get a better grasp at what's happening. "I don't understand..." I search her eyes. "What makes you think you have to give it up?"

"Well b-because..." She rolls her lips. "I can't afford to...I can't....what if you don't want me to have it. What if-" I silence her stammering with a kiss against her lips.

"Love would never require for you to give up something you enjoy." I say to her quietly. "I know I'm a hard man, but I'm not an unreasonable one I don't think. I want you to have what makes you happy. Now, can I have what makes *me* happy?" I tilt my head at her, giving her that grin I know she loves.

"Yeah..." she breathes, running her hands up my arms and to my back, where she scratches her nails down to my ass and then digs in hard, forcing me to snap into her on a grunt.

I bring my hand up, wrapping it around her throat. "This makes me happy, too." I dip my head, licking along her mouth before nibbling on her bottom lip.

She nods, her eyes going wide as I begin a punishing rhythm.

I'm pounding into her now, and she's clawing at me, letting me know she's one hundred percent with me.

"Hudson!" she gasps, before throwing her head back on a hoarse cry that has me tumbling headfirst into my own bliss.

"You're mine. You're mine." I spend half the night whispering these words to her, and early into the morning well after she's fallen asleep.

"You're mine, and I'm never letting you go."

20

LOLA'S POEM

HUDSON

AT MY OFFICE THE next day, I turn away from my paperwork to pull up Lola's blog on my phone. With everything I've had going on I haven't had a chance to read the last couple posts. However, I do my best to keep up with her work because I love it.

My brows furrow as I don't see her regular blog, but instead a simple, short poem.

> Your love was like a gentle osmosis
> Filling me up
> Seeping through intimately into the deepest part of me
> to caress me in ways no other person could
> And in doing so, you ravished my soul
> Tore it apart
> Then you proceeded to weave me back together
> Firmly bending me to your will
> Stitch by stich
> Until I was a new creation
> One that could never be ripped apart again
> Unless it's by you
> The master of my body, the holder of my thread
> The weaver of my soul

Lolita Perez

I pause, fingers curling around my phone so hard that I see my hand shaking and my knuckles turn white.

A hot tear slides down my cheek, then another one. But I leaved them unchecked, letting myself cry for a minute,.

Eventually I get a hold of my emotions and scrub my hand down my face, ridding myself of my tears, and clench my jaw, fighting back a groan.

I love this woman with everything inside me. She's so much a part of me right now the sight of her maiden name agitates and rears that possessive spirit deep inside of me that always vies with my sanity to take over my consciousness.

I tap out a text to my parents, Skee, and Frank, asking them if everything is good for travel tomorrow.

I am so through waiting to marry Lola that it's making me almost physically inept. I pull up her name and hit the call button.

"Hi baby," she says brightly.

Her tone calms me immediately and I smile, hearing her cooking in the background. Something's sizzling, I hope it's fried chicken. "Lolita." I grit using her first name, clearing my throat. "I'm about to come home. Can you do me a favor?"

"Sure. As long as it doesn't require me to be tall to reach for anything," she laughs.

I grin, she knows she doesn't have to reach for anything anymore. "I need you to go back into your blog, and change your name to Lolita Montgomery."

I'm met with silence.

"Uhm... but we're not... we haven't-"

"Uh-uh." I grunt into the phone, grabbing my wallet as I stand up to make my way out of my office. "I don't care. Just do it please. It'd make me very happy." I add.

She chuckles into the phone. "You know, I really shouldn't be giving you all these married woman benefits before we've even tied the knot."

"Oh we've tied the knot baby, you just don't realize it."

"We have, have we?" she teases me quietly.

"Hmm-hmm. So I want the benefits the second I get home. Meet me on the porch."

"So I take it that you liked my poem?" Lola says breathlessly.

I love it.

I chuckle, hearing her breath catch. It makes me hot, and my cock jerks in my pants. "Loved it. As soon as I get home, I'm going to show you just how much. You're in a world of trouble my love."

"Trouble?" she gasps. "What kind of trouble?"

"The kind that's going to require you to soak for a good while when I'm done with you." I reply, making my way into my truck I slam the door and start it, pulling out of my spot and into the evening air. "Have me a whisky shot ready when I get home too, will you? I need it."

Boy I really, *really* need it to take the edge off.

"See," she clicks her tongue. "More married woman benefits."

"You're damn right. You're going to do it too, aren't you?"

"I think I might, I guess we'll have to wait and see won't we?" she teases again.

I say bye, hang up with her, and an hour later she's waiting for me on the porch, naked, with her hair flowing down her breasts. My initials attached to her nipples almost glow in the soft glow of the porch lighting, poking out from her hair.

She has no shot waiting for me, but she does sport a devilish look in her eye. Slamming the truck door shut, I give her a hard look up and down as I make my way to her.

"You wanted it hard tonight, huh?" I call out to her, seeing her lips twitch in amusement.

I'm noticing she does things to purposefully provoke me so she can get fucked hard.

Making my way up the stairs I waste no time unbuckling my pants and pulling them down. Staying silent and eyeing her lustfully as she's already slipping to her knees in front of me, licking her plump lips. And as her lips flow over my dick, bathing me in her heat, I look down at her and pull out my phone, checking her blog. There it is in black and white.

Mrs. Lolita Montgomery

"Good *fucking girl.*" I stress, running the knuckles of my free hand down her cheek as she works to take me deeper on a whimper.

I place my phone on the ladder next to us that holds random knickknacks, seeing the shot sitting there half hidden behind a small pot. I chuckle.

"Bad girl." I pat her cheek roughly and then hike up my leg, bracing my boot on the lower rung, I shoot back the shot, relishing the burn spread through my body and proceed to pound into her face just how she likes it.

How we both like it.

How we need it.

21

FIREFLY WEDDINGS
HUDSON/LOLA

Lola

A COUPLE DAYS LATER I'm waiting for Hudson to get home, hanging out alone in the media room at Montgomery ranch, watching some trashy reality tv. I stretch contentedly, feeling extra relaxed after my surprise spa day yesterday, flipping through more shows to watch, when Amanda texts me she's on her way to hang out.

I smile, so thankful to have a friend to talk to because there's a lot going on.

The fact that I could be pregnant is weighing heavy on me, and I've been sitting here trying to think about how on earth I'm going to deal with a third child, and then all this added drama and shit with Dominic.

Will the boys feel jealous of a little sibling they see being treated better, when they are forced to deal with their dad? And by the way, what the hell can I do to get the boys to admit to the abuse they're going through?

I've tried everything.

I'm at the end of my rope here.

I thought about getting a forensic investigator involved, to see if they can drag information out of them, but will they hate me for it?

God this is getting so messy. Again, I miss my mom during times like this. Miss both my parents....but my mommy?

I need her right now.

Hearing a ping, I look at my phone seeing another text from Amanda come through.

> Hey. You got any pretty dresses to wear? I want to look through your closet! -Amanda

I reply, eager for some company.

> It's Hudson's closet, and he's bought me so many clothes I don't know what's there. So feel free to nab whatever you need. -Lola

I'm a little curvier than her in the hips but it's nothing I'm sure a safety pin or two won't be able to fix. An hour later I hear her come in the front door and yell down the hallway at me.

I'm up fast, headed to her with a big smile.

"Wow Amanda, you look beautiful!" I gush, seeing her in a beautiful v-neck, calf length maroon dress. "Why do you need my closet again? You look fine!"

Amanda graces me with a larger than life smile. "Not for *me*, silly. For *you*. We have a wedding to go to."

My brows furrow. "Huh? Hudson didn't tell me..." My words trail off as I stare at her confusedly, before my eyes widen in understanding. *Oh my God.* Hudson really meant it after all! *"Amanda!"* I squeak, putting my hand to my mouth.

"Don't freak out. He told me to give you this." She hands me a note.

> Soon to be Mrs. Montgomery,
>
> I wanted you to be settled, and to not overthink today. However, I would be honored to have you as my wife. I'm going to

give you a choice, to come willingly. If you don't, you'll come unwillingly.

And by now, you know I'm more than capable.

But can you please do this humble man a favor, and just gift me with the vision of you walking to me willingly? Just this one time? It'll be the best wedding present, and I'll love you forever baby.

Love your soon to be husband or *else*,

Hudson Montgomery

P.S I'm waiting.

I bust out in tears and laughter. "The man is such an *asshole!*"

But on the inside that little girl who want's her parents, and someone to love, is celebrating. Pleasure fills me from head to toe that Hudson really loves me, and will not stop until I'm his completely.

Amanda snickers and rubs my arm. "I don't know two people who are more perfect for each other." I throw her a sharp side eye, I shake my head at her, and she laughs harder. *"I didn't mean it like that, silly!"*

I bring my fingers to my bangs, self-consciously finger-combing them, and anxiously gripping the note in my hands. *Oh my God.*

"Gosh, your hair looks *gorgeous,* Lola!" Amanda gives me a huge hug, complimenting me.

"Thanks." I smile. "Hudson got me another spa day yesterday, so this time I got my hair done."

"I love the honey highlights."

I giggle, and we head up the stairs, thinking about that sex session with Hudson after I came home and he saw it. I didn't know he knew that position, and didn't know I could get my body in it either. I smile broader, loving how adventurous we are together.

He once asked me how adventurous I was, and I certainly wasn't thinking at the time that he meant if I was adventurous in the bedroom.

"I have no clue what to wear!" I admonish, leading the way into the closet I turn off the light and stop, making Amanda run into the back of me, jolting me further in the room.

"Oh shit, sorry girl." Amanda steadies me with a hand to my shoulder, but I don't respond.

I'm riveted by the row of garment bags taking up space in the side of the closet. My eyes widen and I walk up to them and begin unzipping the first bag I can get my hands on. Amanda helps me, and soon we have all fifteen bags open, exposing miles of white fabric to our gazes.

I let out a little huff, placing my hands on my hips. "Now what if I didn't wanna wear white?"

But inside that little girl who wants her mom is melting.

"He said you were going to say that, and he also said to tell you this is something you *don't* have a choice in the matter over," Amanda says.

We look at each other and laugh.

I grumble halfheartedly, and Amanda spends the next hour helping me get ready. I chose a simple boatneck dress, and a veil. Not because I want the veil, but because I know it'll please him to lift it and expose my face to him. So we kept my makeup simple.

I'm standing in the mirror, turning this way and that way, admiring myself when Amanda's phone rings. "Hello? Yes, she's right here." Amanda brings me the phone and shoots me a little grin.

"So what's it going to be baby girl? Do I need to come get you?" Hudson says. He sounds so delicious that a thrill races through my veins, centering my very being.

"No Hudson," I say breathlessly, turning away from Amanda. "I'll come."

"You better. Bye, baby."

"Bye, mi amor."

Amanda whisks me out of the house and we're treated to the sight of a limo parked in the front drive. I look at Amanda in shock and we let out a little squeal, doing an excited dance. When the excitement is danced out, she holds my dress up as we make our way to the limo to keep it from trailing on the ground and then we're off.

I realize for the first time that, though I'm hidden behind a veil, my mask is off.

And it feels amazing.

We're married two hours later, in front of a beautiful pond filled with lily pads and floating lanterns.

His parents were standing off to the side, looking so happy. Frank was there to walk me, and at the beginning of the isle I broke down and cried at the sight of my boys, Skee chartered a private jet to attend, and he and the boys were standing there in their tuxedos looking so handsome.

And guess what? Along with my loved ones, there were a million lightning bugs everywhere.

Because he timed it that we got married right at dusk, staring into each other's eyes, vowing to love each other till death do us part. Giving me my perfect wedding.

Without me having to ask.

Hudson

"Bye buddies. We'll see you in just a couple days, okay?" I ruffle Tuck and Tatum's hair and aren't prepared for when they throw themselves at me in a huge hug. My eyes fill with tears and I lock eyes with Skee.

"Thanks for taking time our of your visit with them to bring them back man," I choke out. Clearing my throat, I take his hand and he yanks me in a brotherly hug, patting my back hard.

"It wasn't nothing but a thing brother, I'm happy to see my sister happy for once. And your parents are amazing!" His eyes do a little once over of my person. "Do you know your dad is into parasailing? We made plans to go when we get back to California. They want to spend time with their new step grandkids, so they're going to stay over my place for a couple days. I'll show them a good time."

I raise my eyebrows in surprise at the news, looking over at the boys now attacking my mother, and my father wrapping Lola up in a bear hug.

"You can just say grandkids, Anthony. *Oh,* these little boys are so sweet." My mothers voice rings out.

She refuses to call Anthony by his nickname. When he heard my parents lived in California, he had a driver bring them to him so they could fly with to Washington with him on his private jet. I overheard him telling Lola how the best thing was, he didn't feel like he had to. He was allowed to offer, and he thanked her for marrying someone who didn't force him to do things for him.

Made me feel good about myself.

Though he did mention it was wild we'd only known each other just a few weeks, but coming from Hollywood, he's seen much weirder things.

It was Frank's approval that sealed the deal. I overheard him telling my father, "I would have *never* gave Lola away to anyone other than a *man.* You did good, Charles."

And seeing my fathers chest puff out with pride well, that's all a man can ask for isn't it?

The boys now claw all over Lola, trying to force her down to kiss them. She bends and gives them each a smacking kiss on their cheeks, making them laugh. The few days in California seem to have done them well, and I realize they've missed their Wednesday visit with their dad, and are probably able to breathe comfortably for the first time in a while.

It solidifies my decision to do what it takes the keep them safe.

I've already met with a lawyer, drawing up a prenup leaving Lola everything in the event something happens to me or my plans go wrong, which they wont.

I've also altered my last will and testament to leave most everything to them, making sure they're taken care of.

I pull Lola to my front with a firm arm around her waist, and we wave at our loved ones as they all drive away. I lean down and press my lips to her bare collar bone, licking along the vulnerable flesh there. She's so sweet, and the look on her face has got me painfully hard.

I need to get her home.

"Mrs. Montgomery, are you ready to go? Let your husband ravish you?" Taking a second to admire her, I watch the blush travel from her cheeks to her chest as she nibbles on her lip.

Fuck it feel so good to finally call her my wife.

Lola gets a timid, shy smile on her face. "All you've been doing since you met me *is* ravish me, don't you think?"

I laugh, bending to kiss her sassy mouth quiet. "Someone's got a smart mouth." I pull away from her reluctantly but keep her hips pressed to mine and rock her, standing close to my truck.

I rake my eyes from her veil down, soaking the sight of her in. Taking in the vision of the only woman who has ever made me feel complete.

My *wife.*

My other half.

"You are a vision, my love," I say to her quietly, holding her eyes with mine I place my fingers to her cheek and slide to the back of her neck and pull her in to me. "God you are so fucking beautiful. I've never seen anything or anyone as lovely as you, and I am so lucky to have you, baby. I feel so honored you accept me as your husband."

Lola's eyes dilate as she stares up at me wide eyed. For a second she looks like a deer caught in headlights.

I get she's scared.

We've known each other a hot second in the grand scheme of things but when you just know, there's nothing that will make the inevitable change. I press my lips against hers and treat her to a little chuckle.

"I cannot wait to take you home and undress you sweet thing. But we got a couple things to to see to first."

She tilts her head "Oh yeah? Like what?"

My hand fists in her hair and tilts her head back. "I'm going to make you mine. *All* mine."

I don't know how it's possible to harden anymore than I already am, but my thighs are tight with strain, and all I can think about is spreading her pretty legs. But I meant what I said.

We've got some other work to tend to.

Helping her maneuver carefully, I get her into the truck, placing her train and her long veil just so before buckling her in and closing the door. Soon, we're back at our house in no time, and like a true gentleman, I pick her up bridal style as I stand with her in my arms at the thresh hold of our front door. A wave of contentment rushes through my body, settling deep in my bones as if it's always been there.

I'm not alone anymore.

She's not alone anymore.

I take the time to press my lips to hers for a deep, lingering kiss. "Welcome to our new life, Mrs. Montgomery. My beautiful bride."

She blushes and presses her cheek to my shoulder, trying to hide. I'm so used to feisty Lola, that the appearance of a more softer, feminine woman in front of me causes me more joy than it should. My words from when we were first talking hit me hard, when I told her she was too deeply enmeshed in her masculine energy.

The irony how, not only did I flip that switch inside of her, she's now my wife a mere few weeks after that first talk. Pride fills me from the tip of my head to my toes, and as I walk us through the house she giggles against my neck.

"Why are you smiling like that?"

I look down at her, furrowing my brow. "Like what?" I drawl, making my way to the door that takes us down to the cellar.

"Like the cat that ate the canary."

"Hmmm..." I hum, hitting the landing and turning towards the glass and iron doors. I push us through silently, thankful I have motion censored lighting in here. "Do you remember what I said to you when we were in here last?"

Lola blinks up at me with a slightly confused look on her face. "You said a lot of things."

"I told you there's a bottle of wine I bought for me and my future wife to share on our wedding night. Now, do me the honor of letting me watch my wife go pick it up and bring it to me."

Lola's lips part and she takes a shuddering breath, mirroring my excitement. "Oh you suave fucker." she whispers, making me laugh as I place her gently on her feet and then smack her ass sharply.

I shrug out of my suit jacket, undo my tie, the first two buttons of my shirt and folding my arms I lean against the door frame. "Come on. Eighteenth row, second from the top. Bring it here."

Lola hurries, and the sight of her fleshy pert ass in her white satin wedding dress has got me seriously suffering to the point I don't know that we're going to make it up the stairs. We need to though. I want to seduce my wife on our wedding night, give her a night that both of us will remember forever.

She's so short that she has to reach on her tip toes, and I enjoy the struggle, I'm not going to lie. I love seeing her strain just a little before I blow her mind.

Goddamn.

"Here," I say, picking her up with a shoulder under her ass I raise her several feet, enabling her to grab the bottle easily. I turn, carrying her just like that back up the stairs and to the living room, where there's a great roaring fire in front of a bearskin rug, and a small table with two wine glasses. I see her fiddling with the rolled paper I've attached to the bottle with a red string. "Read it," I say simply, turning to face her in the light of the fire.

I'm strung so tight that I'm suddenly scared of her reaction; that I'm going to hurt her when I fuck her after this, that she's going to deny me what I want.

I'm scared I'm going to run her away. Because though I've tried my hardest over the last few weeks to show her she's my number one priority, she's not used to being put first.

Lola's eye's meet mine and I melt, seeing she has tears in hers. "Hudson I-I didn't get you anything baby. I'm sorry...I didn't really think that..."

"That I was actually going to make you marry me?" I chuckle, running my knuckles down her cheek. She gives me a shy smile and nods her head. I tilt my own, wondering how to treat this new, docile Lola. *"You're* my present, baby. Just you. You and those boys."

Lola inhales, nodding her head a few times as a tear slips out of her eyes. I reach forward and wipe it away before she can.

"Okay," she takes a deep breath. "You've written me something cute?" she giggles, as if it's a fascinating thought. And as I'm mentally kicking myself for not thinking of writing her something romantic to go along with it, she gets it open and takes a deep, shocked breath. "Hudson!" she breathes, putting a shocked hand to her mouth.

I smile nice and wicked because *oh my God,* I'm going to orgasm with the memory of the way she just said my name.

"This is the deed to a vineyard, and a ...*a winery?"* Her eyes widen. "You own a winery? And you're giving it to me?"

"A small one," I try to reassure her. "I never mentioned it before because-"

I grunt as Lola throws herself at me, sobbing as she clutches me to her. Her hands grip my hair and pull me down to meet her lips, and then she's pushing me towards the couch, making me fall back.

"Wait we're not done!" I admonish her, but she's hiking her dress up and pulling down her panties, ignoring my protests.

I can't think straight as all the blood in my body finishes it's journey to my cock and I growl, grabbing my erection hard and fighting the lightheaded feeling of the viciousness of my arousal. Surprising me, she sinks to her knees and tears open my pants, and I groan as my heavy length is freed, but she gives me literally zero time to acclimate before I'm suddenly down her throat.

"Lolita!" I growl. Roughly gripping her head over her veil, I fist it all in my hands, the delicate white lace, her hair, and hold her still. "Slow the fuck down. *Now!* I can't let you kill me just yet before we sign the paperwork."

My body breaks out into a sweat as she doesn't listen.

Her mouth flows over my cock. The heat is almost unbearable, how tight she has me in her mouth is almost painful it's so pleasurable. She's sucking so hard on her upswing it's causing my hips to lift off the cushion to follow the suction of her mouth.

She reaches forward and scrapes her nails down my abs and I look down gasping, feeling myself swell slightly. She's whimpering and wiggling, and I tighten my hands on her head and begin to jerk her roughly up and down on top of me.

"You fucking naughty little bitch." I chastise her.

She sucks off me so hard I'm seeing stars before she pins me eyes that flash. "That's Mrs. Montgomery to you, sir."

Launching myself off the couch I tackle her to the rug underneath her, and work to yank up her dress before lowering my face to her pussy. "Fuck you're dripping. Greedy ass pussy."

I take my hand and slap her right over her clit, relishing her surprised yelp. I treat her to several more slaps, getting her nice and swollen before I bend down and suck her clit into my mouth.

She arches on a low moan and I bend back her knees, spreading her even wider for me. I clamp my teeth lightly on her clit and tug.

"Yess!" she screams, bucking against me.

"I'm going to spend the rest of my life keeping this greedy ass cunt satisfied." I reach over and grab the wine bottle and, shocking her, I press the tip inside her and begin thrusting hard. I can't trust myself to enter her right now, I'll come too soon.

"H-Hudson!" she gasps, looking down at me with wide eyes. I meet her gaze with a hard one of my own as I press the wine bottle hard, meeting resistance at the thickest part where the bottle flares out from the neck.

"Deep breath." I instruct her, "It's only going to go in about a few inches. Obey me Lolita, take a deep breath."

Lola lets out a little whine, and then I hear her head thump against the floor as she works to wiggle. "Hudson, it's not going to *f-fit.*"

Twisting the wine bottle inside her, I lower my lips to her clit once more and nip at it, sucking and licking at it until I feel her jerk under me. When I hear her squeal with her orgasm I press just a little harder, and see her flesh part around the bottle and I pause, not wanting to hurt her.

"Oh fuck, oh fuck, *oh Jesus, Hudson!*" She whines and I don't even think she realizes that she's gushing all over the bottle, and the floor.

I push and pull slowly, careful not to hurt her.

"God, I wish you could see this," I say harshly Your pussy is so pretty stretched around your wedding gift." I give her a few more shallow thrusts and then pull it out of her slowly. Holding her eye I suck the bottle clean of her juices and procced to open it. I maneuver myself against the couch, and then pull her to settle with her draped across my lap and her head on my shoulder.

I pour us one glass to share and give her the first sip.

Her eyelashes flutter and she moans appreciatively. "Hudson that's the best wine I've ever tasted."

She's not lying.

I take a sip and groan, resting my head against the cushions behind me. "Hmhm. We've got one more step beautiful."

Lolita's head rolls against my shoulder and I turn, finding her eyes. "I already know what you want," she whispers, taking my hand and trailing it up under her dress where she makes me cup her.

"Are you ready? I was going to make you but honestly, I need you to tell me this is okay, sweetheart." I implore her with my eyes and showing her I'm serious. Lola works to unzip the side of her dress and seeing her dress sag open, I help her work it down her body and off, settling her back down on my legs. When she goes to take the veil off I stop her with a hand on her wrist. "No," I say.

I pull her veil back over her and settle her further back over my arm.

She's got a sexy sheer lace lingerie bra set on, and her veil is long enough that it falls past her knees. Her red brown nipples are visible through both the veil and her bra, and I torture myself with the sight of them erect, poking through the material.

"Go ahead, you're licking your lips, I know you want to," she whispers.

My eyes fly to hers because I didn't realize I was damn near drooling over her. She reaches up and wiggles out of her bra, letting it fall to the side. She's glowing under her veil, her sexy round breasts, with it's fleshy, thicker nipples pressed against the veil. My cock jerks hard at the sight of the slight curve of her stomach, tapering off into the v of her bare mound.

"Oh God baby," I swallow thickly and bring my hand up, cupping her pussy over her veil. "You have no idea how much I want you. How happy you make me."

Lola shudders as I bend down and nip at one of her nipples through the material.

She lets out a hoarse, ragged moan.

I suck harder, I know the scratchy material is rubbing, mixing with the wetness of my mouth against her sensitive flesh. My hand rises, and I cup her other breast harder before plucking at her nipple with my fingers and rolling it.

I spend long minutes suffering with my dick trapped between us as she lets me indulge herself on her sensitive nipples. Another gift for me to cherish. "Can I do it now? Can I mark you?"

"Yes," Lola whimpers and nods as I tighten my teeth around her, still not ready to part with her flesh.

I don't know what I did in a previous life to be granted everything I desire, but somehow I wound up with it, and I'm going to enjoy the hell out of this pure, heavenly *bliss*.

22

Our Past Sins

FRANK

Unlocking the door to Lola's old house, I step back and hand the key to Charles, who's standing in the light of the porch with Annabelle.

A *beautiful* specimen of a woman.

She stands there with her brown eyes, light, wavy brown hair cascading to almost the tips of her breasts, still encased in her mother of the groom dress. I blink, locking eyes with her for a second, and her plump lips tip into a smile as the barest hint of a flush graces her cheek.

"Frank," Annabelle says in her soft voice. "Are you sure you don't want to come in and join us for a cup of coffee?"

Something that was left dormant, yet still familiar, stirs inside me. Causing me to lock my body down. I clear my throat, crossing my arms tightly and glancing away out into the cul de sac.

"No," I say. But everything in me wants to say yes. It's just hard for me to open up and let myself get close with anyone. "I'm going to head in, get a hog-"

"Head cheese sandwich," she says with a little grin. She laughs and reaches out a hand to gently touch my forearm, gliding her palm down my skin. My eyes snap to her hand on me, then back up to Charles who's regarding us with an amused expression on his face. "We know. Hudson's already filled us in all about you."

A surprising warmth fills me at the fact that Hudson's been including me in his conversations with his parents. It's been so long since I've felt seen by anyone.

I'm always doing the watching. That's why I've formed a rather interesting bond with Tatum. He's just like I was when I was a boy.

I put my eyes back on hers. They're soft brown. Like a deep caramel color. I roam her face, feeling a ping of jealousy towards Charles because Annabelle has the kind of body I adore. Soft, plump, with a little age on her which means she'll taste better.

I fight, preventing myself from licking my lips at imagining her taste.

I never understood people who do age gaps. No offense to Lola and Hudson. I like my woman my age, with some experience on her, I couldn't do what they've got going on. Lola would've been chained up in the basement if it were me.

Ironic, considering our history. A history she isn't even aware we have.

"Okay Frank, well, thank you for letting us in," Charles says. "You have a good night. Maybe I can come over in the morning for coffee, let Annabelle sleep in."

I nod my head. "Yeah that'd be fine. I'm up about four-thirty, or five."

"Sounds good, see you soon." Charles reaches out his hand to me and I take it, stiffening as something races up my arm.

"Goodnight," I say gruffly, pulling my hand away hastily and turn, making my way down the stairs and across the yard towards my house.

It's been decades since I've felt that feeling. And it coming from a man just fucked up my head. So, it's time to go home.

Letting myself in my home I shrug out of my suit jacket, walking towards the bedroom and hang it up. I change into a regular shirt and pair of slacks, sliding my feet into a pair of moccasins. While I'm walking to the kitchen, my phone rings, and I answer it.

"Malachi." I greet, opening up my fridge and digging through the meet and cheese drawer for my ziplock bags that house my sandwich fixings.

"General Jackson." Malachi greets back, sounding quite official which gets my hackles up. "How are you old friend?"

"Old," I say simply.

"Not too old to give your government a small favor?"

I frown, slapping down two pieces of bread on a paper towel and scoop out mayo, smearing it on the bread. "Malachi, I can't leave. I'm sorry."

"We'll pay you a premium to bring you out of retirement. We just need three weeks of your time. Eight million dollars."

I shake my head. There's no fucking way in hell I'd ever leave Lola and Hudson like this. "No."

"Eleven million."

"Fuck," I snap. "What kind of dog shit did you all manage to step in this time?" I grumble, putting my hog head cheese, tomato, lettuce, and a piece of onion before walking over to the table and then setting it down in front of Gloria's picture.

I stay standing out of respect. I don't have conversations at the table with her present.

"Well. It's a bit complicated, and the President doesn't trust these guys in charge right now. They don't have the tenure or the experience."

"Well Malachi, tell Mr. President the answer is *no.*"

"Do you have a medical reason I can provide-""

"No medical reason, but you tell *Mr. President* I can provide an ass whooping if that would make him feel better. I don't get summoned like a dog. Have him call me if he wants to hear it out of my mouth. The answer is *no.*"

And with that I hang up with a sigh, I know its rude, and it's not Malachi's fault, but if you don't put boundaries up that's how you get ran over.

I wish that's a fact that Lola could have wrapped her head around. She's just like her grandmother, feisty, but too nice for her own good. Too much of a people pleaser. Which is why she's in all this trouble with Dominic. If she would have just chopped his dick off years ago, we wouldn't be in this predicament. But she's too sweet.

Way more decent than that prick deserves.

Sitting down, I sigh deeply and take a bite of my food. "Well Gloria, I'm sorry, but I did it again. Proving you and the kids time and time again that I didn't deserve you guys."

I sit back, and tell my late wife the same thing I do night after night; that I don't mind being ostracized, because I understand the human innate need to protect oneself from disappointment and trauma.

But I do mind. But I can't mind. If that makes sense. I chose my path and walked it the best I could, so now it's up to me to live with the consequences of the decisions I made along the way.

I stare at my wife's blue eyes, thinking about how much she put up with. And as I think about the past, how a lot of it she felt like a single woman for most of our marriage due to my skillset, I also think about Maribel.

Lola's grandmother.

My first love.

Me breaking up with her all those years ago to protect her from the life I was in at the time almost killed me. And while I couldn't get out of it in enough time for her to still be waiting for me when I got back to the states all those decades ago, I still found a way to be close. When

I found out she had to move in with her daughter, Lola's mother, due to her brain cancer diagnosis, I moved us next door.

Paying a premium for this house just to be close to her. To watch over her.

As much as I wanted to, I wouldn't abandon Gloria to be with Maribel. And it killed me, being so close to the love of my life and couldn't actually be there for her. That was my penance I had to pay. The suffering I had to endure in order to make things right with my soul.

Even though Gloria never knew about Maribel, it seemed that every move I made tore my family further and further apart to the point our family unit was unrecognizable.

"Goodnight Gloria dear, I'll see you first thing in the morning." I say, brushing my fingers across my late wife's eyes.

I finish my sandwich, tossing my trash, heading to the bedroom where I decided to lay down a bit early tonight. I pull back the covers and sit on the side of the bed, reaching for the picture frame and pull it to me, giving the glass a kiss.

"Hi Maribel love," I whisper, running my fingertips over her mouth.

Her eyes sparkle as she looks up at me from the photo, and I remember how mischievous her smile was when she'd tease me all the time. Lola's smile. And the look of heartbreak in her eyes when I broke things off with her to protect her. And now, it's all I can do to protect her grandchild.

Lolita.

Who I feel like is mine.

Protecting her is the only way I know how to ask for forgiveness.

I place Maribel back on her spot right next to where I sleep and stretch myself out on the bed, settling against the pillow. I turn my head, gazing into her eyes.

"Maribel, Lo' is giving me a run for my money sweetheart. But that's okay because she found someone who loves her about as much as I loved you. And this time, I'm making sure she gets what we didn't get."

A happy ending.

Goddamn it, Lola will have that happy ending if it kills me.

23

HM

LOLA

I THROW MY HEAD back, eating up the slow, rough laps he's giving me up the seam of my pussy. Usually he's not too rough with me down there because I'm so sensitive, but tonight feels different.

I really appreciate this about him. Because though he does forces me to endure the feel of his mouth on my breasts, which causes me to orgasm just by that alone, *and* he also forces me into really long oral sessions, at least he's not evil about it.

"Uhhnnn," I moan, shivering.

God, he was blessed with a wicked mouth, and knows just how to use it. Licking with the perfect pressure, or tapping my clit with his tongue just right. But my favorite is when he sucks my clit, and then firmly licks the tip of it nice and hard.

It makes me hot, feral for him.

He lifts his head up, and his green eyes pierce into my soul making me feel even more vulnerable. "I'm about to brand us, and It's going to hurt, but you know I'm going to make you feel good."

My heart begins to beat out of my chest. My breathing becomes labored as he holds my eyes, licking up my sex again and again keeping me right on the edge.

"Hudson," I gasp, feeling my forehead bead with sweat.

I work to get my veil off, shoving it to the side desperate for relief, but with Hudson's mouth on me there's no relief in sight.

"Yes baby?"

"Can I go first?" I pant. "I want to get it over with."

Hudson smile's wickedly around his hold on my flesh and chuckles, causing me to stiffen. "Hmm-hmm." he mumbles, sucking me until I seize up, then he pulls away right before I succumb to my orgasm.

I lay here, hot, feeling like a weight is pressed onto my body holding me immobile. I'm so weak, having I don't know how many orgasms since he walked me into our home. But he still hasn't fucked me yet.

The way I'm feeling right now I might not make it.

"Be right back baby girl," he says. Standing up fluidly, he licks his lips clean of my juices and tucks himself into his dress pants. The sight of him shoving his considerable erection into his pants is almost enough to throw me over the edge. "You keep staring at me like that, pretty girl, you're going to be in for one hell of a honeymoon night."

All I can focus on is the muscles in his arms and chest flexing and the sound of his zipper as he works it over himself carefully. He leaves it unbuttoned, the fireplace throwing the dips and lines of his body into sharp relief. He looks dangerous, deadly, and I'm getting ready to let this man burn his initials into my flesh.

"I already am." I retort, giving him a little smile of my own.

To really drive the point home I pull back my lips more, showing him my canines and slick my tongue over one of them. His erection jerks under his pants and his eyes dilate even more. Hudson nods at me and then disappears through the living room door.

I lay there for a second looking into the fireplace. Contemplating where I was just a few weeks ago. Lonely, desolate, without hope.

With nobody.

And now I have someone I cherish, and who I firmly believe cherishes me just as much.

Yes, he's got that bad boy, *different* thing inside of him that likes to come out and play. But it causes me no fear, I trust this man with mine and my boys life. Anyone who is able to win over my boys, can't be a bad person.

He's shortly back in the room with a little bag, and he places it carefully on the side table, beginning to pull out items. I see gauze, tape, alcohol pads, and several metal circular devices with wooden handles.

I swallow hard as he begins talking.

"I'm going to brand you with my initials. One 'H' and one 'M', on the upper right half right above your mound. I was going to do your inner leg, but I don't want your thighs rubbing and it hurting your more than what it needs to." His muscles bunch as he works, and I'm momentarily distracted.

"I'm sorry, *did you just call me fat?*" I can't help it.

He throws me a look and pauses in his actions.

"Oh baby, if you get any plumper I won't let you out of the house. There'll be so much to feast on. So, if you want to put some more weight on and suffer those consequences well... *be my guest*. I'd love to have more to latch my teeth on while I'm fucking you."

And the way he says it, while his eyes pin themselves to my inner thighs and my breasts has got me blushing. He hauls all the supplies over to me and plugs in a device, dropping one of the metal pieces with the handle inside of it and I see it glow, getting hot.

"This is what it looks like." Hudson says quietly, taking the other pieces and shows me.

I see a fancy cursive 'M' that sticks out from the flat metal of the medallion, about two inches in size.

Putting it to the side, he rips open an alcohol pad and wipes the spot on my body carefully. Bending, he blows on the wet area until it dries. Surprising me, he pushes my knees back and sucks my clit into his mouth making me flinch as I'm not prepared.

His hot mouth and tongue sears me, and the burn that subsided slightly with the anticipation of my branding intensifies.

I gasp, whining through this orgasm because I was strung so tight with no release just a bit ago, and my breath soughs out of my lungs. Suddenly Hudson pulls away and shoves my legs together, straddling them, and then clenching them tight between his thick thighs.

My eyes widen, feeling his hands wrap around my wrists and putting them over my tummy holding my wrists together, pinned in his broad hand. I begin to pant, seeing him reach over and pick up the 'H' and holding it up for us both to see. I can tell it's glowing hot, and he blows on it slightly.

But I begin to struggle, suddenly becoming nervous.

The endorphins of my orgasm have me floating, and though I've never done drugs, this is what I'd imagine being high feels like. But I'm crashing with fear.

I whimper, seeing him come closer and my fear overcome me.

"N-No. Wait Hudson, wait!" I'm gasping, trying to arch my hips under him but he tightens his legs and hands tighter, keeping me trapped.

He presses it to me.

I seize up, a desperate scream caught in my throat as I grip my teeth hard to cope with the sharp, burning feeling that envelopes me. Tears escape my eyes, and right when I unlock my jaw to scream at him to take the pain away, he pulls it off me and my hips collapse back to the rug.

I pant hard, feeling my tears drip into my ears. Hudson leans forward, catching my eyes.

"Good girl." He praises me.

I close my eyes, thinking he's about to kiss me, when I feel his wet hot mouth wrap around my right nipple and suck and tug hard. My eyes fly open in shock, and I squirt, wetting the rug beneath me as I orgasm at the contact. My body is strung so tight from the emotions of the entire day, and as my ears pick up on him sucking and manipulating my sensitive flesh, I'm struck with the knowledge that I'm helpless.

Right where he wants me.

Where we both want me to be.

I'm his to do as he pleases.

He lets my nipple go with a pop, leans down for a harsh smacking kiss then sits back, picking up the other handle, holding it to me. I throw my head back once more, arching my neck on a desperate wail. The 'M' feels worse than the 'H' did, kind of like when you get your ears pierced, that second one hurts worse.

But soon, the pain is gone, my hips are back on the rug and I feel boneless, utterly spent.

Despite the heat of the fire I feel chills break out over my body and I look down, seeing myself covered in goosebumps.

"Jesus, look at that." Hudson sounds choked up as he looks down at me, and my eyes leave his face to look down at my lower tummy, right above my pussy.

"H M" is dark, raised, cursive,.

Beautiful.

I blink, feeling tears escape my own eyes.

"I love you." I whisper, my eyes rise, finding his. He looks at me in shock, and I feel ashamed. Because this man has laid himself bare to me with every interaction and he's worthy to feel just as desired, just as *cherished* as he's made me. I tug at his hold around my wrists and he releases me. I place my hand on his cheek. "I'm sorry I've been too scared, too shut down to tell you the way you deserve to be told. But I love you so much Hudson, my husband, my querido. Podría vivir mil vidas contigo y aún así no sería suficiente. Quieres que tenga el deseo de mi corazón, pero mi único deseo eres tú, mi amor. Eres todo lo que siempre quiero y necesito, esposo."

Cognizant he's not understanding, I switch to English. He needs to know how I feel.

I need to tell him.

"I could live a thousand lifetimes with you and it would never be enough. You want me to have my heart's desire, but my only desire is you, my love. You're all I ever want and need, husband."

Hudson lets out a choked gasp and then snatches one of my hands back up and presses the back of my hand to his lips, kissing me there. "Thank you baby. My heart is so full," he gasps, and I feel a tear wet the skin of my palm as his tears rain down on me.

Some people may be turned off by their man crying in front of them, but not me.

The fact that he can so easily show me this vulnerable side of himself, lets me know that he trusts me with his emotions, with his heart. And if I have his heart, I know he's got mine, and will take care of it.

He looks down at me, and the sight of his green eyes tinged with red makes my heart flutter.

"I love your emotion my love, please never ever hold back from me? Promise me?" My hand tightens desperately on him, and I'm suddenly struggling under him, wanting to spread my legs for him. "Let me up Hudson, *please.*" My free hand works to unzip his pants and he falls heavily in my palm, stunning me with it's weight. He shifts, letting my legs free. I hook my legs high on his ribcage and tighten my heels against his back, jerking him to me. *"Fuck me. I need you to fuck me Hudson. Put yourself inside of me, make me yours!"*

He wastes no time ramming himself inside of me, and we let out a groan together at the feel of him spreading me apart. The spot where he marks me burns, reinforcing my thoughts I might like a little pain. Because even I must admit this new sensation is adding to the sharp feeling of his possession of me. Causing me to throb around him.

My eyebrow arches as a new thought hits me. I don't care for pain, but my baby does.

"Let me mark you," I whisper up at him. "I know you like pain, I want to feel you fuck me while I mark you. You can be as rough as you need with me."

Hudson meets my eye and pauses. He sniffs then nods, leaning over to reach back into the bag. He pulls out the collar and chains that he used on me the first time he brought me to his house, and just the sight has a rush of liquid pulsing out of me, licking over my skin.

That night will never leave me.

Just like he put HM into my skin, that night he imparted something inside of me that was invisible, something only the two of us feels. That's the night he gave me back to myself, let me know I wasn't irreparably broken. I raise my head, letting him place the collar around my neck and pull my knees high to attach the chains to the cuffs, tying my knees up and back.

I'm so vulnerable in this position, but I don't care.

He tilts his head and begins to work himself in and out of me. I feel that thread connecting us pull taut, and it causes me to relax, feeling like I'm floating on a cloud. It hits me, I'm married to a wonderful man, we have great sex, we see each other in our vulnerability, we accept each other.

I smile at him and I know it's goofy, because I can't keep up appearances with him. Never could.

Not breaking pace, he reaches over and grabs the new handle and presses it into my hand, looking at it I see an "L" in the same cursive font that's on me. I turn it, facing it the right way and I look at him.

"Ready?" I whisper.

Seeing his nod I press it into his chest and my eyes widen at the sound that comes out of him. His hips begin to fall a bit more heavily into mine, and my pussy twitches at the sudden harsher sensation. His body mists with sweat, and after a few long seconds he's pulling my hand away. The 'L' left behind is beautiful.

He presses the next handle into my hand, and this time I'm the one whimpering at the sharp snarl and the way his hips begin to slap into mine as I press the 'O' into his skin.

Like before, he yanks my hand away and tosses it to the side. But before he grabs the other one, he surprises me by leaning down and fisting his hands on either side of my head, now bouncing off my pussy.

I toss my head back screaming as this orgasm rips through me with no warning.

He takes my hand and makes me press the next to letters in and he's pounding into me so hard I'm temporarily worried, because he's never fucked me so hard before.

"Shut the fuck up," he growls at me, making me press the last of the initials into his skin.

His thrusting deepens making me gasp, heave, and buck under him. At the last initial he cups his hands around my breasts and then traps both of my nipples tight into his fingers, rolling them at the same time he presses as deep as he can into the back of my pussy and then stays there.

He stays there.

"Ohhh," I whine, feeling my chin quiver.

We're both breathing hard, and I squirt on him at the feel of his fingers plucking and pulling at my pierced nipples. But it's the way he's making me take all of his dick the way is he is now, when this is something that so far has been an unspoken rule between us that he doesn't do what he's doing, has got my blood screaming.

My nails dig into his forearms and I let out a gasping sob.

"Hudson!" I choke out, my eyes going wide at how rough this feels. I shake my head at him, unable to speak.

Hudson nods his head and then his eyes narrow, his nostrils flare, and his chest puffs up. He moves, inching up my body, settling his knees higher on the floor on either side of my thighs and pining my hips down even more. My eyes widen at him resting what feels to be all his body weight straight onto my pussy.

He reaches between us and spreads the lips of my sex, flexing his hips even more, grinding into me. I'm completely trapped under him but I realize with him grinding, he's stimulating my clit. I shudder, whimpering.

"M-my pussy-*Hudson, my pussy!"* I yelp, tossing my head back and arching my breasts up to him.

His hands move to cup my breasts, and as he settles even more, what I thought was all of his body weight *before* was nothing. He sits down completely on my pussy and I scream incoherently as he flexes his ass rhythmically, screwing our flesh together tightly.

Pushing my breasts together, he leans down and sucks both my nipples into his mouth at the same time and I freeze, going completely still under him.

It's one thing to have one sensitive nipple stimulated, but both at the same time while he's seated inside me like this? Not even thrusting, just flexing leisurely the way he is. My body is short circuiting at the feel of him pressing into the back of me, and now making me stretch even more to accommodate him.

"It's too much," I whimper. "It's too much Hudson."

But God, that feeling of being taken against my will swirls around us, bonding us even closer together. I let out a harsh gasp, throwing my head back and silently screaming as he tightens every muscle and flexes down even deeper into me. A burning, suffocating feeling works its way up from the back of my sex, up my spine, and exploding through my nipples, the tip of my sex and making my toes and fingertips tingle.

"You're cunt is so hot, Lolita." Hudson pulls away from my flesh to smile at me. "What's the matter baby? My dick too big for you?"

I whimper and nod, throbbing around him. Hissing at his grunt as he leans back down and takes both of my nipples in his teeth and tugs on my piercings, chuckling and I shudder and purr deep in my throat for him. My esposo.

"Hmmmm. That's too bad, isn't it? Because this is my body, and if I want this body to take all my dick, then that's what it's going to do. This is *your* wedding gift to *me*."

He pulls back to the tip, nibbles and nips my nipples before slamming forward so hard it makes me see stars. His thighs over mine keeps me still, and for the next hour all I hear is the dull thudding sound of his outer sex meeting mine mercilessly.

"Yellow." I whisper hoarsely.

"No."

"Peaches."

"No."

"Spaghetti?"

"Uh-uh."

We don't have a safe word, and I'm throwing every word out there to get him to let up.

"Hudson," I gasp through my heart which has firmly lodged into my throat. "I'm too young to have a heart attack." My eyes implore him. "Baby please it's our wedding night, don't fuck me to death. It's not n-nice behavior."

Overcome, I begin to cough through that heavy feeling choking my throat, my bodies fucking response system reacting to being fried. At least I'm not sneezing this time.

Hudson pauses and chuckles into my neck.

"You're so precious. Give me a minute. Do you need to come again before I finish?" His eyes search mine as he finally moves off my thighs and lets the pressure up. I shake my head no tiredly, and revel in the feel of him fucking into my body to find his own release.

It doesn't take long, we're both so worn out.

I get to relax though, as he works to cover our brands with gauze, and then carries me up the stairs to our bedroom where he settles me into bed, working our limbs to get us settled just the way he likes before he slides himself back inside me, and buries his head between my breasts.

I run my fingers through his hair, pressing my lips to his forehead for long minutes. I don't let up on my stroking until I feel him relax into sleep.

I'm in bed with my husband, and life is almost perfect.

Almost.

24

MARRIED FIGHTS
HUDSON/LOLA

Hudson

I WAKE MY BABY up a few hours later and fuck her well into the morning before letting her sleep again. Then, I wake her up again a couple hours later with my head between her legs, licking the taste of her and me off her skin. I press my nose into her vagina and breathe deeply, inhaling the smell of sex.

Just raw, pure, unadulterated sex. I shudder, filling my lungs with our scent.

It's perfect.

I know it's animalistic, but I didn't even book us an actual honeymoon because I knew all I was going to be doing was fucking her, or licking her, and we could do that at home.

Our home.

I catch her standing in the formal room where I keep the knick-knacks of my travels, holding a statue of a breastfeeding woman. It's a primitive statue that I can tell moves her because she stares at it for too long for her to be truly regarding it. No, I can tell she's lost deep in her thoughts.

I come up behind her, wrapping my arms around her body and cuddling her close.

My hands cup her stomach and we just rock there for a second.
Complete.

My chest fills with pride at the sight of her things starting to make
a home next to mine in the formal sitting rooms. Her masks from her
various travels from her parents hang on the walls, and she's set small
busts of Egyptian pharaohs and queens next to my Mayan jade knives
and statues on my side board. It fits perfectly.

I peek around in the room and feel settled, because its me and her
in there. I'm not by myself anymore.

Speaking of not being by myself.

"When should we take a pregnancy test?" I ask, kissing her neck
we just stand there and rock as my hands rub her belly. I imagine
her tummy becoming bigger with our baby, and, as if I haven't been
fucking her like a mad man the last day and a half, I begin to swell
again.

"Probably not for another two weeks or so?" she says, placing the
statue back on the sideboard she turns in my arms and her hands find
their way up my back to pull me even closer to her. I kiss her softly
before I deepen it and groan at the taste of her.

Halfway through the day we're in the media room where she's
giggling at me, watching me do a Michael Jackson impression of
'Dirty Diana'. She's naked, lounging on the plush couch, wrapped
around a fleece blanket. Her hair is loose, flowing over her breasts and
she's clapping and cheering for me while I dance for her.

We're laughing and I'm soaking up the perfect feeling of her being
with her.

"Dance, sexy, *dance*. You really got moves, Hudson! *Work it, baby!*"
She cheers me on, and while I'm entertaining her, unknown to her
she's pulling me deeper into her web.

Her head tosses back on a joyful laugh and for a second it's utter bliss.

We're laughing together, playing around. I snatch her blanket away and cover my mouth with hers in a kiss that's got my blood boiling. Lola's running her hands over me, and she takes a second to lick at my chest, stopping at the tape covering the bandage protecting her name.

"I love you," she says confidentially. In this moment I remember the first time I saw her in the shop and she squeezed my hand a little too hard, challenging me.

I knew then she was mine.

I laugh against her mouth rubbing my nose along hers. "Not near as much as I love *you*, wife."

"Esposo," she whispers back, and I love her speaking to me in Spanish.

We roll around, loving each other all afternoon until we're interrupted by a couple things; Skee calling Lola with the boys to talk, and both Frank and Clayton calling me on a conference call. As Lola kicks back, blanket pulled up to her chin talking to Tatum and Tucker, I step out with my phone to my ear.

"We're on for four am, son?" Frank asks.

"He's back home," Clayton interrupts, and I hear his keyboard typing in the background. "I'll track his car and let you know where he's at."

I grunt. "I'll be at the house with Lola later tonight, and I'll meet up with you at three-thirty. Tomorrow, she's going to hang out with Amanda. So Clay, have Amanda keep her busy. Get them a spa day or something to make it seem less conspicuous. They need to be busy until at least seven."

Clayton grunts through the phone. "Knowing Amanda, that wont be hard, the boys are with our parents and she loves her free days. Trust me, It's not going to take much convincing. What you'll need to be concerned about is if Lolita's going to come home."

"I'll be there at three-thirty sharp, Frank." And with that I hang up and then make my way back into the media room, seeing Lola laughing behind her hand with the boys. I take the phone and I see them, they're hanging out in a game room, their hair is floppy hanging into their eyes, and their eyes are sparkling.

They thrive when they don't have to be with their dad.

"Hudson!" They yell, and I settle next to Lola, pulling her into the nook of my body and stroking her hair. I'm so content I actually hate that I have to pull myself from her tomorrow in order to take care of this fuck up of a man. But we all deserve peace, and a clean slate. And to not feel threatened.

"Boys!" I boom back, making them smile. They look at each other excitedly.

"Hudson we miss you!" Tucker states loudly. More loud than he normally is.

"Yeah! We want to know what our present is!" Tatum says excitedly.

I smile teasingly. "Should we tell them baby?" I look over at Lolita, and kiss her forehead as she giggles.

"Well I think you should do it." Lola tilts her head back to look at me, and that sparkle in her eyes makes me bend down to kiss her plump, deep red lips and I persist, even when the boys start complaining.

Suddenly Skee's voice enters the equation.

"Okay, enough of *thaaattt!*" he chastises, clicking his tongue at us. I pull away reluctantly to turn my attention back to the phone.

"Skee, do you think you can keep the boys a couple more days?"

"Sure," he states, walking into some sort of study. "If you're okay with them being on a photoshoot promo for a movie I'm doing."

Lola shoots up so fast I frown, pulling her back. "Skee, just don't leave them alone-" she looks back at me. *"Hudson!"* She implores.

I turn my attention to Skee, seeing her distress. "Hey, are you going to be able to keep an eye on them?" I ask sternly.

"Yes, either me or my assistant, Monica."

I look at Lola. "You okay with Monica baby?"

Lola nods.

"Then that's okay, but if anything goes wrong I'm coming up there Skee. Enjoy your time with the boys."

We stay on the phone for another minute before we hang up. I look at Lola who glances at me, looks away nervously, then glances at me again before her eyes widen.

"What?" she whispers, wetting her lips with her tongue.

"Are you sure its not too soon to take a pregnancy test?" I know I just asked her this, but I can't help it. I'm anxious. I lean forward and take her lips with my in a deep lush kiss.

"Yes. But you don't have to worry, I'm sure there's a Hudson Jr. baking in there."

I pull back from her. "I want a daughter, I already have two boys. I want a *girl*, one that looks like her mom."

She gives me a surprised look that I've never seen on her face before, but I'm dead serious.

I want a girl.

"How do we know if you're pregnant." I question her.

Working the blanket off her body I ignore her attempts to hold it to her, ripping it off her easily. She leans back with a shy smile, an arm crosses her breasts, and her hand clamps to her pussy. It's cute. Matter of fact I tell her so while I rip her hands away from herself.

"Baby, you've been doing nothing but coming inside of me for the last I don't know how long. I'm pregnant, there's no way I'm not."

I work to tilt her back into the cushions and maneuver my way between her legs. Smoothing her bangs back, I put my lips to hers as I push inside of her body carefully. "If you don't give me a girl, then I'm just going to keep you pregnant until you give me what I want."

"Is that a threat, *Hudson?*" Her brow arches defiantly at me.

"Oh you best believe it's definitely a threat."

My words excite her because she clenches around me, making me groan. I don't thrust, I just give her those flexing drives that I treated her to last night, wanting to be careful not to tear her or cause her damage because of my size.

"Hudson do you have a breeding kink?" she gasps against my ear, making me smile and nuzzle my lips to her cheek.

Her question makes me look down at her and chuckle. "I might. *If you don't give me a girl.*" I smile at her teasingly before bending down to press my lips to hers.

She rolls her hips against me and we laugh together, rocking into each other. "And if I don't give you a girl?"

"Oh honey, do you really want to go there with me?"

I chuckle against her mouth and we spend the next half hour having our first married fight where I basically demand a girl, or else she's going to be pregnant until I decide otherwise.

It's dark when we head back to our house by Frank. We grab dinner on the way, and eat in front of the television watching an amazing movie.

Afterwards I work to get her settled into bed.

She yawns as I crawl in behind her, tucking her under my arm. "What time will you guys be back tomorrow? Four in the morning is crazy, I don't know what's wrong with either of you, but I'm glad you have each other to be crazy with so you don't have to bug me, because can you just *see* my ass in a deer stand? Ugh." she questions.

I smile against her hair because I can't imagine it. "No," I chuckle quietly. "It'd be fun to see that side of you if you ever cared to show me though."

Lola's quiet for a second. "Hudson, can I ask you a question?"

"Sure baby, anything you want." I tilt my head to look down at her, seeing her brows furrowed. "What is it love? What's got you so worried?"

"Do you think that there's just one person on earth for each of us?"

My own brows lift at her unexpected question, and suddenly I am transported back weeks ago when I first saw her in the window of her store. I hadn't seen her entire face, only her profile. But it was enough to set my world so far off course that I know now, that I was just moved from my trajectory and placed into hers.

My fate always was pointing to Lolita.

"Without a shadow of a doubt."

"Really?" she questions.

"Hmm-hmm." I nod and kiss her forehead. "There's only one face for me, that's why no one else ever worked."

She gives me a sleepy smile and I spend the next few hours holding her. And at two forty five I get up, tuck her in carefully and then prepare myself to meet Frank. Who's on his porch at three fifteen sharp, smiling at me like he hasn't seen me in five years.

"You ready son?" He holds the door open, letting me into his lair, and I get the feeling that I've been ready my entire life. I was just waiting for Lolita.

The one person for me.

The only person for me.

Lola

Amanda's eyes are wide as she assess me walking to her car.

"Goddamn, Lola! Are you okay?" she gasps theatrically at the way I climb into her car, ass first, so I don't have to open my legs.

I'm *still* shaking.

"I think my new husband might be a sex addict." I half joke as I close the door and turn to her. She bursts out laughing, placing her hand on her mouth.

"I feel so sorry for you friend." She snorts and chuckles into her hand. Her face is almost as red as mine. "I haven't seen him with a serious woman in the years that I've known him. Seems like he's got a lot of making up to do. How's the kitty cat?"

I bust out laughing. "Purring, *a lot.*"

She gives me a cheeky grin and pulls her shades on. *"Damn I'm fucking jealous.* I need a good dick down."

We're straight cackling as we drive off and get into the highway. Trading stories about men and kinky, fun, sexual adventures.

As we drive, I feel myself so thankful for Hudson. Because of him I now have a new lease on life, and he makes me feel safe. So safe, that I think I might even be able to tackle my fuck up of a ex-husband.

Yeah, I can take on Dominic with Hudson at my side.

Today cant get any better.

Hudson

"There's no one on the street with cameras, and I swept his house for them too. You're good Hudson, he's in there alone, sleeping in his bed. He's naked though. Might want to have him put on some clothes." Clayton speaks through my ear piece quietly, and I pull into Dominic's driveway.

"Thanks man, I'll keep you on but when we get back to my place I'll let you go okay?"

"It's all good bro." I hear the rather comforting sound of him clicking away mindlessly in the background and turn to face Frank, who's sitting patiently with his hands clasped in his lap. Any other person looking at him would see an ordinary older man.

But I know the truth.

This man deserves some sort of recognition for as many weapons as he was able to strap on him and still manage to look inconspicuous. He turns to look at me, both our faces cloaked in shadow.

"You just going to stare at me like a freak or we going to go in?"

I turn my face back to the windshield and shake my head. This man is something else. "Let's go then," I say, stepping out and closing my door softly.

We walk up to the door and I pick the lock easily and pull out my gun.

My eyes take no time at all to adjust to the darkness and I lead Frank through the living room, down the hallway, and into Dominic's room who is sprawled out on his bed completely naked just like how Clayton said he was.

I sneer at the sight of his dick. I guess we can't all be blessed.

I don't fuck around. Not with him. I stride up to his bed, take out my switchblade and shove it straight between his ribs all the way to the hilt.

He wakes up with a scream that I muffle with his pillow before I pull him out of the bed harshly, seeing him hit the floor on his knee.

"AAAHHHH FUCK!" Dominic screams.

I kick him in the mouth hard. He rears back, his head bounces off the mattress before he falls forward and I see him spit out a tooth which I pick up and hand to frank who puts it in a bag that he places in his pocket. Frank reaches over with a gloved hand and turns on the bedroom light.

"What the fuck man?" Dominic looks discombobulated.

"Time to get up," I say simply.

I kick his hand away when it flies to the knife handle. His hands tremble and he stares up at me, blood smearing his lip and trailing out of his stab wound. I take a deep breath.

Fuck, it's finally time.

I want to cry tears of joy.

But I won't. Not yet anyways. But what I will do is revel in the sweet *sweet* feeling of fucking him up for what he did to my three loved ones. My family. Needing to get him to where I can work into him the way I want to, I fight back my impatience and narrow my eyes at him.

"Leave it, and put some clothes on."

He reaches for the knife again and I take out my gun once more, pulling the safety off. Dominic's eyes go wide and then he freezes. "Yo' what the fuck, *does Lola know about this?"* His voice is slightly garbled as he's got blood, saliva, and that missing tooth to worry about.

"Nope, she will though. I can't wait to show her I got your ass. But, first I'm letting her enjoy her day before I let her know I got you." I step back. "Go on ahead and put your clothes on. We're going for a ride."

The look this man gives me is so hateful that if I couldn't match it with my own energy I'd be screwed. It reaffirms what I already knew;

the man's a piece of shit, because I can only imagine the looks that he'd given Lola over the past few years.

Frank and I patiently wait as he drags on his clothes. I guess it's kind of hard to manage when you have a knife in your ribs, but what do I know.

I've never had to deal with that, personally.

I get him into my truck and climb into the back seat with him while Frank drives us to my house back in Bainbridge Island. It's only then when he speaks.

"You a rich fucker, huh?" He spits the words out and I nod.

"Yeah, I do pretty well for myself, and now for Lola and the boys."

"You're fucking sick."

"I mean," I smile at him, because my *sick ass* takes it as a compliment. "I tried to warn you. But you're just so *hardheaded* that I figured I'd show you that I stand on business. Pull up by the shed in the back, Frank."

I wait until Frank draws the truck to a stop before I open the door and unceremoniously kick Dominic out the truck hard, relishing the sound of him hitting the ground. The force of me kicking him sent him flying and he skids. I jump out behind him, kicking him again, making him roll onto the knife and it sounds really painful, if I might say so myself.

"Now Hudson, stop playing with him and lets get him in here please. It's cold." Frank chastises me while he reaches into the bed of my truck and pulls out a red cooler with a white lid. I shake my head. Can the man not go anywhere without his sandwiches?

Other than Lola's lasagna, I've never seen him eat anything else.

"What are you looking at *me* for? He's running," Frank says sternly.

I give him a little look before turning to raise my gun. Dominic's trying to head to the tree line for all he's worth and I aim fast, shooting him in the kneecap and making him collapse. I look back at Frank who gives me a grunt of approval.

"I just like for him to struggle, damn. Can I not have any fun? I've been waiting a long time for this," I say gruffly walking up to Dominic who is now on his back, rolling from side to side and grabbing his knee. He's red faced, covered in sweat and silently screaming.

I snatch him by his other ankle and begin to drag him to the shed past Frank who gives me a stern look.

In the shed I throw him into the chair and make him face the four wheelers I bought Lola and the boys. I came in here yesterday and lined them up just right, so he can see their names while I torture him.

Securing the last tie I stand up, pulling out my spare knife and give his pathetic ass a nice once over.

"You ready?" I ask, matter of fact.

"Fuck you, you psychotic piece of shit!"

"Oh me?" I put my hand on my chest and laugh nice and deep. He might be kind of right though. *"I'm* psychotic? I'm not the one who put out a hit on two children."

I stop laughing and tilt my head out at him, seeing renewed fear enter him. I breathe deeply, this fear smells different.

Desperate.

His eyes are wide. "Wait, what the fuck are you talking about? No I didn't."

I put the blade between my teeth and untie his right arm, put my foot on the chair next to his hip and lay his arm on my leg.

"Wait!" Frank interrupts me and stands up from his chair, taking a handkerchief out of his pocket. He rolls it up and then shoves it between Dominic's teeth, tying it off hard at the back of his head, gagging him. "Okie doke, carry on." He heads back to his little chair and cooler set up.

Without further ado, I look at him and meet his eye. He's breathing through his nose hard and I narrow my eyes. "This one's for Tuck." I move fast, snapping his ulna and radius bones in half. The scream that erupts from him sounds like justice.

Pure *justice*.

I lick my lips and slap him across the face, seeing he's struggling to stay conscious. "You're going to give me that hit man's information. Even if we have to be here all day."

I bring out my knife again and proceed to go to work.

While I cut, my thoughts turn to Lola, I hope she's enjoying being pampered.

She deserves it.

25

A WOMAN'S WORTH

LOLA

"ARE YOU JOKING ME?" I gasp at Amanda, holding a bag in each hand as we make our way into the chilly autumn air. "You're almost as bad as I was!" I tease, snickering at her.

"It was two years ago. I swear!" Amanda gives me wide eyes and giggles at me as we walk out of the lingerie store.

That's the one thing Hudson didn't really buy me, and I know it's because he prefers me naked, but I'd like to give him something more spicy to look at from time to time. So, I let myself splurge with the card he gave me. He added me onto his bank account and having security feels so fucking good that this man is going to get the best blow job of his life just from doing that alone.

Making me feel secure.

"Girl, you better get laid soon. The longest I went was three and a half years and I swear my shit was about to be stuck shut if Hudson hadn't come along."

We bust out laughing, falling over each other. I'm reveling at the feel of having a true girlfriend to talk shit with when I hear my phone ring with an incoming call from Hudson.

I answer it, seeing he's shiny with sweat, and his hair is a bit disheveled. He's also got no shirt on.

"Speak of the devil." Amanda teases and I roll my eyes as we laugh again and I turn back to my phone to greet my husband.

"Hey baby, how's it going you having a good time?"

I melt, he's always so concerned about me.

"I am! I'm on my way back!" I slide into the passenger seat, clicking my seatbelt on. "So did you guys get anything?"

"Oh yeah." He gives me a sexy grin that makes my stomach somersault. "Yeah we got something alright. Speaking of," he turns the phone so I can see Frank. I wave at the old man, loving they've stuck up a friendship. "We're stuck at our house in Bainbridge. Do you think you can drive your car over here? We're going to be busy skinning this thing for a while."

"Yuck," Amanda and I both say at the same time and we crack up laughing again, causing Hudson to look over at Frank chuckling.

He's so damn scrumptious I can't wait to wear my lingerie for him tonight.

"Yeah, give me about an hour and a half and I'll be there. I love you!" I say with a bright smile on my face. Hudson meets my eyes in the camera, making me blush.

"And I love you too woman. Get your ass over here. By the way, we're in the shed."

"I don't want to see no deer!" I say with a scrunched look on my face.

"Doesn't matter, come to the shed and give your husband a kiss. I've been without you all day."

"Fine," I roll my eyes and hang up on him. "Men." I sigh with exasperation.

Amanda and I laugh some more, not even needing music in the car we have so much to talk about and tease each other over.

I didn't think the day could get any better, but turns out it can.

Less than two hours later, I'm busy running my fingers through my disheveled hair and pushing my way into the shed, trying to think of what to cook them for dinner when I stop completely in shock at what I'm looking at.

Hearing the shed door bang shut behind me, my jaw drops open, seeing my ex-husband tied to a chair. Looking...

Unwell.

Not great.

My eyes widen in disbelief, and they turn slowly to Hudson who's standing there looking...great. Happy, even. And so does Frank, like he's really enjoying this shit almost like he's at a movie theater and all he's missing is popcorn and three dimensional glasses. I finally find my voice.

"What the fuck?" I turn, my gaze pinging between Dominic, Frank, and Hudson. *"What the hell is going on?"*

"We went huntin' Lolita!" Frank grits from his folding chair. He's got one boot on top of the cooler, and half a hog head cheese sandwich in his hand.

I groan and squeeze my eyes shut. We're all going to prison.

I'm going to prison.

My eyes open and find Hudson easily, he's studying me hard before he turns smoothly back to Dominic.

"I promised you I would bring you what you needed, baby." Hudson's eyes look like Satan himself as he regards Dominic. He smiles and leans forward into Dominic's face who is sniveling through the gag, shaking his head and trying to get away.

He blinks the blood out of his eye and turns to look at me.

He's obviously terrified.

"I *warned* you what would happen," Hudson says in a deadly serious voice. "And you *still* didn't listen. I warned you *twice* actually, which is generous in and of itself. Now, I'm here to make sure the scales of justice are balanced." Hudson pulls back from Dominic and takes a few steps back.

Dominic starts heaving in his seat.

I glance over at him, seeing a knife sticking from his ribs, his kneecap looks shot, and there's a lone, six inch wide strip of skin missing on the arm that doesn't have a bone sticking out of it. The sight of exposed muscles makes me feel nauseated, and I close my eyes tightly, trying to figure a way out of this that doesn't include us all being hauled off to death row.

Because this isn't just murder.

Hudson's straight up *torturing* Dominic.

Like the epitome of what a lawyer would say is premeditated. I bet Hudson's face is next to that word in the dictionary. I walk up on shaky legs to Dominic, thinking hard. What's the way to this man's soul. Money? Because it sure was never me and the kids.

"How much would it take?" I say, narrowing my eyes. "To buy us out of this? I'll call Skee right now, you'll sign an NDA, you will never speak about tonight ever again. *Do you fucking understand me?*"

Dominic nods his head frantically and I reach forward to pull his gag down.

"Oh Lolita, oh my God help me! Please!"

"Tell me how much you need to keep quiet about this, and *never* contact me about my children ever again?"

Dominic's eyes pierce mine. "Just let me go. Let me go *please!* I'll go away and never contact you again. I don't even need money. *Please.*"

"Oh wow." I tilt my head. "That's something." My eyes shift to Hudson. "Can your lawyer get us a termination of rights document for him to sign before we let him go?" I look over at Dominic. "You're signing away your rights to my children."

Dominic nods as snot begins to leak out of his nose, making me curl my lips in disgust. *"I will. I will.* Oh thank you Lolita, *thank you."* His head bows with how hard he's sobbing.

Hudson steps in, giving him a scathing once over. "Nope. That's not how this works." He looks at me. "Now, do you want *me* to kill him, or do *you* want to kill him?"

I throw him a incredulous look. "What? Hudson, he's going to sign the papers. We won't get in trouble for this! I found us a way out of this! *No I don't want to kill him have you lost your mind?* The both of you?"

Frank just sits there, silently, and takes a slow bite of his sandwich. It's comical, but I can't even appreciate it because it's so fucked up what's going on. I can't believe my neighbor is in on a murder!

"I know he's fucked up, but look! To do this to another *person."* My voice cracks and I just feel a whirlwind of emotions I can't get control of.

And it's really sad, because though Dominic *is* a fucked up piece of shit, an abuser, and yes, he broke my babies arm and he's just overall seemingly a bad person from all the shit Hudson has showed me so far... I don't know that I can justify this.

Don't know if I can sit back and watch the love of my life kill another human being.

I look over at Hudson and my face pales. He's not just the love of my life, he's my husband. Hudson makes a humming noise as if he's thinking about my words before turning his eyes to me and my blood freezes at what I see in it's depths.

"You're a hardheaded woman." His voice is hard, and his eyes flash at me in a clear warning. "And later when I fuck you, I'm going make sure you understand that from now on *you take what I give you without question*."

I inhale on a gasp as our gazes clash.

Everything else fades away, letting me know this man is serious. He didn't even whisper it, he said loud enough I know Frank and Dominic *both* heard him.

We're interrupted.

"Hey, you still haven't told her the other information yet though, Hud," Frank yells out.

Hudson gets a *'oh yeah'* look and then turns, walking to the table. "You're right Frank, I was just waiting for the right moment is all."

"Whatever. You just wanted that man to think he had a chance," Frank says. "That she was going to save him. *It's sick*, Hudson."

This draws a dark chuckle out of Hudson. The one I love, the one that makes me wet.

"That seems to be the word of the day, doesn't it?" He says absent-mindedly.

Hudson reaches into a drawer under the table and pulls out a manila folder with a rare heaving sigh. "I forgot to show you this the other day, baby. I'm sorry, I've just been so busy. You recognize this, Dominic?" He throws the folder onto the table and motions for me to come look at it.

The scream that suddenly erupts from Dominic is enough to make me step back in shock. My eyes flit between the two men, trying to figure out what's going on.

"NO! NO Lolita, don't look at that!" Dominic throws me eyes that are so full of terror that my own eyes narrow as he turns his bloody face to Hudson. *"Oh my God you piece of shit, I'll walk!* I'll walk and you don't have to pay me anything! I'll go! You wanted them, now you have them! Let me go!" he yells, almost hyperventilating with how hard he's begging.

Frank starts laughing. "Aw hell. If it isn't the piper come calling. *Here Lola.*" With a smirk, he reaches behind the cooler and brings out the little black case that I know houses the gun that he tried to give me a few weeks ago.

I scoff. "Oh come *on.* I'm not taking that, Frank. You men are so dramatic. What's in here?"

I walk up to the folder and snatch it up, opening it.

At first, I don't understand what I'm looking at, I think because I *cant.*

I'm just staring at the page, not really able to read too much. Eventually the words start to process and I see it. Photos of the boys and I upfront. Our schedules laid out, pictures of me and the boys doing things together, us in the shop, also times that Frank usually checks in with me.

The information starts to become documented less around the time I met Hudson, and I see the plan had to be changed to accommodate Hudson's presence interfering. My eyes widen, my whole being trembles, and I don't just *feel* my mask slip away; it crumbles and breaks off piece by piece from being petrified from the dirt I've been buried in for so long.

The fucker had a hit on my babies, *and me.* So he could cash out their life insurance as the sole beneficiary. And all the money my brother and I'd been giving him was used to pay for it.

My eyes slowly raise to Hudson and I feel it. I dig myself out of my grave and begin to walk. Straight to Dominic.

Satan's brother.

But I feel no fear, because I'm Satan's wife, and he just brought me my comeuppance.

Dominic sees the change come over my face because he somehow turns even paler and shakes his head, gasping. "N-n-no Lolita, no! Please don't do this! You can't do this Lolita, *you're a good person.* "

"Was. I *was* a good person," I snap. "And might I even go so far as to remind you that at one point I was even a good wife to you. The best wife, as a matter of fact. I was *way* more than you ever fucking deserved you *nasty,* scum of the earth piece of *dog shit.*" I stare him dead in his eyes letting him know I mean business. I hold the folder up between us and slap him across the face with it, following up with a slap from my left hand. I dig my fingers into his jaw and bring his face back to me. "It's one thing, to hurt *me.* But to try and kill my babies, oh motherfucker I'm going to sit back and watch you *suffer.* "

The fear that enters in Dominic's eyes will be enough to sustain me for the rest of my life.

I back away from him, drop the folder to the ground and then walk to Frank, picking up the steel bat he's got leaning against the cooler. Frank pauses in her chewing, meeting my eyes, but wisely keeps quiet for once in his fucking life as I turn back to Dominic.

Do I care that beating a man to death is against the law? No.

Do I care that I've never hurt a fly before, and this is my introduction to violence. No.

Do I even care that this man is the biological father of my kids, and this is truly a fucked up situation to be in? Again, *nope.*

I bend down eye level to Dominic, who is looking at me with equal parts fear and hate.

"With every fucking hit, I want you to think about every time you cussed me out, cussed at the kids, didn't feed my son, was out busy fucking some bitch instead of me, worried about extorting me and my brother for money, breaking my boys arm, manipulating Tatum, and daring to try and *rape me.* "

Hudson makes a rough sound behind me, reminding me I'd never told him that, but I ignore him.

"But most of all, I want you to think about the fact that Tatum and Tucker have a new daddy, and his name is Hudson, and he's twice the man you are, and ten times the father you ever were. And by the way...I'm worth so much more than five hundred thousand dollars."

And with that, I step away and start swinging.

With every sickening crunch and ear shattering scream I feel myself come more into myself. More back to life.

I'm going wild, careful not to hit his head as I don't want him dead just yet. I scream and just absolutely wail on him. I make sure to get him good in his fucked up knee. I hit him where the knife his sticking out of his ribs, driving it deeper and deeper into him until the handle disappears into his ribcage, and then I start working on his broken arm.

Thinking about how he broke Tucker's arm for daring to have a man pay attention to him.

Dominic's screams cease and he vomits on himself, beginning to choke on it he's heaving so hard. I pause, breathing hard myself. The adrenaline fades away and I'm left tired. Just utterly bone tired. The bat hits the ground next to me with a dull clanking noise.

"You did good, Lola." Frank claps and praises me from his chair at the side of the room, but I can't celebrate with him.

I'm numb.

Hudson, taking advantage of my tiredness, clears his throat, takes me by the hand, and pulls me away. Bringing me around to face him he grips my lower back with one hand and tilts my head up with a finger crooked under my chin. His eyes are hard as they meet mine, but then they melt as he softly pushes my bangs back in that way we both love.

Dominic's miserable whimpers fade into the background, leaving just the two of us. Hudson gives me an assessing look before tilting his head.

"Let me finish. You don't have to watch this, beautiful. I will handle this for you, *for them.*" He reassures me.

I nod my head and then whimper into his mouth as he leans down to seals his lips over mine. "Oh God, you think I'm crazy don't you?" I murmur against him.

Hudson barks out a laugh and then rubs his nose against mine. "I fucking love seeing this side of you. You letting out your feminine rage is the sexist thing I think I've ever seen."

I can't help but give a tentative smile at the joy that fills me, seeing he's not turned off by how much of a maniac I must have looked, getting my revenge on my children.

"Here." He takes his jacket off and then places it on my shoulders and I am blanketed in his warmth, his scent. Feeling so safe, like nothing can touch me. "Frank, take Lola inside the house while I finish up here?"

Looking over at Frank he nods his head as the older man stands up and trades a glance with him.

"Come on Lola, I got you sweet pea. Let's go get cleaned up." Frank reassures me as he puts and arm around my shoulders and leads me out the shed.

My arm stretches, and Hudson's fingers glide through mine whisper soft as Frank steers me away from him. Hudson gives me a nod and then turns, his profile hiding Dominic's form from me. For that I'm selfishly thankful.

I don't want to see the man ever again.

"Oh Frank." I break down sobbing as we reach the porch of the house. "He was going to kill my babies. *He was-he was-"* I start choking on my tears. The fear that Dominic was so close to doing the unthinkable to my beautiful boys overtakes me and I begin to sink to the floor, thankful Frank is there to help me stand. *"I can't believe he was going to do that,"* I wail.

But honestly, I'm upset at myself for not seeing this. For not seeing I was letting my kids go with a monster every other weekend. I have so much guilt it almost debilitates me, right there on Hudson's porch.

No, *mine* and Hudson's porch. Because we're married.

Frank wraps me up in his arms and while he's holding me, I hear a muted gunshot. Ironically, with the sound of the bang, my guilt leaves me because I know deep in my heart an evil has been eradicated. My babies no longer have to fear this man, I no longer have to fear him, and then live with the soul crushing worry about my children's safety every time they are with them.

The internal burden that lifts off me is so light that I cry harder.

"Let it out Lola, these are good tears." Frank consoles me.

After a couple of minutes where I'm grateful its Frank that sees me ugly cry like this, and not Hudson, he finishes walking me into the house.

What's he going to do with the body?

Is he okay?

Thoughts race through my head as I climb the stairs shakily to walk into Hudson's-no, *our*-bedroom and I stand there in the bathroom. Unsure as to what to do with myself. I look at myself in the mirror, seeing wild gray eyes, wild hair, small streaks of blood but nothing too much.

I feel like I looked worst after the first time Hudson ravaged me in his front lawn. I pick up a comb and try to detangle the knots in my hair and the errant thought hits me hard.

What if we get caught and Hudson goes to prison?

My stomach drops, and I am filled with a feeling I can't describe. This man put his livelihood, his reputation, and his life on the line to make sure me and the boys felt true safety for the rest of our lives.

The comb clatters to the floor as I let it fall from my hand and I do the only think I know how to do in this moment. I go into the shower, turn it as hot as I can stand it, sink to my knees fully dressed and wait. Thankfully, I don't have to wait long because Hudson comes in soon after, almost so silently that I don't hear him, catches my eye and begins to undress.

He looks a bit worse than me but not too bad.

For someone who just killed another person I would have expected a bloodbath, but I guess not. I stay quiet from my spot on the shower floor and wait until he is completely nude and he steps into the shower with me, hauling me up and beginning to strip my clothes off. He tosses them rather carelessly on top of his, and I briefly wonder why he doesn't throw them in the hamper until it hits me. Our clothes are evidence.

My fear comes back.

"Hudson where...what are you going to do with-"

He hushes me with a finger to my lips. "You don't need to worry about any of that. I got it okay? Don't ask me because I won't tell you." His eyes search mine. "I just needed you to know that you were going to be okay. That you didn't have anything to be afraid of. I couldn't let you and those boys continue with life always being on edge, wondering if he was going to hurt any of you."

He steps us into the spray and is silent a moment, letting the water soak his hair, washing the blood and dirt down the drain.

"Hudson...have you ever...."

Can I ask him?

His green eyes open and find mine, I touch his chest, giving him a pensive look, hating I even brought it up.

"No. But I will admit Lolita, I had plans to kill him even before I found the evidence of the hired hit against you three." He takes a breath and places his hand over mine, pressing it deeper into his chest. "And if you want to leave me because of it... I will let you go baby."

I hear myself let out a shocked sound and I launch myself at him. I throw my short frame and him and yank his head down to me.

"No, please don't! Hudson you can't... *you can't say that!*" My breath hitches. I'm desperate, trying to reach his lips with mine, but he covers the distance between us and captures my lips in a harsh kiss that steals my breath. His hands are hard on my back, pressing me as close as he can. "How can you say that, mi Amor? *How could you?*" My words are garbled as he barely gives me room to get the question out.

"God you're right, you're so fucking right. I wouldn't let you go for the world, Lolita," he says harshly.

Hudson's just as desperate as me. He bends to band an arm under my ass, and lifts me up and lowers me onto his dick with a harsh grunt that has a tear falling out of my eye at the feel of him spreading me apart. His hips churn against me.

We strain against each other quietly, desperately, the both of us trying to prove to the other that we're all we have.

It's intimacy at its finest, to see the worst parts of another person and to still feel this unbearable, burning desire that threatens to burn you down with it in a fiery unforgiving inferno.

It's love. What we have.

In the purest form.

26

THE LAST BUCK

FRANK

FIVE DAYS LATER ON a ugly, dreary early morning, I pull parallel to an old country road about three hours away from home.

Squinting my eyes through the darkness of the morning, I clock the semi-lit, whitewashed brick two-story home down the lane with a ratty yard. The grass is so tall it's swaying in the wind, only illuminated by the little lights on outside of the house.

You'd never know a killer lived inside.

If you're going to be a killer, do you have to be a slob? The fact that Lolita and those boys could have been killed by a man who can't even be bothered to be a clean assassin irks my soul.

"Dammit Squire," I mumble. "What is with you and your generation not taking care of things. That yard is pathetic."

Squire, an older comrade in his fifties who I served alongside during the tail end of my tenor with the marines, turns to look at me from the passenger side. Thankfully he stays quiet, I didn't need an answer no way.

I don't idle, continuing to creep by at a slow pace.

Thanks to my connections I was able to hunt down this hit man in a matter of just a couple days. We're only here three days after that because I had another connection of mine faux contact this man, requesting a hit. Once we confirmed the man's validity as a hit for hire it was game on.

I told Hudson to stay back and take care of his woman. I got this. There's nothing to killing a man, really. If you know what you're doing, it can even be cathartic. Help you work through some things. Like Lolita did.

My brave girl.

She makes me so proud. Seeing her lose it on that piece of shit ex-husband of hers made me happier than I was when I found out my first grandbaby was born. Even though I haven't spoken to her in the better part of a year thanks to her going ons.

I know you aren't supposed to admit stuff like that but hell, my family doesn't care about me, so I'm going to take my happiness where I can. And let me tell you, Hudson's become the son I never knew I needed or wanted.

I'd never thought there would ever be a reason for me to have this much excitement back in my life. I thought when my wife died, I died along with her. But Lolita and those boys gave me a reason to keep going, and when Hudson came around...well...let's just say I've found a new friendship with his parents.

Hudson's pulled me up out the dirt right along with them. Though you may call me a mature, strong oak tree, in comparison to their young sapplings.

Lola's like a willow tree.

"Sir," Squire grunts quietly. "What are you doing?" His voice quivers as I hit a rather hard bump in the ground. I've maneuvered the car in the woodsy area in the south side of the property, turning off the glare of the headlights completely and shutting the ignition off.

I narrow my eyes in irritation. "I don't suppose you want to park in front of the house and walk in with our guns raised, alerting the man we're out to get him now do ya?" I look over at him, arching my brow.

"What's the matter? You too old to walk? It's only about two tenths of a mile to the back of the house."

Squire scrunches his face at me, raising his own eyebrow. "I'm younger than you!" he says, offended.

"Well then *act like it.*" I snap, opening the car door. "And take that fucking coat off, pussy. It's going to slow you down."

"Yes Lieutenant General."

I tighten my lips at the reminder of my time with the military, still pissed I never got a five star ranking, and I was so close before my wife forced me to retire. I get out of the car and roll my left shoulder, the cold and damp settles deep in the joint, reminding me that I'm not young anymore.

Though I feel it, the body lets me know the truth.

I pop the trunk. "Hold the light to the left," I say quietly, opening the tray on the inside that holds our guns and ammos.

I pull his out and hand it to him, before grabbing mine. Making sure to close the trunk softly I turn to Squire, pulling the scarf up on my face to keep my breath from fogging the air. Touching my finger to the annoying ear piece, I clear my throat. "Clay?"

"Yes sir, I'm here." Clayton, who in my opinion is the best of the best when it comes to tech, comes over the little speaker.

"Double check all the security feed has been cut to the house."

"I already did Mr. Fra-"

"Check it *again.*"

These young kids these days. Does no one know how to just listen and keep their mouths shut? *Whatever happened to respect?*

"Sorry sir." I hear keys clocking in the background. "All clear, sir."

I nod, giving the signal for Squire to go ahead. "Thank you Clayton, I'll give you a call when were done."

"I'll be waiting."

The line clicks shut and Squire and I make it to the back of the house in record time. Other than the sounds of leaves crunching under our boots and the occasional critter in the distance, it's quiet.

Heading to the backdoor I hold up my hand and stop Squire. I try the backdoor, seeing it unlatches, creaking open with a groan. My body tightens as I become hyper aware of my surroundings. Why's there a killer in an unlocked house.

I back away from the door. It's bad news.

"No," I say simply. "Another way."

Squire nods but I'm already moving, lowering to my knee and firing off a shot. Seeing the man on the side of the house clutch his chest and then fall forward with a grunt. Squire lowers behind me, facing the opposite direction.

"Damn sir, you still got it huh?" he whispers.

I look over at him, curling my lip. "If you never lose it, you'll always have it son. Remember that. He should have been your first shot. You going to let an old man outdo you?"

Squire just shakes his head. "I see you're still an asshole, sir."

I grin. "Squire, you'll come to the point where you'll be able to take offenses like that as a compliment. Like I do. Now, here's what we're going to do. To the west of the building there's a basement entry to the house. We'll take that and then get to him that way. Take him out silently, then leave."

We stand back up, though my knee protests a bit.

"How do you know about the entrance on the other side?" he asks.

"Checked the blueprints ahead of time."

"Ah."

I tsk at him. "Seriously Squire, help yourself and go old school sometimes. You don't always need this new fangled technology to tell you what to do. Now, let's go get this done. I'm ready to go home."

Entering in through the basement we're in and out in ten minutes. He's such an easy target.

One single shot between the eyes, a gas leak, and a lit match later Squire and I are on the road headed onto the blacktop from the gravel road.

"We're good to go, Clayton," I say into the ear piece before turning on a morning radio news station.

Still feeling the high of the hunt, I look into the rearview mirror as I gun the accelerator. Though honestly, I'm not quite ready to let it go. This is more than likely my last buck, I think, and I want to relish this for as long as I can.

The orange flames look so pretty lighting up the early morning sky.

I smile to myself. I don't know how I'm going to be able to wait three hours to tell Hudson about my adventure. Two bucks ten years after retirement, who would have thought?

Not me.

"You like hog head cheese?" I ask, reaching over to turn the radio up slightly.

"Never had it."

The audacity makes me grin. "Well, today's your lucky day my boy."

And it's a good day, too.

27

WHAT I WANTED

HUDSON

A COUPLE OF WEEKS later it's one o' clock in the morning, and I'm restless.

Not able to sleep, I roll out of bed, throwing on a pair of sweat pants, and make my way out on the balcony to look through Lolita's phone.

> Dominic, are you coming to get the boys? You're running late and they're hungry. -Lola October 30th 6pm

> Hey, if you still want to get them, we'll be at my house. I'm taking them home to feed them. -Lola October 30th 6:30p

> Here are pictures of them dressed up from Halloween, are you getting them this weekend? I haven't heard from you…What's going on? November 1st 2pm.

> Okay Dominic, this is NOT funny. I called your mom and she said she hadn't heard from you either. November 12th 10am

I shove her phone in my pocket and hold my other hand, smiling down at the positive pregnancy test we'd just taken a few hours ago.

The last two weeks have been pure bliss.

The kids ask about Dominic, but when we tell them that no, we hadn't heard from him and we aren't sure if he's going to be there to get them for their visit, the relief on the boy's face becomes more and more apparent as the number of missed visits increase.

Tucker has changed the most, so far.

My gaze drifts from the pregnancy test to the woods beyond the backyard, and I think about how Dominic is in the afterlife burning up for what he did to the three of them. My last words to him before I put that bullet between his eyes was that if I happened to join him in hell for murdering him, that it wasn't over between us.

I'd fuck him up again on sight. Those were the last words he heard before he departed this earth.

I turn, running a hand through my hair and find Lola's sleeping form through the glass double doors.

She's on her back, both arms tossed above her head and the blankets have slipped down some, baring her breasts to the room. Her beautiful breasts; my first indication that she was pregnant. I knew it before she took the pregnancy test just based off how more sensitive they'd become.

That night, a little over a week ago, I was fucking her, playing with her breasts and she wouldn't stop wiggling. So, I tied her wrists together and then attached them to the headboard, subduing her so I could commence to sucking her nipples at my leisure the way I like to do.

I'd never heard a woman cry and beg for mercy so hard in my entire life.

I grunt at the memory, putting my hand to my groin and squeezing at just how swiftly I hardened in response. It was such a turn on, and I fucked her so good that night she passed out.

With my lips around her nipple of course.

Thinking of having a repeat, I push off the railing with my hips and walk to her the doors, intending on waking her up with my head buried in between her silky legs. She can lose all the sleep in the world right now since she's not going to be working for a while.

I informed her tonight that she won't be working until our baby is at least old enough for preschool, and by then, her book/wine shop shop should be ready. She decided to build it onto the vineyard acreage, and her plans are going to take at least a year and a half to build, because I'm the one building it so I'm taking my sweet time.

She hasn't been bored in the least as I keep her days busy with picking out building materials, building plans, interior design, sourcing whatever books she wants from all over the world, and long hours spent fucking the night away.

It's everything I've ever wanted.

Skee has even asked to come down to look at the property, wanted to know if he could invest, thinking it would bring more work if his name was publicly attached to it. He's supposed to be here sometime this morning, along with my parents and Frank for a big family meeting.

Yes, Frank is family.

I'm steeling myself for potential pushback. I want her to be free to be a mother to our children, the only job that she needs to prioritize right now. The thing she always wanted; to be a loving mother.

I put my hand on the doorknob when I feel the hair on the back of my neck stand.

I turn to look over at the boy's balcony and I see Tucker, standing there staring at me. He gives me a little grin that I match and I point my finger down and gesture to the floor, our code for meeting in the pantry.

My romp with Lola's going to have to wait as my boy wants to spend time with me.

Fifteen minutes later we're in the stables mounting Beauty and we take off into the night. I keep us in the lush grass, away from the tree line. Tuck has the reins and he leads us efficiently.

"Hudson..." Tucker starts in his small voice. It's thin, cautious, slightly tinged with worry and trepidation. "Is dad coming back?"

I'm silent for a moment, however, I place a hand on his shoulder and squeeze, acknowledging his question. Beauty stops at a thick tuff of grass and bends her head to chew on it and for just a few moments it's me, him, the twinkling stars in the clear sky above us, and this question between us that I carefully weigh.

"Well son, I'm not really sure. *But-*" I hesitate, unsure of how much to say. What would Lola approve of? "You're going to be taken care of if he comes back or not. I promise. Can I ask you something, Tuck?"

He turns to look at me over his shoulder. His head tilts up until his eyes find mine, and his brown curls ruffle in the breeze around the helmet I make him wear when we ride.

This has become a habit of ours over the last couple weeks.

We do this about three times a week he and I. It's our thing, and I love it. We've learned so much about each other.

We've shared small things from our wants and dreams, our favorite color, the perfect time a day (Tucker's is the middle of the night, a habit he developed from waking up to eat in the middle of the night), our favorite foods.

It's these late night hours that bond us and bring us closer.

Just the other night he shared he was worried that Tatum was going to start sleeping in his own bed now that we're establishing a new household, and a new routine. Their bond has seemingly healed with Dominic out of the picture, and as I stare into his gray eyes, I think to myself that that alone was worth the crime I committed to ensure their safety.

"Yeah Hud?"

"Do you want him back?"

Tucker's little brows furrow, and a small line forms between them as his eyes shift away and then he turns back to the front and loses himself in his own thoughts again. Patiently, because he's just like his mother, I let him take as long as he needs.

Beauty begins to walk again, and we're alternating being illuminated by the light of the moon, and the shadows of the tall spruce trees when he answers me.

"I hope he never comes back, Hudson. *Ever*. And if he does, can you make sure mom doesn't let me go with him?"

My chest tightens at his words. I slink an arm around the cast of his arm, and press my hand into his chest right over his heart.

"I promise, you never have to see that man ever again Tuck. You have my word."

Because it's handled, boy.

We're silent for a few more minutes, and I head us back to the stable, seeing he's shivering and I have no desire to make him catch pneumonia. I'm not sure that Lola knows this has become our thing, but I'm sure she'd be one pissed off woman if he got sick because I had him out here too long inhaling the colder winter air into his lungs.

Back in the stables I dismount first before reaching up and sliding him off carefully, making sure to not bother his arm.

He looks up at me with a serious expression as I work to take off his helmet. His next words catch me off guard.

"Can I call you dad?"

My breath catches in my lungs, because... *did I hear that right?*

Such a simple question, however, I can't be sure over the sudden pounding of my heart.

"What?" I ask, holding my breath. He repeats himself, his eyes welling up with tears. He *did* say it, but again, it's so quiet I barely hear him. I pause, staring at him in his eyes and trying to desperately maintain a grip on my sanity that only the three of them have the power to take away.

I place my hand on the top of his head, brush his curls away, and just stare as he commences to ripping my heart out of my chest.

I'm just resigned to realizing it doesn't belong to me anymore. It's theirs. Always has been.

My eyes well up with tears, and as they fall, I sink to my knees and pull him into my chest on a choked sob as every feeling imaginable slams into me at once.

Pain, because at any given moment anything could happen that's out of my control, and though I will do my damndest to protect my new family, there's always that slight chance that something might happen and I lose them.

Anger, because he's not my blood. They should have been mine, he shouldn't have to ask to call me dad.

I *am* his dad, point blank.

Love, it swells inside of me so bright they can probably see the shit from space.

"Of course you can, son. My boy. I'm so proud of you *Tucker Montgomery.*" I choke out, feeling the tears leak out and fall I don't bother to wipe them away.

No.

Just like I show his mother how she makes me feel, I show him. Unashamedly, and without hesitation.

We stay locked in each other's arms for long moments, and half an hour later I tuck him back into bed with some warmed spiced milk, and crawl back into mine and his mothers bed. I press my lips to her belly and talk for the next hour to my child growing in her womb.

I tell her all about how wonderful the life she's about to be born into will be.

How she's got a mommy, father and two brothers who can't wait to meet her, and that I'm sorry if I knock her around a little over the next eight months.

I'll let her me pay me back sometime in the future.

"Skee, have you lost your mind?" I stare at him wide eyed from my stance on the porch, seeing his face break into a beaming smile so bright that I want to punch it.

"What bro?" he says, "what's the problem?"

"So instead of letting us pick you up at the airport, you hire a *limo* to pick you and my parents up to come here? What are you trying to one up me or something?"

Skee huffs a laugh, taking the stairs two at a time, clasping hands with me before pulling me into the hardest hug I've yet to feel from another man. It reminds me of the first time I met Lola, and she asserted her dominance in a similar fashion.

Must be a family thing.

"What's a little competition between brothers, huh?" he whispers in my ear before turning to walk down the stairs and hold his hand out to my mother to take and help up the stairs.

I roll my eyes, hearing the boys in the house behind me, their thundering footsteps getting louder and louder with their ascent and then they barrel out of the front door and fly down the stairs, throwing themselves into my parent's arms.

"Kids! Come to grandpa!" My dad booms in his baritone voice, taking his hat off and pulling them in tightly. He peeks up at me and gives me a wink.

"Oh my gosh, *are they already here?*" Lola exclaims from behind me and I turn, seeing her fussing with her apron and straightening her bangs anxiously.

Something I've noticed about her? She's gets easily anxious, not able to help letting her nerves get the better of her.

"Now *calm down*, I don't want you stressed for no reason." I reprimand her gently and pull her under my arm, seeing the party making their way noisily up the stairs.

"Oh Alejandro!" My mom trills with a far off dreamy look in her eyes. "Chef Marisa is a dream! Thank you so much for being so generous, but you know you don't have to." My mother gushes at Skee with her arm wrapped around his.

She refuses to call him by his nickname.

He throws me a mischievous grin as they approach, and as my mom and Lola hugs, I sniff and fold my arms. Eyeing him.

"A private chef, Skee? Is that *really* necessary?" I flick him a look and narrow my eyes at his wicked smile.

""Oh come on, *you* don't have to pay the bill," he says quietly, casting a look over at my parents, Lola, and the boys.

"Nope, just *allll* the other ones."

I have a feeling this is going to be our thing, Skee and I, trying to outdo each other financially. Well bring it the fuck on then.

"Oh stop complaining, you sound like a sissy," Skee breathes under his breath, and that bright smile is right back as Lola turns to hug him next. "Oh mami, you look so good!'

"Thanks, Skee." She smiles and faffs self-consciously with her hair. "Well, dinner is almost done. Come in, I've got your rooms together, and Frank should be here any minute, so lets get comfortable."

We all head into the house talking and laughing.

It's noisy, carefree, and damn it feels amazing.

A couple hours later we're relaxing in the lounge after dinner. Frank is here, and we're having a good time talking about the future and what that looks like for us moving forward as a family. Lola is curled up next to me on the couch, wrapped in her favorite dark blue cardigan and she's laughing with my mother.

My father catches my eye, taking a sip of his whisky before speaking.

"Okay, son. Give it to us straight," my dad says. *"Are you sure you want us this close?* We're more than happy to stay in the house next to Frank so you don't feel overwhelmed." My dad's green eyes bounce back and forth between the two of us.

"Nooooo, we'd love to have you move in with us-" Lola gushes, leaning forward to squeeze my father's hand affectionately.

I throw her a little side eye and settle back into my chair, spreading my legs and really getting comfortable.

"What Lola means to say is, we'd like to have you *close*." I correct her. "We plan on having more kids and well....we'd like to have some privacy from time to time and you all being right here to help would be appreciated. The property is plenty big, I can have both homes done within the next year."

My parents finally decided to move out this way, and I wanted Frank close as well for Lola. We decided to build onto my property and move them next to us. So we have three builds to navigate; Lola's business, and our parent's homes.

I love a challenge.

I press the back of Lola's hand to my lips and listen to them all talk amongst each other for a bit. They boys have been hanging all over Skee, and I can see he's getting to be a little weary, probably from all the traveling and the good dinner kicking in.

"Tate, Tuck, go shower and get yourself ready for bed." I instruct, seeing it's getting to be about their bedtime.

"But dad," Tatum speaks up. "We never get to see Uncle Skee and grandma and grandpa! Can we stay up a little longer?" His brown eyes are wide and hopeful, and Tucker adopts the same exact face as his brother.

I smile, leaning forward to ruffle their hair affectionately.

"Absolutely, but you need to get your shower our of the way first so you don't forget. Remember, we shower every day."

Why this has been a fight with them lately, I've yet to find out.

They launch themselves up and I take Skee into the media room, showing him how to work everything and the popcorn machine.

"Hey man," Skee stops me with a hand on my shoulder. His touch is heavy, serious, and I let myself meet his eye instinctively knowing what he wants. "You doing okay?"

"Yeah," I say gruffly, clearing my throat. "To be honest, it's a lot emotionally, all of a sudden having everything you want in life. I want to protect them, never want any harm to come to them. I live with the worry in the back of my head that-"

"One day something might happen?"

I feel my eyes prick. Because I've never really lost anyone, not truly, and this fact has become a fear of mine.

Skee meets my eyes patiently, and the fact that this man lost both parents, and had to methodically cut off all his family members over the years due to his success really sinks home. Though he might be an asshole, he's tough, and he's been through some things.

"We can't predict the future unfortunately, but what we can do is live in the moment." He squeezes my shoulder harder and levels me with a look that touches my soul. "You have nothing to worry about, Hudson. Let that shit go and enjoy this wonderful life you've got, okay? You work hard for it. You deserve to enjoy it."

We stand there and talk for a few minutes. The boys come down and bowl into Skee, yanking him to a spot in the media room and pushing him down.

Skee laughs and throws me a brotherly grin. "I got this." He quips, wrapping an arm around each kid and bringing them in close.

I take off to find Lola and see Frank in the hallway off the media room, staring at a picture of the four of us together.

"You have a beautiful family," he says softly, turning his head to look at me.

It's then I see something new in his eyes I hadn't been privy to until now. Regret and sadness mark his features and haunt his eyes.

"You know, you're part of our family as well," I say.

I turn to look at the picture of Lola, me, and the boys on the wall. She'd wanted to take it a dusk to capture the fireflies. The boys aren't just grinning, they're laughing, and I've got one in each arm as Lola looks up at us adoringly.

In the picture, I'm staring at the camera with a proud smile, not realizing that the three of them were staring at me in that moment.

When I first saw the picture I choked up, because they're looking at me with reverence, respect, and love. So much love. Joy is radiating out from inside me, and for the first time, I see myself as I am. Not my sickness... not the mask I wear that has become my identity over the years.

Just Hudson, full to the brim with love. I don't know how it can get any better.

Yeah I do... there's a baby to be born.

A daughter, if I get my way.

Frank meets my eyes and then looks back at the picture. "You're doing everything right. Keep it up, you don't want to end up like me. An old man, reduced to sitting in his living room and looking out the curtains, trying to pay penance for all the mistakes he made over the years." His voice cracks, and his eyes meet mine, filled with so much sadness it washes over me in waves. "I don't have one single kid to come see about me, no matter how hard I look. Just a granddaughter who takes after me more than I care to admit. So you take your blessings and you run with them. Live your life and be happy with the simple things, son."

My heart breaks for him, because it dawns on me this whole time that Frank hasn't had any family visit. He doesn't talk about his kids. And I guess in a way, he and Lola adopted each other in their trauma and helped fill a void that the other was lacking.

"Frank I'd be honored if you continue to be in our lives, you know, there's a girl coming soon who's going to need a lot of men in her life to protect her."

Frank snorts and looks back at me. "You want a mini Lola?" We share a chuckle and then he turns to face me head on. "I'd love to stay in y'alls lives, if you're sure you'll have me." His eyes are hopeful yet chock full of pain that's a bit breath taking.

I stare into his almost silver irises and I just know, this man has become my second father. Just like that.

We don't even have to say a word about it.

Clearing my throat hard, I pull him in and clap his shoulder. "As long as you promise to stay a pain in the ass, Frank."

We continue to talk as I show him to his guest room for the night, and then make my way to Lola, who's backing quietly out of my parent's room.

She turns and then gives me a slow smile as I approach her. The happiness is radiating from within, and I swear she's glowing. I pull her close, wanting to have some of that magic rub off on me.

"Come on baby, dance with me." I nab her wrist and pull her into our bedroom and out on the balcony, seeing dozens of fireflies lighting up the property.

Lola tosses her head back and laughs as I whirl her a few times on the balcony. I slow us down, pushing her bangs back off her forehead in the way we both love.

"Hudson," she giggles. "What is it?"

I melt into her eyes, taking my time drinking in her features. "Are you happy, sweetheart? Content?"

Lola blinks nice and slow as she stares up at me and takes her time, losing herself into me just as deep as I've lost myself into her. We spend a minute swaying into each others arms.

"You're the only one who's ever made me feel this way," she confesses. "I only ever want to be as happy as you are. I want to share in all life has to throw at you, happiness, sadness. *Whatever* it looks like, esposo, I'm going to be by your side. I finally feel home."

I give her a nice slow grin, the one I know makes her weak. "My baby came home," I parrot back, because she's home.

She's home to stay.

28

EPILOGUE

LOLA

9 months later

I PUT MY HEAD back wearily on the pillow behind me, reaching over for a nice cold sip of water.

A bit of movement in the corner of my eye temporarily distracts me and look over, seeing Hudson rocking gently on his feet in front of the glass door that leads out to our balcony, facing away from me. Feeling a pain in my nipple I gasp, wince, and let out a little whimper, hearing a suction and grunt followed by a cry underneath me.

"Ohhhh, I'm sorry my darling," I coo, maneuvering to place my breast back closer to Tessa's mouth, our three week old daughter. I work to get her to latch on just right and then smile, seeing Tucker reach forward to caress her hair softly.

Tessa makes little soft sucking sounds before her eyes shut and her mouth falls lax in sleep a couple minutes later.

She's the greedier one, just like Tucker.

"Here," I whisper, holding Tessa carefully towards Tuck, I settle her into his arms and then work to find another comfortable reclining position, "Okay Amor, I'm ready."

Hudson turns and gives me that devilish smile before walking slowly towards me with a carefully wrapped bundle secure in his arms.

Tiffany, Tessa's twin sister.

Yes, I had twin girls. What were the chances?

Tessa's a bit harder to feed, very demanding, so while I'm busy with her, Hudson takes Tiff and rocks her, or sings to her until its her turn.

I found out recently that he often takes the boys on midnight horse rides, and when he's done with quality time with Tate and Tuck he puts the girls in each arm and takes them all to the pantry and makes milk for each of them to share.

I've been treated to such wonderful sleep it's hard to believe this is my life now. In another five months our parent's houses will be done, and my new bookshop will be complete in about ten or so months.

I just cant believe that a short year ago my life was completely different. Almost as an unspoked understanding, we don't talk about the life we led before, none of us do. We have firmly and decidedly moved on away from the past to create a new future full of possibility and promise.

I feel my blood race as Hudson draws nearer, leans down and places Tiff in my arms carefully.

He presses his lips on my forehead before he settles himself on the end of the bed with Tatum, who is scowling at a comic book he's reading. Our eyes hold each other for a heartbeat or two longer than proper, and I feel my face heat as he lets me know that he's got plans for me later.

Won't be sex, as that wont be allowed for another three weeks, and he's itching for it.

I saw him mark the day on his phone calendar that we can officially start having sex again, and by the look in his eyes he might start hounding me even earlier than three weeks.

His eyes leave mine smoothly to focus on our children. I look down into Tiffany's light green eyes that are staring up at me and give her a little smile. She startles as her fathers deep voice pierces her momentary peace, causing me to shush and rock her, getting her latched back on.

"What's happened now? Another fight between the one character and his friend?" Hudson asks inquisitively, as he leans over and places his hand on Tucker's shoulder, squeezing before running his knuckles down Tessa's face gently. He moves to put his arm behind his head and then with his other hand he settles it around my foot, squeezing firmly.

Half listening to them talk, I sigh and sink deeper into the pillows as Tucker carefully turns on a cartoon movie while cuddling his sister.

This is our thing, we lounge in bed together as a family while I feed the girls, Tucker holds one of them while Hudson and Tatum talk about his comic book of the week. I close my eyes with a slight smile, cradling my daughter close, and holding every member of my family even closer.

This is joy, this is life. And we live it abundantly.

But all lives hit snags along the way, and we're no exception.

Unfortunately, this isn't the end of our story.

Sneak Peak into Lola Unmasked Pt 3

"LIGHTS OUT!"

I turn my face from the guard as the mechanical whirl of the prison bar doors slamming shut echo loudly across the white cement blocks of my room before fading. I stare at the wall, counting down the minutes like I do every night before I swing my legs over my bed and place my feet on the floor.

My head turns sharply, hearing the almost muted sound of the nighttime guard taking over from the evening shift. I breathe deeply, ignoring the moldy hot rank of the prison air and pretend it's fresh mountain air.

Like my home in the mountains of Colorado. My place of solitude for four years where I was busy hauling in drugs from South America. Working my way up the ranks in the cartel.

I was getting there too. Had the ear of a several powerful men. I was getting to be top dog status, had a different woman on my arm every night during the weekend. But my fuck up of a brother got me caught up in some shit and I had to take the fucking fall for the top dog.

It was either that, or *die*.

So I've been rotting in this prison for the last nine and a half years. With nothing but the words of my encampment to keep me going, and the pictures my brother would send occasionally.

Though he's my twin brother, his fucking attitude burnt my ass up. He took his freedom for granted, while I had to waste away in here. While *he* got to live on the outside, having babies and shit. Babies he didn't even want with a bitch that...well...I sort of wish I would have gotten Lolita for myself if I'm honest with myself.

Dominic.

I snort. Always knew how to fuck up a good thing.

I haven't heard from him in close to a year and a half, and my men said they think he'd been killed.

But I know he'd been killed, because the hit man I connected him with had also been killed as well. And that wasn't the plan. The plan was for the boys and the woman to die so I could have some start up money for when I got out of this fucking place and didn't have to start all the way from the bottom.

But now look, I have to fucking start all the way from the bottom *anyway*.

But here we go.

I'm going to make Lolita pay every cent she owes me and then some.